I0710488

LIGHT'S SHADOW

LIGHT'S SHADOW

RAIDERS OF LIGHT SERIES, BOOK 1

R. ROLAND FINCH

Copyright © 2024 by R. Roland Finch

All rights reserved.

No part of this publication may be reproduced, distributed, or transmitted in any form or by any means, including photocopying, recording, or other electronic or mechanical methods, without the prior written permission of the publisher, except as permitted by U.S. copyright law. For permission requests, contact Finch Fries Press, PO Box 25, Flagstaff, AZ 86002.

The story, all names, characters, and incidents portrayed in this production are fictitious. No identification with actual persons (living or deceased), places, buildings, and products is intended or should be inferred.

Book Cover by Jack Baker

Illustration by Veronica O'Neill

Map and diagrams by Mike Church

First Edition 2024

Identifiers: LCCN 2024909614 | ISBN 9781964521022 (eBook) | ISBN 9781964521008 (paperback) | ISBN 9781964521015 (hardback)

For Caleb and Jane, always

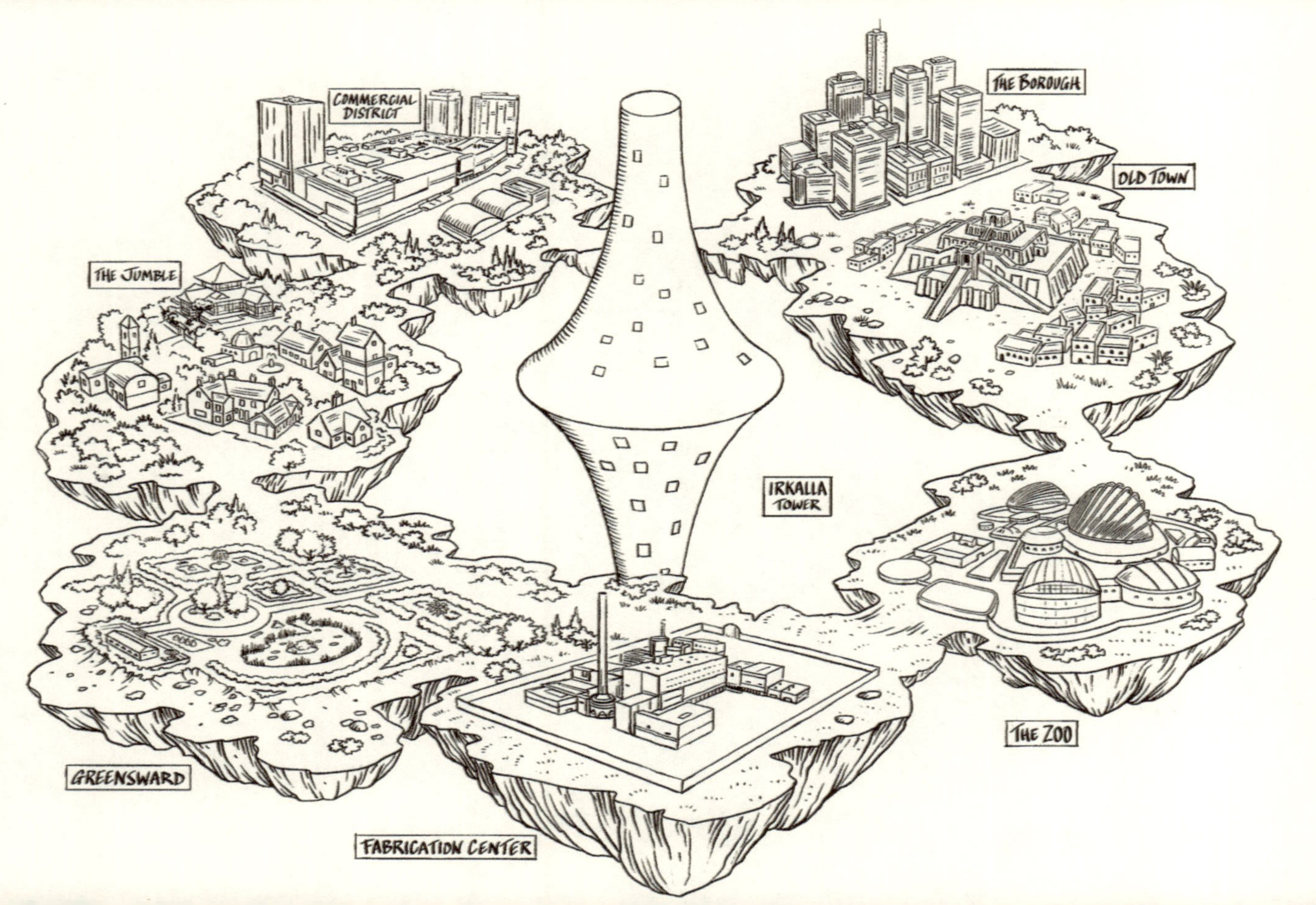

COMMERCIAL DISTRICT
THE BOROUGH
OLD TOWN
THE JUMBLE
IRKALLA TOWER
GREENSWARD
FABRICATION CENTER
THE ZOO

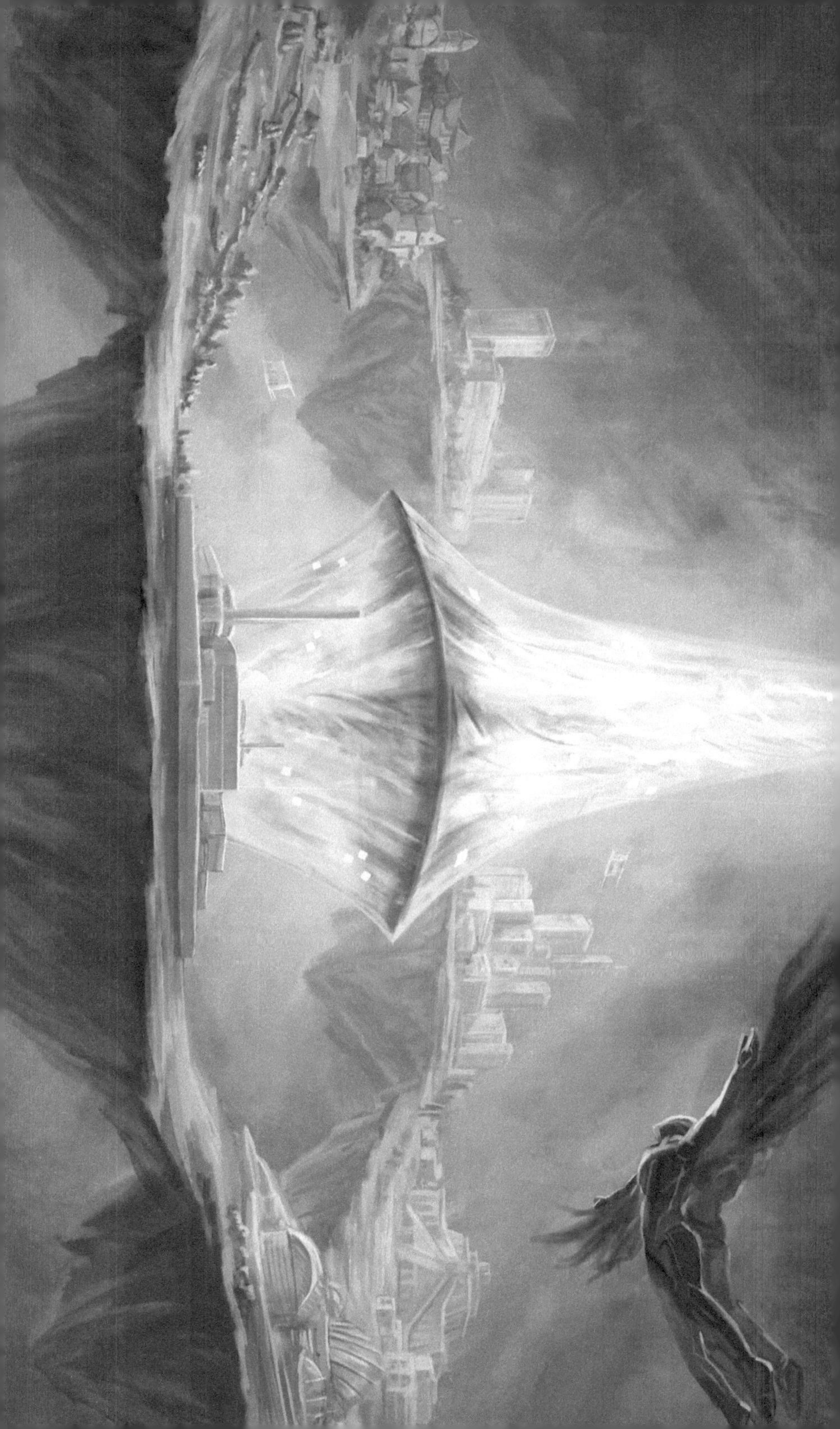

1

THE DARK ROOM

CLICK.

Red light flowed from overhead, painting the walls of the dark room as Lucas Devlin stepped inside. His hazel eyes strained to adjust as he twisted to pull the door closed behind him. Just before it banged shut, he heard the pounding of a hammer followed by a profanity-laced exclamation. "Dad got his thumb again," he muttered.

Quiet embraced Lucas as he stood within the four walls. Drawing dusty air into his nostrils, he ruffled his sandy brown hair. The creaking wood floor greeted him with each step. The dark room's silent tenants watched him, as they had nearly every day for the past seven years: three wardrobe cabinets standing against the left wall, the same number of foldout chairs opposite them, along with some spiders and other critters.

Lucas grabbed a chair, dragging it in front of one of the tall cabinets. He lightly punched a section of warped particle board, replaying in his mind the conversation from ten minutes prior. Again, he had pled his case to his mom. Again, she had shut him down.

I just want to live my life the way I choose. Is that so wrong? My entire graduating class is going to college, working, or taking a break. But not me. It's the "family business" for me.

Lucas's muttering became increasingly bitter. "Oh, a dark room? For photography? Noooo... Heaven forbid."

He went on griping under his breath as he opened the cabinet door. Inside were several empty hangers dangling from a rod and a small box resting at the bottom. One hanger held what looked like a wetsuit of an unusually deep black that seemed to suck in light. Stripping off his sleep clothes to expose his toned frame, Lucas flung them onto the top shelf. Then, he grabbed the black suit from its hanger and pulled it on.

"No, not us. The *family business*. Righhht." Falling backward into the chair, he stretched out his right hand and opened the square container. "What's in the box?!" The joke had been funny once, but now he didn't even smile. It struck him that the movie *Seven* had come out in 1995, almost a full ten years ago. The film reminded him of his childhood friends, Conleth 'Connie' Spencer and Aella Mendoza, whose leaving him behind poured salt in the wound of his situation. "Literally *everyone* is free to do what they want—and here I am, stuck."

Before gearing up, Lucas decided to send a text message to both of his friends. For him, the elation of finally graduating from high school two days earlier had long since worn off. He already missed his friends and mourned for the life he was leaving behind. It had been two days too long since they had last talked. *This is our last summer together—we should savor it.*

Thumbs clicking, he examined the contents of the box. Within it were ten additional pieces of equipment: two small metallic wafers, a utility belt, a set of earbuds, a mouthpiece, a pair of gloves, and a pair of water shoes. They were of a peculiar light-dampening hue, like the wetsuit. If "hue" was even the right word to describe it.

His mind travelled back to the first time he had put on similar gear. Even after seven years, he heard his mom's instructions clearly in his head. He could almost see her no-nonsense frown and laser stare, head cocked slightly to one side and arms folded across her slender chest as she coached him.

"This is training gear, so it's not very sophisticated. When you join the family business in a few years, you'll be fitted with the real thing. It's *much* more convenient."

She then strapped a thin band around each wrist and ankle, one around her neck, and a belt around her waist. Crossing her arms, she tapped the back of her left wrist against the front of her right. In an instant, her entire body was soundlessly covered, clothes and all.

"We Darktouched like acronyms, I guess. We call this KALM gear, which stands for—"

"Knowledge Acquisition and Lifecycle Management. Whatever that means." Lucas flushed in the present as his past self glowed with pride.

"Right. Without it, you can't traverse the dark, so treat the gear like your life depends on it. Because it will someday." She continued, "By the way, define Abzu and Infra for me?"

Lucas answered, "Abzu is dark water beneath the earth. It's how we enter the Abzu Complex, city of the Darktouched."

"And the Infra?" she quizzed him.

"The Infra is like pure darkness way inside the earth," he recited. "Sometimes people call it the Underbelly of the World. The Darktouched explore it looking for artifacts and secrets."

His mom gave him a thumbs up. "Great. There are two things you need to know about the KALM suits and the darkness, even in the simulator. The first: Sight without light is off-putting."

Lucas placed the wafers over his eyes. The red light of the dark room immediately vanished and the room appeared as though well lit, but the edges of his vision grew hazy.

"*See* what I mean?" She winked. She then went on a tangent about the ancient Greeks putting coins on the eyes of the dead and one in the mouth—Charon's Toll—for a moment before returning to the topic at hand. "The second: Movement is going to feel like learning to walk again. It's a little frustrating and miserable. Give it time."

Right on both counts.

Fully geared in the present, Lucas slid the empty container back into the cabinet and closed the door. He got up and walked across the dimly lit room. Crouching down, he pulled a canvas tarp to the side and revealed a hatch in the floor. Opening it with some effort, he slid himself in and climbed down the ladder to the room below, making sure to close the door behind him.

Hard cement walls lined with lead closed in around him. Dizzied slightly by the changeover from seeing reflected light to viewing the world through the KALM technology, Lucas instinctively squeezed his eyes shut and opened them a few times. *Always makes me woozy for a moment. But it's cool how the wafers stay stuck to your face.*

He chuckled to himself as he walked through a narrow hallway, reminded of one of his dad's favorite rants: "Lucas, you might think we see using infrared in the Infra, but of course we don't. It's violet. Or the sky is. But that's just the start. The KALM gear stimulates your brain's visual cortex, if you have one—a brain, not a cortex. And, the training gear has some problems the real suits don't. Sometimes, you can't tell how far away things are. You feel like you're floating. Until you become an official Darktouched by pledging to our laws, you're basically practicing drunk Abzu and Infra navigation. Might come in handy. You never know. Oh, and it's a good thing you can't get lost in the simulator, because you have a very limited HUD."

When he was ten, he asked his dad to explain what a HUD was.

"When you're training, it stands for Hope You Don't," his dad had told him. "Hope You Don't need it, because if you do, something is wrong. It actually stands for Heads-Up Display, but my version is just as accurate. Still, it does at least provide details about your environment like room dimensions and other measurements. Useful for a newbie like you."

Spurred on by his memories, Lucas thoughtlessly flipped through information about his personal health, the environment, objects in his surroundings, and a topographical wireframe.

He continued down the hallway, now unquestionably under the hill that ran along the edge of his family's property. *One more egg in the lead matryoshka doll.* He opened the door in front of him and entered the final room, which the HUD measured as exactly ten feet by ten feet.

At the far end of this chamber was another door in the wall. But, as Lucas had confirmed on many occasions, he was unable to open it. For seven years, he had obsessed over discovering what was on the other side. That particular revelation would have to wait a few more weeks, when he was scheduled to travel to the Abzu Complex and begin his new life.

In the very center of the room was a round hole cut in the floor, beneath which was a massive hollow space filled with water. He remembered thinking as a boy that it was like the hole firemen slid down into, only without a pole... and wetter.

"And now for the fun part," he said out loud to himself.

Above the cavity hung a contraption that resembled a vertical MRI tube. He reached out with his mind and turned the machine on, then raised both arms above his head. Gradually, it lifted him off of the floor until his entire body was in the cylinder, when he then told it to invert. His head was now facing downward, directly above the water. In his mind, he gave one final command: launch.

With a jolt he was propelled through ice cold liquid that—even with the KALM gear on—pricked at his skin, forcing him to full alertness and stirring panic within him. The breath was choked from his lungs, and he had an almost irresistible urge to scream. Lucas had used the machine hundreds of times over the last seven years, but had still not gotten used to the simulation of the Abzu. The sensation unnerved him even after countless hours spent swimming in pools as a competitor.

Within seconds, the water dropped away, and he was falling. And then, just as suddenly, his feet touched solid ground. He could never tell which direction was which. *Feet down, head up. Close enough.*

His legs shook as he collected himself, affected by both dwindling adrenaline and the increased gravitational forces emulated by the simulator. The claustrophobia-inducing walls of the dark room had been replaced by emptiness. The KALM gear interpreted the void as a violet sky with no celestial bodies or atmospheric conditions resting on top of the blackness below. This dark ocean appeared to writhe and shift strangely, as streams of deeper blackness flowed randomly through his vision.

A sudden force slammed into Lucas from the left, mimicking something his parents called a shadewind. Strong gravitational forces within the Infra created bursts of energy, and the Darktouched had invented ways to survive and even harness them. He steadied his body by willing it to lean into the impact.

He remembered more instructions from his childhood, again in his mom's voice: "In the Infra, you control your limbs with your mind. But the rules are different down there. It's kind of like falling randomly in every direction."

As Lucas proceeded, floating islands appeared in the distance. He knew his goal was a few hundred yards ahead and began treading in that direction. But then, off to his right, he felt movement. Swiveling around to see if it was a trick of the KALM gear, he realized immediately that it was not. What he saw startled him because of how unusual it was.

Fifty feet away, a snowy owl perched on a tiny glob of hovering earth. In the deep emptiness, its white feathers seemed radiant. As if calling out to him, it stared directly at Lucas. Its eyes were as black as the dark ocean he swam through, but it exuded mystery and kindness—so if it was an omen, he hoped it was a good one.

Frightened, Lucas turned his gaze away for a second. When he looked back, it was gone.

For a long time, he stood frozen, rattled. *Was it part of the simulation? If not, how did it get there?* It was all he could do to finish the course and return to the surface.

2

Unexpected Company

Smiling eyes and a wagging tail greeted Lucas when he stepped back into the daylight. The scorching sun had just begun its afternoon descent. The air smelled of heated earth and pine, mixed with a touch of canine.

"Hi, Mai! What have you been up to?" The dog brushed up against Lucas's legs demandingly, and he obliged by scratching her behind her ear. A wide smile grew on his face. "How is my coydog buddy?" Mimicking a French accent, he said, "Your mother was a coyote, and your father smelled of prickly pear. But he was a noble breed, right? A couple of mangy adopted mutts, you and I." Mai leapt up and stood with her paws on Lucas's chest, licking his face. "Let's get some food, girl."

Lucas sauntered along the flagstone path toward the Devlins' house. Behind him, the dark room appeared to be nothing more than a simple tool shed. It was sheltered under several ponderosa pine trees, and butted up against a hill that ran along the entire north side of their lot. The backyard was the family sanctuary, nestled between the house and a high fence on three sides, and the hill in back, largely invisible to the outside world.

While they walked together back to the house, Lucas checked his phone for text messages from Connie and Aella. Still nothing.

What the heck! Did they abandon me already?

Inside, his dad was sitting at the dining table, sipping on his customary noontime coffee and wolfing down a breakfast burrito.

"Back in the simulator?" he asked Lucas, who grimaced in reply. "I guess Mom lit a fire under you already. Welcome to the life." He chuckled, and then coughed, exclaiming, "Swallowed wrong. I hate that! He kept on sputtering, his salt and pepper goatee catching food particles as he did. He tossed a piece of flour tortilla to Mai as the coughing subsided. "How about you, girl?"

Lucas rolled his eyes and shook his head. "The first real day of summer after high school. Yay. Going to be great." He ambled to the kitchen island to stand next to his dad, who shot him a glance that asked when he had gotten so tall. Lucas had to jab him. "Yep, I'm a bit over six feet two inches now. Shorty."

He bent down to scratch Mai's ears, whose dichromatic eyes smiled brightly at him even as she went belly up. "You just can't get enough of this, huh, girl?"

His dad breathed deeply, ignoring the quip. "It *will* be great. You have a lot to do." And then, sensing the tension building in Lucas, added, "Look, I know we're hard on you, but it's for a good reason."

Lucas grunted, turning his attention away from Mai, who contentedly slunk off to plop down on the cool tile under the dining table. "I know. I just don't get why I have no say in my own future."

His dad gulped down the last bite of his burrito and noisily cleared his throat, pounding on his chest above the Notre Dame mascot that adorned his navy-blue shirt. "Right. I'm sorry about that. But being Darktouched is both a right and a privilege. Once you're down there, I know you're going to see things differently. By the way, you need a haircut. You look like a hippie."

Lucas crossed the kitchen to the chrome-colored refrigerator, opened the door, and stuck his head in. His stomach groaned. The simulator always made him voracious. *Leftover pizza—nice!*

He forced himself to avoid self-consciously running a hand through his hair, which had started to cover his ears. He grunted again before he said, "Maybe I should just take a year off instead."

"What are you two talking about? Darren Devlin, you better not be putting more fool ideas in his head. He has plenty already." Somehow, Lucas's mom had snuck into the kitchen unnoticed. Broom in hand, she turned to Lucas. "Hurry up and eat. We have unexpected visitors coming over today. If you haven't finished in the dark room yet, you're going to need this broom surgically removed from your colon. Also, close the refrigerator unless you want to start paying the electric bill."

Lucas absentmindedly grabbed a piece of pizza and a two-liter bottle of Coke from the fridge. Closing the chrome door with his elbow, he held the slice in his mouth and reached up to grab a glass from the cupboard. Behind him, Tara rolled her eyes at his methods before dancing around the kitchen island toward Darren, her shoulder-length black hair swaying as she lightly hit him with the broom.

"And you. Get out of the way. Don't you have something to do?"

"Yes, Tara, my dearest," Darren said, tossing his paper plate in the trash and striding toward the door leading into the garage. "Hurry up and do as your mother says."

Before Darren could get out of sight, Lucas took the pizza from his mouth so he could speak and rushed to ask his parents, "Have either of you ever seen an animal in the simulator? When I got down to the bottom, there was a white owl maybe a hundred feet in. It was sitting on a rock just a little off the path."

Tara frowned and turned to Darren, her brown eyes locked on his in a serious gaze. "That doesn't sound right to you, does it?"

Her husband shook his head and gave her a puzzled look. "Are you sure that's what you saw, Lucas?" he asked. "The owl is a very important symbol to some Darktouched."

Lucas nodded, pouring some Coke into the glass. "Pretty sure. Clear as the light of day. Clearer, maybe. I thought I was losing it." He gobbled down half of his pizza slice and took a swig of soda. "Anyway, no idea what it was doing there. No way it was an actual owl, right? Maybe it's just a glitch in the training gear."

"Could be. Very strange," said Darren. "Maybe keep it to yourself when you get down to the Abzu Complex. But I wouldn't worry too much about it unless it started talking to you." He gave a silly laugh and twirled a finger near his right temple.

"Nope, no talking. Not yet." Lucas finished his snack, minus a bit of the crust he tossed to Mai, and returned the bottle of Coke to the fridge. "I need to shower. Be back down in twenty, since I guess we have company coming over?" His mom returned his questioning glance with a nod. "All righty." And then he turned to dash up the stairs.

Once in his room, Lucas jumped onto the bed and closed his eyes. Light streamed into the room through a gap in the blackout curtains, catching particles of dust hanging defiantly in the air. It flitted across the desk placed against the far wall, where there sat a now unneeded heap of calculus, physics, and other textbooks. Next to them, a thick volume of Shakespeare's complete works lay buried underneath clean but unfolded gym clothes. Reflections gleamed off a line of high school swimming trophies.

Lucas let a yawn control him for a moment and then trained his focus on the shadows dancing on the floor near the foot of his bed. His eyes stared through the world as his mind wandered. In a few weeks, the rest of his life would begin.

Am I ready? he asked himself for the thousandth time.

As if in response to his question, three sharp knocks stretched out from the door of his room, slapping him back to alertness.

"I thought you were showering. You need to get your ass moving. Are you decent?"

"Yeah, I know!" he shouted. "And, yeah, I guess. *Why?*"

Relentless, Tara opened the door. "Don't sass me, young man. In just a few days you'll be in the real world, helping the family business." She floated across the room, threw open the curtains, and pulled a cord to raise the blinds. Lucas squinted as the bright afternoon light blew up his momentary peace, then buried his head under the cold side of his warm pillow.

He felt the blood rise to his cheeks and neck as Tara continued her lecture while undoing the locks on the windows and opening them up. A steady breeze slid through the window screen to escape the sun, which was doing its work to cook the outside air.

"Sure, Mom. The real world. *The family business.*" Those final three words ignited his anger like a spark. Lifting the pillow from his face, he tossed it to the side. "Why does everyone else get to choose what they do except me? I mean, Connie and Aella are off to college, and I'm stuck in Bumville, Arizona."

Without turning her head fully toward Lucas, his mom's brown eyes rotated to focus on him and then narrowed.

Here it comes.

"This again? We just had this conversation! Generation *Why.*" She paused to let the words sink in. "College won't help with what *you* will be doing. And very few of us get to choose our path in life. Just be thankful you can lay there and complain about it. Besides, Flagstaff is hardly Bumville. Stop your whining."

"Whatever," said Lucas as he rolled out of bed, the static electricity causing his white t-shirt and gray shorts to cling to his body. As he bent down to grab a corner of the bedding and pull it taut, he looked over his shoulder at his mom. "I get it, okay? I should be thankful to have a job. And be motivated by the great mission I'm supposed to embark on. *Wunderbar.*"

"I'm glad you understand. Now get cleaned up." She turned to straighten a family photo hanging on the wall and smiled. "I remember when Alan took this. We're lucky to have neighbors who are like family."

Lucas peered out the window. "Hey, Mom, speaking of the Linzers, their trash dumpster is still on the curb. Pickup was on Thursday, and it's already Saturday. Nora always rolls it in the minute the truck passes by. Do you think they're okay?"

Still looking at the photo, Tara reassured him, "I know you care about them a lot, but you need to worry less. They're fine. I think they just got out of dodge for a few days and forgot it. Don't stress. I'll have your dad put it away for them while you shower. Now, get to it."

Then she floated away, slipping from sight as she exited the room. Lucas felt himself breathe again as the sound of her socked feet on the steps became ever more distant.

He paused at the door to reminisce about the photo. *I remember the day we took this. The family had gone out driving together, and Nora insisted that Alan snap it because the sunflowers were so beautiful.*

A happy glow lit up Lucas's face as he remembered Mai bounding through the greenery. Holding her in his arms had been the only way to get her in the shot. The photo—while never failing to evoke fond feelings in Lucas's heart—captured a moment where the warm light of golden hour harshly accentuated the stark contrast between his sandy brown hair and tanned complexion and that of his adopted parents, who were dark haired and fairer skinned than he was.

I am grateful, Mom. He shuddered slightly, briefly recalling the disgusting living conditions and absent hygiene his biological father had exhibited the one time they had met three years prior. *You saved me from a life with that guy. I flew halfway across the country just to be disappointed.*

Shelving those thoughts, Lucas dutifully marched into the bathroom.

When he returned downstairs, Lucas was wearing a pair of blue jeans, a black polo shirt, and gray socks. Tara never allowed shoes in the house, but walking around barefoot in front of guests was equally egregious in her sight.

His parents weren't in the dining room or kitchen, and he assumed the visitors had arrived already. Turning right at the bottom of the stairs instead of left, he rounded the corner and passed through a set of French doors.

His parents were in the den along with four others, three of whom he had never met before. Seated on the brown leather sofa with their backs to the entryway were his parents and Alan Linzer, who he had not expected to see. *I guess they're back now.*

Although hidden from view, Lucas knew already that Alan wore his customary Hawaiian shirt and cargo shorts. An Anaheim Angels cap concealed his thin, graying hair. He and his wife, Nora, had recently advanced into their seventies, but looked at least ten years younger.

In two reclining chairs situated to the right of the sofa sat a man and woman. The man's full, untrimmed beard was complemented by a mane of shoulder-length red hair. He looked about forty years of age, and his burly frame spilled over the sides of the small recliner; Lucas was reminded of a time Connie had sat in a preschooler's chair during a community outreach event run by their high school. The man leaned back, tilted onto one hip, with his long legs fully outstretched. His boisterous laughter filled the room.

As Lucas's gaze shifted further to the right, he felt his face flush. The woman's harsh beauty was captivating. She looked about the same age as the man. Even though she was sitting, Lucas could tell she had a tall, lithe figure. Her blonde hair, almost white, was pulled up into a bun. She turned to face him, her mesmerizing green eyes assessing him. The corners of her mouth turned up into a brief, knowing smile.

Remembering himself, Lucas furtively smiled back and then dragged his attention to the final guest, who sat on a fireplace seat next to the brick masonry hearth. His espresso skin, closely trimmed hair, and clean-shaven face was accentuated by fiercely intelligent eyes. He sat leaning forward with an elbow on each knee and a beer in his hands. When he saw Lucas, he stood and moved toward him immediately, his hand outstretched.

"So, this is the man! I'm Asante Washburn, your dad's boss, more or less. Glad to finally meet you."

"Nice to meet you. I'm Lucas."

Asante stood about the same height as Lucas did, but he was more wiry than chiseled. Even so, his strong handshake and the way he moved made it clear he was not someone to trifle with. Still smiling, he returned to his seat by the fireplace.

The blonde woman gave a thin smile. "Oh, we know who *you* are. I'm Fiala. I'm no one's boss. But then, no one's mine, either." Her smile became a quiet laugh, but only her mouth showed any sign of joy.

Lucas knew he was turning red, and there was nothing he could do to stop it. Glad his parents were still facing away from him, he shifted uneasily for a moment. Briefly, he let his eyes dart to Asante, who seemed amused. Anticipating the snag in his voice he knew would fully betray his thoughts, he took a short breath and spoke slowly.

"Nice to meet you, Fiala. You know me already?"

Silence was her only answer. *Apparently, that's rhetorical.*

To distract himself and regain his composure, Lucas shot a glance at the man to Fiala's left before reaching down and grabbing Alan by his shoulder. "Hey, Alan. Hope you're doing well."

Alan extended his slightly wrinkled digits up to his shoulder and patted Lucas's hand. "Doing great, Luc. Nora says hi." Alan, like a grandfather to him, was the only one who called him by the shortened name.

The red-maned man stood and turned to face Lucas, who flinched slightly when he fully comprehended the man's size.

That's what you get for getting twitterpated. Distracted by a pretty face.

The man was at least six feet five inches tall, with broad shoulders and legs that looked like they could kick a full-grown man over the Devlins' two-story house. He flashed a toothy smile, moving alarmingly swiftly for a man of his size, and reached out both hands to grasp Lucas by his shoulders.

"Finally, young man, we meet. I'm Malank—short for Malank. Hardly a common name, but it's the one fate gave me."

For a moment, Lucas felt his feet leave the floor as the man greeted him.

Without turning away, Malank said, "He's built a lot like Alazar, isn't he, Fi? Maybe a little more Black Sea than Red, but..."

Fiala closed her eyes briefly and sighed before simply saying, "He is."

Malank continued, "I digress. You don't know who Alazar is and we don't have time. Let's just say he was a good friend." He reached a hand inside of his dark green Henley and pulled out a small pendant that was fastened around his neck with a leather strap. "He gave me this fate charm. It's like a weather-vane for the winds of destiny. When it speaks, I listen." The oblong jewel was of a deep, swirling teal hue, with a pulsing white light in the center. "Always trust luck more than your head, boy, and you'll be just fine."

Lucas nodded expressionlessly, unsure what to say.

Sensing his discomfort, Fiala chimed in, "Malank, sit. You're overdoing it."

Malank tucked the pendant away with his left hand and ran the other through his wild hair. "You're right. Sorry." He turned away, then turned back again to face Lucas. He reached into the left pocket of his gray canvas pants and said, "Take this. It's a nazar amulet. It never hurts to have someone watching your back."

Made of solid glass, the charm looked like an eye created from layered teardrop circles of black, white, turquoise, and deep blue.

"Thank you," was all Lucas could say before Malank returned to his chair. Lucas slipped the nazar amulet into his own pocket, then shuffled around the sofa to the fireplace, to take the bench opposite Asante. "And nice to meet you all."

His dad winked at him and smiled as his mom cleared her throat to speak.

"Okay. Let's get to it, shall we? Deveras—sorry, Asante. Do you want to do the honors?"

Asante nodded, downed the rest of his beer, and asked, "'How much have you told him?"

"Quite a bit about the Darktouched. Very little about..."

Tara paused, rocking side to side and glancing at Fiala and Malank. Lucas had rarely seen his mom this uneasy.

"Very little about your kind. He knows Nora and Alan are Lightborne, though. We should have told him more, but we wanted him to see you as people and not stories or warnings."

"We understand. We've been watching, and Alan has kept us apprised," said Malank. "It's fine. You were never in any real danger, so there was no urgent need."

Asante sighed. "He's flying a little blind, then. That's fine. Where to begin?" He stood and turned to face the fireplace, one hand on the mantle and the other in the back right pocket of his blue dress pants. His tight-fitting white button-down emphasized each breath he took.

Fiala tapped her foot on the floor. "Just the basics. He'll figure out the rest as he goes."

"Fine," said Asante. "Just the basics. Some of this is probably review, but I don't know what you know. I *assume* you know the Darktouched are the only ones with the ability to reach the Abzu Complex and travel the Infra."

Lucas nodded.

"Not entirely true," quipped Malank. "Technically, anyone can get there. But if you're not a Darksmudged, you can end up lost in the darkness, go stark raving mad, get torn to pieces... or just plain suffocate."

Asante glared at him before continuing, "May I?" He turned to face Lucas. "He's right, though. Anyone can, technically. But only *we* can truly thrive there. And only we can control the technology that makes going there worthwhile." He paced over to the window overlooking the front yard of the Devlins' home. "And then there are the Lightborne. We're not sure who came first, us or them. Once upon a time, we tolerated each other... but now we don't. Haven't for over a thousand years." He looked over at Fiala. "Except for the descendants of a few that broke away from the main group. These two and their friends, primarily."

Fiala tapped her foot again. "And Senna. Wherever she is."

"Unhelpful. But yes," stated Asante curtly. "Anyway, they were banished from the Lightborne seat of power, which they call the Lightwatch. They're being hunted just like us."

Tara added, "The Lightwatch has access to untold volumes of information extending back millennia. While we study artifacts in the dark, they compile information about everything the light has ever touched."

Malank breathed in deeply, saying almost under his breath, "There are limits. It's complicated, and we can talk more later." He smiled at Lucas.

"Keeping up so far?" asked Asante, his gaze fixed on Lucas, who shrugged. "Yeah, I expect so. Well, they want the information we have, and they can't get it without extracting it from one of us or holding us for ransom."

Lucas looked at his mom. "So, they want to rob the 'family business'?" He made air quotes around the words.

"Effectively, yes. And kill us too. There's that." Tara's lips formed into a thin smile.

"But not only the Darktouched," said Fiala. "They want to end us also."

"This is a crash course. You'll learn much more in the Abzu Complex," said Tara, looking Lucas firmly in the eyes. "Now, since you've been asking: you do get to say no, but..."

"We hope you don't," said Asante. "We need every bit of help we can get."

Lucas, still looking into his mom's eyes, said, "Well, that's quite a bit to absorb." He laughed uncomfortably. "So, why are there so many of you here?" He motioned at the room. "Why couldn't my parents tell me this?"

"We wanted to meet you, for one," said Asante. "I personally wanted to try recruiting you into the Seekers. And—"

"And we've gotten reports that Lightwatch Reclaimers are close to finding us," said Alan, who had not even so much as nodded his head the entire time. "They've been closing in over the last month, grabbing up both enemy Lightborne and Darktouched. We don't know why they've gotten more aggressive, but they could be here within days. If they catch us here, we're toast." He motioned toward Malank and Fiala. "Even them, most likely. Your friends Aella and Conleth have been moved already. They're in the wind. Nora's watching over them and their families."

Asante grimaced. "We had a script, man! We need him calm."

"And what of it?" Alan retorted angrily. "We're wasting time."

Lucas felt his blood rise. He addressed his mom. "I thought I had a choice. Guess that was bullshit."

And then the realization dawned on him that his childhood friends were somehow involved in this as well. He knew the Linzers were Lightborne, so their involvement came as less of a blow. But he had grown up with Connie and Aella.

"Actually, it kind of sounds like a good chunk of my life has been." He glared at his mom and dad. "So, assuming you're not insane or lying, when do we leave?"

Just then, Mai, who had been outside, raced into the house and began barking. Fiala rose to her feet and peered through the windows near where Asante stood.

"Now. Our Reclaimer friends are *very* early."

3

BOGEYMAN

WHEN HE WAS ONLY four years old, Lucas recalled asking his father, "Dad, what's a nomen?" He peered up at his dad, bouncing with anticipation.

"A what?" Darren repeated the words. "A nomen? A *nomen*...? Oh! You mean 'an omen'!"

Lucas groaned. "Yeah, that's what I said, Dad."

"Right, sorry. Well, an omen is a sign that something important is going to happen. Like, say for example..." Darren scratched his head, drawing a blank. "Help me out here, Alan."

Alan put his crossword puzzle down and knelt next to Lucas, looking at him from behind a pair of wire-framed spectacles. The little boy stood still, captivated by the hair protruding from the man's long, crooked nose. It had obviously been broken a few times over the years.

Alan pursed his lips. "Like a black cat crossing your path. Some people think that means something bad will happen."

Lucas frowned thoughtfully. "Why? Is the cat bad?"

Alan shook his head and smiled. "No, the cat's not bad. People just think it's a sign of something bad coming in the future."

"Why?"

"Because they're superstitious."

"What's super-tishus?"

"Well, that's when people believe that if they do bad things—*or see an omen*—something will happen to them."

"Okay. Like the booger man."

"Boog-*ee*-man."

"Yeah, that's what I *said*." Lucas was starting to become exasperated. "He sounds like a Lightborne. The booger—bogeyman."

Alan nodded approvingly at this correction and then questioned, "Oh? How's that?"

"Because they steal people away. Geez."

Alan's eyes opened wide. "Ohhh, I see. Well, not all Lightborne are like that, you know. Nora and I are Lightborne."

"Yeah, that's what Mom and Dad said. But you're friends. And you're old," Lucas said innocently. Alan chuckled.

Darren patted Lucas on his bottom. "That's enough now. Give Alan a break and go play with Mai."

From the front steps, the boy whistled for his new puppy, which was playing in the front yard. Lucas remained quiet afterward, only occasionally looking over at the two adults as they talked.

Darren leaned back into a cushioned patio chair, one of a set placed on the Linzers' front porch, and took a sip from his iced tea. "I'm sorry about that, Alan. Tara and I had never met a Lightborne until you and Nora. We grew up thinking of you collectively as the enemy, and I guess our stories rubbed off on Lucas." The boy looked up at the mention of his name and then quickly back down.

Alan, who had returned to his own chair, waved his hand dismissively. "Don't worry about it. As a group, we've been the enemy of the Darktouched for a long time." He crossed his legs. "The Lightwatch leaders live in an echo chamber. Every single one is greedy for data that will fix the future before it's broken. Why help people in need, right?"

Darren took another swallow of his tea. "Tara and I are glad Lucas gets to grow up differently. We appreciate your friendship. And I appreciate that Tara and Nora can go shopping with each other and leave me out of it."

Alan picked up his own glass and raised it to Darren. "Cheers."

Their toast had stuck in Lucas's mind ever since. Darktouched and banished Lightborne together, outcasts of different kinds, fighting against the mythical forces of something called the Lightwatch. As he matured, he had come to understand the real danger the Reclaimers presented to his family, that friendship notwithstanding. But as the months and years of his childhood passed, the probability of that 'if' materializing felt ever slimmer. If not for his Darktouched training, he might not have believed it at all. So, in that moment—as Fiala heralded the arrival of their enemies—Lucas was left staring blankly into nothingness, thinking of a white owl.

4

RECLAIMERS

FIALA CONTINUED, "THEY'VE REACHED the alarm perimeter we set before we came here, Malank. We have less than five minutes." She closed the curtains and blinds, asking Alan to do the same. Surprisingly spry, the old man jumped up and bounded upstairs without questioning her.

Malank calmly stood and addressed the room. "Reclaimer tactics are simple. Fi, can you provide a visual?"

Fi sighed. "Sure, if you think it'll help," she said. "But we don't have much time."

His eyes still focused on Malank, Lucas perceived that the lights briefly grew dim. Then, the living room was filled with a miniature replica of a neighborhood similar to his own. A cluster of six human figures radiating with prismatic light hung in the sky overhead. Malank continued his explanation.

"They work in teams of six. As they approach, they'll put up a concealment perimeter." In the conjured model, a reflective dome materialized over two adjacent houses. Inside of it, as if a switch had been flipped, the light became incredibly bright. "Once they touch down, they'll go house by house within their chosen radius until they achieve their objective. Shock tactics are their default—expect blinding light and extreme heat." The Reclaimer team huddled in front of one of the homes. After breaking down the front door, they stormed inside in single file. They emerged moments later with three captives and, their mission apparently successful, flew away. The scene vanished.

Malank took two steps and stopped in front of Lucas's mom and dad. "Off please, Devlins." As they stood, he bent down and grabbed one end of the sofa, quickly dragging it to the main entryway. "They're arrogant and they don't know Fi and I are here, so they'll use the front door." His right hand reached up to hold the fate charm through his shirt. "I knew luck was on our side, Fi. If we hadn't come early and set that alert perimeter, they might have had us." Like they were paperweights, Malank grabbed the chairs he and Fiala had been sitting on, one in each hand, and tossed them casually atop the sofa. He addressed the Devlins again. "You Darktouched folks have a hidey hole or escape route in that shack out back, right?"

Tara nodded. "We have a private doorway into the Abzu Hub. But Lucas isn't travel licensed yet and won't be able to go anywhere. Our plan was to surprise him with a trip to fix that. We thought we had a few more days." She massaged her temples with both hands. "It's like being able to enter the airport without identification, but not pass security to access the terminals. Or, even if you do, getting to a foreign country and being turned around. There are no exceptions." Her eyes opened wide suddenly. "If we can get to the Abzu Hub's outer ring though, we could at least gain distance by exiting at the Flagstaff station. This is a small city, but our region is the jumping off point for a lot of higher-end Darktouched thrill seeking." She looked up at Asante. "Can you arrange for a car to be waiting once we get there?"

"I already put in the order last week as a contingency. I'll call now to make sure." He grabbed a flip phone from his pocket and hit a number on speed dial, walking into the hallway.

Alan returned to them as Malank began speaking again.

"We'll escape by other means. But you're going to need us to conceal and shield you between the house and that shack. The Reclaimers could end you before you get halfway otherwise. There are four of you and three of us, which means multiple trips." He stroked his beard with his right hand while clutching the fate charm around his neck with his left. "Someone has to be last. For us, that'll be Alan. Fi and I can't afford to be caught. We're not at full strength—we can't fight them and protect you all."

Addressing Tara, he asked, "What's the rest of your plan?"

"We can use the Lava Tubes. It's not ideal, but—"

"But it's insane!" Darren exclaimed. "Even with experience and full KALM gear, it's like skydiving without a parachute."

Tara gave an exasperated sigh. "We don't have time to argue! The hatches will slow them down, but they'll still be able to follow us until we reach the Hub's outer ring. Besides, we used to shoot the Tubes when we were younger."

"Fine," said Darren, shoulders slumped. "I can leave last. I'll guard the door."

Alan interjected forcefully, "Luc needs to be the first out. I'll take him and then come back for whoever's left. It doesn't sound like he can survive without help. Who's going second?"

"Survive what?" asked Asante as he returned to the room.

"Asante can go second, Alan," Tara said decisively, then turned her attention to Asante. "Darren and I are going to help Lucas enter the Infra through the Lava Tubes. You have to go back to the Abzu Complex. We can't lose you right now. Lucas will need to be granted asylum."

Asante's eyes widened and then returned to normal as he shrugged. "I trust your judgment. The car will be waiting at the station exit. Pick up the keys from Maggie—she'll be on guard duty until midnight. I'll make sure Lucas is taken care of. You just get him to safety. I hope you're as quick of a learner as your parents said, kid."

"I guess we'll find out," said Lucas. "But, what about Mai?"

He saw his mom roll her eyes again and shake her head. Fiala tapped her foot louder this time, and Malank took the hint.

"I'll grab her... even though the Reclaimers have no interest in domesticated animals," he said, then paused and guffawed. "Well, not most of them."

Fiala was progressing to stomping.

"Anyway, we have a plan. When the Reclaimer oven turns on, with any luck they'll start at the Linzers'. On my signal, Alan and Lucas will sneak out back and into the shed. Then me and Asante, Fiala and Tara. I'm sorry, Alan, but you'll have to come back for Darren without support from us. We'll sneak out the figurative back door while the Reclaimers do their thing. Good luck, my friend."

Alan smirked and gave a wink. "Don't worry. I've still got it." And with that, the entire group moved to the back of the house.

Lucas knew exactly when the Reclaimers arrived. Even with the blinds closed and curtains shut, the entire house was illuminated with piercing light. He pressed his hand against the sliding glass door that led to the backyard. It was noticeably warmer than a moment before. The display unit on the wall for the digital thermometer outside read 150 degrees Fahrenheit—its max limit. *It could be 200 outside, for all we know. I wonder what these Repo-men look like.*

Fiala snuck on padded feet to the east-facing kitchen window and lifted a slat in the blind ever so slightly. "Good," she said. "It looks like they took the bait. Let's go. A group every five seconds. Malank, grab the mutt."

Mai growled in disapproval when Malank's giant arm swept her up and onto his shoulder.

Alan waved Lucas over. "Stay within arm's reach of me. No matter what."

The older man closed his eyes, concentrating. This time, Lucas paid close attention as the Lightborne used his abilities.

For just a second, Alan's entire body looked different; Lucas struggled to process what had happened. *It's almost like he was more... there. Like the background faded to one dull layer, and he popped forward, his body shimmering slightly.* While Lucas tried to understand what he'd seen, a dark tint went up around them, forming a bubble. Malank's huge hand penetrated the barrier and tapped Alan on his shoulder.

Alan said, "Here we go, Luc. Be fleet of foot and calm of mind."

Alan crept forward, and to Lucas the events seemed to happen in sequence and at once, the beginning and the end occurring at the same time. One second they were leaving the doorway, and the heat blasted his face, the light baked any exposed skin, and the sky was a concave reflection of the land below it. The next, he looked to his right and saw nothing, because the white light made it almost impossible to see; even the fence was nearly washed out. By the third second, they had made it less than a quarter of the way across the backyard, but on the fourth Alan picked up his pace and entered a trot. On the fifth, as Lucas heard Malank and Asante step through the back door, he realized it was difficult to stay in step with Alan, whose head only reached his chest level.

Six. He looked back to see… exactly nothing except his house. But he could hear footsteps following them. *Amazing.*

Seven. He and Alan were over halfway across his backyard. *Maybe we'll be okay.*

Eight. Lucas almost stumbled on rubbery legs but caught his balance just in time to not send himself and Alan tumbling.

Nine. They were only four or five steps away from the shack.

Ten. He knew all three groups were in the yard and his dad was alone in the house.

Eleven. Alan reached for the shack door handle.

Twelve. His fingertips were only a few inches away.

Thirteen. Alan wrapped his hand around the metal handle and began to pull.

Fourteen. Lucas heard Alan wish him luck as he pushed him inside, telling him not to stop until he had gone as far as he could go without Asante or Tara.

Fifteen. He looked back and saw Mai's front paws hit the ground.

Sixteen. He saw the rest of Mai heading back to the house and heard a bark. The sweat had already begun to pour down his face.

Seventeen. Malank shushed the dog and whispered angrily, "You idiot mongrel. You'll kill us all!"

Eighteen. Asante leapt into the dark room's antechamber next to Lucas and told him to keep moving.

Nineteen. He was turning away when he saw his father falling backward through the back door of their house, a person clad entirely in white approaching him.

Twenty. When the white-clothed figure stepped outside into the unnatural light, the brightness became even more blinding. *Reclaimers are almost angelic.*

Twenty-one. He heard a voice speaking, deep and terrifying. It was saying something about paying a debt. As twenty-two became twenty-three, Lucas distinctly heard the words: "Sins of your Forebears."

By twenty-four, he was being pulled into the dark room. A faraway voice was telling him to collect Darren's gear and leave the training equipment. At twenty-five, he was a step from his father's locker with Asante shoving him forward, a sinking feeling sapping his strength and tears welling in his eyes.

And then an explosion of light burst from seemingly nowhere. Behind the shielding of only his arm, Lucas could make out Tara scrambling for cover. She ran the rest of the way, leaping into the dark room between him and Asante.

Near the western fence appeared two glowing orbs that transformed into massive eagles made of light. As though on fire, hues of white, yellow, and orange undulated ceaselessly. The winged familiars stood half again as tall as the six-foot fence boards. Malank and Fiala were silhouetted within the body of the raptors. They lifted into the air, a rush of wind pushed out behind them, and then they were gone into the distance.

A roar burst out from near where Darren lay on his back, and Alan appeared, rushing toward the white figure. Mai growled and leapt at her enemy, the one attacking her family. Lucas heard a scream and a yelp. And then the world went black.

5

ESCAPE

CLICK. FOUR WALLS BLED crimson.

Without thinking, Lucas opened his dad's wardrobe cabinet and grabbed the bin containing his KALM bands. Asante was already stooping down to open the first hatch. Faintly, through the shack door, Lucas heard the din of a struggle—shouting, growling, rending, breaking.

No time to think. He willed himself down the ladder, hearing but not processing the words Tara spoke behind him; he only realized when he reached the bottom what she was trying to tell him. No light. He found his way to the opposite side of the room by memory and knelt down to fumble in the dark.

The box was snatched from his grip. Then, there were hands on his. One held his left digits still and the other placed something into them. Tara's voice sounded wrong in the small room.

"Stand up. Put that around your neck. Quick, hold out your wrists. Asante's getting the belt." Lucas felt her hands shaking. "Suit up. Let's go!"

Suddenly, white light flooded in from above. It was much dimmer than before but no less terrifying. The Reclaimers might be weaker underground, but Lucas knew instinctively that testing their strength today would be his last mistake. Dashing through the door, he veered to the right to avoid the simulator and then tapped his wrists together.

The KALM suit encased his body, fulfilling another boyhood dream. *Finally, a real KALM suit and not just training gear. This feels like wearing the wrong skin though.* His every movement felt awkward and strained.

It struck him that the forbidden door—the portal he had pondered for seven long years—was finally allowing him passage. And now, he couldn't have cared less. Reacting to his father's KALM suit, the door unlocked and swung outward on its hinges. Lucas moved further in as Tara's voice called out, "The Hub's outer ring is still six hundred yards ahead. You'll see the indicator on your HUD."

He heard the hatch slam shut and the locks slide back into place. The word HUD reminded him of his dad. *When you're training, it stands for Hope You Don't. Hope You Don't need it, because if you do, something is wrong. It actually stands for Heads-Up Display, but my version is just as accurate.* He shoved the thought aside.

"Hurry!" Tara urged. "We don't know how determined they are."

The path rounded a bend to the right and then fell away suddenly and sharply before continuing on the other side of a twenty-foot divide. Without hesitation, Lucas leapt and landed safely with more than five feet to spare. He marveled for a second--compared to the KALM suit, his training gear was basically useless. As he moved two steps further down the path, he heard someone land behind him. Asante. His mother was quieter, landing a second later. The only sounds were their footfalls on cement and labored breathing.

Lucas felt his guard dropping. It was peaceful to be this completely in the dark. Quiet and calm, like driving down an empty highway at two in the morning under a new moon.

But behind them, a loud crash shattered any illusion of sanctuary. Lucas ran ever faster without tiring, aided by adrenaline and the KALM suit.

Tara spoke again. "Through the door. Right fork."

They had covered half of the distance to the outer ring when they reached another door. Lucas slowed as it swung open, and then turned right when the path split in two.

"Keep running. We've gained some distance ahead of them, but they're only a half minute behind at most."

Two hundred yards to go. Lucas summoned all of his willpower and surged ahead. The cement turned to gravel beneath his feet as the walls fell away on both sides. Lucas trotted into blackness, his world reduced to a narrow strip of earth. Automated caution warnings in his HUD alerted him that the remainder of the pathway hung over a wide, deep cavern. He cautiously approached the edge and stopped to check his HUD for a way forward. A square icon with bidirectional arrows caught his attention. It was one hundred yards away, and about the same distance below his position. Lucas reached out with his mind, feeling a rush of joy when he latched onto a Darktouched machine. He gave it a command, and soon the HUD showed it was moving closer.

Tara and Asante were next to him now. The lift appeared out of the darkness from below, slowing as it neared where they stood, before settling silently in front of them. Lucas had told it to descend before they were even all onboard. The machine slipped smoothly into the blackness until they were enveloped.

The group took a moment to recover their breath. Asante fully extended his right leg in front of him, heel on the ground, and leaned down over it. Tara breathed in deeply and slowly, her right hand trying to work out a side stitch. Lucas flipped through HUD settings to distract himself from thinking about Dad, Alan, and Mai.

The overlay indicated they were halfway across the chasm. "I don't see anything up top," he said. "Maybe they gave up."

Abruptly, Tara burst into laughter. "You look ridiculous in your dad's gear, Lucas," she said. "It's too wide and too short at the same time. When we get to the Abzu Complex, get your KALM gear as soon as they'll let you. *Please.*"

Lucas, glad for the diversion, laughed along with her. *Everyone has to be alive. We'll get them back.*

No one spoke about his dad or Alan. Silently, they agreed to save the topic for later. Speculating about what happened now would only distract them.

Seconds later, the platform reached the other side. As they stepped off, the area above them was illuminated by a floating light orb. It crept along, mesmerizing them, until it was directly overhead.

Then Tara suddenly screamed, "Run!"

The orb plummeted into their midst and burst, revealing a Reclaimer kneeling where it had landed. Without the KALM gear, they would have been blinded and disoriented; the Reclaimer appeared to have counted on this, because he didn't move with urgency.

While his enemy stood unmoving for a moment, Lucas searched for a weakness. Based on height and body type, he assumed the Reclaimer to be male. The enemy wore full-body tactical gear, including a long, hooded cloak and face mask that left only his eyes and the bridge of his nose exposed. The KALM tech told Lucas it was made of a reflective weave intended to amplify light.

So that's why they turn into camera flash bulbs.

Lucas was also able to see the palms of the Reclaimer's gloves. Embedded in the tips of each finger and the center of each palm was a patch of hexagonal scales. The toe of the Reclaimer's right boot looked the same.

Useless, I can't see enough. I'll just hit him from behind. He tensed his body for the attack.

Asante's voice touched his thoughts. "Don't, Lucas. Just run. I've got this." The Reclaimer remained oblivious.

Asante tapped his right hand to his waist. Like a cephalopod, blackness jetted from his body. It struck and clung to the Reclaimer, who screamed and began rubbing his eyes. Asante took advantage of the moment to flee, and Lucas shouldered the disoriented Reclaimer to the ground as he and his mom followed.

Finger-length needles of green light flew past them in bursts as they ran. One caught Asante in his left leg, and he fell to the ground on his next step. He took in a pained breath and exclaimed, "Paralyzed! He's trying to capture, not kill us. We're almost to the outer ring. Keep going."

Lucas kneeled and put Asante's left arm around him, lifting him upright. "We're right behind you, Mom," he said as Tara ran ahead.

"I'll open the gate," she told him. "Don't think—just jump through it."

More green needles flew by. Lucas felt his right-hand sting and then go limp. The Reclaimer was drawing nearer, but there was no time to look over his shoulder. The final door was within view, calling them to safety. *A few more steps now.* Lucas heard a low humming sound and saw the entire entryway rippling. Tara had already gone inside. As one final burst of needles flew harmlessly past, peppering the door frame, he threw himself and Asante over the threshold, hearing nothing as deep water closed around him and the door slammed shut behind them.

Above, below, and all around without end. Swirls and eddies of deep purple and pink surrounded Lucas, like streams of dinoflagellates hidden inside the earth. Behind him, the metal door was hidden among several large rocks. With no light to catch or reflect, the stone remained a gray color. He suspected that, if he were without the KALM gear, the blackness would be insatiable, swallowing nearly all light no matter how bright. A Lightborne or anyone else unfortunate enough to make it this far would almost surely die. That was if they could make it through the passage and past the barrier in the first place.

Lucas flexed his hand instinctively, but it would only partially close. The feeling, stolen away by the green needle, was coming back slowly.

Tara floated next to Asante, checking his leg. "There's no damage to your suit," she said, continuing her ministrations. *How are they still able to talk? How can I hear them?* "Thankfully, it absorbed some of the light needle. If it hadn't, you'd be hard pressed to swim."

Asante snarled. "Damned Shepherds!" Lucas assumed he meant the Reclaimers. "We're lucky that one was cocky or stupid. He could have had us. We were dead to rights."

Tara beckoned Lucas over. "There's something I forgot to tell you. You've probably been hearing us talking in your noggin, right?" She tapped the top-left side of her head; he tried to verbally confirm, but nothing came out. "Eventu-ally, this becomes second nature, but you should have a display in your HUD that looks like a half sphere with three nested layers. Ignore the other symbols for now." Lucas flipped to the correct HUD view and gave the thumbs-up sign. "Mentally select the second circle. The suit will read your intent and transmit directly into the auditory cortex of anyone within thirty feet, as long as they're also wearing Darktouched gear. Right now, you're muted." Lucas spoke again, but only his own voice echoed in his mind. "No—wrong setting. That was the first layer. Now you're talking to yourself."

"Does it work now?" Lucas asked, again giving a thumbs-up and then tilting it downward questioningly; Tara signaled the affirmative. "There we go! Wow, that's really weird."

"Yep. But it's normally the only way we can talk in the Abzu and Infra, so get used to it. You can also open a direct line that has a range up to a mile. The suit uses compiled data and other metrics so we hear what you mean to say. Just know that it maps and transmits not just words but also pitch, inflection, and so on."

She's always loved the tech. Lucas imagined her grinning as she explained, and briefly forgot their circumstances.

"It's not perfect, but it's better than nothing," his mom was saying. "It can translate too."

"Crazy." Lucas performed flips in the water. "The real suits are way better."

Asante growled. "All right, I'm going on ahead. I want to get back to the Abzu Complex. How in the world did they find us so quickly? Did they send two teams? Something isn't right. Be careful in the Tubes, you two." With a startling suddenness, the purple and pink dinoflagellate-like flecks surrounded Asante, and he rapidly disappeared into the distance.

"This is Darktouched nanotechnology," Tara said, waving her hand through the glow. "They help travelers navigate the Abzu. Try talking to them." She paused for a few seconds. "Your dad likes to say that they're 'a masterpiece of the Abzu's own Beydin Krenneth.'" Her voice trailed off, and she fell into silence.

When Lucas reached out, he was shocked to hear a gruff male voice respond. "Cripes. Another one? Something going on today?" The nanobots surrounded him as they had Asante. "Charon at your service. Ferrybot for the Darktouched, and sometimes for dead surface dwellers. I always get them where they belong, albeit less alive than they'd probably like. Do you have my toll ready?"

Lucas panicked slightly. "Toll? What do you mean? I don't have anything."

Charon swirled angrily, becoming a deep red color. "What do you mean you don't have Charon's Toll? What kind of yokels do they let down here nowadays? Are you even Greek? I should drop you off at the Death Valley Hub and leave you."

Stammering, Lucas replied, "What? Greek? No." *How do I get out of this one? Thanks, Mom!* "My first time." He began speaking with his hands, something he did when nervous. "I didn't know. Sorry." He pleaded, "Could I just bring it next time? We don't have time to waste. How much is it?"

The ferrybot swirled angrily again. "Ingrate! If you were in a hurry, you should've brought the fee." He continued grumbling. "'How much is it?' he says. 'Can I just drop it off the next time I happen to be in town?' he says."

As Lucas's mind raced to find a solution to the predicament, he heard Tara call out. "All right, Charon, that's enough. This isn't Ancient Greece, and we're still alive!"

"I'd say just barely, by the looks of that Reclaimer chasing you. Now, that there would've been a first for me. Carrying one of his ilk." Charon returned to his deep purple-and-pink tones. "That's my fee, boy. A Lightborne to play with." He paused, and Tara cleared her throat, so he finally said, "Fine, fine. I apologize. I was only joking. Your name is Lucas, right? Well, where are we going?"

"The Flagstaff Hub main entrance," Lucas said.

"It seems you have no Abzupass, so that's about as far as I can take you anyway. You too?" Charon asked Tara, who confirmed. "Then let's get going. All aboard!"

With a muted *whoosh*, Lucas felt himself being swept away in an impossibly strong indigo current.

Charon chatted with him casually. "Sorry about messing with you, Lucas. But that Lightborne does sound like a right good idea, doesn't it?"

Lucas let himself smile. "Definitely. I'd like to drown the Lightwatch itself." Dark, rageful thoughts ate at him as he replayed the Reclaimer attack over and over in his mind.

Charon coughed softly. When his passengers failed to pick up on the cue, he did it again. Lucas finally asked what he wanted, noting to himself that the ferrybot had no practical use for doing so other than making conversation. Charon said, "Do you know that before me, the Darktouched *swam* everywhere in the Abzu? Terribly uncivilized. I'm quite amazing, am I not?"

Stewing in his thoughts, Lucas didn't vocalize an answer but instead grunted at Charon. He repeatedly formed the fingers of his right hand into a fist and then spread them open.

The ferrybot continued speaking. "According to Darktouched records, though, there was supposedly a time when they commanded dragons and other creatures of the depths. But that was millennia ago, of course."

Lucas's ears pricked up. "Dragons?"

"Giant serpents. Something like those described in ancient Celtic and Chinese myths, most likely," said Charon. "Fearsome creatures of the deepest depths. If you have an interest in such things, you should seek out my creator. Beydin possesses particularly vast knowledge of the old world and the Deep Infra."

"I will, absolutely," said Lucas excitedly. "I never knew there were things like that down here."

"There likely aren't anymore, lad. Not that want to be found, anyway." Charon sighed. "At any rate, we're almost to the Flagstaff Hub main entrance. It's been a pleasure, young man."

The ferrybot called out to Lucas as it deposited him in front of a rock archway, beyond which was a metal door. "Don't forget to find Beyd. And don't forget my toll next time." Then he swirled around to pick up two new passengers waiting nearby. "Stay safe."

Lucas swam through the arch toward the hatch, passed through, and left the Abzu behind him.

The door opened into a narrow room where two sets of elevator doors stood. Tara entered just behind Lucas and walked over to call the lift. Within a few seconds, the doors slid open and they boarded. There were only two buttons, an *S* and an *A*. Tara pressed the *S*, and the elevator began to climb. Lucas deduced that the *A* stood for Abzu, but the *S* he was less certain about. "*S* for surface?" he asked out loud.

"Yep. That's right." Tara tapped her wrists together, and the KALM suit faded away, revealing her red blouse and black jean shorts.

Lucas did the same. Only once the suit was gone did he notice how cumbersome and bulky his clothes felt. *So, while you're wearing the suit, are the clothes there or not?*

A bell sounded, the elevator settled to a stop, and the doors slid open. They stepped into a well-lit room. An unmanned security station was situated between them and the door. The machinery looked like an x-ray scanner, but Lucas somehow doubted that was its function. Beyond it, there was a small waiting area in front with six plastic-seated chairs. On the right side of the room was an office with a placard on the wall that read security officer.

Tara passed through the exit gate and knocked on the door. "Maggie, are you in there?" She turned the handle and the door swung open. Lucas crossed the chamber to stand next to her, ready to run again as Tara called, "Mags! We need those keys."

A mousy-looking twenty-something woman with her hair partially dyed blue stared at a black laptop, enraptured. She leaned forward with her elbows on the tiny desk in front of her. Occasionally, she sipped at an energy drink. Even though she wore earbuds, Lucas could hear death metal blaring.

"Maggie!" Tara shouted, gesticulating at the security guard to no avail. "All right, fine," she said, yanking the earbud out of Maggie's left ear.

"What the hell, dude?" Maggie shouted. She stood, ready for a fight. Then the light of realization came on and lit up her face. "Oh, Tara. I'm so sorry! But this job," she complained, "Is. So. *Boring*."

Tara folded her arms across her chest. "Not a big deal. But can I get the car keys?"

"Of course," said Maggie. She reached into the desk and pulled out a key and fob fastened to the same ring. Tossing them to Tara, she added, "It's parked in the alley. White Jetta."

"Thanks, Mags. You have a good day, okay?" Tara said, reaching into her shorts pocket. "And, if you could, destroy our SIM cards. We can get the phones later." Lucas followed his mom's lead without comment.

"You too." Maggie's eyes focused on Lucas. "Is this your son? He's cute."

Lucas smiled down at her. "Hi, I'm Lucas." He reached out his hand. "Nice to meet you." Tara opened the front door and called for him to hurry, so he said, "Gotta go. Have a good one."

"Thank you," she said, beaming. "Hope you have fun! Asante didn't say what the car was for."

If you only knew.

They exited into a small storage room with dim, flickering lights. Shelves, boxes, and assorted junk formed a kind of maze. They wound their way out, and then stopped at yet another door. Poking her head out to look around, Tara signaled to Lucas. "All clear. Let's go."

The storage room exited into an alleyway on the edge of downtown Flagstaff, where they found the Volkswagen parked. Tara pressed a button on the fob and the doors unlocked. "Hurry up and get in. We don't know how long it'll take 'em to figure this out." They jumped in and Tara started the car, put it in drive, and pulled away from the curb, heading toward the closest through-street.

"It's about twenty-five minutes to the Lava Tubes," said Tara. They turned right on Humphreys Street, heading toward Fort Valley Road. "But we're not going to the Lava Tubes."

Lucas shook his head and then stared at her. "Are you for real? Why?"

"Because Asante's right. Somehow, they knew where we were. They knew enough to storm our house and the Linzers' at the same time. And they found the dark room right away." With a concerned expression, she continued, "The only thing that saved us was an overconfident, inexperienced Reclaimer. Until we know how they knew, we trust no one but ourselves."

Lucas had to admit that her logic was sound. "So where are we going?"

"To the Grand Canyon. Cave of the Domes." She checked the rearview mirror, grabbing a tissue from her pocket to blow her nose. "We'll pass by the forest service road leading to the Lava Tubes, so we might be able to see if anyone is waiting for us... or following." Her eyes again bounced between the rearview mirror and the road ahead, and she took a deep breath. "I'm sorry we lied to you, Lucas."

"You say that, but everyone's still hiding things. I can tell." Annoyance crept up from his stomach to tighten his chest, but he pushed it back down. "There are so many questions I want to ask, but right now I don't know where to start. Do you think Dad and Alan will be okay?"

Tears welled in his mom's eyes and her voice broke. "I don't know. I really don't." She wiped her face and sniffed. "But they're strong. And they have important information. You heard Asante. The Reclaimer chasing us meant to capture us, not kill us. There's a chance."

Lucas rubbed the stubble on his chin, considering her words, and for the next ten minutes they drove on in silence. Lucas examined his life, staring at the afternoon scenery through dark tinted windows. It had always been clear to him that everything he did was in preparation for becoming a Darktouched. *It's all about the family business.*

But there was more to it than that, he understood now. Lightborne and Reclaimers, Abzu and Infra. He wondered what it all added up to. The Linzers were Lightborne. His best friends, Connie and Aella, probably were as well. Out of everything, the fact that those two had lied to him all of their lives made him the angriest. But then, he had never told them he was a Darktouched, either.

Maybe they were all pawns in someone else's game. But whose? He extremely regretted handing his phone to Maggie without questioning the act.

I miss you guys. And I miss you, Dad and Alan.

Some time had passed, and Lucas had fought the urge to ask for as long as he could. "What do the Reclaimers want? Why are they trying to capture us, specifically?"

"Your dad and I are high-ranking Darktouched. It could be that." Tara seemed to be weighing her next words on her tongue. "But Malank, Fiala, and Asante have other ideas. Today was supposed to be a revelation for all of us." She dried her tears and blew her nose again. "I guess it was, in a way. I'm so sorry, Lucas."

He wished his mom would stop saying "sorry." Every time she uttered it, he wanted to scream at her. But there was no point. The past was past, and now none of them had any choice but to run, hide, and hope.

"We're almost to the forest service road," said Tara. "Keep your eyes open."

Lucas saw nothing through the trees on either side. *But Lightborne can hide in plain sight, so how could we see them even if we tried?*

Suddenly inspired, he latched onto an idea. "Can they track our suits? Can they sense if we use them?"

Tara shook her head. "No, there are various countermeasures to ensure they can't sense us. Some extend from our Darktouched abilities, others from the suits themselves."

Lucas tapped his wrists together, scanned the horizon, and then gave a start. In the direction of the Lava Tubes entrance, above the trees, in a place where they shouldn't have been, he was sure he saw two human shapes hovering. He checked the sky behind and in front but saw nothing. Then, he snapped his eyes back to where he had seen the floating people. *They're gone, if they were there at all.* As he unsuited, he muttered, "I thought I saw something, but I can't be sure."

"Better safe than sorry," said Tara. "We'll stick to the new plan."

Lucas turned his back to his mom and sat facing the passenger side window. He leaned his head against the glass. "So far, at least, I don't think they're following."

He hoped that shred of luck would last the afternoon.

6

PHOTOGRAPHS

LUCAS STARED PAST THE scenery during the drive north to the Grand Canyon. The vibration of tires on asphalt lulled him into a quiet reverie, and he paced a corridor of his own memories. Without intending to, he fixated on the final day he had spent with his best friends.

"I'm so glad you two made me do this," said Conleth Spencer in his customary grumble. "I could've been drinking beer and watching football."

"Well, Connie, your chubby butt shouldn't be drinking beer anyway. Where do you even get it?" asked Aella Mendoza, her curly black hair carried for a moment by a gust of wind.

"Trade secret," said Connie.

Aella looked toward the sky, supplicating some unseen power. When she spoke again, sadness tinged her voice. "Plus, we won't get to do this again for a while. Taking this picture is a tradition. Every year since the third grade." As usual, she was at the front of their trio.

Connie sipped water from his CamelBak gear. "That's true, I guess," he said. "Man, I've gotten out of shape since football season. Linemen shouldn't hike." Sweat dripped down the brim of his camouflage hunting cap and darkened the underarms, neck, and back of his dark red t-shirt. He removed the cap and rapidly ran a hand back and forth through his close-cropped black hair to shake free the sweat. Like the first weeds of spring, gray follicles had already begun to usurp his cranium.

"Dude—Connie! I didn't need a shower," complained Lucas, who was behind, below, and downwind from the other two. "Disgusting."

"It'll wash off," said Connie. "And it's Spence. You bastards always calling me Connie is why I don't get any ladies."

Aella wheeled around to face him. Her nose was crinkled in a way Lucas recognized. *Aella has that look. A sure sign of... that.* She punched her much larger friend in the arm. "Suuuure. That's why." Connie spluttered, turned red, and then laughed. Her work done, Aella clambered up some rocks and continued down the trail.

"Why you always gotta be so mean, Ael?" Connie passed by a prickly pear cluster and stepped around a corner.

Lucas heard her call back to them, "Now I'm beer too? Aella is fine—no need to shorten it."

Connie took another drink. "You know, I wouldn't mind a you-sized beer right now. It's hot!"

In the present, Lucas felt his heart warm as he remembered hearing himself say, "Man, I'll miss this." He may have even spoken the words out loud while sitting next to his mom. "You both have to stay in touch."

Aella rested on an outcrop overlooking white and red sandstone rock formations dotted with juniper, pinyon pine, and other high-desert plants. The sun, high overhead, reflected off her aviator sunglasses and cast a sheen on her exposed olive skin. She wore a green, short-sleeved top and gray hiking shorts. Reassuringly, she said, "Of course we will, Lucas. We're all basically siblings. Blood is thicker than water." She shot a side-eyed look at Connie. "Unless it's been excessively thinned."

"Damned straight," said Connie. "On all counts."

The two boys now stood on either side of Aella. She grabbed a snack bar from her fanny pack, tore it open, and broke it into three equal pieces. "Almost there. Let's go before that group we passed catches up."

"Is it a race?" Connie gestured at her with his palms upturned. "We've got nowhere to be."

"Why waste time?" she asked, and then started down the trail again.

Lucas put his hand in the middle of Connie's back and lightly pushed. "We'd better get going or she'll be on her way down while we're still heading up." His friend grunted and they walked on together.

Five minutes later, they slipped past a trio of girls at a narrow section of trail just ahead of their destination. Once they were out of earshot, Connie whispered to Lucas, "Man, the tall one in the middle was hot." Lucas grinned, then closed his eyes and nodded slowly, agreeing with his friend.

"She was way too skinny. Why do you guys want sticks?" Aella was smiling but her brow was serious. "Whatever. These Greco-Mexican genes are where it's at. Goldilocks right here." She posed and motioned with her hands, pretending to showcase herself. "Just kidding. But I am pretty cute though." There was no inflection in her voice to suggest this was in any way a question.

Lucas turned red, unsure how to respond. Connie simply shrugged and said matter-of-factly, "Maybe. To each their own, I say."

"How about we take the picture, guys?" suggested Lucas, eager to move on. "Before it fills up. Not many people here." He motioned toward a ridge where a few fellow hikers sat resting at the end of the trail. "Maybe we can ask one of them to take it for us. We need someone who knows what they're doing though."

He unslung the strap from around his neck and walked over to the first person he saw with a camera. His dad had often told him, "Never judge based on appearances alone, but don't be afraid to start there either." For Lucas, the point was that you had to start somewhere even when unsure, so why hesitate? In the present, he decided to ask his dad the next time he saw him.

"I'm sorry, the camera's not mine," said the man, pointing with his chin at a woman standing a few feet away. "But my wife can help you."

Lucas walked over to her. "Excuse me. Hi. Your husband said you might be willing to take a few photos of me and my friends on the bridge?" He pointed over his shoulder at the natural arch that locals called Devil's Bridge. At its highest point, it stood roughly fifty feet above the desert below. "Maybe from over there so it shows how high up we are?"

She gushingly agreed to help, and Lucas called Connie and Aella over. Walking single file, they crossed the bridge. Connie stepped gingerly over a cracked portion, obviously afraid it would give way beneath him.

"Okay," said Lucas, "All the way to the narrow part." They centered themselves over the thinnest section of stone, and Lucas put his arms around both of his friends.

"Three, two, one—say cheese!" the woman yelled to them from across the divide.

Lucas slumped in the car seat, his eyes closed as he remembered that the photos were still on his camera's memory card.

Now Lucaas stood in a brightly lit clearing in a darkly shrouded wood. Snow crinkled underfoot. There, perhaps ten feet in front of him, was the white owl from the simulator. It cocked its head to one side, questioning him. Then, wings partially spread, it approached him until the gap between them had been cut in half. Its haunting voice called to Lucas, "Child of Shadow, follow my lead when next you see me." Suddenly, it lifted high above the ground and swooped toward him. Transforming into an eagle of light, wings fully expanded and talons ready, it plunged. He covered his face, bracing for the attack.

The next instant, he was back on the porch with Alan and his dad. "Don't worry about us, Luc. Just take care of yourself." Alan's kind eyes looked down his crooked nose at the four-year-old Lucas. "Nothing can save us now."

Darren finished his iced tea and threw the glass across the yard. "He's right, bud. Once the Reclaimers have you, there's no coming back. We're goners."

"I can save you!" Lucas tried to protest, but nothing came out. His words stuck in his throat, and he frantically flipped through HUD settings as the sun overhead grew blindingly bright and the two men faded from view.

"How, Luc?" Alan asked gently. "You're only one man. They have an army."

Darren encouraged him, "Be strong, Lucas. Our hope is with you young people. Go to the Abzu and explore the Infra. Remember what your mother and I taught you."

Behind him, an ever louder tapping on the window drew Lucas's rage. "Stop! Don't go!" he cried. The tapping became frantic pounding, and he heard the sound of shattering glass behind him. When he turned to look, blackness flooded in around him, filling his mouth and nostrils as he tried to scream.

7

THE LAST CHANCE

"HAVE A NICE NAP?" Tara asked as she made a left turn.

Lucas forcefully closed his eyes and opened them again to push away the bleariness and dull headache.

"The ranger said Grandview Trail is closed due to erosion, which is perfect for us. We can head down as the sun is setting. It's a new moon, so we can wear our suits."

Lucas, still groggy and troubled by the dream, took a minute to process what she was saying. "What about the car?"

"We'll ditch the car," said Tara. "They can't tie it to us. And where we're going, we don't need roads, Marty."

Lucas smiled thinly, unamused by the reference. "Nice..." His voice trailed off. "Do we have anything to eat? I'm starving."

Tara brought the car to a stop in a parking lot that was empty except for a few work trucks. She opened the console and came up empty. "Check the glove box. Maggie always has something tucked away."

Lucas rummaged in the small compartment, lifting a black leather case and checking around it. He popped up triumphantly, holding a Snickers bar in his hand. "Want half?" he asked his mom.

Tara shook her head. "No, you go ahead." She did a double take as he ripped open the wrapper and appeared to swallow half of it whole. "Actually, I'll have a bite. I'm pretty famished myself." Her right hand shook as she held it out to him. Lucas pretended not to notice as he deposited the remainder of the candy bar, still in its wrapper, into her upturned palm.

"There should be water in the trunk." She got out and returned half a minute later with two one-liter bottles. "There are a couple more. We'll save those for the hike down. Here." She handed him one.

"Thanks," said Lucas. He cracked the seal and guzzled half. "Do you think they followed us?"

Tara shook her head. "I don't think so. But that doesn't mean we're out of danger." She drank from her own bottle. "You remember what Dad said about the Lava Tubes, right? Well, these caves are both better and worse. Look." She took a pen and piece of paper from the console and used its lid as a drawing surface. In the center of the page, she drew a horizontal rectangle with multiple lines extending from it. "There are a number of false entrances extending north and south from the main cavern. The Tubes are maybe the equivalent of a class five rapid on a terrible day. These range from class three to six."

"Do you know which one is the right one?"

Tara winked at him somewhat smugly. "If my boss and the Darktouched records are to be believed, then yes." The confident look fell away from her visage. "We used to embed a reactive agent into the living rock as a marker. But when our leaders forbade entry in the 1800s, they removed it so no one could find the right entrance. We'll have to find the trail of breadcrumbs no one else has. And we have a leg up, since my security level lets me know things."

Lucas clicked his tongue as he considered her plan. "Okay. So, we have a better than fifty percent chance of finding the entrance we want. If we find the right one, odds are good we live. If we find a really bad one, then we probably don't." He tapped a finger on the piece of paper. "Why did they forbid entry?"

"Records are sealed, even for me," Tara admitted.

"That's comforting. And there's no other way into the Infra?"

"The entire southwestern U.S. is about the same out to the coast: Tiny Abzu Hubs and caves. The primary Hubs in this country are in Rapid City and Louisville. That's where we can get your Abzupass, but we don't know if we have that much time. Or if..." *Or if Dad and Alan do.* "I can't leave you above ground on your own."

"Yeah, I get it. Then let's find the right entrance," Lucas said.

Tara crumpled up the paper and tucked it in her pocket. "If they *are* following us, there's no point helping them find us. Let's get ready to hike."

The sun was settling low on the horizon when they slipped around the barricades and began their descent into the canyon thirty minutes later. Dusky light painted the sky overhead in brilliant shades of red and orange, casting shadows in the gorges and lighting the tips of the ancient plateau's remnants. The temperature had already started its precipitous decline, and on the canyon rim, the soothing warmth of a late spring day would soon become a near-freezing bite. A falcon soared high above them, out for an evening hunt, and a gecko was sunning itself before night set in.

Lucas recalled Tara's reminder: "We can't wear our KALM suits until the light fades, so it'll be chilly." And then, in a lecturing tone, she had added, "Darktouched have rules. We don't want everyone knowing about us. In ancient times, it was easy enough to invent stories of the Underworld, but now people are harder to fool. Or they think so anyway."

As the sun dipped lower and the pair hiked on, they talked in low voices just in case they happened upon a ranger or trail repair crew. Both breathed easier when, an hour in, the sun had dipped and the light was low enough to don their KALM gear. Were they seen now, the light absorbing material would make them appear like shadows, unless someone stood very close.

Together, they skittered over steep cobblestone riprap and wound their way down into the canyon. Lucas was struck by the KALM interpretation of the scenery around them as they stood atop a section of the trail with views both to the right and left. A purple sky hovered over plants and earth that maintained their daylight colors, and there were no shadows to be seen.

Off to their right, he heard rustling in a juniper tree and the flapping of wings. Moments later, an audible squeaking erupted from the brush as a predator squeezed and tore the life out of its victim. The eerie cry of a coyote floated to them on the wind whipping through the canyon, and Lucas thought of Mai. He had spent so much time worrying about Dad, Alan, and his own situation that she had been squeezed out of his thoughts. Guilt wriggled its way in, and as the light grew dimmer his mood became increasingly somber.

Interrupting his downward spiral, an unfamiliar alert popped up on his HUD. "Accept the invitation," said Tara. "I set up a private comm channel."

"Oh yeah, you mentioned setting up a direct line earlier. Range of up to a mile." Lucas was impressed. "That's handy." He flipped to the communications view in his HUD and joined her.

"No risk of being heard this way," she explained. "So, have you decided on your mission alignment yet?"

Lucas clenched his teeth and disposed of a little venom before answering. "Support of some kind."

"That's noble, but ridiculous with your talent. We didn't raise a short order cook or a mechanic." Tara's voice became almost shrill and Lucas smiled, knowing his response was having its intended effect. "Delve or Seek," she said. "I won't have you working with the Black Hand either. They are... a necessary evil."

"Seek, then. If it's good enough for Dad, it's good enough for me. Besides, you can change your mission alignment." He needed to sound nonchalant even if he didn't feel that way. "I don't get the weird wall between all of these things."

"Because you won't have time to be good at everything. Think about Above-world professions."

Here comes the sermon.

"You can't be a great physicist *and* an influential linguist *and* a decorated soldier all at the same time, right? Besides, you have to stand for *something*. Delvers want to understand the world more fully by examining it. Our goals are focused on gathering knowledge and building a better world." Tara hesitated for a moment. "I'm not trying to push you in either direction—it's your choice.

Your father is a Seeker and a good man. So is Asante. But they're idealists chasing something that might not even be real. Besides, there's no money in it."

"You're doing a great job of not pushing, Mom," Lucas said. "As usual." *I ought to be grateful, right?*

"You know what, young man, you should be grateful we care so much about your future. My parents didn't help me at all."

Bingo. "Maybe that'd be better." Lucas spoke the words in spite of himself. He was incredibly grateful for the life his parents had given him. But some part of his psyche made him fight her.

"Fine," she snapped. "If that's what you want, I'll drop it."

"Thanks." He toyed with the idea of leaving the comm channel, but blushed with embarrassment under his suit at the childishness of it.

Two hours into the hike, they reached the shell of an old building. The signpost declared it to be the Last Chance Mine. Strewn about were old metalworking tools, cookware, and other artifacts.

Tara stepped inside the ruins and began tapping at the stone walls. "Records state that a few containers of the catalyst we need were hidden here. It's what lights up the reactive agent I mentioned before. There are supposed to be few more in the mine itself too. The catalyst was originally synthesized in the Abzu Complex, so it doesn't normally exist up here."

Her tapping became more urgent the longer she searched, and after five minutes Lucas became anxious. He wanted to ask her why someone had bothered to store the catalyst in the ruins of an old mine, but instead simply asked, "Can I help?"

"Sure," she said. "Look for a loose stone in the wall. It should be in a corner. That was the only specific information in the file."

Another five minutes passed before they both knew a decision was looming. Lucas was the one who voiced it. "So do we go into the mine or wing it in the cave?"

Tara ended her futile examination of the rock wall, now standing where she had been crouching a moment before. "Old mines are dangerous. A cave-in could end this trip in a hurry." She paced back and forth as she spoke. "But picking the wrong entrance in the cave means we die, almost definitely. Let's do the mine."

In spite of the circumstances, Lucas couldn't keep youthful glee out of his voice. "I've always wanted to explore an abandoned mine."

"Be careful, Lucas," Tara warned him, hands on her hips. "If you take this too lightly, we could die."

He shrugged. "Yeah, yeah. I will be."

Minutes later, they were inching their way down an adit that showed signs of previous collapse. Old minecart tracks lay underfoot, entire swaths buried under fine red dust. Wooden support beams and shoring had rotted over the prior century, letting loose rock spill onto the paths.

They moved slowly inward for several minutes before Tara spoke, stopping at a junction. "There's supposed to be an abandoned tunnel that was sealed off even before the mine closed. It's this way."

Lucas followed as she veered to her left, and was surprised when a mass of fluttering wings rushed past and around them toward the mine portal. Their presence had disturbed a bat roost. They laughed nervously and then pressed on.

After several more very slow minutes, they stopped in front of a clumsily built wall. It was formed of loose rock and other bits of rubbish. "Help me move some of this but be careful." Together, they set about gingerly lifting and sliding away the wall, stone by stone. When they had cleared the debris sufficiently to continue forward, Tara motioned for Lucas to stay behind while she crawled through.

"Okay," she said once she was on the other side, "you wait there while I search." Lucas watched through the narrow entryway as she disappeared around a corner. He heard her voice say, "Oh, there's a small room here. This must be it."

He sat impatiently as she went silent for an excruciatingly long time—in reality, likely no more than a minute or two. All of a sudden, he heard wood break and rubble fall. Panic had carried him through the crawlspace before he even considered they might both end up stuck in the mineshaft.

"Mom! Are you okay?" he shouted. "Mom!" He rounded the corner and saw her sitting on the ground, back propped against the wall.

Tara began laughing. "Crap! That was close." She held up her left hand. "Got it. I think we're going to be okay. Help me up."

As Lucas bent down to grab her hand, he looked off to his left and almost fell over. Further down the shaft, perched on an abandoned minecart, was the white owl. "Mom, do you see that?" He pointed at the bird.

Tara nodded. "Your owl again. What in the world?" Lucas began to walk toward it as though hypnotized, its words from the dream still deeply affecting him. He barely heard his mom call, "Lucas, don't! The floor!"

In his trance-like state, he had not watched or felt the ground beneath his feet. The sound of splintering wood and a sickening crack were the last things he heard before he fell. He kept falling for a few seconds, and then he was in deep water with walls closing in around him. His fingers grasped for a handhold, but found none on the smoothly carved stone.

"Lucas! Are you okay? Can you climb out?"

"No, the walls are smooth and wet. I can't even do it with the suit on."

"Wait. I'll try to find a rope or something."

He looked up and his heart sank. His HUD showed that it was a little over 140 feet back to the shaft. "I don't think that will work. It's too far." His thoughts turned to the water below, and he dived under. Twenty feet further down, a chamber opened up. It showed signs of blasting and other mining activity. "Mom, I think there might be a way down here. Meet me outside."

"What? Are you insane? Lucas!"

He flipped his HUD settings to the comm view and muted her. *Now I can think, at least.* Paddling deeper and further in, he found more submerged tracks and followed them in the direction of the mine entrance. Or he thought so anyway. But instead of rising in elevation, the path began to descend. It became steeper and steeper.

He abruptly stopped. Again, there in the blackness in front of him, was the white owl. *I am losing my mind.* He pursued, pushing himself faster and faster, but the bird—which was flying unnaturally through the water—eluded him. His heart pounded in his chest as his arms and legs, honed by years spent in competition, churned ever harder. And yet, with each turn and descent, he was further away instead of closer. *I can't stop now. I have to see this through!* As he rounded another corner, he saw only blackness. The owl had left him, and now he was somewhere far beneath the earth, still with no way out of the mine.

He floated slowly in the darkness, searching all around for a way back to the surface. There was nothing. He swam up and found only solid stone. For what could have been several minutes or an hour, he explored the perimeter. Still nothing. Finally, in desperation, he dove.

There, creeping along the floor, were enormous horseshoe crabs that were easily as long as he was tall. Awestruck, he watched them for a moment. Remembering the comm channel, he unmuted Tara. "Mom, are you there?"

"Yes. Are you outside?"

"No, I have no idea where I am. Mom—there are giant horseshoe crabs down here. There's still no way out though." And then he saw it. "Wait, there might be. Talk later."

"Lucas? Lucas! What about crabs? What do you mean? You have no idea what's down there."

A small hole in the floor, barely large enough to fit a man, called to him like a siren. He darted for it without thinking and squeezed through to the other side. Before he really understood what was happening, he was falling again.

The water turned to droplets and then faded away entirely. He fell further and further, until he could no longer tell where he had fallen from. Then, abruptly, he stopped falling and his feet touched solid earth.

He was in the Deep Infra. Someplace where the KALM gear was almost blind and where real danger lurked. There was no purple sky here, only a void dotted with floating masses of earth. He gritted his teeth and then swore. No more than ten feet in front of him, wings flapping and inquisitive eyes locked on his, was the white owl.

"You have done well, Child of Shadow, to find me. But we have much further to go. Follow."

It flew away before he could speak. Not wanting to be left alone, Lucas chased after it once more.

8

INFRA

A HUGE SHADEWIND BORE down upon Lucas from the left and sent him careening into blackness. Hundreds of hours in the simulator had honed his reactions, so instead of flailing wildly, he willed himself to lean into the force and return to solid ground.

As he scanned the distance to see where the owl had gone, he spied a floating mass of earth that was forty feet in front of him and about half as much above. *The simulator never had me jump this far... or land upside down.* He stood still, for the first time noticing the deep, titanic, mournful groan accompanying each surge of energy. Creaking and moaning like an old farmhouse in the middle of a winter gale, the Infra cried out.

Flipping through HUD settings, he now realized the purpose of one of the unknown views. It showed pulsing arrows pointing upward from below and a countdown. Five seconds. Four. Three. Without hesitation, he sprinted and took a flying leap toward the faraway platform. As he soared through emptiness, the countdown hit zero, and another shadewind pushed up from under him. The vibration from the impact penetrated Lucas's entire frame. He willed the soles of his feet to face the mass of earth and bent his knees to soften the landing. Touching down softly on padded feet, he ran at full speed in the direction the owl had flown.

He leapt to the next landmass and the next, each further away and in a different orientation than the last. *This feels so natural.* Joy washed away any doubts and fears as he followed the creature of omen.

Then, some unknown duration later, the chase stopped. The owl stood solemnly before him. "Child of Shadow, from here we leap, spring, descend to the edge of true darkness. Come. Together this time."

As though in a dream, Lucas tiptoed to the precipice and looked down. Darkness reached up from the abyss with thin, claw-like tendrils. It was so potent that he physically felt it scrape and shift his body. Where it touched him, color faded. Where it touched him, he felt cold and weak. Where it touched him, there was only absolute absence.

"Are you serious?" he asked his winged guide. The owl merely stared at him with wise eyes. "All right. It was nice knowing you." Then he let himself fall into the spinning, swirling bleakness of nonexistence.

Strangely, he felt nothing at all. No shadewinds, no sight, no sound, no wind, no sense of falling—utterly nothing. The owl spread its wings and floated alongside him, an infinitesimal bit of white descending ever further. No words were spoken and Lucas felt time cease to exist. He could have fallen for an hour, a day, or a lifetime. It no longer mattered. Deeper and deeper they went.

In the pure calm, they alighted on a perfectly round stone platform. Lucas couldn't tell if it had been there before--it simply was. Upon it was carved a four-pointed star, with three wavy lines extending from between each point. In the far distance, around the platform and erupting from the darkness, stood ten equally spaced pillars also made of stone. They were truly colossal structures, towering so high into the black that they vanished, as if holding up the world itself.

The owl glided down to him from above, landing on the dais in front of him. "Sit. Listen," its haunting voice said to him. "Child of Shadow, Bringer of Light. Welcome. This is a place of great portent to you. Fate will see you returned here one day, so remember it well."

"Where are we?"

"Nowhere. Everywhere. Anywhere. The edge of true darkness, and the birth of true light."

"I don't understand."

"You will. You did. You do. When you return to the world, know that in this place there is no now, no then, and no when."

"So, it doesn't exist?"

"What does it mean to exist?"

Lucas pondered the words in silence, then answered. "To think, feel, and struggle. To need and want things. To believe in things. To experience. That's my view."

"Good. Bad. Mediocre. Your answer is your own. That is existence."

If you say so.

"I do say so, Child of Shadow."

"I guess I should have seen that coming," muttered Lucas. "So after all this trouble, all you have for me are vague words."

"No. I have one more message: Find me once more in the Abzu Complex. Your fate truly begins to unfold there." The owl took to the wing. "Enough talking. Stand. Rise with me."

Through no will or force of his own, Lucas began to fly through the absolute nothingness. He looked down, trying to see the place they had just left, wondering if he could return on his own.

"Do not try to find this place. It will find you."

That is so annoying. I hope you heard that too. Stupid bird.

And then, similarly to how he had come to stand on the dais, Lucas's feet touched earth in a narrow corridor.

"Remember, Child of Shadow. Find me in the Abzu Complex. Farewell."

9

SHADEWINDS HARNESSED

THE HALLWAY EXTENDED IN front of Lucas for fifty feet and for another thirty behind. As was quickly becoming his custom in new environments, he browsed HUD views. The overlay notified him that the walls and floor were constructed from fired mud bricks. It also provided a submenu for accessing a detailed breakdown of the materials and their chemical composition. One data point that particularly interested him was labeled "Object Estimated Age," which was formatted as a running clock. If the readout was accurate, these bricks were more than five thousand years old.

Lucas's mouth gaped in awe for a moment at the implications. *How did this get here?* Any Darktouched-specific learning had always centered more on basic skills and knowledge of different professions. He remembered his dad telling him on a few occasions, "The Infra is *chock full* of tons of cool old stuff, Lucas. You could spend twenty lifetimes just looking at it all." But, citing his pledge to the Darktouched rules, his dad would always shut the conversation down before revealing anything meaningful.

Lucas shrugged off the gloom of wishing his dad was here with him and forced his feet to move. Along the walls hung braziers at set intervals. As he walked along, he wondered why anyone would need torchlight in the Infra, where only the Darktouched traveled. The thought quickly dissipated when he heard a loud thud. Unsure what had made it, he proceeded cautiously.

Lucas rounded the corner, and initially thought to call out to whoever or whatever was in the building with him, but then changed his mind. *Probably best to hold onto my one advantage. At least until I know who they are.*

The hallway widened into a square common area. Shallow, rectangular indentations lined the room's perimeter, and the tattered remnants of partition walls and floor cushions were strewn about. Earthenware pots––some broken––were set into deeper indentations near the center of each seating area. Unseen stairs, perhaps back the way he had come, led to a second storey that shared the same courtyard. He saw no sign of human remains or any other indication that people had ever lived here—at least, not in a very long time.

Lucas could hear choppy voices through the KALM comm system now. *I must be right on the edge of audible range.* His HUD's communications view showed the source was two individuals through the doorway to his left, so he sidled in that direction until their speech became clear. The display clarified that they were speaking in English, and the first words he understood came from a male voice that sounded possibly Caribbean.

"I can't *believe* we're down here searchin' through this junk. There's nothin' here!"

A woman with a Russian accent replied, "You never know, Tuck. We might get lucky with one of these tablets."

The man scoffed. "Yeah, because that's our luck. Noire, the most valuable thing on these hunks of clay is bad poetry written by a drunk scribe."

Lucas moved closer. *These two are probably Delvers. Infra artifact analysis is one of their main jobs.*

The woman laughed. "Like I said, you never know. We get paid something either way, so just keep looking." Her voice trailed off. "Are you registering a third KALM signature?"

"Yep. Hey, you out there," the man called out, "whoever you are, it's not nice to spy."

Relieved to encounter anyone––friendly or not––in this unknown place after his experience with the owl, Lucas responded right away. "Sorry," he said, stepping through the doorway. "I didn't mean to."

The two came into view, both roughly the same height. The woman, Noire, was of an average build while the man, Tuck, was very thin. KALM suits hid the rest of their features.

"Nice to meet you," Lucas said awkwardly.

Noire was the first to address him. "Didn't mean to? Who are you? The HUD shows your equipment is registered under the Darkname of Galan Cadenza. But the person inside is a nobody with no name. Why are you eavesdropping on us?"

Tuck jumped in with a snicker, "Yeah, what's with that gear? Hand-me-downs?"

Lucas flushed under his suit. "I..." *Actually, where do I even start?* He decided to lie. "I stole my dad's suit to go, uh... spelunking. And I fell into a hole. And then, somehow, I ended up here."

Tuck chortled. "Some spoiled, unlicensed Darktouched kid stole his papa's suit and wound up in the Infra? You gotta be kiddin' me."

Noire shook her head. "He's obviously lying. For one, there's no way down to this part of the Infra except through the Funnel. But whatever." Noire shrugged. "Let's keep looking, Tuck. This one seems harmless. Simple, but harmless."

Tuck laughed again and turned away from Lucas to saunter across the room to a shelf built into the wall. Upon it were neatly arranged clay tablets. Noire inhaled as though she'd had a thought and regretted having it. She spoke to Lucas again.

"You can't get back to the Aboveworld without going through the Abzu Complex. Do you know how to get there?" He shook his head. "You can tag along with us then. For now, just stay out of our hair." Then she also walked away, but not before saying, "Don't worry, we won't leave you here. Now shoo."

Lucas returned to the common room, deciding to wander through the building on his own to pass the time. The last thing he heard was Noire ask Tuck, "Do you know Galan? So familiar..."

His feet took him to the doorway on his left. As Lucas walked, he wondered what this place had been. *Was it a library? A monastery? A rest house? And why is it in the Infra at all?* Although his conclusion was that none of the answers mattered right now, he continued musing to while away the time.

The next room was rectangular, with seven rows of long stone benches arranged in three columns. A stage occupied the far wall. There was nothing else of note, so he backed out and looked to his right. The final door on the first floor was the main entryway. Lucas had no need to leave yet, so he paced back down the hallway he'd originally come in from. There were no rooms along the corridor, but he did find stairs leading up, as he'd suspected.

When he reached the second level, he entered the first doorway he came to. The chamber appeared to have been used as an office or writing room. Reed tools for producing cuneiform texts were scattered haphazardly.

Lucas's eyes latched onto a clay tablet with an inscription that looked only partially completed. When he picked it up to look at it, the HUD overlaid the ancient script with modern English. It opened with the words: "Eleventh Year of Tiamat's Fury."

We are beginning to lose all hope that the dragon's rage will subside. It burns more fiercely with each passing day, and the waters below roil. We fear our destruction looms. The great and terrible Tiamat, mother of all, cannot be appeased by any acts of man. Therefore, we have resolved to supplicate our resplendent lords so that

The text stopped abruptly. For whatever reason, the writer had been interrupted and was never able to finish. Lucas held on to the tablet as he wandered back out of the scriptorium and considered the words he had just read.

He was near certain that "waters below" referred to the Abzu. As for Tiamat, he only remembered seeing the name in some videogames, and knew it was typically depicted as a dragon, which would align with the text. The "resplendent lords" could be any gods in any ancient pantheon.

Sum total: No idea. Even so, the find stirred his imagination. Tablet still in hand, he barely glanced at anything in the next room. *It's just a kitchen.* His stomach growled, but he didn't heed it. He allowed himself to be momentarily distracted by a simple contraption for lowering dishes to the seating area below. It struck him that, for such an ancient building, the inhabitants had a number of conveniences bordering on modern. But, very quickly, the words inscribed in clay gripped him again. No longer cautious, and fully consumed by his thoughts, Lucas proceeded aimlessly.

Finally, he looked up. His legs had carried him through the last doorway, and he now stood on a balcony. There, spread before him, was a collection of similar brick structures to the one he was currently in, laid out in an organized fashion with planned streets and alleyways. At the farthest reaches of his vision, backed by the purple sky above and swirling ocean of darkness underneath, were some edifices that looked half missing. What remained was slowly crumbling and falling away into the void below. It looked like an enormous monster had taken a bite and torn away a large section of some ancient city.

Scanning the horizon, he saw what looked like three distinct flocks of birds, each in tight formation, swooping this way and that. They were high above the tops of the buildings and followed no obvious pattern, their movements flirting with the edge of the HUD's range. Achingly slowly, they moved closer until the display finally locked in.

TARGET: Cerberus System (v7.4)
OWNER: Beydin Krenneth
PRIMARY INTENDED FUNCTION(S): Cursory-level identification and/or sampling of newly introduced objects and lifeforms within the Upper Infra.
SECONDARY INTENDED FUNCTION(S): Apprehension and/or eradication of non-permitted personnel and disposal of disallowed foreign objects.

One of the flocks was getting nearer now, each dip and turn edging them to where Lucas stood. He could almost make out the individual creatures comprising each group now. *Just a little closer...*

"Ahhh!" he cried as he was suddenly pulled backward with great force.

"Are you stupid?" yelled Noire. It wasn't really a question. "Cerberus will either kill you or throw you in holding. Didn't you read the HUD?" Lucas was still too shocked to speak, and she gave him no chance to recover. "Three clusters of relentless, all-seeing one-eyed urchins. Getting poked by even one spike hurts like hell."

Lucas finally felt able to speak in full sentences. "But I'm Darktouched, shouldn't that—"

"Unlicensed, nameless, missionless Darktouched. You might as well be a Lightborne or a Severed."

"A Lightborne or a what?"

Noire groaned. "I can't deal with this right now. Learn on your own time." She looked down, her eyes fixed on the tablet in Lucas's hand. "What's that? Let me see." Lucas needed her help to reach the Abzu Complex, so he complied without protest. She read it, whispering a few of the words. "Oh, damn it!" Then, she shoved the tablet into Lucas's chest and stormed away, heading back down the stairs. "Tuck, you were right. Let's leave." Lucas sped down the hallway behind her.

Tuck was waiting for them in the common area. "Told ya so. What happened?"

"This... person," she said flatly, "found a—"

"My name," Lucas cut Noire off only to be cut off himself, "is—"

"Nikto," she said. "Your name is Nikto. Once you pledge yourself to our rules, you have no choice but to follow them. You'd know that if you'd gone through orientation. Now stop interrupting me."

"But I haven't taken the Pledge," argued Lucas.

Tuck then spoke up. "*We* have, though. From the Abzu down, we can't say, hear, or remember any name but your Darkname. Until you have one, you really are a nobody. A Nikto."

"That's not true! My mom was saying my name in the Abzu's outer ring."

Noire kicked and broke one of the clay pots. "Enough! The outer rings are a gray zone, and you have no Darkname. The rules are in place for a reason. If a Shepherd tortured us and we gave up your Aboveworld name, you'd be dead. And so would others, because YOU DON'T LISTEN!" she shouted in frustration. "NOW! *Nikto* found a partial tablet. It's the same as all the others. No new information."

Not wanting to anger her further, Lucas chose not to press the issue. Still, the rule made no sense to him.

"Tiamat this, radiant lords that?" Tuck's annoyance was palpable.

"Right. No specifics, no *names*," Noire said through clenched teeth. Motioning around the room, she continued, "We're cursed. Weeks analyzing this pile of bricks for nothing."

"I guess that's what we get for Delvin' in the shallows. We'll have to go deeper."

Tuck headed for the exit. "Let's get back. We can talk later."

Ignoring Lucas entirely, Noire jogged to catch up with her friend.

The next few seconds dragged for Lucas before Tuck's voice came through the comm, "Are you comin', Nikto? We haven't got all day, man. Let's get before Cerberus comes knockin'."

Air blasted Lucas as the scenery of ancient buildings flew past in a blur, the shadewinds lifting and propelling him and Noire at extreme speeds. *Shadesurfing, she called it. Awesome.*

Steering lines emerging from the hands of Noire's KALM suit—highlighted shining blue by the HUD—contrasted brilliantly with the violet sky and black sea below. They reached up to connect at the wing tips of a shadowy kite outlined in the same color. From her belt extended a center line marked by an equally bright yellow hue that ran up to bridle lines tethered to the kite—the primary means of transforming shadewind power into Darktouched swiftness.

Lucas clung to her back, arms wrapped around her waist, but it was unnecessary. Designed for this purpose, their KALM suits adhered to each other solidly. A platform of shadow supported Noire's feet, preventing her legs from flailing as shadewinds augmented the pair's fierce velocity. Tuck raced along some distance away, ensuring any miscalculation or sudden shadewind gust didn't cause them to collide. At these speeds, that would mean serious injury at a minimum, and death as a likelihood. Noire pulled both lines toward her chest before letting them out slowly; the tandem soared high above the city that was gone from view within seconds. Her touch was feathery on the steering lines unless she meant it not to be.

Lucas roared a battle cry as a shadewind gust came down on them from above and they plunged fifty feet in the blink of an eye into the darkness below; a sudden power dive then caught him off-guard. The HUD showed their speed at over two hundred miles per hour. For the first time, he noticed their KALM suits were outlined in a shadowy haze, which he guessed would ward away small debris if they came into contact with it.

His HUD predicted an extreme downwind blast would arrive in three seconds. Noire pulled the lines taught and brought the kite front and center. The enormous gust hit them from behind and shook Lucas, rattling his teeth, jerking the pair forward with such force that he thought they might be torn to pieces. They accelerated to over three hundred miles per hour before gradually settling back into the low two hundreds.

Rapidly approaching in the far distance, a distortion that looked like severely cracked leather emerged in Lucas's visual field. Noire angled them a touch to the left and let the steering lines out slightly. They slowed as the kite pulled them closer and closer. Two hundred yards became fifty, became nil, and they ran headlong into the odd blemish in the Infra. Lucas heard a loud bang, like a gun signaling the start of a race, and felt extreme pressure all around him. *Maybe I was wrong. Maybe the suit is shielding us from this. Or both.* The weight pressing down on him grew intolerable to the point of choking the air from his lungs and then, with no indication it would abate, was entirely gone the next breath.

Lucas gasped audibly as Noire let the steering lines out even further and began to coast toward an enormous hole in the sky. Concave edges curved into a cone-like shape that persisted in its climb to such an extent that nothing could be seen above.

"So that's the Funnel you mentioned. It's upside down though," he said to her, speaking his first words since they'd left the ruins.

Noire's only reply was a quiet laugh. She brought the kite sail ever more directly overhead until the updraft pushed them into the massive cone. Like a hot air balloon on a cold morning, they rose until a bluish haze became visible. It squirmed and swirled, reminding Lucas of the humming barriers that separated the Abzu from the doorways to the Aboveworld.

Their climb took several minutes to complete. Now, behind the barrier, Lucas saw the Abzu Complex from below. In the very center floated a pseudosphere tower that gleamed with an almost prismatic display of colors. At a substantial distance from it was a floating ring of earth that would have been a series of islands if not for narrow strips of land connecting the larger masses. Countless structures rested upon these. In one section of the city that Lucas could see from his current position, the color of the buildings was diverse, with some earth tones mixed in among both bright and dull ones. It reminded him of a puzzle he and his dad had worked on that pictured a village in the Cinque Terre. He wished solemnly, vainly, that they were seeing this together.

When they were within shouting distance of the blue wall, Noire finally spoke to him. "Let me do the talking, or they'll throw you in jail. Or worse." She veered left as they continued to rise, and moments later a small building inched into view. A narrow cement path ran from the front of the guard station through the barrier and connected to a staircase leading up to what looked like a crisscross of walkways above. Lucas laughed inwardly. *A security guard's shack looks like one no matter where it is.* A man with a black cudgel—the first weapon Lucas had ever seen a Darktouched carry—stood in the window, looking menacing.

"Oh no," Noire said, "It's Caius. I changed my mind—*you* do the talking." She eased them to a soft landing in front of the guardhouse and somehow dismissed the shadesurfing equipment, which was absorbed back into her KALM suit. "Hey, Caius. We picked up an unlicensed Darktouched while we were out. He says he stole his dad's suit and snuck into the Infra via a backdoor."

Caius made a poor attempt at conversation. "Hello, Noire. I just got back after a month away. You should *see* the pile of memos on my desk. Want to?"

Lucas stifled a laugh. He pretended that the guard was almost toothless, with one eye visibly bigger than the other. A handsomer Igor.

"You, boy," Caius said to him. "Galan Cadenza is your father?"

Lucas nodded. *The Darkname thing is so weird though.*

"And you stole his suit?"

Lucas nodded again.

"You *are* planning on getting licensed and registering a mission alignment while here, yes? And, you *don't* have a Darkname?"

Lucas nodded vigorously, since he was responding to two questions at once.

"Fine. One memo I *did* read said that you had been granted asylum. Report at the orientation center right away and you'll be cleared of all offenses." Caius dramatically held up the index finger on his left hand. "One time. Don't do this again."

Why would I do it again, Igor? Lucas nodded for what he hoped was the last time today, or at least the last time during this conversation.

"On your way, then," Caius said, waving him along. "Actually, wait!" Lucas felt a lump form in his throat. "You'd better come up with a placeholder Darkname. Don't use your real one down here. It's against the rules."

In spite of himself, Lucas nodded one final time. "Thank you, sir," he said deferentially.

"Catch up with you later, Caius. One of these days..." Noire mumbled as she grabbed Lucas by the arm and hurried them into the Abzu Complex, leaving Caius with his hand raised in a stiff wave and, Lucas imagined, hopeful words never spoken.

10

IRKALLA TOWER

PAST THE BARRIER, LUCAS was surprised to see a cerulean sky above and a cobblestone walkway stretching in front of him. The false atmosphere, although a natural blue, was devoid of any clouds and absent the sun. Even from below, now that he was out of the Funnel he could see that the entire Abzu Complex was sheltered within an oblong cavern that was wider than it was tall. Scanning the perimeter, his HUD showed him that it was generally circular, with a radius of about a mile. Directly ahead, the pseudosphere tower levitated more than one thousand feet above the ground, looking like an enormous spinning top. Above it, barely visible, was another blue barrier.

The lattice of pathways he had seen from below ran along the entire floor of the cavern, and there were circular platforms placed at some intersections that served as lifts to the buildings above. Each causeway was bordered with white stone markers placed at set intervals. In the spaces between them, there were pools of clear water and manicured beds containing an unusual, luminescent flower. They resembled a spider lily, transitioning gradually between shades of red and white. Blood Amaryllis, his HUD labeled them.

Noire recalled her KALM suit, surprising Lucas. When she seemed to be fine, standing before him in a pair of blue jeans and a teal V-neck shirt, he withdrew his own gear.

"How can we see and breathe?" he asked, astonished. "We're *between* Abzu and Infra, where we need the suits to survive. But we don't need them here?"

Noire replied matter-of-factly, "We're not really sure why. The creators of this place are long gone, and the Seekers have found zero trace of our origin. Beydin thinks it has something to do with Irkalla Tower." She pointed at the pseudosphere building. "You can ask him during orientation. He should be there." Then, after looking him up and down, she added, "You look much better in your own clothes, Nikto."

Lucas winced inwardly, still annoyed at the false name. Outwardly, he chuckled at the no-nonsense way in which she spoke the words, and then simply said, "Thanks."

Now that Noire was no longer in her KALM gear, Lucas could see that she wore her brown hair in a short, feathered cut that complemented her button nose and somewhat round face. A barely there, sarcastic half smile matched her questioning brow line and blue eyes. Strolling up to greet them was Tuck, whose bony frame and dark features were accentuated by a white spandex shirt and black sweatpants. He kept his hair in short, natural curls. A wide grin stretched across his face. "How was Caius today?" he asked Noire.

"Go find out for yourself, if you want," said Noire. She now bore an expression that was slightly more sarcastic than her resting face.

Tuck giggled. "No thanks. What's next?"

"Well, we should head to Irkalla Tower and report our findings to Brasa. Once we have our money, maybe we hit up the Deadman's Straw," Noire said. "It's been a while."

Like waking up from a dream, memory fragments of Lucas's flight from the Reclaimers and of Tara, Asante, and the others wormed into his conscious mind. He remembered the odd name his mother had accidentally called Asante.

"I need to meet someone with the Darkname of Deveras. Or, I think that's what my mom called him. Do you know him?"

Tuck cackled, and then with one hand rubbed his eyes and pinched the bridge of his nose. "Wait, wait. You need to talk to Deveras Turin, leader o' the Seekers?"

Lucas blushed, embarrassment mixed with a pinch of indignation. "Yeah, I met him in the Aboveworld. He said he was my dad's boss. So what?"

"Next thing you're gonna tell us, kid," Tuck expressed doubtfully, "is that your mommy is Reina d'Martest and your grandpa is Kilk Branthum."

Lucas felt himself blush an even deeper red. "Who are they?"

Now it was Noire's turn to snicker. "They lead the Delvers. Our boss's bosses, so to speak."

Thunderstruck, Lucas suddenly recalled a memory from when he was in the second grade. His parents were arguing about something. He was in his room, and they were downstairs, but he could faintly hear their voices through the aging ductwork. His dad was, as usual, the louder of the two.

"Kilk isn't the one running the Delvers. *You* are! You need to stand up for yourself. He's never even around. What does he do?"

"It's Mike in the Aboveworld, Darren," she chastised him. "He does more than you think. Besides, I don't think I'm ready to lead the entire operation. They only listen to me because they respect him."

His dad groaned noisily in disgust. "Oh, for the love of..." He paced to a different part of the house and his voice became inaudible. Lucas cracked his bedroom door so he could hear. "...not the point. I've been hearing about 'Reina the Great' since we were teenagers." His voice was oozing contempt. "I'm fine getting shit on. I'm just a lowly Seeker. But all you have to do is reach out and grab what's yours, and you won't *do* anything."

His mom shushed his dad. "Keep it down. Lucas doesn't need to hear this." She lowered her voice, but somehow a faint whisper bounced its way off the walls and up the stairs. "It'll come in time. Mike won't be around forever. For now, I'm happy being free to Delve wherever and whenever I please."

Their conversation continued in hushed voices for some time, and Lucas heard little more. Finally, though, he overheard his dad admit, "I guess you're right. No one else can do what you do. Especially that one thing, if you know what I mean."

At the time, this had all meant nothing to Lucas. But now he both mentally congratulated and flogged himself, elated that he had remembered his mom's Darkname and revulsed that he had stumbled upon those last few words spoken by his dad.

Gross. Now I'll never forget. The last part was what I didn't need to hear, guys!

"Helloooo," he heard Noire say. "Where did you go?"

"You there, kid?" Tuck questioned him, waving a hand in front of his face.

Lucas took a deep breath and slowly let it out. "Yeah, I just remembered something. I think my mom's Darkname *is* Reina. Is there more than one?"

Noire shook her head. "Not allowed. Darknames currently in use have to be unique," she explained. "And are you *serious*?" Lucas thought she was going to smack him and took a half step back.

"Wait. You're tellin' us Reina d'Martest *is* your mom?" Tuck probed, incredulous. "Noire, maybe we can get some money out of this after all!" The smile faded from his face when she shot him the same look she had given Lucas. "I'm only kiddin'. So serious, geez."

"We'll find out if he's lying when we report back at the tower. Let's go."

They strode along a wide cobblestone path leading directly to the center of the cavern and beneath the tower. A few minutes later, they stepped onto a lift platform. Silently and swiftly, it conveyed them up. They rose with no walls or protective barricades around them, and Lucas was compelled to peer over the edge. The height quickly became dizzying, and he inched back.

"Some people jump off and glide down for fun," Noire said to Lucas. "Over and over and over." She eyed Tuck, who shrugged.

"A guy needs free entertainment with the kind of money we make," he said, prompting a laugh from Noire.

Lucas turned around to watch as the bottom tip of the pseudosphere tower reached eye level. Irkalla seemed to exude—not reflect—pools, webs, and swirls of the entire color spectrum. As they went higher, he saw that the center of the tower was a mysterious black that looked as though it was oozing streams of bright hues from its edges, lending the entire structure the appearance of an elongated prismatic eye. Subconsciously, his hand reached down into his left pants pocket where he had placed the nazar amulet that Malank had given him. Perhaps someone *had* been watching his back, in a fashion. Because, so far, fate or luck had been on his side.

"You know," Noire mused, "maybe we *will* get in good with Reina and get some better jobs."

"Now you're talkin'," Tuck said cheerfully. "And here we are."

The elevator glided to a stop, and they stepped off. Before them, a set of revolving doors led into the iris. Inside, a hanging footpath ran the entire perimeter of the middle section of the tower. Dispersed around it were a few people strolling, others sitting on benches overlooking the cavern floor below. From up here, the beds of Blood Amaryllis were enthralling. Crimson seemed to seep through the white, the very life of the world waning only to be renewed once again. The rough curves of the cavern wall wrapping around and shielding the Complex were also more plainly visible from this vantage point. Because of the shape of the tower, Lucas could see the blue gates above and below.

The floors and walls were fashioned from a material so black that the room appeared to be a hole over a deep abyss. Lucas was afraid at first to step on it because it seemed transparent, like walking on nothing. He had to blink when he noticed that the faint ribbons of color layered within it were actually moving.

Perceiving his unease, Noire told him, "It's Nabucite, an incredibly strong mineral that's mainly found right here in the Complex. It messes with your head at first, but you'll get used to it."

Lucas fought his instincts and proceeded gingerly, step by step, his brain not convinced that the next one wouldn't be his last. "I hope so. This is freaking me out."

To distract himself, he digested his surroundings. The room was empty of furniture except for a round service desk just to the right of the entryway. Behind it stood a man sporting black spiked hair with frosted tips, and a woman with auburn hair pulled back into a tight bun. Lucas found himself casting judgement: *Man, this guy needs to leave the nineties already.*

A wide staircase protruded from the wall and spiraled in a clockwise fashion, giving access to the many rooms above. To his left, Lucas noticed that it also continued downwards, seeming to disappear into the Nabucite floor. In the center of the room, an elevator shaft ostensibly ran the length of the tower. Walkways extended from it in different directions depending on the level, and their varied length created an almost haphazard visual effect when looking upward inside the tower. The Nabucite, although giving the appearance of translucency, hid the bottom level from view.

Noire grabbed his attention and pointed to a pillar on their left. "We don't have time zones down here, and the sky kind of does its own thing, so that shows date-time for each time zone in the Aboveworld. We're closest to Zulu time plus three, probably. Handy for me, since it's the same as Saint Petersburg. I have family there."

Lucas stepped over to the time-zone clock. "So, do people live down here year-round?"

Noire nodded. "Most do. Irkalla draws every Darktouched to it. We're meant to be here. Besides, this place is where our work is." She pointed up subconsciously. "Some maintain an Aboveworld presence. Surface Affairs, and people with mixed families or kids who aren't old enough to take the Pledge. Some others. Tuck and I have been here since we were younger than you."

Lucas scanned the board, looking for Mountain Standard time. Absent-mindedly, he asked, "Who decides when a kid is old enough?" But when he saw the date listed, the whole world vanished for a moment. *I graduated on Thursday, June second, and we escaped the Reclaimers two days later. But...*

"We all do. We vote every fifteen years on the rules. Our next one is..."

Ignoring her, Lucas declared more than asked, "This can't be right. It's June ninth?" Panic overcame him and he could barely speak. "There's no way."

"Time moves strangely when you're in the Infra," Tuck reassured him, having caught up while Lucas stood in shock. "The board is never wrong."

Five days. It's been too long. Dad and Alan could already be dead. Did Mom make it? What if she didn't? What am I supposed to do now? I have to talk to Asante!

"And there he goes again," grumbled Noire. She snapped her fingers. "Hey, Nikto! Wake up."

Still, Lucas heard nothing but his own thoughts, until he suddenly felt a painful sting on his ear. Whirling around, swatting at the side of his head, his anger erupted when he saw Tuck laughing.

"I had to get your attention somehow," Tuck said. "Sorry. You were off in la-la la—"

Lucas, entranced by his own fear and doubt, punched Tuck in the face, cutting off his words and sending him reeling.

"Whoa, what the hell?" shouted Noire, scrambling over to check on Tuck, who was wiping blood from his bottom lip. She looked back at Lucas. "What's wrong with you?"

Dazed and ashamed of himself, Lucas couldn't find words.

Tuck appeared unfazed. "I don't know what's eatin' you, man, but you need to figure it out. I'll give you a pass this time," he said warningly, "but never hit me again." And then he looked Noire in the eyes and said provocatively, "Besides, we need his mommy's help."

Noire was stone faced, her anger cold when she said her next words to Lucas. "We'll take you to Deveras, but then we're done. Come on, you spoiled child."

Deveras's office was on the twenty-fourth floor and was adorned with a placard that read Deveras Turin – Seeker Mission Leader. Noire knocked on the closed door twice, and Deveras appeared moments later.

Lucas blinked several times at him, unsure if he was looking at the man he had known so far as Asante. Among many other small changes, his cheeks appeared fuller, his frame wider and shorter. Vexingly, Lucas couldn't remember Deveras's appearance from before, only that this was not it. He mentally compared it to hearing the wrong note in a song and being unable to recollect the true melody.

When he saw Lucas, Deveras examined his face closely, and a moment later relief emanated from his entire body. His fierce eyes glistened, calling attention to the deep, dark bags under them. He shook Lucas's hand, hugged him, ran his hands over his own hair, then moved back into the office and slouched into his chair. For a moment, the trio thought he had fallen asleep and that they would have to return the next day. But, after a fashion, he beckoned them into the room and commanded them to shut the door.

As though he had never seen them, Deveras eyed Tuck and Noire. "Why are you here?"

Noire opened her mouth, but Lucas spoke first and she closed it. "They helped me," he said. "If not for them, I don't think I would've made it to the Complex at all. They need to talk with my mom. Where is she?" Still regretful, he couldn't bear to even glance in their direction.

Deveras barely lifted his finger and pointed it at Lucas. "Looking for you. It's been almost five days since you were separated." He let his chin fall onto his chest. "Damned fools, both of you." Admonishing Lucas with a side-eyed look, he continued, "She should be back tomorrow or the next day. She has a five-person search party with her, but they're far into the Deep Infra. It's dangerous."

I doubt they're as far in as I was. But then, I cheated.

Deveras stood and walked over to a small whiskey table, pulled the stopper on a decanter, poured himself a drink, and swallowed it down in one go. Then he poured another and returned to his seat, glass in hand. He motioned to Lucas's companions. "You two should go. We have things to discuss."

Lucas, compelled both by guilt and feelings of friendship toward Tuck and Noire, protested. "Can they please stay? I trust them."

Deveras sighed deeply. "If that's what you want. But you both have to engage a non-disclosure Edict." Tuck and Noire wordlessly examined each other's faces and nodded. "Good. Here are the implants. If you speak a word to anyone other than us, his parents, or a few others we'll name, you'll enter a coma until I bring you out of it. *If* I do."

Noire shrugged. "We know how Edicts work, Deveras. I'm game. What about you, Tuck?"

"Might be good money in it," Tuck answered. "Why not?"

Lucas stared numbly at them. This was more serious than he'd ever imagined. He watched as the two inserted small pill-like objects into their right ears. Noire showed no sign of discomfort, but Tuck grimaced and put his palm against his ear like he was trying to relieve pressure.

"The Edict is valid for up to two years," Deveras said, "but I fully expect to be able to remove the implants sooner."

Lucas looked over at Tuck and Noire, managing to muster up heartfelt words. "I apologize for earlier. I lost my mind for a second."

Tuck looked him in the eyes and shrugged. "No big deal. Not the first time I've been slugged." Noire just huffed, not yet ready to let it go.

"I see," said Deveras. "Y'all will have to figure this out another time." He sipped from his whiskey. "I've been working to contact Malank and Fiala, but so far it's been silent since the Reclaimer attack."

Noire, wide-eyed, now looked in Lucas's direction. Yet she still said nothing.

Deveras continued, "I don't know if your dad is alive. I also haven't heard anything from Nora Linzer, but I didn't expect to." The glass touched his lips again. "What I do have is Marfisa. You met her at the Flagstaff Abzu station. She's got feelers out trying to find them. But so far, nothing." He drained the glass and began running his finger along the rim. "So, where have you been the past five days?"

Lucas began recounting his tale, starting with the Reclaimer attack. *I might be crazy, but I don't even know what's normal to them.* As the false sky turned red and then black beyond the walls of Irkalla Tower, his recounting was met with many skeptical looks and probing questions. He did his best to answer them. Details about the owl and the dais, however, he kept to himself. Because while it had felt like a dream, he regarded the experience as profoundly personal. Instead, he accounted for the lost days by saying he had been wandering alone in the dark and only by chance found his way out. Whether they believed him or not, by the time the story ended, Deveras wasn't the only one taking part in libations.

11

A Shortcut

Lucas awakened the next day refreshed, despite having gone to bed just as the sky gradually became a lighter shade of blue. At first, he forgot where he was. This room could have existed anywhere in the Aboveworld. Still, he couldn't shake the feeling that something was missing. He sat up from the beige suede sofa with deep, soft cushions that he'd sank into. An alarm was nagging from a coffee table a few feet in front of him, and he reached over to turn it off.

Nine a.m. already. I guess I better get showered and go. Getting up, he gazed through a window facing a cobblestone courtyard with a fountain in its center. Early morning greeted the Abzu Complex, but the place looked much like it had the night before.

In that instant, Lucas understood clearly what his intuition had hinted at earlier. Something *was* lacking. No light streamed through the blinds. No shadows danced on the floor. Outside, the colors of the buildings and the paved walkways were the same now as they were at the darkest hours of night.

His stomach growled, but there was no refrigerator, no oven, and only a few utensils. On the counter was a note from Deveras:

Organizing meeting with Darktouched leaders. Back late. Talk to Zane Sibard at info desk in tower. Grab food at place around corner. I have a tab.
—Deveras

He would need to hurry if he wanted a shower and breakfast before reporting at Irkalla Tower. Letting out a long sigh, Lucas marched down the hall to the bathroom where Deveras had laid out some toiletries and towels for him. *Time to get orientated.*

As he showered, Lucas recalled the end of their conversation the night prior.

"I think we both need rest," Deveras had said to him. "Maybe all of us do. Tomorrow..." He paused and then corrected himself, "*Today*, I want you to report for orientation at ten a.m. I'll send word to Beydin."

He rubbed his eyes and stood up, looking out the window at the sundry creatures floating in the air beyond the tower walls. They lit up the cavern with flickers and trails of blues, greens, and yellows.

"They consume darkness, you know?" Deveras had said to Lucas, who was now standing next to him. "The light they emit is, to them, waste. They excrete it like we do toxins. It's beautiful, but it also puts things in perspective."

Noire had started awake, having nearly tumbled out of her chair. She muttered inaudibly and then slipped back into slumber.

Tuck had laughed. "Typical Noire. Lightweight," he slurred. "Light! Even down here! Can't escape it. It's a losing battle." He was beginning to lose his own battle with whiskey and tiredness.

A drunk and half-asleep Deveras had replied angrily, "And that's why we have to find the Source! We'll never be strong enough to resist those bastards in the Lightwatch without it!""With all due respec', sir," Tuck had said, "there's no guarantee it even exists."

Deveras had spun around and slammed his glass on the desk. "Bullshit! We're living proof that it does. It's in the Infra somewhere. Way, way, way down." His hand dipped closer to the floor with each utterance of the word "way."

Tuck had held up his hands in acquiescence. "All right, all right. I been hit once today. That's enough for me. But I believe in things I can grab hold of."

"I guess that's why you're a Delver," said Deveras. "But you"--he tapped Lucas on the shoulder--"could be a great Seeker. I hope you consider it."

Lucas had smiled halfheartedly. "Definitely. I'm keeping an open mind," he said. *But I really have no idea what I want to do.* "Speaking of, it's only seven hours until I report in. Can I crash at someone's place?"

Lucas walked briskly, the hot shower having cleared his head and loosened his sore muscles. Other than an overly tight black t-shirt, he was still wearing dirty clothes because Deveras had had nothing that fit him.

"I let Beydin know to have Fabrication put something together for you. They'll do that once they fit you for your KALM suit," Deveras had instructed. "Leave your dad's bands and belt here. Your mom was right—truly awful."

The small, single-bedroom house was located in a quiet recess, hidden amongst taller buildings in a hodgepodge of architectural styles ranging from villas to Minka to adobe. It blended together in a strange but not unwelcoming patchwork quilt of building culture.

A slight right after crossing the courtyard led him down a narrow street where he saw the café that Deveras had mentioned in his note. The smell of freshly baked bread made Lucas's mouth water and stomach groan. Above the front door, a signboard was hung that was written in a curved script with prominent loops wholly unfamiliar to him. By some means, however, he immediately understood not just the message but the spirit of it: "The Ravenous Raptor – Come try our famous khachapuri!" And there, above the words, was the cartoonish image of an owl hungrily eyeing a cheese-filled bread boat with a fried egg on top.

Lucas remembered his feathered omen's final words: "Find me in the Abzu Complex." *Could this really be it? Tricky bird.*

Excited, he burst through the doors and ran headlong into a strongly-built man about his height. Perhaps in his early twenties, the man's dirty blond hair was trimmed down almost to the skin on the sides, with the top cut longer and slicked back. When Lucas slammed into the man, Turkish coffee spilled down the front of his gray dress shirt, staining the entire left side. The stubble on his chin, prominent bridge line, and clenched square jaw made him appear angry; thin, unsmiling lips and cold gray irises marked it a certainty.

The only words Lucas could manage to speak were, "Oh no." He could do nothing but gape at the damage he had done.

The man closed his eyes, clenched his fists, opened his eyes, looked up, looked down, and shook his head. He spoke in a language that sounded Germanic to Lucas's ears. But, as with the sign out front, the man's intended meaning was clear to him even though the words he spoke were not.

"What are you thinking?" the man asked, then held up a hand as though objecting with himself. "Never mind, you look too stupid to think. You have to be a Seeker. No, not even. Maybe Support. Maintenance or something." The muscles in his arms were tense, a vein in his right temple swollen to the point of bursting. If this man struck him—something that seemed a certainty—Lucas knew the hits were going to land precisely and relentlessly.

He entertained striking first even while speaking an apology. "I'm sorry. I was in a hurry and didn't see you."

"Because you are *blind*! It's impossible to clean this," snarled the man, shifting his weight to the balls of his feet and turning his hips slightly.

Lucas prepared to hit and run. This fight, win or lose, would be costly. He was winding up to strike when, from a corner table hidden behind a partition screen, a girl who looked the same age as him ran over and put her hand on the man's shoulder. She wore a well-fitted black uniform that covered everything from her neckline down. Lucas noticed that a scar ran behind her left ear, across her neck, and disappeared beneath her button-down jacket. The image of a hand was embossed over her left breast.

"Vorin, you should wait," she said quietly, almost in a playful manner. "Your orientation starts today, and I have a feeling his does too." Lucas felt her examining him, saw her thin eyebrows lift in shrewd deduction. Jet-black hair framed high cheekbones, and tanned skin accentuated full lips formed into a confident smile. "You can beat him into a pulp tomorrow and not break any rules." She gripped Vorin's shoulder firmly, coaxing his rage back into confinement. "Go get changed—there's still time. I'll pick up the tab." Vorin melted and slipped past him with a glare.

Lucas searched the girl's face for a moment, trying to discover if she was an ally. "Thanks," he said, "I'm... new." *I almost said Nikto. Cripes.*

The girl's glinting brown eyes met his. "Don't thank me yet. I only bought you a day," she said, holding out her hand. "I'm Corynna Darkspear. Rynna or Rynn, as you like."

Lucas searched for inspiration as he took her hand and spoke the first thing that came to mind. "I'm Arden," he said, his hand still touching hers. *As You Like It.* "Last name to be determined. Nice to meet you, Rynn."

She smiled, slowly pulling her hand away. "I need to finish my food. Want to join me?"

Lucas glanced at the clock hanging above the counter to his left. He only had fifteen minutes to get to the tower. "I shouldn't. I'm sorry," he said, resenting his luck. "I just got here last night and don't know the way."

"I know a shortcut. Sit with me for five. The khachapuri is amazing. I'll share."

Tip-a-tap, tip-a-tap, tip-a-tap.

Lucas ran faster with each footfall, his lungs burning, always two steps behind Rynn. *Her shortcut is to run crazy fast!* The khachapuri had been delicious, but now the bread swelled in his stomach and made running immensely more difficult. They had left with exactly ten minutes to spare, and the tower was still far in the distance.

"I'm not sure," he called ahead to her, panting, "that the breakfast was worth it." He gasped for air. "Don't get me wrong, it was amazing. And the company was great, but... Oh damn, I'm going to throw up."

Rynn doubled back to urge him on. "No time for that! We're almost to the shortcut." Lucas saw nothing ahead but a park bench, ornamental bushes, and the tower behind it.

Rynn stopped, not even breathing hard, and waved him closer. "You don't have a suit yet, so you have to hold on." She grabbed him by the hand and led him to the hedge, slipping through a small notch and up onto the knee-high wall behind. "Okay, wrap your arms around me and clasp your hands. Don't let go." Lucas stood behind her and did as he was told, unsure if his hands were shaking from the sprint here or from what was coming next. "We're going." She never looked back, never hesitated, only shouted in delight as they tipped off the edge.

For the first few seconds, they were in freefall. The moment played out for Lucas in slow motion as he screamed from his belly. He interlaced his fingers and squeezed Rynn's waist, considering whether it was self-preservation or something else. Their plunge continued until, with a stomach emptying jerk, Rynn tapped her wrists together and her KALM suit sprouted wings, transitioning into a slow glide. The tower was closer now but high above them. Lucas saw her point at something in the distance, and then his heart fell into his feet.

From the latticed walkways at the bottom of the cavern, the central elevator was rising, and they were on course to land on it during its ascent. He felt Rynn shift into a more downward angle and did what he could not to fight her. Their speed increased for a moment before she tilted back hard. Hovering now more than gliding, they easily touched down on the lift. A surprised worker riding to her office muttered insults under her breath in their direction.

Rynn reached down and pulled Lucas's hands apart, smiling back at him. "Still not sure if it was worth it?"

Lucas, exhilarated and nauseated at the same time, knelt down on the edge of the platform and heaved. "Let me get back to you," he managed to eke out between discharges of vomit. "I didn't know we can fly."

Rynn smirked. "Not really fly. But we can drag out a fall for a really long time."

Perhaps a minute later, they strolled into the tower together. The clock showed that they were still two minutes early. Vorin, clothed in a clean version of the same dress shirt, was already standing at the information desk when they walked up. Rynn waited until he was watching before saying to Lucas, "What if we go out tomorrow for dinner and drinks? Would that make it worth it?"

Lucas flushed, the blood rushing to his head as he answered, "Totally worth it."

No matter what happened, he didn't foresee the smile fading from his face. But while his eyes were glued to Rynn as she disappeared down the lefthand stairway into the bottom of Irkalla Tower, he missed Vorin's deathly stare piercing his back with a hundred daggers.

12

Darkname Selection

Lucas was seated in a small, gray-walled waiting room with two others: Vorin and a middle-aged woman. Not wanting to speak to Vorin, or even look in his direction, Lucas caught the woman's attention and smiled kindly. "I'm Arden. Nice to meet you."

She glanced at him expressionlessly. Gray strands accented her black hair, and wrinkles touched the corners of her mouth. Slightly upturned dark brown eyes peered around the room, perhaps revealing uncertainty about this place and how her life was changing. She frequently reached a hand up to her round nose to scratch it, which Lucas assumed was a nervous habit.

"Nice to meet you," she said, offering nothing more.

Lucas wondered how much she knew of this place and its rules, since the only context he really had was himself. "Have you picked a Darkname yet?"

"Phosop," she said. "After the Thai rice goddess."

"Any idea what mission and discipline you're interested in?" he probed.

"Surface Affairs. Merchants or Finance. I like money!" At the mention of money, Phosop at last flashed him a smile. "What about you?"

"I don't know. Surface Affairs might be interesting," he said, looking briefly at Vorin. "If he's going where I think he is, not the Hand." Phosop gave him a veiled look while his mind wandered to his parents, concern for both weighing heavily on him. "My folks want me to Seek or Delve, so probably one of those."

Phosop bobbed her head in recognition. "It's good to respect your parents. But you have to do what's right for you. I used to think differently but recent events... changed my mind." Pursing her lips, she looked down at the floor and then back at Lucas again, deciding what to say next. "My son, he..."

But she never got the chance to finish her sentence because a teacherly woman strode into the room, her horn-rimmed glasses much larger than suited her slim face. Her footfalls barely made a sound on the carpeted floor, while her shoulder-length hair––mostly gray––bounced with each step. Lucas immediately recognized her as the office worker from the elevator.

"Good morning," she greeted them. "I'm Vidaya Murtabak of Surface Affairs." An aquiline nose dominated her countenance, and sharp, narrow eyes gave her an eagle-like appearance. "Beydin Krenneth, Support Mission Leader, was unable to make it. That is why *I* am here. *You* are here because the Dark-touched Right passed to you at some point in your life." The weight of her glasses caused them to slip down toward the end of her nose, and she frequently pushed them back up as she spoke. "This *mandatory* orientation runs for exactly one week. By the end, you are expected to have chosen a discipline." She paused for effect. "Which can be changed, yes, but not easily. So do not take this lightly."

Facing away from them, she pressed a few buttons on a kiosk, and a black display panel descended from a compartment in the ceiling. In her hand, she now held a small device. With each click, words in white appeared to be impressed onto the panel rather than projected or written with an implement. Vorin raised his hand while sitting tall in his chair, and Vidaya sounded annoyed when she told him, "We are not schoolchildren here. Please just speak up."

Vorin turned a shade of crimson Lucas had only seen in cartoons. "Sorry," he said, eyes downcast. "I was wondering when we'll get to the practical part. We all know the rules by now, right?" He looked at Phosop but not Lucas.

Phosop shook her head. "Actually, I don't really know. I'm very much looking forward to learning."

Vorin took a deep breath and clenched his jaw. "Sounds good," he said with a false smile. A furtive glance between Lucas and Phosop caused them both to grin.

Without speaking a word, Vidaya clicked forward in her presentation. The screen displayed the words *Darktouched Pledge Rules*.

"These that you will see," she said, "are the most important of our laws. We obviously do not have time to cover the entire legal code. Before we proceed, you must either pledge to these few rules or leave. If you choose the latter, you will be labeled Disavowed, transported to the surface, and forever lose your right to be Darktouched. You will not have any memory of this place or anything related to us. Your abilities will be sealed via Edict."

She again paused for effect, and a wave of guilt slammed into Lucas. *I really can say no. I guess it wasn't bullshit. But then, what would I do? I could go to college. Would that make me happy without Connie and Aella? So many people are counting on me now, and this world is exciting. And then there's Rynn.*

His inner dialogue continued until Vidaya pointed at him. "You. Puking boy. Did you hear what I just said?"

Now it was Lucas's turn to be embarrassed, but he kept his emotions level mostly out of spite. In his peripheral vision, he could see Vorin tittering. "We have to take the Pledge to the most important rules," he recited. Years of staring through teachers and retaining a reasonable degree of information while still daydreaming were serving him well now.

Vidaya nodded, satisfied for the moment. Click. The display showed the rules grouped into four categories. She explained, "The Unbreakables are absolute. Violations result in severe Edicts. It will be as though you said no to our Pledge, but worse. The others come with varying levels of punitive action, which is enforced by the Black Hand."

Lucas shifted anxiously in his chair. He was guilty of at least five punishable offenses, depending on how strict the interpretation of each law was.

"The *bonus* rule at the bottom of the list only applies to one of you, so far," said Vidaya, looking askance at Lucas. "Of course, this is not something that you must pledge to, but it *is* a matter of common decency."

He felt himself shrink even further into his chair. *And this is why I always sat in the back of class.*

Phosop leaned forward in her seat. "In the Abzu Complex, what is the definition of an Edict?" she asked, drawing a loud chortle from Vorin.

Vidaya quieted him with a stare. "Perhaps this young man would like to explain."

Vorin smugly turned to Phosop and said, "A Darktouched Edict requires insertion of an implant. If you break the Edict, you enter a coma or die."

"Indeed, an Edict is not a trifling matter." The eagle-woman nodded solemnly at Phosop, who appeared troubled. "You have five additional minutes to digest the Pledge rules."

Lucas thought of the Edict that Tuck and Noire had taken as he progressed through the lists. They read:

DARKTOUCHED PLEDGE RULES

Unbreakable

- **Do not** commit murder or maim another Darktouched

- **Do** have a Darkname that is in accordance with naming rules, approved by your orientation instructor and logged in the Compendium

- **Do not** use your Abovename in the Abzu Hubs, the Abzu Complex, or the Infra

No Exceptions

- **Do not** have more than one child

- **Do not** enter forbidden areas of the Infra

- **Do not** harm life forms in the Abzu or Infra

- **Do not** bring artifacts from the Infra into the Abzu Complex

- **Do not** damage Darktouched property of any kind

Exceptions Allowed—Approval Required by Guidance Committee

- **<u>Do</u>** participate in our society [voting process, economy, etc.]

- **<u>Do</u>** spend at least half of every calendar year in the Abzu Complex

- **<u>Do not</u>** consort with Lightborne

- **<u>Do not</u>** tell anyone that you are Darktouched, unless they are also Darktouched

- **<u>Do not</u>** let Aboveworlders see you enter the Abzu

- **<u>Do not</u>** wear your KALM suit anywhere above ground

- **<u>Do not</u>** let anyone else wear your KALM suit

- **<u>Do not</u>** take items found and/or Fabricated in the Abzu or Infra to the Aboveworld

Vidaya's Law—Bonus

- **<u>Do not</u>** use KALM wings in residential areas—descending from Irkalla Tower is permitted (if you must)

After exactly five minutes, Vidaya called for questions. She noted that many would be answered during the practical portion of the orientation later in the week.

Lucas could think of only one. "What are the forbidden areas of the Infra?" he asked. "Doesn't that limit what the Delvers and Seekers can accomplish?"

Vidaya answered carefully, "Yes, it's very possible that worthwhile artifacts—and perhaps even the Source that our Seekers covet—are in or accessed through those areas. However, the risks are high." She leaned against the kiosk. "As for which zones are off-limits, *that* can be changed through the vote! And the next one is two days from now. If you take the Pledge today, you will be eligible."

Phosop put the tips of her fingers together in front of her face and then covered her nose and mouth, engrossed in thought. Vidaya called on her, but she stayed quiet for a long time before saying, "I don't feel ready for this anymore. The Darktouched Right came to me only a few days ago. It's so much. What if I can't see my friends and family again?"

"Yes, it is a leap of faith," acknowledged Vidaya, her expression one of pity and understanding. "But I promise you one thing if you don't take the leap: The pangs of longing you will feel are nearly unbearable. Most who deny the Pledge live out their days deeply unfulfilled, as a best case. I know because I'm responsible for keeping watch over the Disavowed."

Phosop remained absorbed in her thoughts, and Vidaya took the silence as a cue to move on to Vorin. "What about you, oh Hurried One. Any questions?"

"Yes," Vorin responded. "Who is the guidance committee?"

Vidaya's eyes lit up. "Ah, an easy one. The five mission leaders. You can learn their names later if you don't already know."

Vorin was turning crimson again. "Wait. Why does the Hand's leader have to ask permission from the other four, exactly?"

"I'm not even going to dignify that with a response. Let's move on to the Pledge," Vidaya declared over his remonstrations. Click. "If you are willing, enter your Darkname in this kiosk. You can use a temporary or partial one until the end of orientation."

Vorin was the first to input his Darkname. As he typed, Lucas watched the letters appear on a black panel that was a smaller version of the one displaying the Pledge rules. *It's almost like the words are imprinted on the darkness. How strange.*

"Welcome, Vorin Nordlim," Vidaya announced when he had finished.

Lucas peered at Phosop, who still looked confounded. Placing his hand on her shoulder, he whispered, "Let's go together?"

This seemed to break the spell over her. A warm smile graced the corners of her mouth, and she rose from her chair. Soon, they stood by the kiosk together. Lucas watched her punch the keys and celebrated when Vidaya proclaimed, "Welcome, Phosop Makmay."

When it was his turn, Lucas hesitated. His thoughts turned to his dad, to Alan, and to how, as a boy, his difficulty with the surname Linzer had been a joke among the adults. Settled on a name, his fingers stroked the keys. Uncannily, the moment his Darkname was accepted, he could no longer remember his Aboveworld name. He was so consumed with trying that he barely heard Vidaya say, "Welcome, Arden Arinza."

13

A Vision of the Abyss

THE THREE FLEDGLING DARKTOUCHED were now gathered two floors further down in Irkalla Tower, the proud owners of temporary Abzupasses and Darktouched license numbers.

"For all intents and purposes," Vidaya had said, "you are full members of this society. You can work for money and discipline rating. Both things will be recorded in the Compendium henceforth." Arden had a burning desire to ask what the Compendium was but decided to save it for later.

The final orientation item for the first day was the most exciting: KALM suit fitting. Vidaya introduced them to a short, heavy-set woman in her thirties with a bright smile, rowdy laugh, and unrivaled energy.

"Afternoon, everyone! I'm Zarinda Aneveh, leader of the KALM department. You can call me Zari." A stylus was tucked behind her ear, almost hidden in her wild dark brown hair. "Today you'll each go into one of the booths over yonder. For this, you have to be totally naked." She made a silly face, and then went on. "But don't worry, because no one can see but me." She let loose a peal of laughter that Arden was afraid would leave him deaf, forced to wear the suit just so he could hear. "I'm only kidding. But maybe not for you," she said to Vorin with a wink.

"Zari, please behave yourself," chided Vidaya.

While this was going on, Arden was scanning the lab. There were five human-sized booths made of Nabucite connected via thick tubing to a large cistern that filled one corner of the room. Cables ran from each one to a central control panel where Zari's lunch was sitting half-eaten. Behind them sat seven lockers, presumably one for the occupant of each booth and two extras for Support team members.

Vidaya waved to them all. "I have to do my real job now, but I'll see you all tomorrow morning at eight. See yourselves out after Zari's done with you." A chorus of appreciation followed her as she left the room.

"All right, I need you to stow your shoes and anything in your pockets that emits light," Zari directed, motioning to the lockers. "Everything else can stay on." While they complied with her order, she explained the process. "The tank in back holds liquified Nabucite—almost the same stuff your KALM suits are made of. It's the perfect conduit for our talents as Darktouched." She sat down in a roller chair in front of the control center, half facing them while she prepared the equipment. "Its properties are unusual. When it comes in contact with one of us, it basically dematerializes anything we're wearing and becomes an extension of our skin."

Arden remembered taking the suit off after escaping the Reclaimers. He had asked himself whether the clothes remained underneath while the KALM gear was active. *And the answer is: No clothes under the suit! Sort of.*

Vorin walked over to stand by her. "Then why the lockers?"

"Because," said Zari, "let's say you're stupid enough to be carrying a phone or digital watch from the Aboveworld. That can throw off the measurements." A disgusted look darkened her face. "And shoes make the booths nasty. After you're fitted, it doesn't matter. Do what you want."

Arden and Phosop were clustered next to Vorin now, awaiting further instructions. Zari led them each individually to their assigned booth, taking several minutes to begin the process.

Arden was last, and when it was his turn she said to him, "Beydin told me to have Fabrication make some clothes for you. Dark colors and jeans are fine?" Arden nodded. "Okay, I'll have them make a week's worth and a duffle." Her eyes met his. "He has high hopes for you, you know." She strung leads to his forearms, shins, and temples. "Let's see how you do." Arden felt the door close behind him and, not long after, he was hearing Zari's voice in his head.

They ran through a preliminary check. "Blink if you hear me. Good. Now raise your right arm. Great. I'm going to start filling the tank now."

He felt the familiar feeling of what he now knew to be Nabucite flowing around him. As it surrounded his face, the walls transformed into blurred images of a place he had never seen. He heard Zari's voice: "So far so good. Your body is adjusting quickly."

The images became clearer. He was somewhere in the Deep Infra looking down on an ancient building. It made the ruins where he met Tuck and Noire seem newly built. He heard Zari say, "Amazing. This level of attunement to Nabucite is on par with the best I've seen. Maybe better."

As he passed through walls in the images, something was coming into view—a cocoon of darkness so intense that it reminded him of the stone dais in the Deep Infra. The vision showed him the silhouette of a person sealed within. Arden no longer heard Zari. A hand extended before him. His hand. Vainly, he tried to reach inside and pull the figure out. Not to save but to know. He thought he heard speaking. *Who or what is it?*

"Arden! Arden, are you okay?" Zari's cry pierced the blackness and the Nabucite fell away. Her round face loomed over his, and he blinked several times. He lay crumpled on the floor of the booth.

"I saw something," he heard himself mumble. "Or someone. In the Deep Infra. Ancient ruins."

Concern was thick in Zari's voice. "That makes no sense. This is only supposed to assess how your body reacts to the Nabucite and collect other measurements. All you should have seen is four walls and darkness."

"It spoke to me, but I can't remember."

Arden saw Zari reach for something, felt a pinch, and then drifted to sleep.

When he woke up, Tuck and Noire were standing next to him. *Where am I?* Blurry eyes made it difficult to orient himself.

"Hey there, sunshine," he heard Noire say. "We heard you failed the easiest test."

Tuck's signature giggle met his ears. "Yep. You had one job to do. Just stand there. Couldn't even do that!"

Arden raised himself up on one elbow. He was in what looked like a hospital. "Where am I?"

"Still in the tower," Noire told him. "Medical Services is just one floor above where you passed out. Zari had instructions to get us on a direct line if anything happened. Deveras's orders." She motioned in the direction of a bin sitting on a shelf across the room. "Your stuff is in there."

"I feel like dog crap," said Arden. "How long was I out?"

Tuck smiled in spite of his swollen lip. "Only an hour. But Zari was really worried. She said you were spoutin' some kinda nonsense about a vision."

"I did. I was. But it's kind of hazy now."

Noire looked down on him with smiling eyes. "You know, there's a cure for this."

Tuck grinned at her. "The Deadman's Straw?"

"The Deadman's Straw."

14

THE DEADMAN'S STRAW

ARDEN ROLLED HIS NECK in circles, trying futilely to piece together his vision from the KALM fitting booth. Realizing that he wouldn't succeed, he instead watched his surroundings.

They strode casually along the tower's outer walkway. Other than the elevator that serviced the cavern floor, there were eight ways out, and each of these led to the floating ring of residential buildings and shops surrounding Irkalla Tower. His thoughts were pulled to the morning's events and the shortcut Rynn had shown him. He let the scenes replay in his head, and they brought a smile to his face.

"What's with him, Tuck?" Noire asked as they boarded a passenger cabin and the doors closed behind them. The smooth motion of the gondola bearing them along lulled Arden almost to sleep, and he plopped down on one of the cushioned seats while his companions stood on either side of him. They were the only ones in the cabin, which had seating for ten.

Tuck inspected him out of mock concern. "Hm. Definitely something different about him. He looks happy."

"I was thinking the same thing. Must have been *some* vision." Noire tapped Arden on the shoulder, interrupting his daydream. "Or maybe... something else."

They were just slipping over the edge of Irkalla Tower now. Arden was still smiling when he answered, looking past them both at the tower growing smaller on the horizon. "I met someone on the way in this morning. At a café near Deveras's place. The Ravenous Raptor, I think?" If the front of the tower was south, he considered, they were moving in a northeasterly direction. Deveras's apartment was west. As they moved further away, he noticed that absolutely nothing supported and guided the gondola on its path. Or nothing he could see at least.

Noire rubbed her brow and right temple. "Wait. Tuck, isn't that a Hand hangout?"

"Yep," said Tuck. "Great food though."

"Wow. Off topic, but sure." Noire tilted her head back and brought her arms across her chest. After stifling a yawn, she nudged Arden. "Be careful. If your story's true and the Lightborne *are* being more aggressive, the Hand will be pushing its anti-Lightwatch agenda. Stay out of it."

Arden looked up at her. "Are you warning or telling?"

"Yes," replied Noire, her brow wrinkled. "Trust me. They're not bad people, but their leaders are ruthless. Especially Daryala Gindir, the Black Hand mission leader. You'll be in over your head before you know it."

"Okay. Understood, Mom," said Arden derisively, and then sheepishly added, "Sorry. I'll be careful." *But there's no way I'm bailing on drinks with Rynn tomorrow.* Their ride into the residential ring was nearing its end as Arden asked, "So, what is a Deadman's Straw?"

Tuck chuckled. "Nice changin' the subject. And you'll see soon enough."

The cabin doors opened and the three walked onto the exit platform and down a flight of stairs. Unlike the melting pot of architectural styles in Deveras's neighborhood, the buildings here were mostly uniform. Arden glanced up at tall structures made of steel and glass, some faced with brick, feeling like this could have been any modern city in the Aboveworld.

On one corner, a group brandished signs adorned with the Black Hand emblem, which was depicted wearing a wristwatch. These were imprinted with the words *Time's Up for the Lightwatch*. Others showed a hand pinching a candleflame and were captioned *Stop the Terror! Snuff Out the Light!* Avoiding them, Noire ushered Tuck and Lucas down an alleyway. "We always cut through here into Old Town. It's just a little further."

After another few minutes, the cityscape suddenly gave way to a village that looked very similar to the ruins where Arden had met them both.

"Here we go. The most popular brewhouse in the Complex." She pointed in the direction of a sign written in cuneiform with the image of two skeletons in ancient garb sipping from straws that extended down into a clay jar. A green door below the sign beckoned them.

The Deadman's Straw was arranged similarly to the common room of the ruins, with ten seating areas around the perimeter divided by partitions. Floor cushions ran along three sides of each space, leaving an area for staff to maneuver within as they served food and refilled drinks. In the center of the room was a table with two chairs on opposite sides, nested within a depression in the floor. Four L-shaped sofas enclosed and offered a clear view of the table. A bar ran along the wall farthest from the entrance, and there were two other groups of patrons already seated against the right wall in adjacent areas. They talked in quiet voices while waiting for their beverages.

When they entered, the musty odor of stale beer floated up to greet them. Tuck took a seat in the back corner of the room on the left side, and Noire dragged Arden along with her en route to the bar. "Hey, Stig. Where's Yel?" she said to a baby-faced man not much older than Arden.

Stig stood behind the bar, a rag in his right hand and a spray bottle in his left. He looked up through brown eyes, smiling and shrugging at once. "Oh, hey, Noire! I see you brought the other wino." He motioned with his head to where Tuck was sitting. "And an aspiring talent." He freed his right hand, rubbed the palm on his pants, and held it out across the bar. "Nice to meet ya. I'm Stig." Arden shook his hand and introduced himself.

"Well, Noire, what'll it be?" asked the bartender.

Noire tapped a finger on the bar. "Just the usual, I guess."

Stig shook his head. "We're fresh out of the usual."

"How can you be out?" Noire complained. "All you have to do is run the Fabricator in back."

Stig's mouth gaped, and he smacked himself lightly on the forehead. "I forgot to tell you. That's why Yel stepped out. Lately, I've been callin' her Yelyn, because she's always yellin' about the damned— Oh, sorry." He stopped and massaged his neck upon witnessing an unamused look conquer Noire's face. "Our Fabricator's busted. No idea when that'll be fixed, but I have a barley and emmer brew in the refrigerators that's quite nice!"

"Fine. Start us off with a gallon," Noire relented. "Put it on *his* tab," she said, pointing at Tuck with her thumb. Stig sighed in relief and told them it would be out shortly.

Moments after they sat down, a server delivered their beer. Instead of a clay jar like Arden expected, she carried an enormous glass vessel with two vertical handles. It was filled with a cloudy, light-tan liquid. Three large brass straws were held in position against the glass by soldered clips.

"They hang the straws," Noire explained, seeing Arden eye them, "so you don't end up drinking the sediment." She leaned forward and took a pull from one of the brass tubes. Her face wrinkled and she smacked her lips. "Go ahead and try it," she said to him.

As Arden bent down slightly to take a drink, he thought of his dad, who often enjoyed two fingers of scotch in the evenings. "Cheers," he said. Lifted by emotion, he drew in a huge mouthful of beer and glugged it down. A look of surprise covered his face, and he stuck out his tongue. "Blech. What is that? It's kind of sour and fruity."

Tuck laughed and slapped him on the back. "Ancient brew is *tart*. You get used to it. Gets you tipsy, if nothin' else."

Arden took another drink and was already feeling a little light-headed, having had alcohol only on a few prior occasions.

"Cheers to Arden," Tuck said as he took a sip.

Arden laughed. "I'm almost not a nobody now."

Noire flashed a wry smile. "Aww, don't worry. Everybody's a nobody to somebody." She lifted her straw and clinked it against the glass container. "Cheers, Arden."

Half an hour later, they were well into their second gallon and snacking on flatbread, goat's cheese, and olives. Arden had recounted the morning's events, prompting his companions to spend most of the time ribbing him.

"Swooning over the Hand's rising star," Noire said, then laughed. "I take back what I said earlier. You're already in over your head."

"Rising star?" Arden asked, his voice tinged by uncertainty. "She looked maybe even younger than me."

Noire's expression turned serious. "Rynn's been here since she was ten, I think. The committee granted an exception to the Pledge age, and Sabrath Nulne took her under his wing. He's the Hand's second-in-command. Her adopted family was abducted in a Reclaimer raid, from what I've heard. Damned Shepherds."

Arden frowned. "She was adopted too?"

Tuck shot him a quizzical look. "Wait. You don't know how it works yet? What did your parents teach you?"

Arden felt insecurity begin to worm its way into his psyche. *With all the "family business" talk, why didn't they tell me more?*

"Best to learn before the vote happens," Tuck added.

Noire read his mind again. "Your parents probably wanted you to form your own opinions. It's a touchy subject." She lifted her eyebrows at Tuck and exhaled loudly. "There's no time to learn like the present, I guess. You or me, Tuck?"

Tuck pointed the index fingers on both hands in her direction. Noire rolled her eyes, mouthing the word *Typical.* She popped an olive in her mouth, ate it, and took another drink before speaking again. "Everything begins with the Darktouched Right. When one of us dies, that person's power transfers to a random individual somewhere on the planet. Young. Old. It doesn't discriminate."

Arden remembered Phosop saying that she had just inherited the Right a few days prior. "Totally random? How do you find them?"

"Darktouched naturally yearn to find the Abzu Complex and Irkalla. The urge grows the longer you have the Right and don't exercise it... or the older you are when it comes to you." She took another swallow. "Some of us find it on our own, but Surface Affairs identifies most of us. I don't know how—some kind of Compendium analytics. For most, not much convincing is required." Her cheeks puffed out as she exhaled another deep breath. "Usually within days of a Darktouched dying, we can locate the new person."

Arden bent his right knee and rested his elbow on it. "Okay. But what does that have to do with Rynn and me both being adopted?"

Tuck chimed in. "The interestin' part is that almost *all* Darktouched kids are adopted. Both of us too." Arden tucked his chin into the crook of his arm, his eyes fixed on the glass vessel as Tuck continued, "It's probably for the best. When we do leave 'em in mixed families, a lot of times they end up twisted."

With a jolt, Arden sat upright. "Do you... Do we *steal* them? The kids?"

Noire looked somber. "Not *steal*. We liberate. If there's no other choice, then yes. Only if the family is rotten or the child is in real danger. That's one role of the Hand." Arden sat in stunned silence as she went on. "Like I said earlier, it's controversial. Every fifteen years, the vote decides whether we keep the practice. It comes and goes, but we've done it for most of our history."

Arden felt the blood pounding in his ears. "But, how can people... That's seriously messed up."

"Is it?" Noire asked flatly. "Governments around the world have child services that do almost the same thing."

Arden remembered meeting his birth father, recalled vividly the squalor and obvious signs of addiction. Still, even if it was the right outcome in his case, that hardly justified the policy.

Noire added, "But if you don't agree with it, then vote that way. That's your choice now."

Tuck stretched his arms and yawned. "The world's full o' problems. No end to 'em and no fixin' 'em all! Before the night's up, you'll find two or three more." He stood up and ambled over to the table in the center of the room. "Let's play Tower Race. I'll show ya how."

Not wanting to dwell, Arden balanced on wobbly legs and joined Tuck as he pressed a button hidden on one side of the tabletop. The entire surface dissolved to reveal a gameboard made of Nabucite, measuring two feet by three feet. Eighteen separate squares comprised the playing surface, arranged into three rows and eight columns. The third through fifth columns only had squares in the center row. On Tuck's side, near his left hand, rested seven human-shaped game pieces wearing blue helmets, as well as a six-sided die. Arden's side was a mirror of Tuck's, except his pieces donned red helmets. An image of Irkalla Tower was impressed on the table between each player's seat and the gap left by the missing squares in columns three through five. Shimmering arrows and a guideline directed the red player to move pieces in a counterclockwise manner and for the blue player to do the opposite, starting and finishing at the tower. Additionally, on some spaces, pictographs were embossed and glowing.

Tuck picked up his die, blew on it and rolled. "Highest roll goes first. The goal is to move your seven pieces onto the board, along the center line, and back to the tower without being knocked off. The first player to save all seven wins the race."

Noire was spectating on Arden's side. She informed him, "In the Aboveworld, they found a version of the Tower Race and called it the Royal Game of Ur. Whatever its origin, the Darktouched have played this version for millennia. The Compendium says so."

Arden picked up his die and tossed it. "I win, my six to your five. Now what?" he asked excitedly.

"That's the spirit. Just enjoy the game," Tuck said with a chuckle. "Roll again and move one of the seven pieces onto the board. Just follow the arrows and line."

Arden rolled a three and reached out his hand to move a game piece. Tuck corrected him gently, "Don't touch the pieces. *Think* at them, just like you do machines." Arden reached out mentally to one of the seven pieces and jumped in his seat.

"Good day, Arden. We seven share the consciousness of Dart the Dashing. You can simply call us Dart," the game piece said with a wave. "We see you have no Compendium data for the Tower Race. Would you like to keep our commentary on while you learn the rules?" Arden nodded. "Very well," said Dart. The game piece summoned a mini-shadesurfing kite and then, as though shadewinds were actually propelling it forward, moved to a square with a wing pictograph. "This piece has engaged the float effect, which lasts for one turn. You also receive an extra die roll." The miniature Darktouched began levitating a foot above the gameboard.

Arden rolled a six, and the piece moved to another square with the same wing icon. Dart announced, "This piece has engaged a second float effect. Float will now last for two turns, and you receive another extra die roll." Arden rolled a five, and the game piece raced to the Irkalla tower on Arden's side of the board. It disappeared upon contacting the pseudosphere image, which sparkled with red light. Dart praised him, "Only six more to go until you win! It is now your opponent's turn."

"Damned beginner's luck. We'll see." Tuck blew on the die, rolled, and swore when it showed four. "Never gonna win a random roll in my entire life," he grumbled. His piece moved onto a square with a question mark icon and he rolled again—a two this time. He cursed even louder when his piece instantly moved back to the Irkalla Tower on his side.

Ten minutes later, Arden had saved six game pieces. Meanwhile, Tuck had two on the board and one that had just been reset to the beginning after being pushed off by a dark tsunami.

Dart instructed Arden, "You need exactly a six to win and a four or five to reach safety."

Arden flashed Tuck a cocky grin. "Loser buys the next round, right? Watch this." He put his left hand over his eyes and rolled the die. Before he ever saw the number, he knew he had won. His pieces cheered and Dart proclaimed victory: "You, Arden, are a natural. Even the great Kilk Branthum should watch out for you." Then the board blinked and the pieces reset, ready for the next game.

Tuck threw up his hands. "That's enough for me. Let's go back to the beer. I'm better at that."

After two more hours, the bar was overfull and the clientele rowdy. A group comprised mainly of Black Hands had been playing Tower Race for maybe an hour, and their hoots and shouts grew louder with each game. As they played, they debated the upcoming vote. One man, whose voice boomed, proclaimed, "Bollocks! Spendin' untold amounts of time and money on the Seekers and Surface Affairs when the Reclaimers are on our front doorstep. Only the Hand will see us through. Strike first and strike hard. That's the way."

A woman, almost equally loud, rejoined to a chorus of laughter. "Sterculius, the hardest strike you make every day is the toilet seat on the way down. And your opinion is worth as much as what comes after." On and on they continued, never tiring of the banter.

Arden sat cross-legged in the corner. On his left, Tuck leaned against the back wall and, on his right, Noire lounged on the cushions with her left arm propping up her head. They were now on gallon number four of the ancient brew, and Arden had been watching the world spin for the last ten minutes or so. "How do most Darktouched kids learn to navigate the Abzu and Infra?" he slurred.

Noire shrugged. "Their families live in the Aboveworld *and* down here. They learn by practicing. Why? How did you learn?"

"Well, I never came down until recently, so I learned in a simulator in our backyard," Arden replied, pounding his chest to release a belch. "I never really knew we had our own doorway into the Abzu's outer ring until a few days ago."

Tuck giggled and shook his head. "Rich kids. You had a private simulator and your own doorway down? Ridiculous."

"Like I said, I never knew. I wish I could've come down sooner like you two." Arden turned bright red and tried to hide it by taking another drink. "I need to take a leak," he said.

"Again?" Tuck said incredulously. "It's like every ten minutes with this guy."

Arden nearly tripped and fell leaving the seating area, barely saving himself by thrusting his left hand out and slamming it into the wall. Blood trickled from a scraped knuckle. Staggering slightly, he passed in front of the bar and nodded to Stig on his way to the restroom. Footsteps followed behind him a few paces, so he held the swinging door for a second and then ambled inside. No one followed him in. Veering left from the hidden entryway, he assumed his customary stance in front of the urinal.

At least the bathrooms aren't old-world style. Tiled floors, stalls, and running water are fine inventions. But the urinals were different than in the Aboveworld. Instead of water or a sanitary cube, they had a round contraption about the size of a basketball underneath. When he had asked Noire about it earlier, she called it a Reducer. *Re-deuce-er. Questionably sanitary, but absolutely efficient.*

While washing his hands, Arden viewed himself in the mirror. A sound drew his gaze to the left, but he saw nothing and returned to self-examination. Dark bags under his slightly bloodshot eyes, disheveled hair, and a bit of peach fuzz were maybe his best features at present. A cupped right hand gathered water to splash on his face. The room continued to spin as he held the wall up with his left.

Feeling suddenly and violently sick, he whirled around looking for a trash Reducer or clean stall, realizing too late that someone was standing in the way. In the blind dash to find a place to hurl, he kept his focus on the floor while shimmying past. Desperately, he turned his shoulders and tried to slip by, but the person side-stepped into his way. A familiar voice berated him, "You really *are* blind! And weak." Through watery eyes, he looked up just in time to see a gray button-down shirt before spewing caustic vomit all over it.

Arden saw Vorin's face twist into a monstrous purple-and-red mass of abhorrence. A large hand reached out to grab him by the collar. And then he tasted saltiness--a second upwelling was coming. This time with some intent, he doubled over and painted black slacks and shoes with his sick.

Vorin erupted in a rageful scream, which was cut off when, seeing no good outcomes left, Arden cheap-shotted him with a jab to the groin. With his opponent briefly stunned, Arden summoned every ounce of force he could and swung with an uppercut. It was a weak punch, but Vorin was caught flat-footed and tumbled to the floor.

Arden seized the opportunity to run, but he was slowed by drunkenness. He pulled the handle—the door didn't budge. *Locked? I guess the idiot was after revenge.* Unbolting it, he burst into the seating area. Vorin was almost upright again when Arden's feet carried him past a bald man who was dancing in front of the restroom door.

Tuck was leaning against the bar and looked in his direction with a grin. "I heard a scream and thought you fell in."

"I'd better go," Arden told him. "Little accident. Meet you back at the gondola."

Tuck wrinkled his nose and curled his upper lip as Arden sprinted toward the entrance of the Deadman's Straw. Just as he reached it, he heard something slam against the wall behind him. Vorin bellowed, "I'll end you!"

Without looking back, Arden pulled open the green door and stopped cold. Standing there was Deveras, flanked by a woman wearing a blank expression and a man with a shaved head who was clothed in a Black Hand uniform. Something about the woman was familiar. Vorin stormed across the room and then, covered in stinking mess and sporting a bloody nose, abruptly stood at attention when he saw the trio.

"What in the world...?"

Arden heard the woman's voice and it clicked. His mother!

Deveras laughed. "Looks like your boy is learning about the best parts of the Complex first, Reina."

The unfamiliar Black Hand let a thin smile steal onto his face. "And making new friends among my recruits." He moved his eyes, but not his head, to address Vorin. "Go get yourself cleaned up. You haven't even donned the uniform and you're already a disgrace to the Hand."

Vorin looked like a kicked puppy crossed with a wolverine, his entire visage contorting strangely as shame, sadness, and rage tried to work their way out together. "But, sir. It was him. He..."

"Yes, and you let him," said the man. "Out of my sight. Now!"

Vorin saluted by bringing his right fist over his left breast, where the embossed hand he so desired to display would have been. Then he walked stiffly into the early evening light and out of sight.

"That was a little harsh, Sabrath," Reina said to the Black Hand officer, who responded with a shrug. "And you," she said to Arden. "You have a lot of explaining to do."

15

REINA'S STORY

"TAKE THIS." DEVERAS HANDED Arden a pink capsule and an espresso. "The pill will help sober you up and keep the hangover at bay. The caffeine will wake up your mind."

Five of them sat around a small dining table. Sabrath Nulne, the Black Hand's second-in-command and Rynn's adopted father, had excused himself at the Deadman's Straw.

"It's a good thing you live close by, Noire," Deveras added. "You three really tied one on. Walking to the other side of the Complex would've been tough."

Within moments of taking the medicine, Arden was feeling better. "That's amazing," he said.

Tuck clapped him on the shoulder. "There's gotta be *some* benefits to living in the dark, right?"

Deveras crossed the kitchen and stood in front of what looked like a pantry door. When he opened it, Arden saw a Nabucite floor but an otherwise small and empty room. Deveras issued a silent command, closed the door, and waited. When he looked inside again, there were was a bottle of whiskey and a tray of glasses on the ground. "And very nice that you have your own Fabricator," he said to Noire. "I don't even have one at my place."

Reina rolled her eyes. "That's because you're never home."

"Speak for yourself," said Deveras.

"Fair." She turned her attention to Arden. "Deveras told me about your adventures after the mine. Did you really use the HUD's shadewind indicator to jump rock to rock?" Arden grinned proudly and Reina said, "Are you insane?"

His grin stayed, but embarrassment gripped him. "Well," said Arden, "it's not like anyone ever showed me shadesurfing. Or taught me that we can glide." He ground his teeth and then spat out, "Or that we abduct children. Sorry, I meant *liberate*."

Reina's face fell and Deveras choked on a sip of whiskey. Noire and Tuck glanced at each other but remained silent.

"Okay, since we're going there..." said Reina. "Yes, your dad and I could've told you more. But we wanted you to have a relatively normal childhood. Plus, with our Lightborne connections, we didn't want you to feel... overly Darktouched."

Arden shrugged. "Doesn't matter now, does it? I'm catching up."

Reina rested her elbows on the table and leaned forward. "Did you tell them everything?" Arden shrugged again. "What does that *mean*, Arden?"

"Yes, everything. Maybe I left out minor details. I can't remember for sure," he hinted.

She closed her eyes and grimaced. "You need to tell them about the bird."

Deveras's face lit up, and he set the whiskey and tray down on the table. "Bird? Not an owl?" It was Arden's turn to be wide-eyed. "It was! Why didn't you say anything? The owl represents wisdom and is the symbol of the Source! What happened?"

Reina banged her fist on the table, rattling the glasses. "Stay focused, Deveras. The Source isn't the point right now. We need clues we can use—something that explains why the Lightwatch is more active. Maybe we can figure out where... Galan is." Arden was sure at that moment she had tried calling him Darren first. Holding onto that thought, he told the rest of his story.

Deveras stayed enraptured during Arden's entire recounting, and he looked like he was going to pass out while listening to the description of the stone dais and the ten colossal pillars. While Arden had expected the Seeker's behavior, his mother's reaction gave him pause. She was far away, staring blankly into the whiskey Deveras had poured for her.

"It said something about the number ten. Seven of Ten?" she murmured, barely perceptible.

"What did you say?" Deveras narrowed his right eye and turned his ear toward her. "Did something happen while you were looking for Arden?" He watched her face carefully. "Or before that?" Arden noticed no visible tell from his mom, but Deveras seemed to. "It must run in the family then, to hide things. What really happened after the mine?" Arden felt his ears burning.

Reina spoke slowly at first. "After I lost Arden"—she held her gaze on her son—"I stayed at the mine entrance for maybe an hour. I guessed that he made it to the Infra but wasn't sure how." Pushing up from the table, she paced around the living room, folding her arms across her stomach and unfolding them as she did. Arden tried to imagine things through his mom's eyes as she told the story.

Since we'd gotten the catalyst, I knew my chances of finding the right way down in the Cave of the Domes was decent. After deciding what to do, I reached the false entrance in less than twenty minutes. The real entrance wasn't much farther on, but the hard part was knowing where to look. Compendium records suggested that the way down wasn't through a crawlspace or natural cave. They mentioned a carved door that was now sealed.

Something Arden did when looking for Lightborne along the road made me wonder. What if there was a clue only visible in a certain HUD view? A wireframe seemed like the most logical option, but the solution actually ended up being simpler. Whoever did the work back then did a sloppy job. They'd hidden the door but left bits of the old mechanism for opening it. I guess they figured there was no point, since they sealed it shut and removed the reagent to mark it. Over time, Darktouched adventurers gave up and found other places to go diving.

Once I found the mechanism, it was only a matter of time and having enough catalyst. Imagine how excited I was when I finally found the door. But after all of that, I couldn't open it. I considered everything, even running back to the old mine to see if there was dynamite lying around. Then I opened the HUD wireframe view and saw it. A small channel led within a foot or two of the tunnel I needed, so I flagged the coordinates. I barely squeezed through the crawl hole, knowing for sure it was a one-way trip. If it hadn't worked, who knows...

Wriggling and sliding deeper, I arrived at the location. Someone had found it before me. At least one. There was a skeleton. So I used the femur to dig. When it broke, I used another. And then I switched to the fibula. It took hours, but we—me and the corpse—managed to break through.

It killed me to leave you behind, Arden, but now I had real hope. When I dropped in, I expected a manageable dive. But even on the way down, I knew something was wrong. There was nothing tranquil in that place. The shadewinds battered me, cut me. I felt a presence in the depths even though the KALM gear detected nothing. That far down, there are no sensors and limited ability to navigate. One wrong move, and I was dead. I knew that.

Sparks of light like static electricity burst and flickered. Above, below, all around. The darkness was so potent that I could feel it. But even worse, it burned my skin like frostbite. Like it was stealing me away from myself, ripping pieces of my soul away and consuming them. Yet the void remained enough at a distance that I lived. I couldn't understand why.

I felt a writhing in the deep. I saw into the void and watched as mere shadow was overtaken by terrible darkness. A rumbling voice spoke to me, "Child of Shadow, why are you here?" I passed it off as a trick of my own mind, mercilessly punishing a dead woman. And so, I didn't reply, merely waited for the end.

Then it spoke again, more forcefully, "Why have you already returned? This was not supposed to be. They moved me here only a century or two ago. I had just found slumber."

"Who moved you?" My voice was trembling.

"Children of Shadow did. Why, I cannot say. But the ancient covenant has now been broken twice, and my kin will not suffer a third time." An earthquake shook throughout the entire cavern.

"What covenant? Who are you?"

The earth screamed around me. I wasn't sure whether it was out of pain, fright, or joy. The voice spoke further, "I remember now. What was my name? Nuzum? Yes, that was my name." As the titanic creature shifted, I saw light of many colors illuminate a cavern bigger than the one this city calls home. "After the Reshaping, a covenant was made. A contract never to be torn. A question never to be asked." The darkness swirled more rapidly now. "We creatures of the deep and Eresh struggled and failed. They all, the Seven that were Ten, failed utterly."

I listened as the rumble became a groaning, angry growl. "Child of Shadow, leave this place now. I will allow it, but this is the last time."

Even though I was afraid, I called out, "Who were the Seven? Who were the Ten?"

Lightning sparked from everywhere. I felt severe heat even through the KALM gear. Flame ignited where life should be extinct. Yet this voice was attached to an existence greater than all of the Darktouched. It replied, "The Ten were. But the Seven might still be. While they live, their machinations shall never cease."

The sound of deep breathing vibrated through my entire body. "Once, we ruled the earth. But ever since the Reshaping, we have subsisted on scraps from their cursed table." The cavern again grew suddenly bright. "Leave me now, before my mind changes. Never return here, or I will personally consider the covenant broken. That day will not be kind to those who once sheltered beneath Her wing."

A path opened in front of me, and I left. But on my way out, I saw seven heads growing out of the body of an enormous winged serpent.

Reina looked around the room as she finished her story. Then, she said, "When I heard your story of ten pillars, of course I drew a connection to what Nuzum told me. But there may not be one. Deveras, you seem to have something on your mind..."

Deveras scratched his right eyebrow with the index and middle finger of his left hand. "Nuzum doesn't appear even in restricted files. So what you're saying could be fake, could be new, or..."

"Or someone tampered with the Compendium records," concluded Noire.

"Correct. And frightening," Deveras said. "The other name you mentioned though," he continued, sipping from his glass, "should be familiar to all of us. Eresh was the Darktouched founder. According to our beliefs as Seekers, she was the one who found the Source. If this is true, then there's a chance she's still alive somehow. And that means the Seekers have been right all along! We have to find her."

Tuck looked up at them. "Doesn't it also mean that there are nine others just like her? People who can wipe the floor with us? I vote we stay away."

Deveras appeared about to burst, but Reina had returned to silence. Arden looked around and then said, "It doesn't seem like it'll help us find Dad and Alan, Deveras. Doesn't that mean it has to wait?"

Deveras stood up and stretched his long arms above his head. "Maybe not," he said, pointing at Arden, Tuck, and Noire. "What if the three of you track this down while Reina and I work on finding Malank and Fiala? I'll pay you for your trouble. And Arden can get some practical Delver and Seeker experience on top of orientation."

Reina nodded. "Makes sense enough to me. Are we agreed?"

"Sure, after orientation," replied Arden, not forgetting his plans with Rynn.

"We could use the money, right, Tuck?" said Noire.

Tuck poured himself another glass of whiskey. A big one. "You four are gonna get me killed." He giggled. "Start tomorrow?"

16

ABZUBALL

"GOOD MORNING, EVERYONE," SAID Vidaya cheerfully. "Welcome to the second day of orientation." The group was gathered in front of the elevator on the main floor of Irkalla Tower. "Consider this a friendly reminder that the vote is tomorrow. Participate here at the tower or any voting center. They are all within a short walk of the eight gondola stations."

Arden felt alert even though his sleep had come in fits and starts. He had hoped to find Rynn at the Ravenous Raptor that morning, but the proprietor let him know that she had come and gone before half past six. "She was with the mean-looking guy again," was all the man told him.

When Arden saw Vorin at orientation, the only sign of the prior day's animosity was a fleeting sneer. *Not even a vengeful stare.* Phosop, though, smiled at him brightly and waved when she saw him.

Vidaya motioned for them to follow her onto the lift. Once they had boarded, it began to descend on its own. She informed them, "Today, we will be spending time in the recreational area. There, you can find free weights, simulators, and many other facilities free for your use. For today's KALM suit instruction, we will be using the Abzuball arena."

Upon exiting the elevator, Arden saw a side door on his left that led into a sprawling gym setup. In the opposite direction, a sign on the wall pointed to lockers, showers, and restrooms. Their group, however, walked straight ahead and ascended a long, enclosed staircase.

When they emerged from the tunnel, the floor leveled out. There was a railing not far ahead. The huge room in which they stood was precisely square and had four entrances set at each cardinal direction. To the right and left of each entrance were stairs leading into a seating area. The center of the arena was filled with an enormous sphere of water.

Rectangular viewing boxes were hanging high on the ceiling. In his mind's eye, Arden imagined them filled with spectators and slowly descending, stopping within feet of the top half of the sphere. Fans were cheering from the stands, and he felt a familiar churning in the pit of his stomach. He had gotten butterflies before every swim meet.

Vidaya turned to the right and directed them to the first row of seats. There, marked with name tags, were their KALM bands and belts. "If you already know how this works, please feel free to equip yourself. If not, I am happy to assist."

Arden and Vorin were both suited up in less than thirty seconds. Phosop learned by watching them and was cloaked in Nabucite not long after.

Arden marveled at how perfect the suit felt—each muscle, tendon, and joint optimally supported. His movements were precise and smooth. Perhaps he was imagining it, but the HUD views also felt faultlessly tuned to his vision and the way he looked at the world. The suit knew him at the molecular level. But it also knew *him,* anticipating what he was going to do and how, optimizing itself to best support his choices.

Arden was so absorbed that he failed to notice three people coming up the tunnel behind them and taking places at the railing nearby. When he finally looked up, he saw Vorin showing off to Caius and Rynn. The third person was Zane Sibard, the information desk operator with frosted tips who Arden had seen his first day in the tower. Zane held himself slightly apart, standing off to one side.

Vidaya was helping Phosop acclimate to the gear. With the rest of the group occupied, Arden examined the spherical playing field. His HUD told him that it measured one hundred feet in diameter. His eyes were drawn to the solid vertical and dashed horizontal lines bisecting it. They were now vibrant gold. Without the suit, they had been barely visible. Goal zones measuring ten feet long, six feet wide, and six feet deep were situated opposite each other, perpendicular to the vertical midline and centered on the horizontal midline. Designated areas of some kind were situated halfway between each goal at the top and bottom of the sphere.

"Please, everyone, we need to get started with the game," Vidaya called out. "For those that don't know, regulation Abzuball is played in a bigger sphere with teams of five players. But today we'll be three-on-three. How do we want to team up?"

Rynn offered, "Me, Arden, and... Phosop. We'll be orange. We can't have three of the Hand together."

"Sounds good to me. For the new people, please gather around and look at the diagram for a moment." Vidaya unfolded a piece of paper and used it to explain the rules.

"Abzuball is the main sport in the Complex. We are playing to help you learn more about your new suits. And because it's fun!" Vidaya let a rare, awkward smile flash across her face. "The objective is to win more periods than the other team. You win a period by scoring more points within the time limit. And you score points by picking up Abzuballs and returning them to your team's goal zones." Vidaya pointed at the ball icons on the diagram. "The *farball* in the opponent's goal is worth five points and the *midball* is worth one point. Remember also that one person has to stay on their team's half to remain onside." She paused, seeming satisfied, and then added, "If you break any of the rules, say going out of bounds by leaving the sphere, you automatically go to jail for thirty seconds. You'll learn the rest as you go." She slapped her hands together excitedly. "Guests, please help our orientees. Let's play!"

Everyone suited up, and Rynn leapt from the railing into the play area, doing flips in the water. Arden and Phosop followed close behind. Via a group channel for their team, Rynn told them, "Phosop, you play defense. Just stay close to our goal zone and slow them down. Don't stand inside. If you can, try to push them out of the sphere."

Phosop flexed her right arm. "I won't *try* to push them out. You'll see. I know a trick or two."

Rynn laughed and went on coaching them. "Use your suit's weapons. If you tap your belt, it'll emit a shadescreen and blind them. You get two per period, so use them carefully."

"What do you want me to do?" he asked Rynn.

"Are you a fast swimmer? The midball isn't as strategic in three-on-three, so let's attack the farball at the start. I'll pincer from above and you from below. Follow me." She swam over to the orange goal zone and grabbed the ball. "Here, get a feel for it." She tossed the oblong ball to Phosop. "Heavy, right? When they touch a KALM suit, Abzuballs become charged. That's what lets us throw them underwater. These are regulated at thirty feet. After that, they'll slow way down, so don't try long passes. Like Vidaya said, the rest will come naturally."

Phosop threw the ball to Arden with a full charge at close range. It twisted out of his fingers and spun toward midfield, away from them all. He swam casually and it disappeared before he could grab it.

"They reset on their own?"

Rynn replied, "Right. They reset to mid or whichever goal zone. That happens after five seconds if they're left untouched, or instantly if they go out of bounds."

From midfield, Arden surveyed the opposition as they swam on their half of the sphere. Zane and Caius tossed the purple farball back and forth while Vorin swam around the goal zone.

Vidaya proceeded to midfield and shouted over the comm system, "All right, let's begin. Please tether to your team's goal zone to set colors." Arden reached out mentally and did as she instructed. An orange glow surrounded his body. The other players were doing the same. She then announced, "Modified rules. We'll play two periods of seven minutes each. No timeouts. Begin on my mark."

Rynn called out to him, "Arden, move back toward our goal. Line up with me." She was about halfway to midfield from their goal zone. "When the count gets to three, tuck your knees in like you're doing a cannonball dive and push off in the direction you want to go. Your suit can boost you a few times per game."

Vidaya began counting down from five. Arden tucked his legs at four and pushed off at three. Propelled by the suit, he crossed the center line before she reached zero. As a horn blared to signal the beginning of the game, he was instantly and forcefully pulled into the cage at the bottom of the sphere. Vidaya's voice boomed, "False start on Arden. Thirty seconds of penalty time."

"Sorry. Bad way to start the game," he heard Rynn say as she continued pressing forward. "You're a faster swimmer than I thought! Phosop, remember what I told you."

Arden spectated from a private jail cell. The HUD displayed a game clock and a timer for his penalty. *Still twenty-seven seconds to go.* Helplessly, he watched both Zane and Caius bearing down on Phosop. Their strategy was brute force. Rynn was racing along the outside edge of the sphere toward the purple farball, but then sharply changed direction. Her fingers reached out to clutch the midball, eventually cradling it under her left arm.

The hopelessness of watching a clock tick to zero reminded Arden of his escape from the Reclaimers only a few days prior. *Twenty seconds to freedom.* He returned his attention to Phosop, who was within feet of both opposing players now. She tapped her belt and blackness jetted out from her entire body—thanks to Rynn, Arden now knew it was called a shadescreen. With sudden and unexpected force, Phosop grabbed Zane by the leg, curled her body up, and threw him out of the sphere. He flew into a barrier like a safety net that Arden reasoned must have materialized when the game started.

As Phosop grappled with Caius, who was much larger and stronger than both her and Zane, Rynn raced back with the ball and scored. They were ahead 1–0. *Ten seconds.* Arden prepared to race toward Vorin and the farball as Caius and Phosop tumbled out of the sphere. Rynn sped back to mid in a beeline toward the opponent's goal zone, while Phosop was detained in a cage next to his.

"Nice throw, Phosop. You destroyed him," he encouraged her, eliciting another flex. *Three seconds.*

Arden timed his burst perfectly, and the jail walls dissipated just before he slammed into them. He and Rynn were synced for the attack.

"Arden, you go in first. Vorin will chase you, so swing in front and distract him."

With all the speed he could muster, Arden surged from underneath the purple goal zone. Vorin was waiting. He boosted, moving with alarming power toward Arden. Stubbornly, they both held course—the collision was imminent now.

Arden saw stars and the breath was knocked from his lungs when they impacted. Vorin doubled over, arms wrapped around his diaphragm. While they were incapacitated, Rynn snuck in and dashed away with the purple farball. Soon, Zane would be released from jail. Arden gathered his strength and pushed to reach the midball before anyone else could take it. Before he could gain any momentum though, he felt a hand grip his ankle and pull him backward. A foot swung toward his face, and he blocked the blow with his forearms. He heard a whistle over the comm system.

"Kicking on Vorin. One minute of penalty time."

Arden seized the opportunity. When he reached the midball seconds later, Rynn was already on the edge of their goal zone. She crossed coolly over the line and the scoreboard now read 6–0 in their favor. A chime rang in Arden's ears and he looked up to see Zane roaring down from the purple jail. Desperate, he chucked the ball as hard as he could toward Rynn. It fell at least ten feet short, but she was able to pick it up before it reset. She scored again and the HUD showed 7–0.

They earned the period win by amassing a 22–7 lead.

"We still need to win the second," Rynn reminded them. "Start fast like last time, Arden."

Vidaya began the countdown. Arden boosted at three, this time almost in his own goal. The horn sounded the start of period two exactly as he crossed the midline. He followed the curve of the sphere near where the jail was, screaming ahead and seeing too late that the purple team was playing a shell defense. Vorin and Caius guarded their goal zone while Zane raced straight to the midball.

Caius was upon him first, trying to pin his arms and wrestle him out of the sphere. Arden expected Vorin to barrel into them both, but he maintained discipline and waited for Rynn. She was faster, but Vorin managed to grab an ankle and swing her out of the field of play.

Now it was two-on-one. Zane was already speeding back with the midball, and Caius had Arden inches from the boundary line. Vorin came at them, now in a blind rush. At the last second, Arden slipped free from Caius and angled his body in an attempt to glide past the incoming blow. He swore he heard an "Oof" when Vorin crashed into Caius.

Somehow, Arden was still inbounds, with the edge of the sphere now on his right. In the tangle of limbs, he saw a fist just before it jarred his left cheek. Zane had already scored and was back on the offensive, heading for the orange farball. Rynn was in jail and Phosop, unsure whether to move up or not, was totally uninvolved in the action.

Maintaining the smallest bit of composure, Arden engaged his shadescreen. Angry now, he used the brief moment of disorientation to grab onto someone's arm with both hands. While holding onto the limb, he brought his knees up and launched off the first thing his feet touched. Mimicking the move Phosop had used earlier, he torqued to his left and wrenched the arm as hard as he could. One of the two bodies nearby was sent flying into the safety barrier and quickly pulled into jail, while the other was several feet away and scrambling to recover. Not caring who he had flung, Arden raced to the first glint of purple he saw, grasping for it.

Arden now held the farball tucked under his right arm. He saw Zane returning from the orange side, Phosop trailing behind him. Rynn broke free from jail and called for a pass. He released it just before a ferocious hit from behind snapped his head back, dazing him. Rynn caught the ball and boosted to the orange goal zone. As Zane raced by Arden, he vainly reached out an arm that was easily slapped away. Phosop crossed the midline to help and, when no penalty sounded, she grabbed onto the person who had tackled him. The reprieve was what Arden needed. Believing the farball Zane was carrying a lost cause, Arden dropped back to midfield and took the easy point.

The board now showed a 6–6 deadlock.

With under a minute left in the second period, the score remained tied at 8–8. Following successive failures to capture another farball, both teams had gotten caught up in a battle over midfield.

"I have a plan," Arden stated calmly during a lull. "Phosop, move up halfway to mid. If they attack our end, pretend to fight but let go after two seconds."

He curled up and dashed for the purple goal zone, taking the other team by surprise. They were playing so far up that slipping in behind them required no effort.

"Rynn, pop a shadescreen in mid!"

The inky blackness deployed just as Arden grabbed the purple farball and sprinted toward center sphere. Uncertain what to do, Zane broke free and went for the orange goal zone. As planned, Phosop struggled with him briefly and then let him free. Rynn dove for the midball, but Caius put up his own shadescreen in desperation and tried to incapacitate her. Vorin spun around to chase Arden, who veered sharply away while simultaneously slowing. Sensing the distance between them closing, Arden knew his ploy had worked. He braced himself for the hit as he let the ball fly toward Phosop, who stood with arms outstretched.

To Arden's shock and horror though, Caius came out of nowhere and intercepted the ball as Zane reached the midline. And when Vorin struck him, he lost sight of the play. His HUD showed the clock at five. He looked back to see Zane alone, racing against time. *There's no way he makes it. We're going to tie.* But he did make it as the clock hit one and, also to Arden's surprise, so did Rynn at the other end.

The second period ended 9–13. They had lost.

They stood together near the stands. "Truly amazing game," applauded Vidaya. "I hope you enjoyed it and got a taste of what your suits are capable of. It is now time for the last item on today's agenda! Which is—"

Phosop interrupted her. "Wait. It can't end in a tie!" The entire group agreed in unison.

Vidaya shook her head. "I'm sorry, but we are out of time. Both teams tallied a period win, so use overall points as a tiebreaker." She sniffed. "Or finish the game on your own time. If you must." Her eagle visage and abrupt retreat to her default setting of disapproval made it clear that fun time was over. Work had to resume. "Now, as I was saying..."

Arden glanced in the direction he'd last seen Rynn, his focus on Vidaya's droning voice dwindling, but she was already gone. Disappointed, he picked up the thread of Vidaya's schooling where he had left it.

"...choose three disciplines to gain practical experience in. These do not have to be your final selections, so please explore options. Here are printed lists of available opportunities."

Arden took a sheet of paper from Vidaya. He had already decided that anything with the Delvers and Seekers would be redundant. As for the Hand, he had reasons to argue both sides of the question. But, boiling it down, it made no sense based on his upbringing and outlook. One conflict versus another mattered little to him. He would fight if he had to. For the ones he loved. For the things he believed in. If fate brought him those things. *Apparently, my fate is to lecture myself in my mother's place.*

Arden forcefully pulled his mind back to the list. Discounting Delvers, Seekers, and the Hand, he was left with Surface Affairs and Support. Even so, he reviewed each line:

DISCIPLINES WITH AVAILABLE PRACTICAL OPPORTUNITIES

Black Hand

- Child Liberation

- Defense, Search & Rescue

- Law Enforcement

Delvers

- Aboveworld Knowledge Acquisition

- Assessor

- Biological Studies

Seekers

- Analyst

- Arbitrator

- Depths Explorer

Surface Affairs

- Child Assignment & Disavowed Support (CADS)

- Finance

- Merchants

Support

Fabrication

- Equipment

- Building Materials and Other

- Private Use

General

- Accounting

- Compendium maintenance

Hospitality

- Bar and restaurant owners

- Other service

Maintenance

- Equipment Help (KALM and other)

- Irkalla building and facilities (including pathways, barriers, lifts, gondolas, etc.)

- Complex buildings and facilities

Research and Development

Arden made decisions as though he were throwing darts at a painting. *R&D because I want to meet Beydin Krenneth. CADS because I have a bone to pick. And... Merchants because it sounds interesting.* He gave it no more thought, even as he punched the keys on yet another touchpad to make it official.

17

THE LEDGE

ARDEN DISEMBARKED THE ELEVATOR at Floor B6, one level below the recreational facilities. Tuck and Noire had told him to meet them there after orientation because it functioned as the main access point for Compendium records. They'd called it the Ledge, but left it to him to guess why.

Arden fought with his own expectations as he surveyed the place. Following a crude map Tuck had drawn, he meandered his way along, seeking the private study room where they were waiting. His imaginings of the Compendium had been far from this—it looked like a common library but without the actual books. Study rooms tailored to different group sizes consumed the majority of the floorspace, with a number of booths designed for individual use scattered throughout. The rooms were furnished with ergonomic chairs and desks, paper and pens, display panels, and tablets for accessing Compendium files. Signs pointed to a lecture hall, offices, a café, and restrooms. The Darktouched had even gone the extra mile and somehow replicated the woody, earthy smell of book stacks.

Arden wound this way and that, turning corners and slipping down narrow pathways, occasionally having to double back and scan the map. When he finally found the room, he knocked lightly and peered through a small window in the door. Noire saw him first and motioned him inside.

Tuck looked up from a tablet and grinned. "You look like you got in a fight," he said, drawing a finger across his left cheek.

Arden reached up and touched his own face. The spot where he'd been punched during the Abzuball game felt a little tender. "Hadn't noticed. I think my buddy Vorin got in a cheap shot. More than one." Arden laughed it off. "So, why are we here instead of the Infra?"

Noire shook her head. "Do you think we just randomly go digging in the dark? Every Seeker and Delver job starts here. That's why we call it the Ledge. We all want to jump off, literally and figuratively." She added, "The majority of our work happens *here*, not the Infra."

"C'mon now, Noire. I wouldn't say the *majority*," argued Tuck. "You're gonna scare him away. I bet he signed up with the Hand already."

"If that's what he wants." Noire shrugged.

Arden pulled out a chair and sat down. "Nah. I went with R&D, CADS, and the Merchants. I don't think the Rynn thing is going anywhere," he added. "We were supposed to do something tonight, but she left right after the Abzuball game without saying anything. I think she forgot. That or she's pissed I blew the Abzuball game." He forced out a chuckle.

"Who knows, kid," Tuck said. "People are hard to predict, 'specially complicated ones like her. It's probably for the best."

Noire learned forward with a serious look on her face. "If she did ditch you, I don't think it's because of a game," she said, eyes on Arden. "It's because you're *annoyingly* unfocused. For example, we have a job to do right now." Her customary smirk returned. "Can we please get to work?"

Arden felt a smile spread across his face. "Yeah, let's do it. Before that, though, any news about my dad and Alan from Deveras or my–– Or Reina?"

"Not yet," Tuck answered. "They're supposed to meet with the other leaders today, seekin' support for a rescue op." Arden bobbed his head in recognition. Tuck added, "This might sound harsh, but don't get your hopes up. I think our chances are better with the banished Lightborne."

"Let's find some info," Noire said.

Tuck gave a thumbs up. "Metis said she can dig up anything we need from restricted records."

"What'd that cost you?" Noire asked knowingly.

"Dinner. Time." Tuck giggled, running a hand through his curls. "I don't have money, so it had to be somethin' I *do* have." He looked up at the display screen across the room from where they sat. "All right! What're we lookin' for? We know Nuzum isn't in the records. But we could try keyword searches for dragon, Eresh, the Seven, the Ten... Anything else?"

"What about mentions of owls or the Source?" suggested Arden.

Tuck motioned in the negative. "We'd pull every Seeker file, memo, and ticket stub. They're obsessed with both things. That's basically their job description."

Noire cleared her throat. "Dragon and Eresh are also too broad. We'll be sifting for days. For Arden," she continued, "just pull up *On the Myth and Materiality of Eresh*. The author was a hack, but the intro is a decent summary."

Tuck typed in the title and pulled up the first page on the display screen. The author's name was listed as Ziglaf Chaucer. *This person must have been an English teacher Aboveworld.* His musing allowed *The Canterbury Tales* to sneak out of his collection of repressed memories, making his skin crawl.

"Here you go, Arden. Take a look at the first two paragraphs," Tuck instructed him. He began reading carefully.

For many Darktouched, in this age of accelerated industrialization in the Aboveworld that has seen the "invention" of technologies such as the steam engine and electricity, the principles we hold dear and the sense we have about our place in history have been shaken. Multitudes of our brethren have long questioned the veracity of our fundamental beliefs, and this inevitably threatens the fabric of our social order. In contemporary times, many treat even historical figures as myth, regarding our origin texts as mere children's tales. But is this a fair treatment? Eresh is perhaps foremost among these debated persons, and certainly the most contentious. This is not without reason.

Eresh, likely the final Darkname she employed prior to expiring, was known for millennia as the one who discovered the Source. Texts describe her as the founder of an ancient Darktouched society that helped rebuild the world following a nigh apocalyptic disaster. This event, labeled by Darktouched scholars as the Reshaping, forever altered the trajectory—and the memory—of the sphere called Earth.

As is common knowledge, the Reshaping purportedly culminated in the Abzu and Infra erupting on the surface, rending asunder the land and leaving a trail of ruined societies in its wake. Some evidence of phenomena described in the Reshaping tales certainly exists in the Infra. We can interact with objects pulled into the abyss when the dark tide swelled and receded on a smaller scale. Yet we know next to nothing about the causes of the larger, mythological event. Further, we know even less of Eresh's role leading up to and during it, if she indeed had a role. The question, really, is whether she existed at all. By extension, we must also ask if the Source itself exists.

Arden let them know he had finished reading with a question. "So, when did this Reshaping event happen, if it did?"

Noire snorted. "He's going Seeker on us, Tuck." Then her tone became more serious. "If the Reshaping did happen, researchers say it was *at least* twelve thousand years ago. The Darktouched themselves have existed that long—minimum. You can imagine how many studies have been done, explorations undertaken... and still no answers. Seekers are chasing a needle that never existed in a haystack that rotted and blew away before they started looking."

Tuck rocked in his chair and nearly fell over backward, drawing laughs from the others. "What I was gonna say..." he mumbled at first, still sorting himself. Then he started over, "What I was gonna say is that I see it differently. If ya really believe in it, why do ya need proof?"

Noire looked at him as though seeing him for the first time. "Where is this coming from? Mister I-need-money-this and Let's-make-money-that. I think you've been spending too much time with Deveras."

"That could be, Noire," Tuck said. "Anyway, if Eresh is still alive, she's one old, old lady. The rest of the tale goes that, before the Reshapin', she gathered the original Darktouched to her and bound them to the Source to save 'em. After it happened, somehow the Source was lost to her and the rest of us. We've been down here ever since. That's what the Seekers believe."

"And the Lightborne?" asked Arden.

Noire stood and leaned with both of her hands on the table. "We know almost nothing. They're maybe more secretive even than us, and they protect information to the extreme. I doubt even Deveras knows much about them, and he's colluding with the banished bunch."

"Okay, I'm good for now. Thanks." Arden felt as though he had endless questions, but he decided it was time to let their research lead them.

"Great," Noire said, returning to her seat. "Let's dig in."

Arden paced one side of the room, rubbing his eyes, while Noire drained her third cup of coffee in as many hours. They'd started with document searches on variations of "the Seven" and "the Ten," but ended up buried in records. A phrase search for "Seven that were Ten" flagged a single restricted record that gave them hope only to destroy it soon after. Even an hour later, Tuck continued to grumble.

"The Seven that were Ten," he complained, "isn't cryptic enough. Now we have a Nine."

The file had referenced the Nine Saviors of Y'sham, whose deeds had impressed a king, scribe, or someone.

"Had to pull Metis out of a meeting, and that's gonna cost me. We should find an Eight so we can have a small straight."

"Nice rhymes, Tuck." In a rare turn, Noire's laughter was stifled by an angry stare from Tuck. "Yep. Not that funny anyway."

Arden verbally summarized their searches and outcomes, seeking direction. "The numbers have gotten us nowhere. Dragon, winged serpent, seven-headed dragon, multiheaded dragon. All junk. Eresh and the Source. Worse than junk." Abruptly, he stopped pacing and grabbed a handful of his own hair. "Wait. Nuzum said something about being moved."

Noire laid both of her arms on the table and let her head bang against it. Without moving, she said to Arden, "So what? Reina already looked at those records. We've been over this."

"But she looked at them trying to find a way down," Arden reasoned. "What if she missed something?"

Tuck reached his hands above his head and stretched. He shrugged and began typing. "It was the Cave of the Domes, right?" Arden nodded and resumed pacing, now with his hands clasped behind his back. "Not a whole lot here. Let me see." Tuck sifted through records while Arden watched on the display panel. "Closed as an Infra backdoor in 1855. Entrance sealed citing extreme danger. Yeah, more nothing."

Noire looked up with one eye. "Does it say who ordered the closure?"

"No," Tuck answered, and Noire closed her eye again. "Wait. It does. Some guy named Oswald Adnemos."

Noire shot out of her chair and walked over to the display panel. "Damn! You're right," she said, then began muttering to herself. "I'll never hear the end of it now. Should have paid more attention. Wait!" Grabbing the tablet from Tuck's hands, she frantically entered a search. "Tuck, you know how obsessed my adopted family is with their Darktouched lineage, right? I mean, how stupid. They're not even blood related." Results appeared on the screen under the heading "Izmir Council of 1857."

Tuck turned his palms up and slightly wagged his head. "Sure, but what are you talkin' about? I'm not followin'."

Noire raised both arms triumphantly. "There!" She called their attention to a photograph, then walked over to point out two specific individuals and their names listed below it. A clean-shaven man with a gentleman's frock coat, top hat, and monocle was shaking hands with a younger man who wore traditional Turkish dress and a fez. Their names were listed as Friedrich Pedersen and Binnaz Demir. "Friedrich Pedersen *was* Oswald Adnemos. In my Darktouched family, he was my great-great-grandfather. The man he's standing with had the Darkname Eldras Shurali. Well?"

Tuck and Arden stared at each other blankly. For an uncomfortable period of time, they both searched the room, the floor, the table, the ceiling, and Noire's face for answers. Her normally cool exterior now resembled Vorin's raging red.

"Ugh! Eldras Shurali was leader of the Delvers for decades. His grandson always speaks fondly of him, every chance he gets."

"Oh, you have to be kiddin' me!" The sound of Tuck's palm slapping the table made Arden turn and look. He saw Noire smile for the first time since the night before, conviction in her eyes.

"Not at all. We need to talk to Kilk Branthum," she said. "But first, we have to find him. And I think I know where to look."

18

KILK'S STORY

T HE SIXTEENTH FLOOR OF Irkalla Tower, like most above the fifth, only
housed office space for senior leadership. They stood in front of the office
of Brasa Langiles, who owned the job title of Delver Personnel Leader.

Tuck had explained the Delver leadership structure to Arden in a few words:
"Reina leads the Delver operations day to day, Brasa deals with the personalities,
and Kilk has a lot of free time for politickin'."

After failing to pull Deveras into a call, Noire decided the next best option
was to ask Brasa for help. Her expectation, shared with the others, was that the
mission leaders were finally meeting to discuss a rescue operation for Darren.

Arden briefly recalled the night before. After Deveras's fervor regarding owls
and Eresh had subsided to a degree, he'd stressed the difficulties of organizing
the gathering.

"Reina and Sabrath are in almost the same situation. They lead, but their
bosses are the ones with decisioning rights on big issues. Kilk and Daryala
are both impossible to track down." The evening had already turned to early
morning and the whiskey bottle stood nearly empty. "If it were up to me and
Beydin, things would already be moving." Even so, he'd proclaimed confidence
that the group would convene today.

Brasa sat behind a wide, ornate desk piled with papers that were placed in tidy,
uniform stacks. His entire workspace, in fact, seemed immaculate beyond practical means, crossing the line between high organization and inefficiency. This
belied the appearance of the man himself. Brown hair fell onto his shoulders,

seeming to resist the very act of being combed. Wild, patchy stubble covered his face and neck. A faded blue t-shirt and ragged jeans covered his thin frame. Flip-flops dangled from feet that were propped up on his desk as he leaned back casually in an office chair, listening to rap that filled the room and penetrated the thick door. When he saw them, the music stopped suddenly, and he waved them in.

"Hey, guys. It's been a minute," he said to Tuck and Noire. "As for you, I don't think we've met. You must be Reina's son." Instead of reaching out his hand, he merely gave a wave and a half smile. Arden returned it in kind as Brasa asked, "What can I do for you?"

"We need to talk with Kilk. Any idea where he is? Or Deveras?" Noire asked.

Brasa brought his legs down and sat up in his chair. With his feet lifted off the ground, he began alternating between left and right half turns, his eyes never leaving the group.

"Deveras is in a meeting on the top floor. Kilk just got back in sometime last night. Brighid in Medical Services said he had a broken arm and some other wear and tear, but he's otherwise unharmed."

"Wow. I'm glad he's fine. What happened?" Noire asked concernedly. She received only a shrug from Brasa in response, so she said, "I guess we'll just wait then."

Brasa spun around as he answered, "Nope. I'll take you down to B2. I can get you in to see Kilk."

At the entry to Medical Services, visitors were met immediately by a long, curved desk with three attendants staffing it. Brasa walked up to the middle one, a man with a shaved head and a pot belly. "Hey, Graf. I need to get these three in to see Kilk."

"Brasa, my man. I can do that. That's everything you wanted?"

"Yep. I have to talk to Carmen, so I brought them down. Thank you." Brasa rapped his knuckles on the desk and strode away down a hallway to their left. "I'll see you later. Hope you get what you need."

Graf glanced quickly at them. "He's in Room 106. Do you need help getting to it?" Noire shook her head. "Okay, you can head on back."

When they entered the room, Kilk was sitting up in bed tearing tiny pieces from a sheet of paper, rolling them up, and tossing them toward a half-empty cup sitting on a table a few feet to his right. A cast covered his left arm. His white hair, wispy on top, was ruffled to cover a hairline that had receded long ago and then begrudgingly held on. Weathered skin blemished by brown patches and skin tags crumpled around a subdued smile, which called Arden's attention to a large mole near the right side of his mouth. Blue eyes sparkled and persuasively debated against an otherwise wizened and brittle countenance.

Kilk's steady hands continued their work even as he sagaciously sized the three up. "I know you two," he said in a gravelly voice that Arden found oddly disarming. "But this one not at all." A bony finger pointed at Arden before collaborating with the others on his right hand to toss another piece of paper. "Missed again. You three are the ones looking into Eresh?"Noire opened her mouth to speak, but Kilk continued. "Certainly you are. Otherwise, why would you be here?" Another ball of paper fell short of its mark.

"We found a connection to your grandfather in some Compendium files, and we hoped you could help us," Noire hurriedly stated.

Kilk took another shot. It hit the rim of the cup and fell off. "Bah! This is a terrible game. I'll have to have a word with the inventor." Bushy eyebrows covered his eyes like willow branches as he laughed. "Which grandfather?"

Noire began to answer and then stopped herself.

"Grandpa Eldras, obviously," Kilk supplied for her. "You wouldn't have found anything about the other in the Compendium, complete wastrel that he was." Finally, a shot went in. "Good, I win. Now I can focus. *What* about Eldras?" Noire remained silent, but she leaned forward slightly in anticipation. "Well?" Kilk asked. "I can't deduce something from nothing."

Arden analyzed the scene as Noire began speaking, convinced steam was coming out of her ears. "Reina d'Martest told us she descended via a backdoor in the Cave of the Domes. Underneath—"

"Nuzum. Yes, Deveras informed me," Kilk interjected. "I think I see now. One of you is connected to Oswald Adnemos." Noire's mouth remained as it was when Kilk interrupted. She closed it and nodded her head slightly. Kilk continued, "I believe he was leader of Surface Affairs when that backdoor was closed. Grandpa always spoke kindly of him."

Tuck rapidly snuck in a question. "Nuzum said someone moved it before the door was closed. Do you know why?"

Kilk smacked his lips. "I do. And Nuzum is a him, not an it."

"Does he—"

"Have anything to do with Eresh? No, not really. The Seekers won big in the 1855 vote. Forbidden zones changed." Kilk scratched his beard. "It's of no interest to your search."

"Pardon, sir," Tuck said, "but why not just start with that?"

Kilk frowned at him. "Being of no interest to your interests doesn't make the information *disinteresting*. That said, I have something for you."

Noire added quickly, "About Eresh, right, sir?"

"Who else?" Kilk asked. "For decades now, I've been poking around in the extreme reaches of the Infra. Before you ask, my goals are my own." A bony finger wagged at them warningly. "As the Lightwatch becomes more aggressive, I become more desperate. So, when I heard from Deveras about the attack on... you and yours, I believe,"--the bony finger again pointed at Arden--"I sallied forth, as it were." Scratching his nose, he tacked on, "You should sit."

They each found a place to rest, prepared for the tale.

"Have any of you heard of Göbekli Tepe?" Kilk inquired. "No? Well, it's one of a collection of hill sites in Turkey. Very old by Aboveworld standards—close to twelve thousand years. Awe inspiring." Arden imagined the ancient sites, stepping through them in his mind as Kilk explained, "Compared to Deep Infra ruins, they're nothing to write home about. I've been exploring sites nearly half again as old." Forgetting his cast for a moment, he tried to gesticulate with his left arm and grimaced. "They're so old I've had to work with Beyd on a specialized translator. I call the zones where I've spent most of my time Eldrastan and Branthumville." Blue eyes narrowed at his audience's audible silence. "What? They're forbidden zones, and I'm the only one there. Or that's what I thought until two days ago."

Arden listened intently to the old man's words as he recounted events from the past week, eager to hear a different perspective.

The day after Deveras came back, I left Irkalla in the afternoon. The fifth of June. Let's call that Day One. Reina wasn't back yet, and I was of course worried. But like I told you, I've been searching those grids for years now. They're massive, ancient cities. We're not talking about skyscrapers. No steel and glass. There are some buildings that surpass Ancient Sumer and Egypt, but these people were more in tune with nature. Anyhow, I've wandered off topic.

Shadesurfing hurts at my age, so I like to settle in for a few days once I'm there. First thing I did was find a place to rest for the night. These people used some kind of plant-like material to sleep on—I've never slept better in my life. Every time, it makes me wish I could bring some back with me.

I headed straight for a cluster of buildings I've hunkered down in before that are on the edge of the explored zone. As I approached one, I saw the usual door markings and headed toward them. The structures are made of a greenish-blue stone, like a dark amazonite. The markings are white, and doors are signified by three notches above them in the shape of a narrow-bottomed letter H. Now see, the doors in these places react to a certain chemical signature. It took me and Beyd years to figure this out. When the right stuff gets near a marked entrance, the living stones move to the side and let you through. It's technology that feels a bit like magic.

Inside, there was a circular chamber with stair markings leading up to a loft area. When I approached the marks, stones floated into place to form a wide staircase. I wasn't there for giggles, so I climbed up looking for a bed. Found one too. There was little else to find, and I was tired. When I Delve at those depths, I carry an Explorer's pouch to stay alive. I took the pills, and Day One ended pretty unceremoniously.

I woke up in the morning on Day Two and set out for a part of Branthumville I'd never been to. I picked my way slowly through the streets. It's so far into the darkness that one wrong step or a second of carelessness can be the last thing you do. There are creatures down there too. Things that consume darkness. Things that abhor light. After hearing about Nuzum, you might be thinking of dragons. But these are worse.

Some hide in the preserved remnants of manmade, nearly eternal trees that were pulled under by the dark tide's swell. They appear humanoid. Maybe in a different era they were a weaponized form of defense. Gorged on darkness, though, they mature into enormous, obese giants. Nabucite stirs them into a frenzy. Thankfully, they're slow. And if you avoid the trees, you can skirt past them. But there are others. There's one type that appears to be some kind of twisted dog with razor-like fangs that can run both forward and backward. They move with alarming speed and are relentless. When they run in reverse, their head screws up underneath it to face you. In my younger days, a pack cornered me in an old shithouse for two entire days.

The scariest, though, is some kind of enormous human-dragon hybrid that can separate in half horizontally along its abdomen. Killing is like breathing to them. They're one reason you don't want to shadesurf too far in, especially where you haven't been before. Whether they were manufactured or bred, I can't say. But after being pulled down into the Infra, they clung to life and survived in the darkness. They're death personified. Imagine you're starving and you see your favorite meal. We're that to them. Semi-solid Nabucite wrapped around blood and bones. A Darktouched chocolate-covered ice cream cone.

It took me half a day just to reach the target. My analysis suggested it was some kind of depot attached to a military installation. I'd stumbled across a memo in an old outpost a couple of months ago. It described the chemical signature to open a special door, so I asked Beyd to synthesize it for me. Three weeks ago, I finally figured out which door. I won't bore you with how.

The place was massive. From the outside, it looked like an inverted V. The greenish-blue walls stretched from the ground high into the sky. It was surrounded by sheer cliffs on two sides. My HUD estimated it at over three hundred feet tall and two hundred thousand square feet at the base. For you Aboveworld sports fans, that's about two and a half soccer fields. Still, there were no signs of overland transportation. There were no markings for gates and no vehicle tracks.

I slipped in through a worker's entrance and began searching for the door to my key. Really, I had no idea even where to begin. I walked around for half an hour or more before I saw the answer to one of my questions: Enormous white markings on the ceiling and ground. I surmised this civilization had somehow harnessed both flight and belowground travel. But it didn't help my mission, so I moved on.

My HUD showed it was already late afternoon. The suit lessens water and nutrient loss, but thirst and hunger were setting in. I had almost thrown up my hands, ready to call it a day, when it came to me. Large flying somethings coming in through the ceiling could mean smaller flying somethings for individual movement. The doors would be up high. Higher than I could reach. Shadesurfing normally doesn't work indoors. It's also dangerous. But I figured if it could work anywhere, this was the place. I summoned the kite and hoped. And voila! In a darkness so powerful, the shadewinds never stop.

As methodically as I could, I scanned the depot walls, climbing as I went. Within minutes, I'd found the door. It's impossible to remain totally stationary with the kite, so I floated up high above it and hung in the air, slowly easing myself lower. I'm old and rickety, so imagine doing this with one arm and one leg. The living stone gradually gave way and I swung forward, stepping ever so gracefully inside.

Right, well, I thought that would be the hard part, but I was wrong. The ceiling was cut too low for flying, and there were hundreds of stair steps ascending in front *of me. There were markings on the ground though, and I wondered if riding an ancient escalator was perhaps in my future. Alas, it wasn't to be. I was exhausted by the time I reached the top. In the first enclosed spot I could find, I plopped down, swallowed another round of pills from the Explorer's pouch, and fell asleep.*

It was just after midnight on Day Three when I woke up. My body was sore and my mind foggy. The floor I'd climbed to was a control center with a footbridge that led further into the installation. I poked around in the vicinity for information but found nothing useful. As I crossed the bridge, I was able to look through small windows at the cityscape below. I discovered then that this wasn't a bridge at all. Instead, a path was carved into the cliff I had seen from outside.

The passageway began to cut into the rock and descend swiftly. At the end was an elevator that thankfully responded to the same chemical signature as the door. When I reached the bottom, I was elated. A research lab stretched out in front of me. I felt that this could be everything I'd been looking for. I found documents, schematics, and even operable prototypes! It truly was a goldmine. Technologies that were thought to be lost forever.

And yet, my real target eluded me. Maddeningly. For that entire day and most of the next two, I scanned, read, searched. Until Beyd and his team parse through the data, we won't know exactly what was there. But I found so much! I might be the greatest Delver ever, you know?

It had been basically five days, so I decided to head back to the Complex. The return trip was uneventful until I reached the bottom of the stairs. It was then that things began to unravel. My heart beat faster and faster the closer I got to

the door markings and the way out. In a few hours, I'd return triumphant, my legacy assured. The stones slid to the side, and I was near to leaping off the edge and calling my wings. And then I saw it.

This was the first time I had been close enough to analyze one thoroughly. Unknown entity with unknown origin. Partially synthetic chemical structure. It hadn't seen me yet, so I concealed myself further inside the entryway and studied it.

The upper half was humanoid, with wyvern wings protruding from its back. Its lower half was something between a bird and dragon. A strong tail balanced its movements, and four talons as long as my forearm grew out of each foot. I could see more clearly from this distance the line at the bottom of its torso showing where the top and bottom parts of its body were joined. And where it would separate while murdering me. Strangely, the farther it flew away, the louder the flaps of its wings became.

Even in my youth, I don't think I could have outrun it. So I waited. As my shock wore off, I began wondering how it got inside in the first place. My answer arrived a while later. A small dragon, like a winged serpent, appeared through a portal in the ceiling. My guess is a malfunction in the chemical receptors, but I can't say for sure. Whatever it was, it gave me an opportunity. Like a fly through an open window, the half-humanoid monster escaped before the hole in the ceiling closed. I'd traded devil for demon, but now I had a chance.

Once the dragon was out of sight, I jumped from the doorway and waited a second to open my wings. I was trying to reach the ground fast, and I did. I landed with a thud and began running back to the side door I'd come in through. I heard nothing, saw nothing, and calmly stepped outside. No wing flutters. No trees. No backward-walking dogs. I was home free.

Relieved, I decided to sneak back a ways, hidden between the buildings, before shadesurfing out. There was nothing. I became more confident with each step, but I'd done this so many times that I never really let my guard down. All was well. By the time I reached my little private guesthouse, I felt safe to summon my kite.

I called it, and within seconds the flutter of wings came directly overhead, rapidly growing quieter. The hair on the back of my neck stood on end, and I felt the creature's presence. I had little chance to escape. Fortunately for me, it struck the kite first. I was thrown against a tree and heard a sickening crack. I knew immediately that my left arm was broken.

Across a field that was probably a park at one time, I saw the three white marks of a doorway. Desperate, I ran into the open, knowing that the tree was also a death trap. An obese giant landed behind me, shaking the earth beneath my feet and almost causing me to fall. My arm ached. Each step worsened the agony. With every bit of strength left in me, I ran. And ran. And ran. But not fast enough. The monster behind me fell away, but the ever-quieter flutter of wings came upon me from the right. In sickening rhythm with my footfalls and breathing they flapped, until I almost felt the synthetic beast touching me.

My vision dimmed and I felt myself stumble. Then, in front of me, I saw a doorway form and a figure emerge from it. A woman's voice screamed, and a sudden burst of darkness pulled the monstrosity's focus away from me. I caught my balance and staggered to her, falling through the doorway. I collapsed on the floor and passed out.

When I came to, I was lying in one of those miracle beds. My arm had been set and there was some kind of leaf wrapped around it, firmly holding it in place. Thanks to the mystery woman, I was alive.

My HUD showed that it was early morning on the tenth of June. Day Six. I rose from bed and followed my nose. The smell of food wafting from down the hall called to me. Perhaps ironically, this building that looked to have once been a small house was still functioning as one. I rounded a corner and saw her. Really saw her. I was surprised, because she had no KALM suit or other gear.

She must have understood, because she said to me, "There's a barrier around this place. You can take off your suit. Please, sit and eat."

Not sure if I was truly alive or just dreaming, I did as she said. A fire was burning in the hearth opposite where I rested. I had never seen a fire in the Infra before then. Never thought it possible. Carefully, she moved her waist-length black hair to the side as she stooped over the fire. When she handed me a bowl of soup, I devoured it without so much as a thank you.

She spoke again, wearing a thin, knowing smile. "I only have a small Fabricator, so the ingredients are mostly greens and spices."

I could no longer hold my thoughts down. "Thank you, it's delicious. But... is this real?"

"Very real. Although your disbelief is understandable. Not many Depths Explorers know how to set a barrier. Maybe none." Her tone was casual, like it was nothing out of the ordinary.

I nodded, not really understanding. You know as well as I do that no one knows how to set a barrier in the Infra. "That makes sense," I lied. "Do you have a Darkname?"

The firelight cast shadows on her face. She was really quite fetching. "I did, a long time ago," she said. "You can call me Persephone."

"Well, Persephone, thanks for the rescue. I was dead."

She simply nodded. "You're welcome. And you were."

"Do you live here?" I asked.

"For today." Her smile hadn't lapsed the whole time. "Perhaps not tomorrow. May I ask why you're down here?"

I wanted to be honest, but not too much. "Looking for ancient tech. I found what I hope are some good things." Her brown eyes never left mine, and the smiling began to put me off, so I asked her, "What about you? Are you a Seeker who gave up the Complex? Or maybe a Delver looking for the Big One?"

Her answer came after a brief pause. "Neither. I'm just a wanderer of the depths. It's quiet. I find it comforting." Still, she kept smiling. It became a personal goal to make her stop.

"With a name like Persephone, people will start to think that you're some Eresh fanatic. Maybe it's her you're after?" I was certain that would do it, and yet the infernal smile remained.

"Eresh. I have no need of her. That woman died a long time ago."

I considered whether that phrasing was peculiar or simply awkward, but I had a mission. An idea came to me. "Perhaps you're lamenting a long-lost love?" That did it, if only briefly. And then I felt terribly guilty, because in that split second, I saw the most profound sadness I had ever encountered. "That was cruel. I'm sorry."

Her guard was back up, and the smile returned. "No, that's okay. Love is never really lost, after all. Don't you think so?" she asked, addressing me by my Abovename.

My jaw must have hung open for a minute before I recovered. Hearing a stranger speak my Abovename—in the Infra no less—truly shook me. "What did you say? How could you know that?"

Her expression turned cold. The room turned cold. Smiling. Staring. "Insulting those who hold your life in their hands is foolish. You are foolish. But you are not truly malicious, I can tell." The room felt warmer again. "Let's begin again. I'm Persephone. It's nice to meet you..." She let the words hang in the air as an invitation.

"Kilk Branthum. It's a pleasure. Could I please get another bowl of soup?"

As we sat and talked, the time passed strangely. She agreed to help me travel home before the day was over but asked me to stay with her for a while and chat. We spoke of past and future, life and love, things found and things lost.

Before we departed together for the Complex, she said something that stayed with me: "When I was young, I hoped to fix the world. When I was older, I hoped the world would spare me loss. And now, I simply hope to leave something worthwhile behind as I exit. You and I have the freedom to define our own legacy, and that's a blessing. Yet true freedom is a lonely thing. Everything has a cost."

How could I argue? By appearance, she could have been my daughter. But sometimes you get a feeling about people. In her presence, I felt like a snot-nosed kid again. For the first time in a long time, I was totally honest with someone.

"In my advanced years, I know I don't have long to live. And after spending the better part of a lifetime searching for answers in the dark, the old junk I found in that ancient building is my greatest legacy." In the end, I smiled back at her. "I have to believe it's worth what I spent to find it."

Persephone saved her reply until leaving me at the Funnel. "I'm sure you've finally found your legacy, Kilk. Thank you for talking with me today."

"I hope you find yours, Persephone." And I watched her fade into the blackness.

19

BEYDIN KRENNETH

LIKE THE POWDERY SNOWFALL of a cold January night, silence blanketed the world for the occupants of Irkalla Medical Services, Room 106. They found solidarity in the emotional impact of a story that meant something profoundly different to each person. No one desired to be the first to dispel the enchantment. Yet the moment passed. A knock on the door signaled its end.

The shining crown of a bald head ringed with black hair pushed into the room, pursued by skeptical eyes and a bulbous nose. The body of the stocky middle-aged man it belonged to followed shortly after. He sported a full beard that reached his chest and a handlebar mustache. In his right hand, he clutched a tablet similar to the one Vidaya toted everywhere. A tweed suit, red bowtie, and oxford shoes gave him a professorial look. Everyone stared at him in surprise, each for their own reasons.

Bounding across the room, he raised the tablet to his chest and spoke to Kilk in a New Zealand accent. "We started the analysis, Kilk, and we've found an anomaly already. A strange relic. We can't tell how old it is. But by the looks of it, it's possibly older than the ruins themselves. Take a squiz at this." Sausage fingers gripped the tablet by its edge, handing it to the elderly man.

Kilk grabbed the device and turned it over, holding it a distance from his face and squinting. When his forehead crinkled into a confused look, Arden wondered how the old man could see through his dangling brows.

"But, Beyd... This is a picture of me!"

The man—who Arden now understood to be Beydin Krenneth—let out a deep, growling laugh. "Is it? I couldn't tell. I should inform the lab, eh." With a serious look on his face, he bounded out of the room only to walk back through the door seconds later.

"Cheeky bastard," muttered Kilk, glaring at the three others who had erupted into laughter. "This is the thanks I get? Little whelps." Then he himself began laughing.

Beyd dipped into a small bow with a hand flourish. "You were too tense to hear what I have to say." Making a face as though tasting something bitter, he said, "The guidance committee won't organize a rescue attempt. And," he continued over their disapproving looks, "if Deveras is to continue partnering with the Lightborne in the search effort, Daryala and Toyotama both want daily reports henceforth."

Kilk let his head fall back onto the pillows wedged behind him. "Daryala sees an opportunity to push her anti-Lightwatch agenda," he stated. "But Toyo... Why would Surface Affairs want that information?"

Beyd ran his fingers along the hospital bed's footboard. "Doesn't trust the Lightborne. Her words were, 'How can we be sure what this relationship will cost? Do we really know what their agenda is?' Other than being a risk to her business dealings, she's worried it'll turn us from pacifism."

"Legitimate concerns," said Kilk. "What did Deveras say?"

"He said yes, of course. They never told him what he was supposed to report, because he didn't *exactly* tell them the full nature of the relationship." The corners of Beyd's mouth turned up into a barely visible grin, and Kilk reflected a brief half smile.

Arden understood their rapid back and forth but quickly grew tired of his head snapping back and forth along with them, so he stared at the floor until they had finished. He knew from experience that Tuck and Noire were reading the looks on each other's faces. When he glanced at them, they seemed neither impressed nor concerned. Kilk looked like he was falling asleep, and Beyd was eyeing the door.

Using just his arms, Arden lifted himself up from the chair and extended his hand to Beyd. "Nice to meet you, sir. I'm Arden Arinza." Awkwardly, the bald man shook his hand, offering him only a thin smile. Arden pulled back feeling a little crestfallen, having built Beyd into a legendary figure he wanted to befriend. "I signed up for the R&D practical tomorrow. I was hoping we'd get to talk."

Beyd was still reticent, replying with only a nod. He seemed to be struggling with something. After a long time, he finally turned to face Arden. "Sorry for being rude. Kilk looks knackered. Walk with me?" Arden agreed but sidled to stand by Kilk's side first.

"Thank you for the information, Kilk," he said quietly. Then he looked toward Tuck and Noire. "Meet you up top?" Both agreed and said quick goodbyes as Arden walked away.

Beyd held the door for him. When he was halfway out of the room, Kilk coughed and held up his good hand. "Wait. Before you three young fools go looking for Eresh, don't you think it'd help to know where I met her?"

Arden spun around, taking two steps back toward the bed. "I thought you said her name was Persephone."

Kilk took an exasperated breath, letting it out slowly. "I thought you were smart enough to know she was lying. It was obvious. I'll give directions to your friends here. You can go now." As Arden thanked him and again began walking away, Kilk said, "Young man. Good luck."

"We appreciate your help," said Arden. "I hope you recover soon."

Beyd picked up a gray felt fedora from a table just outside the door, closing it behind them. He signaled for Arden to walk with him down the hall to their left. They ambled in silence until reaching the reception desk. "Let's take the elevator up," Beyd said. Once they reached the main floor, he led them to a bench on the outer walkway. Below them, the Blood Amaryllis played out their gradual transition between sanguine and alabaster.

"You've got great potential, Arden. Such a high Nabucite attunement is very rare." Arden searched for words but stayed silent as Beyd continued, "Zari told me what happened. Tomorrow, I want you to try some new gear we've been prototyping."

Arden grinned like a kid at Christmas. "That sounds great."

Beyd took something out of his suit pocket. He unwrapped some white parchment paper and proffered it to Arden. "Biscuit? Gingernuts. Made them myself."

The crunchy texture and sweet, gingery flavor reminded Arden of how hungry he was. "They're awesome. I think I could eat a whole plate," he said.

Beyd flashed a full smile. "Cheers. I overheard Kilk saying something about Eresh. My guess is you and your friends are headed to Branthumville soon. The new gear will help."

Arden finished the cookie. "About the booth. Do you have any idea why it happened?"

Beyd nodded and said plainly, "Yeah, I have some ideas. We can work through those tomorrow."

"Looking forward to it," Arden told him. "I have a couple of other questions for you too. Let's see... Charon told me I should ask you about dragons. And Noire mentioned some of your theories about Irkalla Tower that I was interested in. Things like that."

"Sure thing. Branthumville. What a dag Kilk is. I never get over it." They both laughed and Beyd offered Arden another gingernut. "Go on. I have plenty more." He folded the paper and put it back in his pocket. "I need to head out, Arden, but it was good to finally meet you. Until tomorrow."

They shook hands and Arden watched him walk away, then looked around for Noire and Tuck. Since he didn't see them, he leaned against the window and watched the flowers' ever-changing blossoms. *Nothing ever stays the same.* The sight reminded him of Connie and Aella, and he began to daydream.

Seven-year-old Aella sat on the molded blue rubber seat of a chain swing in a small park near her house. Lucas, the same age as his friend, was nearby hanging from a set of metal monkey bars. He suddenly had an idea. Hand over hand, he crossed to the other side and climbed until his feet were on the upper-most ladder rung. Then, with a tall leap, he grabbed ahold of the support bars and pulled himself up. A moment later, he was standing on top and waving at his friend.

"Aella, look!" From her seat on the swing, she peered up at him as he said, "I bet you can't do this."

Aella frowned. "I could do that when I was five. My cousin showed me something else though. I bet *you* can't do *this*!"

Her toes barely touching the ground, she built momentum and then raised her legs. On the backswing, she pulled the chains toward her and tucked her feet under. Similarly, on the upswing, she pushed the chains forward and straightened her legs. With practiced timing, she was soon dangling so high that the chains went slack and caught slightly when returning down. "Watch!" she shouted. On the next forward movement, she jumped from the seat and landed cat-like in the wood mulch spread across the playground.

Lucas let himself slip down between the metal bars to hang from a rung, then dropped to the ground. "I can go even higher," he proclaimed, landing himself in the seat next to her. Within a minute, he had mastered the swinging technique. Higher and higher he soared, until he thought he might flip backward over the swing supports. It was time. He leaned back, felt the chains sag, and recovered momentum on the way down. At the peak of the next upswing, he let go. Gravity held no power over him for a glorious moment. His stomach lurched, and he had never felt so alive.

Unfortunately, the moment ended. Isaac Newton grabbed him and slung him to the earth. Limbs flailing, he sailed to a crash landing. Tears filled his eyes as the pain response reached his brain. Frantically, he strug-gled to draw breath.

Aella ran over to him, patting him on the back. "Don't worry. You just got the wind knocked out. It only hurts for a minute."

Just then, a large boy riding a bike rolled up to taunt Lucas. He pointed and laughed. "What a wuss. Poor widdo baby is gonna cry."

"Shut up, fatty. If you jumped off the swing, the whole world would explode." Aella's taunt made the grown-up Lucas smile at the memory. "Go ahead. Try."

The boy shrugged. "I don't need to prove anything to you," the boy said. "My mom said so. But fine. Just watch!" He balanced on his right leg, awkwardly swung his left over the crossbar, and put the kickstand down. Haughtily, he planted himself on the swing where Aella had been and slowly gained steam. By now, Lucas was on his feet and breathing normally again. Lifting a hand to his forehead to shield his eyes from the sun, he watched the boy climb.

Higher and higher the boy went, his greater weight giving each swing more force than either Lucas or Aella could muster. "Here we go!" the boy shouted. At the apex, he rocketed as though shot from a trebuchet. A panicked scream escaped him. By the time he was heading back to the ground, his head was tipping below his thrashing arms, and he landed flat on his face with a dull thud. Blood trickled from his forehead. Gasps for air soon became ear piercing wails. Lucas wanted to laugh—he remembered that Aella actually *did* cackle for a second—but instead he jogged over to the boy and tried to help. He took off his white shirt to dab blood from the boy's temple.

Maybe ten minutes later, they were sitting together under a gazebo talking. "What's your name?" Lucas asked him.

"Conleth," said the boy. "Conleth Spencer. What about you guys?"

Aella wrinkled her nose. "That's a weird name. I'm Aella Mendoza."

Conleth spat blood on the ground from his cut-up mouth. "Ay-luh? That's a weird name too." Aella's glare made Conleth turn away and look at Lucas. "What about you?"

"I'm Lucas Devlin. Hey, Aella, what if we call him Connie?"

Conleth turned beet red when Aella chortled loudly and began rolling on the ground. "Because he screams like a girl?" she asked.

"Hey, shut up!" the boy, now nicknamed Connie, barked at them. Soon, they were both laughing and pointing at him.

Lucas remembered Connie storming off only to return minutes later. They had been almost inseparable ever since.

And now I have no idea where you both are. Please be safe. You too, Dad and Alan.

When the afternoon light had faded into early evening tones, Arden decided it was time to return to Deveras's house. Maybe he would finally get some decent sleep.

As he circled the tower heading for the western gondola, he still saw no sign of Tuck and Noire. *I wonder what's held them up.* Shrugging away the thought, his feet plodded while his mind wandered. Without remembering having boarded, he disembarked the passenger cabin of the gondola, descended the stairs, and wound his way through narrow streets until he saw the welcome sight of the Ravenous Raptor.

When the fountain plaza came into view, he began daydreaming about a hot shower, food, and early bedtime. He was passing by the fountain when a voice called out to him from behind.

"Arden! Wait up!" Rynn ran toward him. "I'm so sorry. I meant to talk to you after the Abzuball game, but I was so angry we lost that I forgot."

As tired as he was, seeing her made him smile. "Hey. No worries. Sorry I screwed up the second period."

"No way! We had to do something. I was the one who rushed in like a dumbass and got jailed right away." Her cheeks were flushed. Arden noticed that she was wearing a green jumper and white undershirt instead of her Black Hand uniform. "Go ahead and get cleaned up. I'll wait. I want to show you around."

Arden knew he was blushing, but it didn't matter. "Great! You want to wait inside while I shower?"

She shook her head. "Nah. I want to be outside for a while. I've been in the tower since a little after six. Sabrath had me go in and make Vorin run laps after your little tiff last night." Mischievous eyes twinkled in the dusk light.

Arden grinned. "Poor guy. He's an idiot though, so whatever. I'll be right out."

"He is. And okay. I'll be here. Don't take too long though or we might not have a place to eat," she said, sitting down on the edge of the fountain. Arden acknowledged, walked away with some effort, and headed inside. The day had turned out okay after all.

20

THE COMPENDI-YUM

DEVERAS HAD ADDED ARDEN to his home's security settings, and the door unlocked when he touched the handle. Inside, he was surprised to see his mom and Deveras already sitting at the kitchen table, snacking on dried dates. He reached between them to grab one and popped it into his mouth. Deveras greeted him and asked if he wanted a drink, but he declined and headed for the bathroom. Reina called out to him.

"Arden, come here and sit for a minute. We need to talk," she ordered. The domineering way she spoke rankled him.

"Not right now. I'm going out," Arden said harshly, wanting her to feel his irritation fully.

Reina sprang from her chair and followed him. He stopped but didn't turn to face her as she said, "We need to talk about the guidance committee's decision. And—"

"I already know, *Reina*. We were in the infirmary, and Beyd—"

She floated around him and blocked his path. "Don't interrupt me, young man. And we're aware, because *we're* the ones who asked Beyd to tell you. We need to talk. *Now*."

Arden could feel her eyes trying to bore a hole into him, so he glowered defiantly back into them. "About what? More lies to tell?"

Reina slapped him across the face, stunning him into shocked silence. She had never struck him before. "I'm sorry," she said, stepping out of his way.

"Do what you want." He walked down the hall and into the bathroom without saying a word.

Arden let the hot water run over him, thoughts simmering in his rage. Between his parents, his mom had always been the one pushing him ahead, forcing him to make decisions, signing him up for things when he failed to, and holding him to account when he fell into mistakes. He knew it was because she cared for him. Still, resentment muddied the waters of gratitude, and the older he got the angrier she made him. In his heart, he understood the reasons she and his dad had withheld certain information about the Darktouched and Lightborne from him. Yet feelings of being controlled—thoughts that he was in many ways just a chess piece—aggravated him.

At the same time, he fumed because the person who had been the hardest on him had failed to prepare him for the last week. For Darktouched, the possibility perpetually loomed that the Reclaimers would strike, but his parents, Deveras, and even the Linzers had done nothing. Complacency had rendered them flat-footed when it mattered most. The secrecy, collusion, and lofty goals boiled down to empty words. Now, they were waiting for news from two rogue Lightborne that they knew next to nothing about. That they didn't even know were alive. His dad and Alan could still be out there, and he was stuck wasting time in a pointless orientation and chasing after myths that meant little to him.

And what could I even do? I'm useless. The thought incensed him further. *If they'd taught me more, I could actually help! Instead, they kept the most important things from me.* "We wanted you to have a normal childhood." *For what? Just so I could come down here and be worthless?*

The water cascading over him stirred awake the memory of a high school swim meet. In terms of his personal swimming highlight reel, it wasn't an important race. But it had been his first time competing on the varsity team—and as a freshman.

A fusion of exhilaration and dread, swagger and diffidence, had coursed through his veins and languished in the pit of his stomach. His limbs felt at once rubbery and overflowing with energy. In the stands, he could see his parents and the Linzers sitting together. Dad and the older couple were cheering him on, while his mom sat quietly watching, her arms folded across her chest. Alan waved at him, and Nora shouted to him through cupped hands, her normally raspy voice made more so by the exertion.

The referee whistled in three short bursts, drawing the swimmers' attention. A longer blast with varying pitch followed, and Lucas rose onto the starting block, readying himself. Shaky legs had found their strength. He was ready.

"Take your marks," shouted the official, and then signaled the start of the race.

In a violent and efficient movement, Lucas pulled with his arms while pushing off his front foot, making sure to extend the thrust through his back leg. Honed technique saw him enter the water with hardly a splash. Balanced, strong overhand strokes and powerful legs propelled him forward.

This felt different, like he'd reached another level. Adrenaline carried him—he had three strokes to the wall. Looking to his left and seeing he was far in the lead, for a brief moment he lost focus. Panic set in and he tumbled forward, staying perfectly tucked into the flip turn. But even with his legs fully extended, his feet barely touched the wall. He had begun the turn too soon and lost nearly all momentum. Soon he had fallen to the middle of the field, and he never caught up. He recalled vividly how he had mentally kicked himself afterward. *Fourth place in my heat. Because I'm an idiot.*

That evening, they had gone to dinner together at the Linzers' insistence. Nora, her graying blonde hair slightly tousled, consoled him, "It's okay, Lucas. It was the first of many."

"That's right, Luc. You just need to learn from it, and pretty soon you'll be winning races." Alan patted him on the back. "It's a common mistake." Lucas's dad echoed the sentiment, but his mom remained expressionless. Alan glanced at her and continued, "We were really tough on Jamie when she was growing up, but now I wish we'd been more easygoing. You'll get it next time."

Lucas remembered his mother being mostly quiet until they were alone later that night. He said to her, having by then rationalized the outcome in his mind, "I lost, but I did my best. Next time, I guess. Like Alan said."

She folded her arms across her chest and frowned at him. "You did your best, but today your best wasn't good enough. Now, you need to work even harder."

A knock on the door ended Arden's remembering. Deveras's voice reached him. "Don't keep that girl out there waiting, Arden. Your new clothes are in the cabinet left of the sink. And splash some of my cologne on. Works like a charm!"

"Almost done. And will do," he said, turning off the water. As he toweled off, he considered how much that otherwise insignificant race and its aftermath had changed his mind-set about life. His mom was right. His best was subpar relative to the competition. Her ability to prod him to greater heights was something he appreciated even while he hated it. And he knew part of his anger stemmed from the fact that she'd failed to prepare him for what was happening now. *And she's—no, they're all—still hiding things.*

Tossing on jeans and a dark blue dress shirt, he examined himself in the mirror. If nothing else, he looked better now than he had a day prior at the Deadman's Straw. Grabbing the cologne bottle from the counter, he sprayed some near his Adam's apple.

Reaching into the left pocket of the dirty jeans he had discarded on the floor, he put his hand around the nazar charm. Inspecting it, he noticed a small crack across the surface for the first time. "How did that happen?" he wondered out loud. Shrugging, he slipped the amulet into the pocket of his new pants.

When he exited the bathroom, Deveras was the first to see him. "Looking good, man. You're gonna kill it."

Arden laughed as he stooped down to put on his shoes. From his peripheral vision, he saw his mom approach and heard her say in a conciliatory tone, "Who are you going out with?"

He suspected she already knew but answered anyway. "Rynn Darkspear."

She smiled softly and patted his shoulder. "Look at you after only a day!" He blushed at her cajoling, his anger having diminished, and she said, "I'm sorry about earlier, Arden. There's no excuse for that."

A smile conquered his face despite him taking pains to fight it. He snuck a sideways glance at her. "I'm sorry too. Do you have any new info? If not, can it wait until after I get back tonight?"

"Yeah, tonight is fine," she said. "But don't come back here. I'll send you the coordinates to our house. It's not far." Clearing her throat, she told him, "Rynn's cute, but be careful. Sabrath is... brutally honorable. You'd better get going. And behave yourself."

Deveras shouted at him from the kitchen. "Good luck, kid!"

Fifteen minutes since leaving her, Arden rejoined Rynn at the fountain. They walked north instead of heading back toward the gondola station, winding down narrow cobblestone streets and through the architectural hodgepodge that she called the Jumble.

Rynn pointed out her favorite homes along the way. The first was a three-story Victorian-era house painted brown with a red-tiled roof and a prominent turret, the top of which was open beneath the spire. Some distance further, she stopped in front of one that seemed plucked from a fairytale. Built into an enormous tree, it presented almost no straight lines. Stairways wound around the trunk and through the boughs, stopping here and there to allow external entrance into several rooms. The main entryway was tucked beneath some bushes clustered to the left side of the base, with a staircase comprised of roots and stone leading inside.

Arden looked forward to each subsequent house Rynn drew his attention to, growing more engaged the longer they talked. The pair alternated in creating the history of those they liked most, making up stories of the people who had lived in them over the centuries, possibly millennia. For others, they simply daydreamed about sipping wine on a particular veranda under the warm sun, or staring into a woodfire on a dark, crisp night filled with stars.

Arden had never considered how life would be growing up in the Complex, every day absent such basic experiences. As the medley of the Jumble transitioned gradually into a more suburban residential style, Rynn explained the layout of the Complex.

"Northeast is the Borough. It's like any big city, minus the traffic." Arden recalled the modern cityscape he, Tuck, and Noire had passed through on their way to the Deadman's Straw. "Most people live there. But high-rises are boring, don't you think?" Rynn talked with her hands, pointing to things in the air as though Arden could see them. "The Complex grew up organically at first, and it's changed a lot over time. A century or so ago, the Borough was part of Old Town, called the Stacks back then. That was a maze of stairways and elevators I would've loved to have seen."

Arden said, "That sounds so much better. Why did they change it?"

Rynn rolled her eyes. "Why else? They voted. That reminds me!" She clapped her hands together. "There's a ballot initiative to expand the Borough further into Old Town. Vote no, or I'll never talk to you again. I mean it. And neither will the regulars at the Straw."

He held up the little finger on his right hand. "Pinkie swear," he said with a grin.

She wrapped her finger around his to seal the deal with a wink and then renewed her running description.

"So yeah, Old Town is south of the Borough. Most of the Complex used to be like that area. Except that nowadays, even Old Town is revival architecture, not the original buildings." The scenery around them had begun to change again, now looking more like an outdoor shopping mall. Streamers, banners, and signs related to the upcoming vote hung from most of the structures. "You know the Jumble. It covers the western quarter of the ring. And to the north, where we are now, is the Money Pit. Or that's what I call it. Shops, restaurants, and an arena."

Arden mentally drew a picture of the Complex, trying to figure out what was missing. "What's to the south then?"

Rynn smiled at him. "Due south is the Fabrication Center. That's where they make larger stuff that's too big for the bottom levels of Irkalla. Building materials and stuff. Southwest is the Greensward and southeast is the Zoo. Don't spoil those. If tonight goes well, I'd like to show you sometime."

He nodded and returned her smile. "Sounds good. Thanks for showing me around."

"Anytime. Maybe someday you can show me where you're from." They turned to their right down a promenade at the end of which was a series of brick buildings that looked like old warehouses. Hand-painted cursive script scrawled across a rustic signboard read The Compendi-yum. "This is my favorite place anywhere, so I hope you like it. The name is a little silly, but don't let it fool you. It can be confusing, so everyone just calls it the Yum."

They descended a dingy flight of stairs and proceeded through a solid metal door that groaned loudly when it opened and slammed when it shut. After passing through a narrow tunnel, the room opened up into a wide seating area with a lofted ceiling. In the center of the room, a chef sat in front of a large griddle. It reminded Arden of a teppanyaki grill. Opposite the entrance, along one wall, was a stage where musicians were readying their instruments. Seating primarily consisted of simple wooden chairs and round tables, with booths around the outside edge. Multiple stairways led up to a second level where there was overflow occupancy, which Arden guessed would be needed based on the crowd already filling the lower level.

Rynn waved to a waitress she apparently knew and then led them to a table close to the stage. "Self-seating," she said. "I know it doesn't look like much, but it's pretty special." Arden listened attentively, waiting for her to continue. "The ingredients are made by Fabricators in back. You can order anything edible that's ever been logged in the Compendium, guilt-free."

Arden frowned, asking her, "But I thought *all* Fabricators could do that. Not true?"

Rynn shook her head and excitedly began to explain, "Fabricators are special-ized to do a variety of things. The first models from way back could only produce basic plant material. Today, most in-home and smaller Fabricators can produce a wide variety of things from simple meals to beverages to inorganic materials, like utensils and cups. The more complex the item, the better the Fabricator you'll need... and the higher the cost. Most restaurants and places like the Deadman's

Straw use specialized ones that can make copies of a meal or brew that they've created already and scanned in. It's basically proprietary."

"The khachapuri at the Ravenous Raptor is like that too, right?"

Rynn nodded enthusiastically. "Right! But the Fabricators in the Yum can synthesize any ingredient down to the exact molecular makeup and age you want. Fresh fish or even whale? Done. Aged steak? No problem. Bear, ostrich, lion... anything. Vegetables too. Even things that don't exist anymore, like it was just picked from the garden. And the best part is that they cook everything right here! There are also ovens in back if you want baked dishes." Her excitement carried her away, but Arden didn't mind. "And the music! Any instrument or style, and any piece of music that's ever been written down—they play it here live. Sometimes they do new stuff too. The only thing they don't do is larger scale performances. So no symphonies, big band, that kind of thing. There are other places for that."

Arden made sure she was finished before he said, "That's unbelievable. I can see why it's your favorite. I love it."

Rynn flushed. "Sorry. I didn't mean to go on like that. But I'm glad you like it."

"You're fine! I'm having fun. Can't wait to try something new. But I have to admit, there are almost too many options. Any recommendations?"

Half an hour later, their meals were resting on the table and the band was performing a perfect rendition of "Stand by Me." They had played their way through multiple eras already, having opened with a Yum tradition by playing what Rynn said was an old Babylonian drinking song. Customers on both levels sang along and tinkled their drinking vessels jovially.

Rynn held her wineglass up and Arden toasted with her. They were drinking Madeira, a fortified wine she told him was popular in colonial America and Europe for centuries.

"Malvasia or Malmsey, this one is called," she told him, eyes sparkling. "It's supposed to be a dessert wine, but who cares?"

Arden held the glass to his nose briefly. It had a strong, pleasant scent. He tipped the cinnamon-colored liquid to his lips and tasted a sweet, almost coffee-like flavor that lingered on his tongue. The strong alcohol made his head fuzzy almost right away and left him with a pleasant warmth in the pit of his stomach. "That's tasty!" he exclaimed. "I think I like it more than the ancient brew at the Straw."

Rynn's eyes widened. "Right? It's so good. You should try the food."

Arden surveyed the meat on his plate with a touch of uncertainty. "I imagined whale to be more like fish, but I guess it *is* a mammal," he said. The flesh appeared similar to other kinds of red meat. As he cut into it, the tender muscle parted easily. With Rynn watching him, he slowly raised the fork to his mouth and tasted the lightly seasoned protein. His face lit up in surprise. "Wow. That's not what I expected. It's really good."

She drank some wine and giggled. "It really is. My birth family was First Nations. Even though I never met them, I feel like this brings me closer. It's not really accepted to hunt whales in the Aboveworld anymore, but the Darktouched don't have to worry about that!" Then she cut into her own meal of Fabricated milkfish, asparagus, and potatoes.

Arden talked between bites. "I met my birth father once, unfortunately. He's a piece of work. I guess I'm lucky that I'm a Darktouched and was adopted."

"At least you know. I lost my adopted family in a Reclaimer raid. Sabrath found me and took me in. I owe him a lot. He's a good person, but maybe a little too harsh." Arden wanted to ask about the scar on the left side of her neck but decided to save it for another time. Rynn's fork plucked a potato from her plate and delivered it to her mouth. "I joined the Child Liberation wing of the Hand because I want to help other kids like me."

The air seemed to evade Arden's lungs for a moment, and different parts of him internally grappled for the right to speak. "I still don't know how I feel about it, you know?" he finally said. "I mean, it worked out for both of us, but don't you think stealing babies from their parents is kind of evil?"

Rynn nodded slowly, her eyes shifting left and right. "I understand what you mean. Many people feel that way." Her finger drew small circles on the table as she continued, "I see it like this. Darktouched don't get to choose to become one, and their families don't either. But we're from two different worlds. The Complex is a nation formed from all nations. And we're tiny. There are less than ten thousand of us at any given time. Child liberation—or stealing, if that's your perspective—is a necessary thing. Good or evil." Arden could tell a thought was on the tip of her tongue and she was deciding whether to say it. She almost pleaded, "We genuinely care for them, Arden. I hope you understand that."

"I... need to think about it for a bit."

Arden couldn't find words after that, and Rynn left him to his thoughts, occasionally looking up at him with concern. *Say something, you ass!* Again and again, he willed himself to reignite the conversation, but nothing came out except an occasional platitude unless manners dictated. They ate the rest of their meal in virtual silence. When it was time for dessert, she ordered a roll cake wrapped in banana leaf. Made of sticky rice, chocolate, and coconut milk, the sweet's appearance was of alternating bands of black and white.

Rynn broke the silence. "It's called morón. It's from the Philippines." A sigh escaped her. "Arden, I'm sorry I brought up child liberation. I wasn't thinking."

Arden felt the emotional dam break at last and shook his head apologetically. "I'm such a jerk. I've been sitting here trying to think of something to say, and I just couldn't. I didn't mean to ruin a good time. I know you've been through terrible things and have good reasons." He took a breath, and then went on. "This world is new to me. My parents never told me anything." Looking around, he leaned in and began to speak in a whisper. "A few days ago, Reclaimers attacked my home and took my dad and a man who's like a grandfather to me. I'm having a hard time, and I apologize."

Rynn held a hand to her mouth, her eyebrows raised. "Oh no, I wish I'd known. I never would've... Can we start over?"

Relief lifted Arden up like a shadewind gust. "Yes, please. I really like spending time with you, Rynn. I thought I messed it up."

"Me too, Arden. To everything you said. Want to try the morón?"

After that, dinner concluded much like it began. They laughed, they talked, and afterward they strolled along quiet streets, occasionally seeing another person or couple doing the same.

The coordinates his mom had sent him were in the north-central part of the Jumble. *Headquarters of the family business.* Arden and Rynn stood outside of the cottage-style home, Rynn tucking strands of black hair behind her right ear, opposite her scar. "I had a really good time. I hope we can do this again."

Arden smiled, genuinely happy. "I did too. I'd like that a lot. Actually," he pressed, "how about breakfast at the khachapuri place tomorrow?"

"If you can be there at seven, then definitely."

"I'd be there at five if that's what it took," he joked, then wondered if it sounded too desperate.

"I'm not sure I'd give up that much sleep for you yet." Rynn laughed, fanning the flames of his insecurity. "Goodnight, Arden." She leaned in, kissed him on the cheek, then turned and walked away.

He heard himself say, "See you, Rynn," and went inside.

21

AWAITED WORDS AND A WARNING

THE DEVLINS' TWO-BEDROOM HOME in the Jumble consisted of a single level with a connected open living and kitchen area. Unlike Deveras, they owned a Fabricator and stove. The interior was decorated with sand-colored walls and ornate walnut furnishings. Throw rugs covered large sections of the wooden floor.

When Arden entered, he found his mom sitting in blue pajamas on a beige-cushioned loveseat sipping from a cup of tea. For some reason, it struck him again just how different she looked in the Abzu Complex versus the Above-world.

Arden watched her "other" face look up at him. "How did it go?" she asked.

"Good. We're having breakfast tomorrow at the Ravenous Raptor." He walked over to the Fabricator and opened the door, reaching out to the machine with his mind. After mentally inputting his order, he closed it. A few seconds later, a sound emanated from the contraption, letting him know his goods were ready. When he again opened the door to the pantry-sized, Nabucite-floored interior, he welcomed a bottle of Malmsey and two glasses.

"Want some wine? Rynn and I had this at the Yum." Arden plopped down next to her on the small sofa.

"No, thanks. You go ahead, but don't overdo it," she told him. "I think you and I need to clear the air, Arden."

"I agree. Shouldn't we start with the plan to rescue Dad though?"

"That can wait until tomorrow. Deveras said he was expecting word from Malank and Fiala soon. Go ahead and ask whatever you want."

"So how about we start with an easy one. Was I... *liberated* as a baby?" He poured some wine into a glass and glugged without letting it rest.

Drinking from her own cup, Reina replied, "No. Your biological parents gave you up for adoption on their own, thankfully." She took another sip and went on. "Your parents weren't bad people, I suppose. But they couldn't care for themselves, much less a baby—especially a Darktouched child. Your birth mother was a store clerk from Indiana who died after you were born. She overdosed. And your birth father... Well, you met him."

Arden nodded slowly. "Rynn works in Child Liberation. I still can't wrap my head around it all, but it's not an easy issue. Now I get why you didn't say anything."

His mom finished her tea and walked into the kitchen. "That's progress. Your father and I view it as an unfortunate but necessary thing. I was adopted too, but Galan was raised in a mixed family. I think it was pretty terrible. You'll have to ask when you see him. Okay then, what else?"

"How did you, Dad, and Deveras start working with the Lightborne?" Arden asked.

His mom returned with a fresh cup of tea. "Deveras came to us the day Surface Affairs identified you, asking us to care for you. Part of the arrangement was growing up around Lightborne. The Linzers moved in when you were about a year old."

"I remember Alan saying that both he and Nora are Lightborne..." His mother nodded in reply. "Are Connie and Aella too?"

She shrugged. "I don't know for sure. On that point, I know as much as you do. The first I heard of it was from Alan when the Reclaimers showed up."

Arden groaned and polished off half of a glass of wine. He felt his head buzzing again. "Why are you working with them in the first place?"

His mom shifted on the sofa to look directly at him. "All Deveras ever told Dad and I is that you might be the key to finding the Source." She paused to let him digest that, and when he asked no questions, she continued, "He said Malank and Fiala are certain of it, but not how or why."

I knew there was something else. "Beyd said I have unusually high Nabucite attunement. Is that why?" he pressed.

"Part of the reason, we think. But not all." Her eyes turned misty, and Arden felt a lump forming in his throat. "Deveras told us before we adopted you that their plan was risky... for you. We never told you about it because we started to hope after a while that the whole thing would go away. Why worry you? That's what we told ourselves anyway." Tears trailed down her cheeks. "I think we all tried to shield you in our own way. Your dad babied you." She snorted and snot came out of her nose. Arden grabbed a tissue off the side table and handed it to her. "Thanks. The Linzers treated you like a grandchild. We never really found out their story, only that their daughter Jamie passed away when she was a little younger than you." She blew her nose and wiped her cheeks with her forearm. "And I pushed you. Trying to grow your Darktouched skills in an Aboveworld way. Swimming, physics, language, literature, and technology. Daily sessions in the simulator. I know it wasn't enough, but it was a compromise Galan and I made."

Arden shook his head and thumped the sofa arm with his hand. "It sounds like you played with fire, and now I'm the one who gets cooked. Thanks."

His mom's composure had returned by now, and she admitted in a clear voice, "You're right. We were thinking of ourselves when we said yes. And, maybe arrogantly, we felt like we could protect you from it."

"And then the Reclaimers came," said Arden. "I don't know what you think, but it seems like they have to be after me. Not you, not Dad, not anyone else."

She dipped her head in agreement. "Based on our limited information, that seems probable. There could be things we don't know though. The bigger question is, how did they catch us so off-guard? You might not see it this way, but we were already being proactive. We'd accelerated our plans—we just weren't fast enough."

Arden bounced his right leg anxiously. "Does anyone else know? Kilk or Beyd? Who can we trust?"

"Kilk is aware and mostly disinterested," she answered. "He's busy trying to leave a legacy, as I'm sure you gathered after hearing his story." Arden motioned his agreement with her. "Beyd knows. Probably more than me. Him, you can trust. Marfisa—you met her in Flagstaff—knows a bit. You can trust her too. As far as I know, Vidaya is on our team. No one else in Surface Affairs knows. And we don't want the Black Hand to know. Daryala would have her pet scientists running experiments on you within the hour."

Arden said, "One final thing." His mom smirked, seeing the lie in those words even if he didn't yet. "Do you believe in all of this? Do you trust Malank and Fiala?"

She sighed and grabbed the bottle of wine from Arden's hand, took a long pull, and handed it back to him. "I believe Eresh is somehow in the Infra looking for or protecting *something*. Take enough trips into the deepest depths and you'd start to think so too. Since I believe that, my guess is the Source is real in *some way*. But I don't know what that means." A second time, she pried the bottle from his fingers. This time, she kept it. "For me, it's hard to trust any Lightborne. I believe you're important to those two, and I know I believe in you. If it takes my life, I'll see you through, Arden." The bottle tipped once more to her lips. "Do I trust them though? Enough to feel uneasy."

Arden got up, put in a Fabrication order, and reluctantly called to her from the kitchen, "Should I stop seeing Rynn?"

She shook her head. "No, but be a little careful about what you tell her. We can't know how much goes back to Sabrath and Daryala." The wine bottle hit the table with a muted thud as she set it down. "One thing I forgot to mention... Deveras didn't tell the committee everything. They think we're trying to meet with Malank and Fiala for the first time to organize the rescue. He sold them a bill of goods about us chasing a rumor. They think we're seeking rebel Lightborne for hire and don't know about the Linzers."

Arden smiled widely. His brain was fixated on the one thing he wanted to hear, and the rest faded to background noise. "Good. I really like her. I'll be careful."

But uttering the word "careful" triggered his mind to process the rest of what his mom had told him. In his head, he replayed the conversation where, earlier that night, he had told Rynn about the Reclaimer raid.

"I might have said too much already," he confessed. "I told her there had been a Lightborne attack, and that Dad and someone like a grandfather to me had been taken."

His mom scoffed. "Amazing, loose lips." Her derisive tone clashed with her thoughtful visage. "It does give me an idea though. Let's see if the info gets back to Sabrath or Daryala. Then maybe we'll get a sense of how much they share with each other."

Returning with a bag of pistachios, Arden sat down. "How can we know?"

"We probably can't. But since we can't 'un-tell' her, I'm looking for a silver lining," she said dryly.

Arden stretched his legs in front of him and sunk low on the sofa. "I should go to bed in a bit. R&D practical and the vote are tomorrow. The three of us might poke around in Branthumville too."

"I'll make sure you're cleared for those areas. They're forbidden zones unless that changes during the vote tomorrow. There's a two-strike rule for entering without sanction. One warning, and then the committee moves to Edicts," his mom said with a deadly serious countenance.

Arden looked at her wide-eyed. "Damn. Thanks."

"Yep. Be very careful. That place is scary, even for me." She blinked a few times before adding, "I can't lose you, Arden." He knew what she was feeling exactly. "And I'm so worried about your dad."

They talked and sipped wine for another hour before going to sleep.

Sometime in the middle of the night, a rapping on the door stirred Arden from a vivid dream he could only remember snippets of. He awakened to find Deveras entering the living room, his mom shutting the door behind him.

She said, "This better be good. What is it, Deveras?"

Deveras paced the floor this way and that, a hand rubbing his brow. "Marfisa received word from our Lightborne friends an hour ago," he stated.

Arden was wide awake now. "What did they say?"

Deveras continued pacing, now running his hands through his hair. "The message was brief, delivered through a courier. One of their people." He sat down and then stood up right away. "They've been on the run since retreating from your place a week ago and couldn't safely contact us. They're closing in on locating your dad. Expect further instructions in two or three days, they said."

Reina shot Deveras an inquisitive look and said, "There's something else. What is it?"

He sat down again and, as he had when Arden first met him, leaned forward in the chair with his elbows on his knees. "The last words of the message were hard to hear," he said breathily. "Watch out for the Linzers. They gave us away. Nora and the two kids are missing."

Minutes later, Arden was still reeling in shock. *There's no way Alan and Nora would betray us!* He could only manage to think the words. *Connie and Aella are fine. They have to be.*

"I don't believe it, Deveras," his mom said firmly. "There has to be more to it."

Deveras stared fiercely at the floor. "I agree. Do you have any idea where Nora might have gone, Reina?"

"No, not at all. Arden, any ideas?"

"All I can think of is that Alan said my friends had been moved. But that could mean anything," he conceded.

"In the wind," Deveras said, amending his words. "He said, 'They've already been moved. They're in the wind.' It's probably a dead end, but what do we have to lose? I'll have your friends work on it while you're in orientation tomorrow morning. Let them know if you think of what it might mean."

Reina leaned against the wall, arms across her chest. "Other than that, do we have any kind of a plan? Or are we just waiting on the Lightborne?"

"I'm going to see if Vidaya can help. Disavowed Oversight has surveillance everywhere. We might get lucky. Otherwise," Deveras said, "I have no idea what to do."

"If that's what we've got, so be it," stated Arden's mom. "Let's hit it in the morning. Maybe sleep will bring us some ideas."

After talking for a bit longer, they had said their goodnights and Deveras was gone. Arden slept poorly the rest of the night, too restless even to dream.

22

BREAD BOAT AND THE VOTE

ARDEN HEARD HIS MOM leave the house before he got out of bed. He quickly got ready and, seeing no message from her, concluded she must be working on securing the forbidden zone clearances they'd talked about the night before.

It was half past six when he left the house, heading for the Ravenous Raptor. His parents' home in the Jumble was further from the restaurant than Deveras's place, and he wanted enough time to walk leisurely and clear his head.

"In the wind" could just mean that they're free and fleeing, like we first thought. Racking his brain, he tried to pull a memory from the ether. While growing up, he would often spend time with the Linzers, since his own parents were working and Alan and Nora had both retired relatively young. *Retired from what? Their actual jobs might have been to watch us. To watch me.* Arden knew those thoughts would draw him down a dark path, and he pulled his focus elsewhere.

Every day without fail, the Linzers would work through the *New York Times* crossword puzzle. Arden so badly wanted a clue to be hidden in Alan's words. The shock of loss—and now possibly betrayal—was causing him to grasp for anything that might stabilize him emotionally, give him some kind of direction. The fact that the riddle might not be one at all was crystal clear to him, yet seeking the answer comforted him. His feet carried him down the cobblestone streets and footpaths, but his mind was far away.

Alan and Nora were, according to what they had told him, born in the same year and month in Bakersfield, California. In stories that had made him cringe as a boy, they would go on about how they were made for each other. *Birds of a feather. That's what they always said. Wait...* Lucas's heart began to beat faster. He recalled a term paper Alan had helped him with during his junior year of high school. As part of his thesis, Lucas had summarized the impact of large wind farms on bird populations and their migratory patterns. California owned several wind farms of note, one of which was in Tehachapi Pass. *Alan definitely remembers that paper. Could it be that? It's so flimsy.*

Making a mental note to bring it up with Tuck and Noire, he moved on to other possibilities. The Linzers were enthusiastic outdoorsy types, and would often talk about their favorite places. One of these was the Wind River Range in Wyoming. *But does that even make sense? Alan said Nora was watching over the families too.* And then there was Chicago, the Windy City, that the couple visited often.

The more time Arden spent on the exercise, the less hopeful he felt. The Linzers—and his childhood friends—really could be anywhere. For now, he decided not to think about it any further. Part of him, he knew, didn't want to find them. If he did, there was a chance they would reveal another major portion of his childhood to be a lie.

Arden rounded a now familiar corner, and the khachapuri-obsessed owl came into view. He subconsciously picked up his step. Rynn stood next to the front door in her Black Hand uniform. When she saw him, a smile lingered on her face for a few seconds. After exchanging pleasantries, they stepped inside. As he scanned the menu above the counter, Arden remembered that he hadn't actually placed an order last time. The options were straightforward: They were khachapuri, and coffee or tea.

Two minutes later, he sat down opposite Rynn at a small corner table with his cheese-filled bread boat and a cup of Turkish coffee. A soft chuckle escaped him when he considered it was just like the one that had ruined Vorin's gray shirt. Arden looked around, surprised not to see the glowering face he'd become accustomed to.

Rynn read his body language perfectly. "Your buddy is starting the Law Enforcement practical today. It runs for three days, unlike most of the others." She broke off a piece of bread with her hands, dipping it in the cheese and yolk. Arden mimicked her, even though forks were laid out on the table. "Good," she said. "It's tradition to eat it with your hands. Zane coaches anyone who will listen on Georgian customs." As the warm, fresh bread dipped in butter, egg, and cheese touched his taste buds, Arden's senses came alive.

"How do people not eat this every single day?" he asked himself out loud.

Rynn giggled. "Darktouched can still get clogged arteries, you know?" Her fingers worked at tearing off another piece of the boat's edge. "I should warn you, Sabrath knows we went out last night. He was asking a lot of questions," she admitted. Arden felt a searching look spread across his face. She noticed and added, "Don't worry, I didn't tell him about your friend."

Hearing this, Arden leaned back in his seat. "Thank you," he exhaled. Bit by savory bit, he devoured the khachapuri while sipping at his coffee. "Any election pointers other than to vote no on expanding the Borough? I'm surprised they let us vote without telling us anything. Not even a pamphlet."

"Most of the proposals are very straightforward. They have to be by law. So, not really. Just vote your conscience," Rynn said plainly. "The general vote doesn't apply to leadership roles. You can learn about that some other time." She took another bite of food and went on while chewing. "Removing the forbidden label on some areas would make Deveras happy. And maybe you too." She winked at him.

Does she know something about our Eresh hunt? He swallowed the wrong way and began to cough.

"Are you okay?" Rynn asked, and Arden held up his right hand to signal he was fine while thumping his chest with the left. Rynn went on, "Also, the proposals with the highest number of supporters are shown first on the ballot. Those listed as Cooperative Proposals are sponsored by more than one mission leader. Watch out for those. It can be dangerous for the entire Abzu Complex when they agree."

Arden thanked her and glanced at the clock. They still had a few minutes. "I was wondering earlier," he said, choosing his words carefully, "does Sabrath disapprove of us?"

"Of us... what?" Rynn questioned, a serious look on her face.

He spluttered, "You know. Going out."

Rynn broke into a mischievous laugh. "I'm just messing with you. His other faults aside, Sabrath is fair. I don't think you'll ever have anything to worry about, Arden." He was learning that, with Rynn, the more he pondered her words to ascertain their meaning, the more uncertain he became.

"Unless we take the shortcut today, I think we have to go soon. Walk with me?" he suggested.

Rynn smiled and told him, "Yep, let's go. No shortcut today. They don't like it during public events. The lifts fill up."

They headed southeast toward the gondola station. As they walked, Arden wondered out loud, "Lightborne are this big enemy, right?" Rynn shrugged noncommittally. "But, other than the raid that day, I know nothing about them. Do they teach you anything in the Hand?"

She stopped walking for a moment to look him in the eyes. "I know some things about them."

"Like what?" Arden asked. "Anything is more than I know. Even what kind of toilet paper they use."

"Well, they don't use toilet paper, for one." Her grin stretched from ear to ear. "White uniforms too." Then her look turned somber. "Lightborne power is different from the Darktouched Right. Theirs is given as a gift—one time. The further down the figurative family tree, the weaker they get."

Arden stroked his chin stubble. "So the newer ones are weaker. What if they die?"

"We don't know for sure, actually. But we don't think it works like the Darktouched Right," Rynn explained, resuming their walk to the gondola. "What we do know is that they aren't limited in number like we are. At some point, though, the math becomes quantity over quality." A mischievous smile crossed her face. "Maybe that's because we lost the Source." She chortled.

Arden, unsure what he believed, laughed along with her. "Maybe we can talk more about it on our second date," he quipped.

"I hope not," she said, smiling. "As for the second date, I already know where we're going."

When they reached the gondola station, the entire area was filled with people. A yellow haze that reminded Arden of Charon's purple-and-pink luminescence filled the center of the platform. Around it, a group held signs depicting a burglar stealing a baby and another with a bloodied stork. They were chanting, "Hope is left, Stop the theft!"

Rynn rolled her eyes and shook her head. "Your people. Anti-liberation protestors."

Arden was jostled forward from behind and stepped into the unnatural cloud. He was greeted by a female voice. "Good morning, Arden Arinza. You may call me Minerva. Would you like to place your vote now?"

Arden peered around for a half minute in wonder. He no longer saw the gondola station or Rynn, but instead was seated in an ancient Greek amphitheater. A lone figure held the stage. She was clad in a peplos, her hair tied with a cloth band. The same voice spoke again, "Arden, do you wish to vote now? Time passes slowly here. Ten minutes here for one outside."

"Can I have just a second?" he requested. "I was with someone."

Like taking off sunglasses, he was back at the gondola station. Rynn was already gone. Arden mentally reached out to Minerva. "Can you bring me back?" Flick. He was in the amphitheater. "Minerva, before we do voting things. Where is this, and how did I get here?"

"This is a visual representation of the voting process generated from Compendium information about you. Physically, it does not exist. The Darktouched connection to Nabucite allows for the difference in how time flows."

Arden looked around again, felt the stones beneath his feet, and shook his head. "Beydin Krenneth invented this, right?"

"No. We have existed far longer than he has been in the Complex."

"I understand," he said. "I'm ready to begin voting now."

"Before you do, please take a moment to listen to a message from each of the mission leaders."

Abruptly, Minerva was no longer Minerva. Where she had been, there stood a young woman who had straight black hair with auburn highlights. She wore a gray pantsuit with a collarless black blouse and low-heeled pumps without socks. She spoke in a deep voice that belied her small frame.

"Welcome, fellow Darktouched, to the six hundred and second vote. I am Toyotama Inari, leader of Surface Affairs. This cycle, I encourage you to consider the increasingly turbulent waters we must navigate together. The Aboveworld has become fraught with risks for our kind, yet we have never been more integrated into surface society. We of Surface Affairs implore you to vote with wisdom, prudence, and foresight. Any choice we make must be for the sake of continued economic prosperity, an ever-improved quality of life and, especially, aimed at ensuring a bright, *peaceful* future for the Abzu Complex and its citizens. Thank you."

Then Kilk Branthum appeared in place of Toyo, wearing full Delver gear with an Explorer's pouch slung around his waist. His gravelly voice uttered, "I am Kilk Branthum, leader of the Delver mission. This vote is about building and preserving our legacy as a people. We ask that you make Project Everdark a priority. Also, we want you to consider the anti-Lightborne measures we are co-sponsoring with the Black Hand as a way to ensure our existence, without which our only future is that of a defeated people."

Next up was a woman that Arden did not recognize. Olive skinned and roughly in her forties, she wore her black hair tied into a braided ponytail. From the neck down, she was covered by Black Hand battle gear that to him resembled what the Reclaimers had worn. Her most striking feature was her left eye, made of solid black. In a modulated, commanding tone, she said, "I am Daryala Gindir, leader of the Black Hand. Every proposal on the ballot is intended to protect the people of this city-state. The Lightborne might seem a distant threat, particularly in the depths of the Abzu and the Infra. Yet, I assure you, the scars beneath this suit and my Nabucite eye are testament enough to their capabilities and their will to do us harm. With their attacks intensifying, we are not safe."

Now, Deveras's fierce countenance bore down on him. "I am Deveras Turin, leader of the Seeker mission. This is an era for returning to our roots. This is an era of unearthing the wisdom entombed with our ancient past. This is an era of uncovering the Source and mastering the Darkness. With your help, we can finally achieve the purpose for which our society was created, and master our fullest potential. Through this strength, the goals of the other missions will be made possible."

Beyd stepped forward awkwardly, speaking in a casual tone. "I am Beydin Krenneth, leader of Support. No matter what you choose, we will do our best to enable and support. We ask only for patience as priorities shift."

Minerva returned, and Arden welcomed her understated grace after the awkward postulating most of the mission leaders had displayed. "Thank you for listening to these messages, Arden. Do you have any other questions?"

Arden shook his head. "No, I think I'm good."

"Very well. For any proposal shown, please do not hesitate to ask questions. I am here to assist." Then, suddenly, a list appeared in front of him. "Items with the most petitioners are shown first. Merely tell me your decisions."

KEY AND POPULAR INITIATIVES

General Proposals, Anonymous Sponsorship

- Proposal to allow two children per household

- Proposal to disallow child liberation

- Proposal to disallow relinquishing of non-Darktouched offspring

- Proposal to remove forbidden restriction for:

  - Zone Abaddon

- Zone Branthumville

- Zone Eldrastan

- Zone Nostrand

- Zone Tartarus

- Proposal to allow retrieval and examination of Class 0 – Benign artifacts

- Proposal to remove six-month residency requirement for Darktouched

  - Counter proposal to eliminate possibility for living in the Aboveworld

- Proposal to remove exception requirement for wearing KALM suit aboveground

- Proposal to expand acceptable classes and annual volume of Fabricated items taken into the Aboveworld for personal use (not sales)

- Proposal to restrict use of KALM wings in residential areas

Black Hand Sponsored

- Proposal to allow Defense, Search & Rescue personnel to carry anti-Lightborne weaponry at all Abzu Hub station entrances, Abzu Complex guard stations, and Infra outposts. Does not allow weapons within Complex barriers.

- Proposal to expand Cerberus System capabilities:

  - Add additional systems at unpatrolled backdoors

  - Add lethal, anti-Lightborne capabilities

Delver Sponsored

- Proposal to expand oversight of Aboveworld internet and other information sources, within already established privacy and detectability standards

- Proposal to increase funding of Deep Infra Assessment Drones (DIAD) and expand pilot program

Seeker Sponsored

- Proposal to expand investment into Deep Infra Exploration Technologies (DIET), such as foldable Fabricators, Explorer's sustenance medications, etc.

Surface Affairs Sponsored

- Proposal to implement Disavowed Automated Surveillance Helper (DASH) bots

- Proposal to expand scope and scale of the Aboveworld Replacement Artifact Sales (ARAS) program

- Proposal to market the Irkalla Tower Race game as an Aboveworld boardgame called Irkalla Escape

Support Sponsored

Abzu Zoning

- Proposal to expand the Borough south and replace impacted existing structures in the area called Old Town

- Proposal to expand the Fabrication Zone west into the Greensward

Hospitality

- Proposal to designate establishment registered under the name of The Deadman's Straw as a Darktouched cultural heritage monument

Research and Development (R&D)

- Proposal to expand research into the Darktouched Right

Cooperatively Sponsored Proposals

- *All Missions* | Proposal to approve Project Everdark, which will leverage artificial intelligence and Compendium resources to construct persistent personas of key Darktouched individuals

- *Delvers, Black Hand* | Proposal to allow biological studies on Deep Infra lifeforms, such as those found in Branthumville

- *Delvers, Black Hand* | Proposal to increase funding for anti-Lightborne research and development, as well as contracting of Delver resources to further said research

- *Delvers, Black Hand, Seeker* | Proposal to increase funding for development of KALM Expanded Range suit (KALM-ER model)

    - *Related – Black Hand Only* | Proposal to increase funding for KALM Enhanced Shadow Taskforce suit (KALM-EST model)

- *Delvers, Seekers, Support* | Proposal to seek further sources of Nabucite in forbidden zones Kigal and Gehenna. **Note:** No proposal is being made to remove the forbidden label on these zones.

Arden's eyes glazed over as he read through the proposals. *I might spend all week in this place and all day in the gondola station.* He dutifully began working his way through the list, trying to make quick decisions. For perhaps ten minutes, he sat agonizing over the first three proposals related to child policies. Being no closer to even one selection after such a substantial amount of time, he chose to save them for last. After doing so, he found the exercise relatively straightforward.

With a handful of exceptions, he voted to approve every ballot measure. The first thing he looked for was the proposal to expand the Borough. Keeping his promise to Rynn was a priority, and he voted no immediately. Seeing Vidaya's Law, the one she had mentioned about not using KALM wings in residential areas, made him laugh. It had seemed a joke during the first day of orientation. *I can't believe she actually got enough petitioners. No on that one.*

Further down, he saw the Black Hand proposals to increase the number of Cerberus Systems. These initiatives gave him pause. Noire's warning about the technology made him skeptical of the flocking urchins. *Making those things lethal sounds like a bad idea, even if the proposal does say anti-Lightborne. I wonder why Beyd created Cerberus in the first place.* Arden took a mental note to ask him during his R&D practical later that morning.

He scanned the ballot a second time. Feeling like he knew too little about residency requirements, he abstained from voting on both. In review, some of his choices did prick at his conscience. Because the Black Hand leaders made him nervous on reputation alone—even though his personal views favored anti-Lightborne measures—he voted no on their proposals. *I wonder if Kilk's Delving in Branthumville is helping their efforts.* Even as an unintended consequence, the prospect caused him worry. *Not all Lightborne are bad people.* Again, the Linzers crept into his thoughts, and he had to push them back out.

Removing the forbidden restriction on some zones also made him uneasy, but he couldn't fully rationalize why. Hearing his mom's story of Nuzum and Kilk's recounting of the monsters of the Deep Infra scared him though. Some things were better left alone. Surprising himself, he changed the votes to no.

That left him with the child policies. *What do I really believe?* Everyone close to him—his parents, Tuck, Noire, and Rynn—all regarded it as a necessary practice for the survival and health of Darktouched society. *A few days ago, I thought it was only evil, but now...* He felt a realization setting in and played the words out in his head. *Judging past decisions out of context is questionable. But aren't bad decisions bad even in context? Is a decision bad if it leads to a good result?* In the echo of the empty amphitheater, he paced ceaselessly, contemplating the answers.

"Minerva," he finally said, thirty minutes later, "I vote no on the three child policy proposals."

Ultimately, he decided to trust the past and those he believed in. Perhaps in fifteen years, if he survived that long, his choices would be different. Certainly, the circumstances surrounding them would be.

"Very well," said Minerva. "Would you like to progress to pages two through seven, to vote on the remainder of proposals? Only seven actual minutes have passed so far."

Arden felt numb as he spoke just two words to the artificial being: "Why not?"

23

DEEP INFRA PREP

V IDAYA'S EAGLE EYES SNAPPED to Arden the instant he set foot on the main floor of Irkalla Tower. She stood waiting for him next to the revolving doors as the rest of the chamber was bustling with people. Minerva clouds were situated around the room in coordinated locations. Without breaking her stare, Vidaya tapped the index and middle finger of her right hand against her left wrist.

Arden glanced at the world clock behind her—8:07 a.m. on June 11, 2005. In most of the Aboveworld, it was Saturday. But in the Abzu Complex, it was not only voting day but also the third day of Darktouched orientation. And he was seven minutes late. The clock seemed to look down on him, to criticize, to lay bare his guilt. It said, "You took a full eighteen minutes to vote. The equivalent of three hours! Why do we even bother with Minerva?" No one, not even his own conscience, came to his defense. He dragged himself across the room to stand before Vidaya.

"Sorry," Arden told her, "I've never voted before, and it took me a while. I was hung up at the western gondola station."

Vidaya's irritated stare turned into a surprised one. "You *already* finished? How long did you spend with our Minerva?" she asked with a hesitant fondness in her voice. Arden told her, and she began to grin in a way that made him uneasy. "I am impressed, Arden. And I'm sure you made responsible decisions. Perhaps you even recognized the error of your ways and voted for my little contribution, hm?" He knew, of course, that she was referencing the proposal banning KALM wings in residential areas. With a coy shrug, he danced around the topic until Vidaya sniffed and once again became an eagle-woman.

"Should I head down to R&D?" Arden asked.

"No. Since you are late, we shall go together," she intoned. "Today, we take the stairs. Floor B10 is our destination. It is good that you showed up today. The practical sessions are mandatory, and missing for any reason can result in you being forced to repeat the entire orientation."

She steered him to the left and they descended the spiral staircase. When they reached the next level down, Arden noticed for the first time a sign that read B1 – Waiting Rooms, Law Enforcement, Child Liberation, CADS Offices. *This is the floor where both Rynn and Vorin work. And maybe Vidaya too.*

They passed through a security gate similar to the one Marfisa had been supervising at the Flagstaff Abzu Hub station. Thinking back to the first day of orientation, Arden remembered wearing a slightly disappointed look when he'd reached the other side. Vidaya had asked him against the backdrop of Vorin's squawking laughter, "What? Did you expect something more magical? The device merely confirms that you are in the Compendium and have appropriate security permissions."

Arden already knew that B2 housed Medical Services, where he imagined Kilk was still convalescing, tossing tiny bits of paper into a cup or a Reducer. And B3 was Equipment Services, where Zari had fitted him for his KALM suit. As they spiraled down, he hoped a memory of his vision from that day would suddenly return. But he was again disappointed.

When they reached the next floor, the sign read B4 – Arena Box Access, Confections. *Abzuball. I have to play again to get the bad taste out of my mouth.* Rynn had shown him kindness, but he knew the muck of defeat was his to wallow in. He recalled with some embarrassment how one time, after losing a fiercely contested game of touch football, he had sulked for an entire week. In the end, Connie and Aella had set firm guardrails around all things competitive. Aella had chided him, "Pity parties longer than one day demand payment to your friends. That's us. In the form of ice cream and servitude." Ever since, he had avoided any outward expression of his internal self-bludgeoning.

Vidaya quickly led him past the recreational facilities on B5, noting that Lucas and the other orientees had already seen it when they'd received their suits and played Abzuball. Level B6 was the library known to Delvers and Seekers as the Ledge, where he, Tuck, and Noire had spent long hours learning the limitations of Compendium keyword searches. Below it, on B7, was Compendium Restricted Records. Arden remembered that Tuck's girlfriend, Metis, worked in this department.

Vidaya urged him along before he got a chance to take a peek into the area. "There's nothing to see on B7, Arden," she droned. "However, B8 is quite interesting indeed. Would you like to take a look?" Arden gave her a single nod, trying not to look overly excited by the invitation.

When they reached B8, Arden saw that it was labeled only as Compendium Maintenance. Vidaya warned him, "Stay close to me or you may end up stuck." Passing through multiple sets of metal doors, they entered into a round room made completely of Nabucite. He noticed, however, that the colors in the dark mineral were more vibrant here and moved more swiftly.

Crouching down, he discovered that he was able to see further afield within the substance. There were three-dimensional, almost life-like images of people, animals, creatures of the Deep Infra, buildings, and tomes. Occasionally he witnessed globs of text etched on the darkness fly past. In the center of the room was a pseudosphere, like a miniature version of Irkalla Tower. The mesmerizing colors and imprinted images were being pulled from the outer walls and floor toward its lower portion and flowing into the ceiling, forming a reverse-cascading stream. Two Darktouched wearing red uniforms both wielded tablets that were, on a smaller scale and lower volume than the pseudosphere, drawing data into themselves.

Vidaya put her hand on his arm. "This information stream is the Nabucite's greatest asset to us: The Compendium itself. From here, roughly the center of the tower, it flows to the very top. The elevator is mere camouflage. In a sense, this room is a scale model of Irkalla and the cavern it inhabits."

"And the reason Beyd thinks Irkalla and Nabucite are the keys to everything," Arden concluded, connecting the dots. "But if Darktouched have been around for millennia, why didn't anyone look into it sooner?"

Vidaya's grip on his arm tightened. "Many fear the implication that our power is equally mechanical and spiritual, as invented as it is primordial. Others neither care in the least, nor would they understand if told. However, my young friend, *very few* ever get to see this. Consider yourself fortunate," she said with a half-smile. "We should be going."

Taking in one final view—this being perhaps the only time he would see the Compendium—Arden spun on his heel to walk away. He caught a glimpse of the ceiling on his way out of the room and stopped. *I must be losing my mind, because that looks just like...* He squinted, lifting himself onto the tips of his toes. *It is. Why is she in the Compendium?* He was certain that there, above and to his right, hovered an imprint of a young Nora Linzer.

"Is something wrong, Arden?" Vidaya asked him, beady eyes searching for what had captured his attention.

Arden, although unsure why, lied. "I thought I saw someone. But it wasn't them."

"Hmm. There are perhaps millions of individuals logged in the Compendium, so that would be very unlikely. How interesting if it was though. What a small world." With that, she motioned with her head for him to follow, and they stepped through a metal door.

The sign on the next floor's doorway read: B9 – R&D Showroom, Seeker and Delver Tech, Unrestricted Items. Vidaya held out an arm to halt him, then gestured with it as she spoke. "Research and development spans two floors. The first houses general access items. Most people do their R&D practical on this floor with Ming Fuzi." She lowered her arm but remained stationary. "You will be working in *restricted* R&D, which is one level down. If you were paying attention during the vote, then some of what you see there should be familiar to you." Using her fingers to designate the remaining floors, she said, "From there, B11 through B13 are Black Hand facilities, B14 is Biological Studies, and B15 is for large-scale Fabrication. However, if the vote to expand the Fabrication

Center on the residential ring passes, that floor will be retrofitted for larger-scale biological analysis." With a superior tone, she said, "Quite a tour, wouldn't you say? Let us proceed."

Another security checkpoint and multiple steel doors awaited them on the way into restricted R&D. As they passed through the final one, Vidaya said quietly to Arden, "It was a pleasure, Arden, but now I must leave you to Beydin. I also wanted to let you know that an optional shadesurfing training session is available tomorrow at six a.m. sharp. Do try not to be late, if you plan on attending. The instructor is one of our best. Meet at the Funnel near the guard station. Afterward, I will see you in the tower for your CADS practical at nine. Have a wonderful day."

Arden thanked her and she disappeared behind the metal door.

Arden found Beyd stooped over a workbench, tinkering with a mannequin wearing a KALM suit. "Kia ora, Arden." His right hand held a device that looked like a blowtorch, but instead of flames it emitted charged Nabucite. When the particles came into contact with the suit, they appeared full of colorful specks that faded quickly into the light-absorbing shadow Arden was accustomed to. Seemingly satisfied, Beyd grabbed a tablet similar to the ones the Compendium technicians had wielded. Holding it over different parts of the suit—first the head, then the neck, thorax, wrists, and down—he sampled Nabucite.

"Running some tests to see how she'll hold up in the Deep Infra. This model is the KALM Expanded Range, or KALM-ER suit. Another Branthum term. Kilkism, I say." Shaking his head, he continued with his diagnostics.

"What does it do that the other suits don't?" Arden asked.

Beyd didn't reply with words but by making the suit retract. Instead of the KALM bands Arden expected, the mannequin wore only a Nabucite wristwatch. A miniature tablet was secured in the palm of its hand. "Give her a try, eh, Arden? Watch on the left wrist, phone in the pocket."

That is a strange-looking phone. No way that catches on. Arden strapped the timepiece to his wrist. As he rotated the dial, a series of icons—a suit, a shield, a fishhook, and a sun—moved across the display until returning to a clock face. The phone's interface was similar to the KALM suit's communications HUD view. When he slid it into his pocket, Beyd instructed him, "Turn the watch dial 'til you see the suit icon, then tap the watch face."

When Arden did so, the suit deployed around him. Excitedly, he tried the shield icon and felt the suit stiffen. The same shadowy haze surrounded him as when he had clung to Noire's back while shadesurfing. As he walked around the room, he recognized the tradeoffs of engaging the stronger armor. Movements felt sluggish and more difficult. Raising his arm required more force. But it was more than that. He felt himself growing fatigued after only a minute. In his HUD, he flipped through the views until he found the one showing his vitals. None of the readings looked unusual, but he was definitely feeling physically drained. Reaching down, he tapped off the armor and a very real weight was lifted.

Beyd cautioned him, "Let the last two be surprises. I guarantee they work."

Still thinking about how the armor had drained his stamina, Arden asked, "Why did I get tired so fast?"

"That's the price of power. The KALM-ER suits use a special Nabucite. The wearer can take in more darkness, but it strains their body," he explained. "The other prototype––we call that one KALM-EST––isn't even wearable yet."

Arden nodded. "Okay. So use the extra features sparingly. How often?"

"Depends on the person. The phone is a mini-energy source too. For you, I'm guessing every five minutes," Beyd said with a shrug. "In the Deep Infra, down in the wop wops, is where she shines. Not many places you can't go, as long as the baddies don't turn you into a snack."

"Are you letting me use this?" Arden asked him hopefully.

Beyd smiled briefly. "Needed to properly test it at depth anyway." Arden frowned, causing him to laugh. "Don't worry. I'm sure she'll be all right."

Waving Arden along behind him, Beyd marched down a corridor toward a plain wall with a single door. Off to their left, Arden saw into a room with two mannequins wearing KALM equipment that looked more like tactical gear than wetsuits. One held a spear with a dull, semi-transparent gemstone embedded into the shaft where the tip connected. But his guide bounded between him and the open door, slamming it shut. "Black Hand projects in there. Another time, eh?" Beyd said.

Unperturbed, Arden thought this might be his only chance to ask questions, so he cleared his throat and said, "I was wondering about Project Everdark. Is that Kilk's legacy?"

Beyd nodded solemnly. "Old fool. I'm afraid he's sold out to Daryala to make it happen too. He wants to be the first one we put in Everdark. Then the dag can talk to himself all the time and never have to listen to anyone else."

Arden clasped his hands behind his back and stretched his arms. "I'd like to see it someday. It sounds pretty damned cool. Like being immortal almost."

Beyd replied with a grunt, then strode to the door ahead of them and opened it. They stepped inside, and he closed the door behind them. The room was empty except for a Nabucite reclining chair in its very center. On its seat were a pair of goggles and a set of earbuds. Beyd said, "This room is earmarked for Everdark, but I want to try something else. First, in the KALM booth the other day, did you have anything in your pockets?"

Arden began to shake his head, and then reached his left hand down to his thigh, feeling the nazar charm. "Only this," he said, taking it out of his pocket. "One of the Lightborne gave it to me."

"Malank, no doubt. Always on about luck and fate. Hold up," he muttered almost to himself. "Do you reckon this crack was there when he gave it to you?"

"No," Arden answered. "But I wasn't sure how it got there."

Beyd took a deep breath and rolled his eyes around in his head. "Mind if I keep it?" Arden shook his head in reply. "Cheers. I want to try exposing you to a boatload of Nabucite. When you had the vision, I think the nazar charm did its job. Legend has it that a nazar breaks when dark energy blasts the wearer. If you want, hop in the chair."

Without hesitation, Arden sat down and put on the goggles. Before he put in the earbuds, he said, "Will I remember this time? And you'll be just outside in case something happens?"

Beyd dipped his head in confirmation. "Me and a cuppa."

Minutes later, Beyd's voice came through the earpieces. "Nabucite incoming." The room began to fill with the abyssal substance that was neither liquid nor gas. It flowed around Arden, crawling up his legs, covering his abdomen and arms, until it encased his entire body. "Vitals are solid."

Arden began to doubt anything would happen. The only thing he remembered from last time was the Nabucite covering his eyes. And then he had blacked out, remembering the experience as one did the emotions of a dream, failing to retain more than a few fragments of visual memory.

Reaching up, Arden removed the goggles and let the Nabucite fill his eyes. In that instant, he was returned to the building where he had stood previously. The walls were made of greenish-blue stone, which he recognized this time: They were exactly as Kilk had described the structures in Branthumville. Above the door, three white marks in the form of a narrow-bottomed letter H signified a doorway. He stepped toward it, and the stones parted. A long corridor opened before him, and he inched cautiously forward.

A man's voice called out to him. "Arden, Lucas. Two and one fates, all true. Come closer." As though his body were being summoned, Arden felt himself be pulled once more through walls until he again saw the figure sheathed in an abyssal cocoon. "In my youth, I sought out darkness. Away from the blinding folly of light, I thought the truth could be found. The secret to unravel mankind's curse. And ours as well. Yet I found only shadow, the mere imitation of darkness borne of light."

Arden recalled the words of the owl: "Child of Shadow, Bringer of Light." He reached out his hand through the blackness and pulled the figure closer to him.

The face of a young man appeared. His body was frail, and his expression pained, as though exhausted to the point of death. And yet, a wellspring of strength and tenacity shone in his eyes.

The man in darkness spoke again: "The owl's story is for another time, so listen to *me* now. In a past that is ancient to you and as yesterday to me, I journeyed into the depths with hope in my heart. Our reality in the Aboveworld, I reasoned, is a mere reflection. But of what? Is there not something extant before the light shines upon it? There is. I have glimpsed it."

Arden tried to respond, but he was incapable of speaking. *Are you the Source?*

"I am not. I am but a conduit."

Then who are you?

"I will not give you my true name, but long ago I took up the name Ninazu. And my bride named herself Eresh. Together, we explored the depths. We found a way to subvert the light, to learn the truth. But we fell short. Everything was lost to us."

If everything is lost, why are you talking to me?

"Fate. In the grand tapestry, no one can ignore the push of the past or the pull of the future. Even if you were born before all other men, in so many ways you are subservient to the inevitable flow of time and the follies of what becomes history. A tale that unfolds in so many ways but always ends the same. Yet the threads held in your hands could end our suffering. If you grasp them. If you use them well."

I don't understand. Why me? I'm no one. I'm unimportant. I'm not powerful.

"You are correct. Like every human, you are a mere mortal. But what makes a man important? Who puts the reins of power in his hands? In the flow of time, all who came before you. Those whose threads of fate were intertwined with ones you now hold, who believed in you or despised you, who right or wrong put their faith in you. They made ready the stage upon which you now act."

But that wasn't my choice. I didn't ask for this.

"No man can choose his role. Not you. Not even the Ten. We are slaves to the nature we were born with and the circumstances that defined us. The choice we have is to play our role well. I cannot linger with you any longer. Find Eresh. Tell her I spoke to you. She will know what to do."

Wait. Where can I find her?

"Merely look where she has the most to lose."

The vision ended abruptly, and Arden felt empty inside, no closer to understanding than he had been before. As the Nabucite left the room and he saw Beyd enter, he felt tears streaming down his face. For a moment, he wept bitterly, utterly lost. If what the voice had said was true then, as always, there was no freedom in his existence. Before he was even born, a path had been laid before him. Whether it was a worthwhile road or not mattered little to him, because it was not of his choosing.

As though he understood, Beyd wrapped an arm around him and said nothing.

24

ANCIENT GROVE OF Y'SHAM

"That's quite a yarn, Arden," Beyd commented. Arden had just described what he had seen while in the Everdark chamber. He sat recovering near the workbench where the Support leader had been tuning the KALM-ER prototype. "Hope you don't mind. I called your friends down from the Ledge. They'll be here soon."

Arden held a hand over his eyes and nose, and spoke a muffled, "Okay." Beyd left the room and returned minutes later with a cup of coffee and a plate holding chocolate-covered fish-shaped cookies. Arden bit into one and sipped from the coffee. He thanked Beyd, who sat on the workbench twirling his fedora. "This helps. I'm already feeling better," he said, just as Noire and Tuck entered the room escorted by a woman he didn't recognize.

Beyd waved at her and said, "Thanks, Ming."

With a smile, Ming turned and left them.

"I'm sorry to ask, Arden, but can you go over it again?" Beyd asked.

Noire and Tuck listened intently as Arden told them about his second encounter with the man who called himself Ninazu, saving their questions for the end.

When he was done, Beyd spoke first. "This is unexpected, eh? Darktouched myths tell that Ninazu died during or before the Reshaping. Some texts say he caused it."

Tuck frowned in thought. "Didn't he say Eresh was his bride? That makes him one of these number people, right?" Arden laughed at the term "number people," which pulled him further from the grip of dismay.

"Right," remarked Beyd. "The Ten, you mean." Noire gave him a curious look, as if to ask how he knew that term. "Malank told me a yarn years ago. He said it was a myth he didn't know the origin of. In that tale, a war was raging. In the midst of it all, ten souls took it upon themselves to end the violence and stop the world from teetering over the edge. It might make sense that Eresh and Ninazu were two of them."

Noire chimed in. "The story helps, but it's so thin. Nuzum said, 'Seven that were Ten.' What happened to the other three?" Beyd shrugged in reply, shaking his head.

"Let's skip the Ten for now," Arden stated. "Do we have any idea what Eresh might have left to lose? In Kilk's story, she had a home on the edge of Branthumville. Do we start there?"

Tuck glanced at Noire before saying, "Never got a chance to tell you yesterday. After you left, he told us more. Said he found somethin' about Eresh down there. Said Beyd might be able to help." He handed what looked like a glass square to Beyd.

Beyd's brow lifted. "Oh, I see. Let's take a look." Dropping his hat and bounding across the room, he waved them along behind him. He came to stand in front of a contraption that reminded Arden of the transparency projectors his teachers used in grade school. The machine was primarily comprised of a square-bodied base with a depression to insert the glass square. A thick cord ran from the body up to a black display panel hung from the ceiling.

"This is an Uldu scriptstone," Beyd said as he held up the glass square. "Uldu is a mashup of Sumerian words for 'ancient' or 'perfect'. Scriptstone is obvious. Those are Beydisms." He grinned at Arden, genuinely excited for the first time since they had met. When he dropped the scriptstone into the machine, it began to whir, and Nabucite filled in around it. Slowly, words formed on the screen. "This hunk o' junk is a bit of improvisation. The Uldu would've read these texts some other way."

Beyd entered something into a tablet, and the text enlarged. "Old eyes," he muttered. "Or Uldu eyes, eh?" His laughter hung in the air as he scrolled. One passage in particular stood out to them:

Our allies in the depths are running out of time. If the Lady of Dark Water cannot muster the forces we contracted, then we will suffer grave misfortune. We have sacrificed too much to fall short. Were she to abandon the cause now, the enemy's retribution would be swift and complete. Her abyssal domain will become a tomb and everything she claims to hold dear ripped from her. At this late stage, half measures will only bring totality to her grief. Tell her to remember the words I spoke when last we met in the shadow of Y'Sham's ancient grove, where her sons now lay interred beneath the giants. All is not yet lost. She still has a role to play before the end.

Arden read through the text slowly, looking for anything that might be actually useful to their search. He had just reached the words *abyssal domain* when Noire slapped her hand on the table. "Tuck!"

Startled, Tuck looked at her askance. Noire exclaimed, "Guys, please! Y'Sham!" She rolled her eyes when both Tuck and Arden still wore confused looks. "The record you had Metis dig up yesterday mentioned the Nine Saviors of Y'Sham, remember? It was unknown date, unknown origin."

Arden stood from his chair, placed one knee in the seat, and rocked against the back. "What if the Ten were powerful Darktouched? People who wanted to save the world from disaster, like in the story Malank told Beyd?"

"And Eresh was their leader?" Tuck wondered out loud. "And maybe one died, so that's why there are nine? That could be Ninazu." Beyd closed his eyes, pondering the idea.

"That still doesn't explain the Seven that were Ten," Noire pointed out. "But it did say she lost sons. So maybe that's why."

Arden's rocking had become more like bouncing. "And this ancient grove of Y'Sham could be a clue to finding her. Beyd, do you have any idea where it might be?"

Beyd ran a hand through his thick beard. "Y'Sham turned up no other hits in restricted records?" Noire, Tuck, and Arden shook their heads in unison. "Well, I have a model of the explored areas in Branthumville and Eldrastan. Let's take a guess and say they were both part of Y'Sham." He finagled with his tablet, and a three-dimensional rendering replaced the text on the display. Stepping up onto a chair so he could point at the screen, he said, "Kilk's guesthouse is about here. Let's call that west. Quite a distance on is the depot he searched. Down here in the south."

With a look of disgust, he fiddled again with the tablet and a blinking indicator hovered over an area on the map. "Sometimes I forget about features," he admitted. "Eldrastan is way over here to the east. The further in that direction you go, the more rural. I'd search these grids here." He highlighted an area on the easternmost edge of Eldrastan. "Kilk never had an interest, and no one else ever goes that far."

Noire clicked her tongue. "It could take days instead of hours if we can't shadesurf in. We don't have that kind of time."

Beyd's eyes lit up. "I have KALM-ER prototypes for you both too," he informed them. Looking toward Arden, he added, "I forgot to tell you earlier. The new suits have expanded HUD range and improved stealth. Almost undetectable and faster shadesurfing. Finding Eresh will be a piece of piss!"

Half an hour later, the three were suited up and descending the Funnel. They waved to Caius at the gate, calling their wings and gliding down into the depths. For the first time in perhaps weeks, Arden felt free, and his lifted spirits made him insist on shadesurfing solo.

Summoning the kite using his HUD, he watched as dazzling blue-and-white lines extended from the gloves and waistline of his suit. In his excitement, he pulled too hard for too long and shot ahead of his companions. Feet dangling behind, he began to flail in panic. Noire yelled at him over the comm to release the steering lines. When he did, the kite coasted gently upward and he began to sink. More gently this time, he pulled the lines toward himself and began to accelerate.

Growing more confident in his skills now, Arden tried a sharper pull on the right steering line followed by a quick return to center. When the kite didn't move, he again pulled the right steering line toward himself. The kite's natural lag compounded by the second tug sent him on a collision course with Tuck, who dodged at the last moment, saving them both.

Noire's voice in his ear oozed annoyance. "That's enough, Arden. Get some practice before you kill someone. Most likely me." Then she swooped in ahead of him, snapping the order to withdraw his shadesurfing gear and grab onto her back. Reluctantly, but humbled enough not to argue, Arden did as he was commanded.

The rest of their journey went smoothly, and they neared another cracked leather-looking fissure in the Infra. Arden felt the expected compression of his body as they passed through and the longed-for relief as they emerged on the other side. Darkness surrounded them for another ten minutes, with only a small island occasionally dotting the violet sky above or the black sea below.

When the first greenish-blue buildings came into view, Arden felt his apprehension grow. *I sure hope Beyd's right about these suits.* As with the ruins where he had met Tuck and Noire, the edges of the structures and the island they rested on seemed to have been chewed on by some enormous monster. He imagined the dark waters of the Abzu and abyssal black tide of the Infra swelling, rising up to devour portions of the Aboveworld and then swirling downward with them in tow. Nuzum and Tiamat soared vengefully, bursting through fissures in the earth's crust and ascending through ocean depths to lay waste to civilizations and unleash pitiless torment on their terrified enemies. *Only to lose in the end, apparently.*

Then he remembered Kilk's stories and began watching his HUD for dragons and worse. On tenterhooks, he listened for the *th-wak-th-wak* of giant wingbeats, recalling how they grew quieter as their murderous owners drew nearer. Flying beasts with the ability to tear their torso from the lower half of their body, ready to gorge on flesh and blood. Tearing, ripping, and glugging while Darktouched victims twitched, the last breaths of life escaping from their shredded lungs.

Arden and his friends flew over the depot where Kilk had at last Delved his Big One. From above, Arden thought it looked oddly like a cathedral. On top of the cliff that sheltered it, he spied what he suspected was the ancient equivalent of an air traffic control tower. Around it patrolled at least three of the winged horrors Kilk had described. The monstrosities seemed not to notice the trio as they flew past in the distance.

To their left, an ancient complex of ornate temples and palace buildings was laid out in a clear grid. These structures were intermingled with natural rock formations, synthetic vegetation, and the remnants of parks and gardens. In the distance, Arden could make out the edge of an old lake that now stood empty, and likely had for millennia. As they traveled further east, the land opened up into rolling fields that resembled a soundless, sandy desert. Although the shadewinds were not blowing the loose soil around, the constant shifting of the entire island as it bobbed and swayed in the Infra had over time given the landscape a unique, rippled appearance.

As they progressed, he would occasionally see what looked like a flock of birds and be reminded of Cerberus. The improved HUD labeled them as flying scorpions, and their measurements were frightening. Each one was as long as Arden's forearm, according to the dimensions the suit provided. He imagined a stinger as long as his finger sinking into his skin, and he shuddered. On the ground, they saw packs of wild dogs racing this way and that, perhaps seeking a source of potent darkness to sustain themselves.

Tall hills began to rise around them. According to the HUD overlay, the three of them were on the edge of the grids that Beyd had suggested they search. As they pressed deeper, Tuck broke off on his own so they could cover the area more efficiently, and Arden began to breathe easier. Now that they were out of the city, he expected fewer monsters and an improved ability to see and hear more clearly if something did take interest in them. For an hour, they swept over the landscape and climbed with the terrain as it changed from hills to mountains.

A little more than halfway to the eastern edge of their planned search area, Lucas and Noire spotted a strange shimmering in the air far ahead.

"Tuck, are you seeing that weird visual disturbance maybe twenty klicks downrange?" Noire called out over the comm.

"Yep. Other than that, though, this is a big bag o' nothin'." Lucas imagined Tuck shaking his head pessimistically.

"Let's head for it. It seems as likely a place as any."

"Copy that. Let me poke around in there first."

"Copy. Let us know what you find," said Noire. She sped up and angled them directly for it. "By the way, Arden, we couldn't find any info on your Lightborne friends in the Compendium. I'm sorry."

Taken aback, Arden questioned her, "Are you sure? Vidaya acted like it was a big deal when she showed me the Compendium earlier. I swear I saw a young Nora Linzer in there."

"Are you serious? Seeing the Compendium *is* a very big deal. Only top leaders have clearance," she said.

"Okay, I feel special." Arden laughed. "Nora isn't a Darktouched though. Why was she in the Compendium?"

"Not only Darktouched records are kept there. Anyone we consider important for any reason can be logged. Not to say we monitor them. It could've been a one-off image or file. If it was her, she was probably dealing with someone in leadership," Noire said, pushing out slightly on the steering lines to slow them down. They were less than thirty seconds from the shimmering they had observed earlier.

"Could she have used a maiden name, or a fake?" he asked.

Noire shrugged with her voice. "Could be, yeah. We're close, so pay attention."

The HUD alerted Arden that they were ten seconds from impacting whatever was in front of them. He sensed something but couldn't see it. The landscape looked the same no matter which HUD view he flipped to.

Noire slowed further, bringing them almost to a hover, and steered parallel to the disturbance. Reaching out a gloved hand, she touched it. "Tuck, anything?" she asked. "Tuck, can you hear me?" They heard a crackling on the line, but it went dead soon after. "Shit. Hold on—we're going in."

Noire steered them hard to the left and they picked up speed. Arden felt ice water wash over him, and then stared in awe as the barren landscape transformed into a lush forest. They swooped down, both quickly realizing they were passing through the boughs untouched.

"It's an illusion," said Noire. "But watch out, we still can't see anything." Her voice was calm, but Arden could tell she was distressed. "Tuck. Can you hear me?"

A crackle sounded on the comm, and then Tuck's voice broke through. "Yeah, I'm here, Noire. Are you seein' this?"

"We are. I'm going to swing over to your position and set down. I just picked you up on the HUD." Noire steered to the right and brought them gradually lower.

Arden marveled at the enormity of the trees—titanic live oaks that were at least three hundred feet tall and seemingly twice as wide. As he scanned the forest, he saw the breathtaking yet subdued beauty of what had long, long ago been a natural wonder. Up close, he noticed the veins of the leaves shone with a dewy silver.

Descending further, they quickly fell beneath the boughs and under the giants' embrace. The trunks were as pillars of the world, fed by a gently flowing stream that wound around and among them. Grass and clusters of vibrant blue flowers took shelter under the vast canopy. There were no creatures on the ground. No monsters, dragons, or people, save for themselves. Alighting in a small clearing where Tuck already stood waiting, they planned their next step.

Noire took the lead, saying, "If Eresh has gone through the trouble of somehow creating this illusion, she might know we're here. We need to be careful." Even in the suit, Arden could see her eyes scanning the area, flipping through HUD screens. "If they exist, the graves are likely half a mile over that way. Let's cut straight across. Keep a HUD view up that lets you see through the illusion.

You could still twist an ankle or step in a hole." They set off in the direction she pointed, walking single file and keeping a short distance between them, Noire in front and Arden in the middle.

Arden observed how complete the illusion was as Noire's feet made indentations in the grass and moved fallen twigs aside. It was so realistic that he reached down to touch one of the blue flowers; he was able to pluck it and hold it in his hand before it dissipated into nothingness. Tuck called from behind them, and Arden dodged as a stone flew past his head and bounced into Noire's leg.

"Oh, shoot. That was a real rock," said Tuck. "Sorry, Noire. And Arden."

Noire grumbled, "Somebody is about to get a real rock shoved right up his— What is that?" She had stopped in front of a hollowed-out stump with a sod roof and makeshift door. "It looks like an old witch's house from a fairytale."

Tentatively, they moved toward it. Noire reached out her hand, almost in jest, and knocked three times. With an ominous creak, the door swung slowly open, and a young woman with flowing black hair that reached her mid-back stood in the entryway. Arden checked the HUD to see if she gave off a heat signature, only to find that she was just another part of the illusion.

She spoke softly to them, beckoning. "Please, come inside. My name is Reshenu." No one moved closer. Noire began carefully rotating through her watch icons as the woman spoke. "There is no need to fear. I cannot harm you and would not if I could. Please. We have important matters to discuss."

Arden, thinking of the conversation with Ninazu, and in a way not caring what happened, strode forward and into the room. Tuck shrugged and followed on his heels. Noire, even after seeing her two friends walk inside, hesitated until the voice spoke again. "Come inside, Noire Ouranos. You have my word that you will not be harmed."

Noire tossed her head back, laughing. Then, looking uneasy again, she jumped across the threshold. The door shut behind them with a groan.

Reshenu invited them to relax, saying, "This place was prepared for you by Eresh. Please, sit. Remove your suits. A barrier was set when the door closed."

Again, Arden acted immediately, even while knowing that darkness in the Deep Infra would tear an unsuited Darktouched to shreds within a few seconds.

Let's see what happens to my threads of fate if I die here. He recalled his suit and—feeling surprised, relieved, and disappointed—was fine. Noire and Tuck removed theirs a moment later, and gave each other a lingering, concerned look.

The floor of the large room was covered in a downy white plant which Arden had never seen before, with woven mats laid on top. There were no chairs or tables, but there were seats carved into the wall. Noire carefully lowered herself into one of these notches and seemed thankful that it held her up. Tuck sat in a different one near her. Arden instead lowered himself onto one of the mats and ran a hand across the fluffy plant material. Again surprised, he felt it move under his fingers, tickling the palm of his hand.

Reshenu crossed the room and stooped down, ladling what appeared to be water into three wooden cups. She brought one to each person, then offered a chewy, sugary substance to them on a plate. "This liquid and crystallized sap once sustained large populations. It was given by the gentle spirit in whose remains you now rest. The spirit was called Hulpa, and it took the form of a magnificent weeping willow. At one time, the Hulpa was a vibrant and blessed being that existed in the Lightwatch, Infra, and Aboveworld simultaneously. The ancients called it the Tree of Life... which is an exaggeration. It was, though, a symbol of our cooperation. And of hope."

Arden took some candied sap and bit off a tiny piece. His immediate reaction was that if umami was a fifth flavor, then this was a sixth. It tasted like everything he enjoyed most, separate and yet mixed together at the same time. As he swallowed the first bite, his body coursed with energy. His mind became sharp and alert, and he felt sated. With a touch of guilt, he tore away another portion and chewed slowly, savoring every atom. Similarly, the cold, clear liquid was the freshest water he had ever tasted, complemented by a hint of earthy sweetness. With a single sip, he no longer felt thirsty. Looking up at Tuck and Noire, he knew they were experiencing the same things.

Reshenu sat down on the floor opposite them, legs crossed, and continued speaking. "I am here to guide you to Eresh, Arden Arinza. But not your friends. Rather, there is another that Eresh wishes to see. One named Corynna Darkspear. You are to come together on the morrow to the place I will show you how to find." Arden nodded, resisting his desire to reel in shock. Tuck and Noire, as usual, exchanged a long glance, shrugged, and turned their attention back to Reshenu. "Before that, however, I am to tell you about the past. Please listen, consider, question, and learn."

25

ERESH AND NINAZU

As RESHENU BEGAN HER tale, Arden considered that, in ancient times, the sun would have been high overhead in the land of Y'Sham. The trees around them and the water flowing past would have kept this place cool. For the Uldu, as Beyd called them, this had been a sanctuary. And now it was again for him and his friends.

Arden found Reshenu's voice soothing and at the same time melancholy. She began by saying, "Eresh bade me to set a condition for you all. Stop searching for and seeking to learn about the Seven and the Ten. All will be revealed in time. As one of two founders of the Darktouched who has your best interests at heart, she asks that you trust her. If you do not agree, please leave now and never return." She paused, and when no one moved, she continued, "Know that if you break this agreement, Eresh will know. Now, listen. This tale has never been told."

The stories of Eresh and Ninazu are essentially one. They were born more than seventeen thousand years ago, with names that no longer matter in lands that no longer exist. Like many in that era, they were torn from their families at a young age by warfare, thrust into a conflict not of their making and forced into roles they neither wanted nor felt equipped to perform. Through battles and trials, they

found comfort in one another and hope in a few like-minded souls around them. Once the violence subsided, they recognized this peace to be tenuous, and believed the trajectory of the world and its nations pointed to imminent and catastrophic outcomes. They foresaw utter devastation in every possible future.

Examination of a then-ancient past revealed to them the possibility of finding answers not in the Aboveworld but in the world beneath—in light's shadow, entrenched within the world, in places where darkness remains untouched. For the Infra is not only beneath the world but also within it—it is ether, it is quintessence. Together, they uncovered what the Darktouched now call the Source, and bound themselves to it. Shucking off the light, they wended deeper and further, until at last they reached their own limits. Yet, for their purposes, this was not enough. The secrets of the abyss remained frustratingly out of reach.

So Eresh and Ninazu looked to the world above, and in this the Darktouched had their beginnings. They sought out the powerful, the rich, the skilled, and the strong, binding them to the Source and teaching them how to survive deep water and cold abyss. In a cavern far below the earth, they strove together with these handpicked allies to build the heart of a society aligned to their interests. And still, after everything, the path to true darkness remained shut. Wars came and went, nations rose and fell, the Darktouched of yesterday were replaced by those of tomorrow, but the answers Eresh and Ninazu sought—the keys to true peace and the lasting future they hoped to find—eluded them.

The Lightborne, in a way cousins to your kind, eventually approached them with a warning and an offer. Combining the knowledge borne of all the light touches with the wisdom drawn from the abyss, they would save the world from itself. Inevitably, war returned to the land as its rulers resisted control, fearing loss of power more than death. Forming a covenant with the creatures of the depths and their mighty queen, Tiamat, Eresh and Ninazu returned to battle. In the chaos, however, they lost their family once again. Two sons, both willful and strong, were taken by the flames of conflict.

In the end, their efforts failed, and the catastrophe they had foreseen unfolded. In desperation, they called upon Tiamat to summon the dark tide and cleanse the earth. Mighty kingdoms, broad swaths of land, entire civilizations, and creatures of every kind were pulled into the depths. Much was lost. The price was steep.

In their grief, the two believed their sons might be revived if they could find a way further down. Desperate, Ninazu pressed into the blackest depths. Enraged by repeated misuse, the darkness and its denizens pushed back, and the door to true wisdom began to slam shut. Ninazu, like a block of wood wedged against the jamb, has held it barely open ever since. Without his sacrifice, the Darktouched would be no more.

With her connection to the Source diminished, Eresh was no longer able to bind new individuals to the darkness. Yet, by the will of Ninazu, the power of those individuals already tethered to it never returns to the Source when they perish, and instead seeks out new ownership. You call this the Darktouched Right.

Eresh has remained since that time ever vigilant, an invisible protector and guardian of the Infra's secrets. Shielding the unaware Children of Shadow from breaking the Second Covenant she forged. Waiting for the right moment to reveal the truth. This is the legacy that she wishes to pass on to you and those around you, Arden Arinza.

Reshenu ended her narrative by saying directly to Arden, "Eresh commanded me, Arden, to give you this bracelet. She said that it will be the key to convincing Corynna Darkspear to journey with you."

From a cubby in the wall, she picked up an object and strode across the room to pass it to him. Made of woven strips of cedarwood, it was plain but intricate. Since it was too small for his wrist, he slipped it in the pocket where the nazar charm had been.

"Do you have any questions?"

Arden ran a hand across the patchy stubble on his face. "It's so much to absorb. For now, I have two. We found cuneiform texts that were only about five thousand years old in some ruins. They mentioned the rage of Tiamat. Can you explain why? And the second, a... colleague of ours met a dragon named Nuzum. Are other dragons still in the Infra?"

Reshenu replied, her countenance pleasant but unreadable, "Before and since the event I just described—that which Darktouched call the Reshaping—the abyss occasionally erupts. This brings Abzu and Infra to the surface on a smaller scale. The effects are the same, but not nearly as final. Also, in the cultural and subconscious memory of those who live on the surface, the fury of Tiamat and her children lingers still. I believe that answers your first question." She allowed them an opportunity to inquire further, but no one did and she went on. "Some of Tiamat's children were trapped on the wrong side of the door. They are angry and vengeful, but hold to the Second Covenant. Others chose to stay for their own reasons. Most are older and more powerful than any human, but you are unlikely to have the misfortune of meeting them."

"Thank you, Reshenu. That's all I can think of," said Arden. Looking up at his friends, he asked, "What about you two?"

Noire shook her head and remained silent. Tuck, though, raised his arms into a stretch and giggled. "I just can't believe the stupid Source is real." Arden and Noire laughed with him.

Reshenu rose to her feet and walked to the door. "Then our time together has ended. Eresh asks that you do not share this information with others yet, except for Corynna Darkspear. The time for silence will soon pass." She opened the door to reveal a blue barrier and stepped to the side. They suited up and passed through single file. "I bid you farewell. May you find the truth and the freedom you seek, Arden Arinza. The coordinates and instructions that you need to reach Eresh have been sent to your suit." Arden checked his HUD and saw a message with the information she mentioned, then thanked her again.

As the group stepped into the forest, Arden reached down to touch the grass. Unlike Reshenu's home inside the carved out remains of the spirit Hulpa, it wasn't real. He heard a door close behind him, and the illusion dissolved before his eyes. They stood in silence on the barren mountaintop, looking out over the purple firmament.

26

THE WAY HOME

CONFIDENT IN THE NEW stealth technology built into their KALM-ER suits, they quickly made their way back to Branthumville. They had reached the depot when intermittent flashes of light to the north caught their collective attention. Noire and Tuck agreed to swing around and discover their origin, and Arden felt his stomach lurch when Noire pulled the right steering line hard into a power dive.

They raced forward, passing over the elaborate temples and palace complex they had seen earlier. From above, the largest set of buildings looked like a spinning star with seven points spiraling toward a central structure that reminded Arden of a round ziggurat. This main tower had ten levels and a smaller shape, perhaps an observation tower, jutting from its top. The HUD measured it, top to bottom, at nearly four hundred feet tall.

From the ninth level, they saw more flashes of light and drew closer, circling around the uppermost floor. After a full revolution, they finally saw two human-like figures emerge from a covered enclosure. Behind them, a pack of five dog-like creatures chased their prey toward a flying torso, the bottom half of the body nowhere to be seen. *Now we have different types of monsters working together. Wonderful.*

Knowing they had at most ten seconds, Arden flipped to the fishing lure icon in his HUD and engaged it. A circular target interface appeared. Unsure what would happen, he centered the effect area over the winged monster and deployed it. An orb of darkness larger than Arden was tall formed to his left and shot toward the beast. The HUD began a countdown from thirty seconds the instant it reached its mark.

Unable to resist the immense dark burst, the creatures hurtled toward it, gorging on it. The Darktouched on the ziggurat looked around in bewilderment, and when they saw the three in the distance, a voice panted over the comm, "Please, help us! We're running toward the opposite side of the tower. Can someone pick me up? I'm too clumsy to outrun them." Arden instantly recognized the voice. It was Vorin Nordlim.

In their group channel, Arden said to his friends, "I have maybe five minutes before I can deploy another lure. Tuck, can you toss another in about fifteen seconds? Then swing around and pick up the one who just talked."

"Copy," Tuck said.

"Noire," Arden said urgently. "When they go for the second lure, can you try the sun icon? No idea what it does, but I'm hoping for a blast of light."

Noire answered, "You do know the feature has a tooltip, right? Can't read?"

"Deployin' in five seconds!" Tuck exclaimed.

Arden shouted over the comm to the two Darktouched on the tower. "On my signal, the other person has to shadesurf out immediately. We'll escort you until you're in the clear."

A dark orb whooshed from Tuck to a narrow pathway directly between the Darktouched and their pursuers. He then rushed down and snatched up Vorin, racing off into the distance.

"Got it. Awaiting your signal," responded a woman whose voice Arden didn't recognize.

The creatures were now huddled around the second lure. Suddenly, a solid beam of light burst from Noire, burning everything living that it touched. Without even waiting for his word, the second Darktouched summoned her shadesurfing kite and fled. Noire chased along behind, maintaining a steady distance between them.

Arden breathed a sigh of relief only to shout in distress the next instant. From his peripheral vision, he saw the legs and talons of the winged horror hurtling toward the female Darktouched. Not knowing what else to do, he engaged the light beam, targeted it, and deployed. At first he missed his mark, but was able to recover quickly and torch the enemy.

The act, however, came with a steep price. His vision began to grow dim, and the last thing he saw before passing out was burned flesh plummeting to the ground. After that, a stream of blurry images Arden barely remembered faded in and out, and concerned voices hurt his brain. He felt nauseous and exhausted, and then passed out again.

When Arden awoke, he knew immediately where he was because he had spent so much time there in the past three days. *Medical Services, my home away from home... away from home.* He tried propping himself up on an elbow but was too weak.

Noire was sleeping in a chair at his bedside. Roused by his stirring, she jumped out of her chair and loomed over him. He blinked uncertainly a few times. To his astonishment, she looked angry.

"You idiot! You could've died. You've been in and out of consciousness for hours," she said, her fury transforming into concern. "The doctors say you'll be fine in the morning. Darktouched medicine is better than the Aboveworld's."

Tasting bitter sourness on his tongue, Arden smacked his lips. Noire reached over to a side table, grabbed a small bottle, and helped him take a sip of water. "What time is it?" he asked groggily.

"Not late. Only eleven o'clock. The idiots you saved with your stupidity are out in the hall. They want to talk to you."

"Tuck asleep?" he asked.

"No, Tuck had a date. He said you'd better not die, especially now that you made him an honorary Seeker." She laughed. "'Deveras is never gonna let us hear the end of this when he finds out.'" Arden tried to laugh with her, but only managed a weak chuckle. "Well, I'm going to get some rest. I'll let those two and the staff know you're awake."

"Thanks," Arden rasped. He watched as she left the room. Seconds later, Vorin and a blonde woman in her twenties approached. They both wore Black Hand uniforms, but Vorin's lacked the embossed hand emblem.

The woman spoke in a hushed, apologetic tone that increased in volume the longer she talked and the crosser she became. "Arden, I'm sorry this happened. I'm Astarte Matraque. We were training at a guard outpost along the route you three took, and this... recruit... Well, he saw it was you and followed you against orders. Through the portal! Before I knew it, we were being chased every which way. We'd been holed up in some corner of hell for I don't know how long when we decided to make a break for it. Bad idea. If not for you three, we'd be pâté."

Arden smiled and motioned with his hand. "No worries. I'm glad you're both okay." He looked up at Vorin, who wore a neutral expression. Resisting a dark urge to be snide, he instead took a breath and said, "I'm sorry about your shirts and everything else. Can we call it even?"

Vorin at first clenched his teeth, accentuating his pronounced jawline. Then his look softened, and he held out his right hand. "You saved my life. I'd be an ungrateful shit if I held a grudge now. We're good." Arden shook Vorin's hand, then let his own fall back onto the bed.

"I'm pretty fried, but thanks for sticking around. I'm glad you're both safe. Maybe we can grab some brews at the Straw," Arden mumbled sleepily. "I promise no puking this time. At least not on you, Vorin." Then he felt the world slowly fade away, and he once again drifted to sleep.

Lucas blinked, peering at the late afternoon light painting the Linzers' porch with a soft glow. It was a warm summer day, and his dad leaned back in a chair with his head against the wood siding, snoozing. In the yard, Nora and Alan were playing horseshoes while Mai ran circles around the pit each time a shoe landed.

Without moving, Lucas was suddenly standing next to Nora, readying a pitch. "I thought we were family," he said to her, flinging the shoe. It flew high into the air and disappeared.

Nora had tears in her eyes. "We are, Lucas. Alan and I love you from the bottom of our hearts. We would never do anything to harm you or your friends."

"That's right, Luc. We're always on your side. Even if it costs us our lives," said Alan, popping into view next to the pit Lucas had just thrown toward. "Nice one, by the way. It's a ringer!" The horseshoe spun down from the sky like a boomerang and swung around the stake.

Aella and Connie cheered behind him, and Lucas turned toward their voices. They now stood on the porch in front of his sleeping dad. Connie fidgeted with his baseball cap and said, "Nice one, dude! Don't worry about us. Nora has us hidden away where no Lightborne will ever look."

Aella grinned and gave him a quick thumbs up. "You take care of business, Lucas. We're always going to be here for you. Just make sure you stay safe. Something about this place makes me nervous."

Arden frowned and slightly shook his head. *This place?* He suddenly wasn't in the Linzers' yard anymore. The carved walls of Reshenu's home rose around him, and Kilk sat on a woven mat directly in his line of sight.

The old man spoke in his gravelly voice, "Sometimes, if you want to achieve great things, you have to take even greater risks. I spent my whole life taking chances before they finally paid off. And now look at me. What a legacy! Everdark will be glorious."

Arden heard three knocks on the door behind him. He opened it, and Beyd stepped into the room. "Ignore that old muppet, Arden. He's gone daft. Trust in me, cuz. I'll see you through, eh." He winked a slitted yellow eye.

Now Arden was soaring through the Infra, but not with wings or by shadesurfing—he was truly flying. A silent scream left him, lighting up the purple sky with blue lightning. Behind him, two Reclaimers were drawing closer. Panicked, he called out for help, but none came. Cracks formed in the abyss in front of him. Green needles flew past him, and two struck his abdomen before he passed through the portal.

The living room of his home in Flagstaff appeared. The Reclaimers stripped off their masks, revealing themselves to be Malank and Fiala. "Luck will see you through, kid. You can't trust people—not even me—but you can trust the winds of destiny," said Malank, playing with the oblong fate charm around his neck.

Fiala tapped her foot on the floor. "Speak for yourself. No one that looks like this could possibly betray anyone."

Deveras yelled at them from up the stairs. "If we find the Source, I don't care what it takes. Let's just hope this plan works."

Malank laughed from deep in his belly. "What plan? I'm just making it up as I go."

Arden backed out of the room and fell, and fell, and fell. The cold, dark water of the Abzu reached up to grab him, pulling him under. Swimming with long, powerful strokes, he swam until he saw a door in the living rock. Jerking it open, he plunged through the barrier and spilled onto the cobblestone streets of the Jumble. Rynn smiled down at him.

"You can't trust anyone, Lucas. Arden. Whatever. Trust will just break your heart. Why bother? Besides, your buddy is over there." She snickered, pointing to Vorin. Urgently, Arden turned back to Rynn, but she was gone. Sweat dripped from his brow, and he ran. The Reclaimers were behind him again. He had to get away. Irkalla Tower hovered in the distance. He was jumping from a ledge now, flying with wings unfurled, gliding down to the lift.

Vidaya's eagle stare locked onto him before he was even halfway to the rising platform. "Quite a tour, wouldn't you say?" And then he started to fall, faster and faster. Soon, he would crash into the Blood Amaryllis. Who would ever notice? He let go, giving up on life, passing peacefully into nothingness, allowing the threads of fate to slip from his grasp. With a soft thud, he fell into the plush cushions at Deveras's house. Someone was knocking on the front door, and he wanted them to go away. Knock. *Stop it!* Knock. *Leave me alone!* Knock. *I said, go away!*

He opened his eyes. Standing at the door to his hospital room was Rynn, smiling mischievously.

27

A DUBIOUS INVITATION

ARDEN STILL HADN'T SEPARATED himself from the emotions of his dream, and he looked at Rynn doubtfully. Lifting her left eyebrow, she asked him, "What? Something on my face?"

Arden felt the cobwebs shake loose, and he let a smile form. "Sorry. Bad dream."

She sashayed across the room and stood next to where he lay. "About me?"

"Part of it," he replied. "'Dream you' was telling me not to trust anyone. 'Trust will break your heart,' you said."

"Dream me said, you mean," she corrected him, eliciting a laugh. "How are you feeling?"

Yawning, he said, "I'm feeling surprisingly good. I don't remember seeing a doctor or nurse, except maybe once. Must've slept like a rock."

Rynn's expression became serious. "Good, because Sabrath and Daryala want to meet with you. Right now, if you can manage it. They found out about your excursion yesterday and want to know more." She added with a pleading look, "Please don't be mad at me. I'm just the messenger."

Arden eyed a bin resting on a small shelf across the room. Based on his last stay, he knew it held his clothes, and the bracelet that Reshenu had given him. *I shouldn't talk to Rynn about the bracelet until the Black Hand leaders are done grilling me.* Consumed by his own thoughts, he distractedly waved off her entreating. "Oh, no problem. I'm not mad."

She looked at him inquisitively. "Where are you right now? You seem miles away."

He shrugged, masking his concern over meeting Sabrath and Daryala with nonchalance. "I'm still waking up. Yesterday was... educational."

Crossing the room, Rynn reached for the bin. *Don't open it.* Arden wished so forcefully that he wondered if she heard him. Setting it down at his feet, she said, "I'll wait outside while you get dressed. You can tell me about it on the way down to headquarters."

Without looking back, she walked out of the room and closed the door. Arden checked the pockets of his jeans, making sure the bracelet was still there before breathing again. Sliding out of bed, he took a towel bath before tossing on his clothes.

On a stand at the foot of the bed, he noticed a tablet and inspected the words displayed on it. *Results of the vote. And it's only five in the morning! What the heck?* Grabbing a piece of bread from the food tray placed on a nearby table, he reviewed the outcomes.

VOTE RESULTS

Approved Proposals

- Proposal to allow retrieval and examination of Class 0 – Benign artifacts

- Proposal to expand acceptable classes and annual volume of Fabricated items taken into the Aboveworld for personal use (not sales)

- Proposal to remove forbidden restriction for zone Abaddon

- Proposal to expand oversight of Aboveworld internet and other information sources, within already established privacy and detectability standards

- Proposal to designate establishment registered under the name of The Deadman's Straw as a Darktouched cultural heritage monument

- Proposal to increase funding of Deep Infra Assessment Drones (DIAD) and expand pilot program

- Proposal to expand investment into Deep Infra Exploration Technologies (DIET), such as foldable Fabricators, Explorer's sustenance medications, etc.

- Proposal to expand scope and scale of the Aboveworld Replacement Artifact Sales (ARAS) program

- Proposal to approve Project Everdark, which will leverage artificial intelligence and Compendium resources to construct persistent personas of key Darktouched individuals

- Proposal to increase funding for development of KALM Expanded Range suit (KALM-ER model)

- Proposal to seek additional sources of Nabucite in forbidden zones Kigal and Gehenna

- Proposal to expand research into the Darktouched Right

Rejected Proposals

- Proposal to allow two children per household

- Proposal to disallow child liberation

- Proposal to disallow relinquishing of non-Darktouched offspring

- Proposal to remove forbidden restriction for:

  - Zone Branthumville

  - Zone Eldrastan

  - Zone Nostrand

  - Zone Tartarus

- Proposal to remove six-month residency requirement for Dark-touched

  - Counter proposal to eliminate possibility for living in the Above-world

- Proposal to remove exception requirement for wearing KALM suit aboveground

- Proposal to restrict use of KALM wings in residential areas

- Proposal to allow Defense, Search & Rescue personnel to carry anti-Lightborne weaponry at all Abzu Hub station entrances, Abzu Complex guard stations, and Infra outposts

- Proposal to increase funding of anti-Lightborne research and development, as well as contracting of Delver resources to further said research

- Proposal to increase funding for KALM Enhanced Shadow Taskforce development (KALM-EST model)

- Proposal to expand Cerberus System capabilities:

  - Add additional systems at unpatrolled backdoors

  - Add lethal, anti-Lightborne capabilities

- Proposal to implement Disavowed Automated Surveillance Helper (DASH) bots

- Proposal to market the Irkalla Tower Race game as an Aboveworld boardgame called Irkalla Escape

- Proposal to expand the Borough south and replace impacted existing structures in the area called Old Town

- Proposal to expand the Fabrication Zone west into the Greensward

Rynn will be happy. Old Town and the Deadman's Straw had been saved, and the proposal to expand the Fabrication Zone had also failed. *I guess the bottom floor of the tower isn't getting retrofitted either, like Vidaya said it might.*

Given the heated discussion surrounding the anti-Lightborne proposals and Kilk's open support, he was shocked to see none had passed. Navigating further into the data for several ballot initiatives, he had to double check the narrow margins. *They almost won all of them... The child liberation ones weren't even this close.* Beyd had said the Surface Affairs leader, Toyo, feared an end to Dark-touched pacifism. Others in the Complex seemed to share her perspective. He set the device down and finished getting ready.

One of the attendants at the main desk called after Arden as he and Rynn made their way out of Medical Services. "Sir! Please sign this release form. This isn't a hotel, you know?"

Absentmindedly, Arden began to write his Abovename, only to find that he couldn't. Having never signed anything with the name Arden Arinza, he absentmindedly squiggled the initials *A. A.* with a tail at the end.

"Thank you. Have a great day," the attendant said.

Glancing at Rynn, Arden commented, "I didn't know you couldn't even *write* your Abovename down here."

Rynn called the elevator. "Bizarre, right?" The elevator arrived and they stepped into the compartment. "Before you talk to Daryala, you need to know something. She's having Beyd work on tech that could make the Lightborne vulnerable. We need your help. If you found anything yesterday, please tell her."

Arden was surprised that her words reminded him of the vote more than anything else. He asked, "Didn't those proposals get rejected?"

Rynn scoffed. "What? Who cares? We're not stopping because of the vote. I doubt you are either."

He raised his hands in mock defeat. "Okay, okay. But we didn't find anything. I do need to talk to you after this meeting though." The elevator stopped at B9, two floors above their destination. When no one got on, they continued talking.

For the first time, Rynn looked very irritated with him. "Fine, if that's your story. But you should meet with her anyway. We need people like you."

The elevator doors closed as Arden's trepidation grew. *She keeps saying "we" like it's her asking and not Daryala.* He did his best to maintain a calm demeanor and strike a conversational tone. "People like me? Incredibly handsome and charming?"

"Connected. The other mission leaders are lukewarm at best. You can help us make inroads," Rynn said, leaving the lift.

They passed through a large room where there stood a circular, walnut-finished table with an open center. Showcased in the opening was a Black Hand emblem emblazoned on the gray carpet that covered the entire floor. Along the sides of the chamber were doorways into offices, meeting rooms, and a small officers' lounge. At the very back, a short corridor led to a staircase. They passed by a guard and climbed up the flight of steps.

In the office, a woman that Arden recognized from voting day as Daryala Gindir sat behind a carbon-steel desk. Her left eye, made entirely of Nabucite, was even more unsettling in person. Sabrath, whose bald head Arden recognized from the Deadman's Straw, was seated on a corner of the desk talking to her, his back turned to the door.

The woman raised her eyes to look at them, and Sabrath turned to see who had arrived. Rynn brought her right fist across the Black Hand emblem on her uniform. "I've brought Arden Arinza, as ordered," she declared.

Sabrath stood in proper decorum and returned her salute. "Good. You're dismissed, Lieutenant Darkspear."

Rynn turned to leave, but Daryala motioned for her to stop. "You should stay." A firm, controlled tone lent her words gravitas. "At ease. There's no need for formalities right now." Standing, she introduced herself: "Daryala Gindir."

Arden reached out his hand partway across her desk, hesitated, and then pulled it back. "Arden Arinza. Nice to meet you, ma'am." He extended his hand to Sabrath, who squeezed it like a vice, penetrating his skull with intense, large gray eyes. "And sir."

"Don't be so stiff, boy. You're not in the Hand," Daryala said to him with a welcoming expression. "Nice to meet you. Let's chat. Everyone, please sit."

They did as she directed, and Arden noticed that Sabrath was the first to obey. He was also the first to talk. Unlike Daryala, his natural speech was quiet and rapid. "May I, Commander Gindir?" Daryala nodded, giving him the floor. "We received a report that two of our officers owe you their lives, Mister Arinza. Thank you."

"You're welcome. I was able to speak with them last night. I'm glad they're safe," Arden said.

Sabrath sat perfectly upright, his hands on the chair's arms and his feet squarely on the ground. "I'll be direct. What were you doing in forbidden zones Branthumville and Eldrastan? Passage into them is not typically sanctioned. We know Reina d'Martest pulled strings with Kilk Branthum."

Without a pause or taking his eyes from Sabrath's, Arden said, "Kilk hurt himself on his last expedition and needed help. We were exploring unmapped grids in those zones. He wouldn't tell us why, but I think it has to do with Project Everdark."

Arden watched painfully as Sabrath stretched his lips into a thin smile. The Black Hand's second-in-command probed, "And did you find anything?"

Shaking his head, Arden responded, "Nothing other than barren earth and monsters."

Daryala scratched her left temple, calling his attention to the sable eye. "I believe you. Thank you for your honesty," she put forward. "You have a sincere look, like an old friend of mine. I'll be honest as well. We need your help to locate certain artifacts and schematics in the Deep Infra." She pressed on, sensing correctly that Arden was about to say something, "You won't be the only one looking, and we know you're not the most experienced or best Explorer. Maybe you will be. But you already have a strong network of Seekers and Delvers. We'd like to build bonds of cooperation with someone who could become the next great leader of one of those groups."

Arden picked his words carefully as he reacted to her offer. "May I ask what kind of artifacts and schematics? What are we looking for and why?"

"I can only tell you *that* if you agree to help us," Daryala said, her good eye seemingly focused on something behind him. "What if, as advance payment, I give you something in return?"

He ran a hand through his hair, pretending to consider her offer. "Like?"

"Like, for example, we can commit off-the-books support to help find Galan Cadenza," she replied, her mouth scrunched. "Or, perhaps, safe harbor for these supposedly banished Lightborne that Deveras has cozied up to. After all, we already granted *you* asylum. You have no reason not to trust us."

Arden glanced up at her, his focus switching between her intact eye and the artificial one. "That would be great, but something seems wrong. Me helping you—me, who's only been on the job less than a week—is what it would take for you to change your mind and help us?"

Daryala shook her head. "Don't misunderstand. This isn't a one-for-one trade. If we agree to be friends, then we expect a *lasting* relationship."

Arden nodded slowly. "This is a big decision then. I'm going to need more time to think it through. Is that okay?" he asked, feigning deference.

"Very well. Understand that an offer like this does not come often," she said. "Your asylum can still be revoked. Orientation isn't over yet. Also understand that Deveras, your parents, and your little Delver friends can be brought on charges of colluding with Lightborne. And a host of other offenses that could see them in cells for years, if not get them executed."

Arden felt his blood rise, and in spite of his better judgement said, "In that case, wouldn't everyone in this room be guilty of developing anti-Lightborne technology without approval?"

Daryala leaned forward. "We would, but a day is coming when none of that will matter." She slammed a fist on the desk, leaving an impression in the metal. *How strong is she?* "The Lightborne left me with half of a body and no eye! They steal our people away, killing and ransoming them, and we still haven't figured out the reason! All the while, you idiots scurry in the dark while they wrap their fingers around our collective throat." Striding around the desk, she menaced over him. "There will come a day when you'll need our strength. When you'll regret not collaborating with us. Actually, no! You're standing in our way at each step. That day of reckoning can be never, years from now, or tomorrow. And if you won't choose, I will." Her tone said without saying, "Don't toy with me, child."

Arden moved his jaw, but the words stuck in his throat. He looked at Rynn, who only shook her head and wore a miserable look on her face. For a brief moment, Sabrath let pity sneak past his guard, saying without words that he was regretful. That he knew the spider had its prey trapped, and there was nothing left to do but watch the feeding.

Arden knew that if he gave in to Daryala now, he would have no choice but to play her game until its end. A contest with an objective and rules he had no knowledge of. *If I refuse, will she really go after me? Or my friends and family? Can she? Can it really hurt to pretend we're feeding her information?* The conversation so far hinted that she neither knew nor suspected of their meeting with Reshenu.

"Well," said Daryala, "what do you say, my new friend? Will you roll the bones with me?"

The way she called Arden her "new friend" rankled him. In defiance, he gritted his teeth and stated resolutely, "No, I won't. Leave me and my people alone."

Daryala was silent for perhaps a minute before smiling and uttering under her breath, "My, you really are the same." Returning to her chair, she slowly eased herself down. "I'll give you until tomorrow to choose your path. Leave us."

Legs shaking, Arden propped himself up and strode out of the room. Behind him, he heard Rynn call his name and her footsteps approaching rapidly. "I had no idea, Arden. I really didn't know. Sabrath said she wasn't always like this. What happened to her was... You can see it yourself."

Arden believed Rynn, but he resented her more. For dragging him down here, for being complicit in the ambush, and for sitting silent while it happened. Reaching into his pocket, he pulled out the woven cedar bracelet. The shocked gasp he heard a second later made him sick with guilt and egged him on at the same time.

"Where did you get that?" Rynn asked incredulously. "That's... Some northwest First Nations peoples make those. I had one like it when I was adopted, but I lost it during the attack when they were taken."

Arden answered coldly, feeling only his own fear and inefficacy, "Ask your masters. Or maybe you sold out your family too, like you did me and mine." Throwing the bracelet on the ground in front of her, he marched away.

"Wait! Please," Rynn cried behind him. "I never meant for any of this to happen. They told me they wanted to talk—that's all. I would never wish any harm on your family or friends. I lost mine, remember? Please tell me where you got the bracelet. Why do you have it?"

Halting his steps, Arden called back to her, "If you want to know, come with me. I'll tell you on the way. I can't threaten anyone you care about, so you'll have to make up your own mind what to do." Swinging around to look at her, he added, "If you come along, we'll work together until I get what I need, and then we're done. Trusting people like you just leads to betrayal. The real you, not the dream one."

The sound of Rynn's footfalls let him know she was coming along for the journey. He already regretted most of what he'd said, but knew it was too late to undo it. The absurd thought crossed Arden's mind that the shadesurfing lesson would begin soon. Without it, he would be totally reliant on a person he had likely just made into an enemy. But, he rationalized, she probably was one before he did anything at all.

His words rang down the hallway. "I have orientation until later today, and don't want to repeat the whole thing. Not that it really matters if I'm tossed in prison. I'll call you when I'm done."

Rynn's footsteps stopped without a word, but Arden thought he heard sniffling. Fighting the urge to care, he got on the elevator and left her where she stood.

28

INDEPENDENCE UNLOCKED

WHEN ARDEN ARRIVED AT the guard station beneath the Abzu Complex, he found Vorin and Phosop already waiting. Having left Rynn no more than fifteen minutes prior, he had to work hard at mustering a wave to Phosop and a nod at Vorin. They both greeted him in kind, and the three engaged in small talk while waiting for their instructor.

Arden let his mind wander as they conversed. Only ten days ago, he had graduated from high school. The capstone event was, as he looked back, inconsequential in the grander scheme of his life. At the time, his worries had centered around missing Aella and Connie when they moved away to attend college. Beyond that, he dreaded readying himself for his still-un-chosen Darktouched discipline. His entire life had become an exercise in latching onto a bit of freedom while a multitude of decisions were being made for him.

Now, his father was captured and possibly killed, and the neighbors he considered grandparents were likely in some way responsible. Aella and Connie had been missing the entire time, Daryala Gindir had upended his entire existence in the Abzu Complex, and every day consisted of an orientation leading to an uncertain future. The one certain thing was that his opportunity to choose becoming Disavowed had passed. The burden of life had grown immensely heavier, and his choices even fewer.

And then there was Rynn, who along with Tuck and Noire had become a sliver of sanity and happiness in his life. After the morning's events, he wasn't sure if his relationship with her was salvageable, or if he wanted it to be.

Vorin or Phosop would frequently say or ask him something, and he would have to request for them to repeat it. Thankfully, they were patient with him, because he was grateful for the companionship.

When their instructor arrived, Arden reflexively groaned out loud before his brain engaged. His mom casually walked down the steps from the criss-crossed walkways above and called out to them all. "Good morning. I'm Reina d'Martest, and I'll be teaching you the basics of shadesurfing this morning. And you," she said to Arden. "We need to talk." Reina turned her attention to the whole class. "Now open up your wings and float down to the bottom. Wait for me on the platform down there."

Vorin signaled to him with his chin. "Race me down?"

Arden nodded. "Sure."

Phosop jumped up and down. "Me too. I can take you guys."

"All right," said Vorin. "On three. One, two, three!"

The three unfurled their wings, and Arden dove to an early lead. Converting his frustration and rage into momentum, he surged forward ever faster. Plunging recklessly, he covered half of the distance from the barrier to the ground below in ten seconds. Shifting his body to take a brief glance up, he saw Phosop in a faraway second place and Vorin struggling to keep up in third. And then, a flash that he could hardly believe was a person swooped down, passing Vorin and Phosop in less than a second. Refocused, he mustered his strength and streamlined himself into a human projectile. He was seconds away now. *I have to pull up. No way she catches me.* Before he finished the thought, in a way that reminded him of the Abzuball loss, the blur raced by him and under the small platform at the bottom, then surged twenty feet above it and floated down gracefully. Meanwhile, he and his two fellow trainees barely managed to stay standing when they landed.

Phosop cheered loudly over the comm. "Wow! Amazing! You are so fast, Reina."

Vorin clapped exuberantly. "Unbelievable. I didn't know that was even possible. Rynn is the fastest I know, and she's not even close."

Reina bowed. "You might be good in the water, Arden, but I own the dark."

"Then it's about time you taught me something useful," Arden quipped.

"So," said Vorin slowly, "you two obviously know each other."

"I'm his mother," Reina said nonchalantly.

Vorin and Phosop both began to giggle and tease him. "You got smoked by your mom, bro!" exclaimed Vorin. Arden found himself laughing along with them, even though he was a touch mortified.

"All right, listen up," said Reina. "First, I want you to stand in a line and practice without gear. Keep your arms relaxed and pretend like the lines are connected to your fingertips. Hold them together very lightly. Keep your hands in a center position. Every movement should be gradual." She modeled very smooth, gentle motions, and her students followed along. Arden and Vorin studied carefully, the prior day's hard lesson of how little they knew fresh in their minds. "Keep a slight bend in your knees for now. I want you to imagine a target with the bull's-eye centered on the horizon. That's your power zone. Closer to the center is where you get the most zip, and the outsides are more for coasting. Since shadewinds can originate from any direction, you have to account for vertical gusts too."

Arden remembered his trips clinging to Noire's back and could see the target clearly in his mind's eye. "What do we do if the shadewind comes from behind us at an upward angle and our kite's high in the power zone?"

Reina answered quickly, "We'll get to that. But the basic answer is you do one of two things. One, you adjust the angle of your kite to meet the wind. Or two, you briefly release the kite by fully unclenching both hands." He practiced the motion, imagining how it would feel with the lines extending from his palms.

Reina continued her coaching. "Stand with your feet pointed perpendicular to the direction you want to go. The board is under you, supporting you. Gliding along the darkness." Again, she showed them with her body what she wanted them to do. "What most rookies don't know is that the shadewinds have stable currents. They flow down along the outside edge of the Funnel and continue that way in all directions. There's a gentler one that flows directly up into the Funnel. The HUD can show you the current stream, which makes this whole thing much more predictable. Usually."

Arden was thankful he could now connect Reina's teaching to his solo shadesurfing experience, regardless of how painful it had been. "Yesterday, when I pulled on the lines, the kite didn't do anything for a few seconds. Then I pulled again and almost killed Tuck and me."

"Common mistake. That's why I'm having you practice gradual movements. At first, like most things, shadesurfing is about patience. I know two of you who could learn the definition of that word," she said dryly. Phosop began giggling again, starting up another round of chuckling from Vorin. Soon, Arden had forgotten entirely about his argument with Rynn.

They moved methodically through the training. After a few more minutes of practice without gear, Reina had them summon their kites and boards. She taught them to pull the steering lines back to gain momentum and then to center them quickly. Arden pointed and laughed when Vorin pulled too hard and kept the steering lines tight against his chest, only to be dragged along behind the kite as he himself had been the day prior. Then, he did the same thing a moment later. Phosop caught on quicker than either young man, her movements calm and easy on the lines.

Eventually, they were stable enough to fly without much supervision, and they began racing against each other. Reina followed along behind, ensuring that no one careened into the darkness or smashed into a floating island. Arden's worries and cares subsided as his motions became more fluid, more natural, his keen, innate sense of what to do and not to do growing sharper with each run. While still clumsy, with the HUD and his mother's instruction, he felt a sense of belonging for the first time since arriving in the dark. Speeding along, Arden felt truly free, acting of his own volition. The purple sky overhead welcomed him home, and the darkness below pushed him along. Of all the moments in his life, he wanted this one to last.

And then he saw the owl perched on an island off to his left. He awkwardly steered toward it and alighted upon the small bit of land. Its haunting voice reached out to him. "Be cautious, Child of Shadow. The threads of fate are unwinding, fraying, unraveling. Do not let them slip from your grasp. You have but one chance, opportunity, hope to set things right with Rynn." *But can I trust her?* "More than anyone. More than you know. More than she knows. I will come to you again, so worry not. For a moment, let your heart be unburdened."

Phosop called out to him from the comm. "What's the matter, Arden? Tired already? You're young and fit! This is no time for breaks! Wooooo!" Hollering, she blew past him back toward the Funnel.

Two hours after they started, the three orientees walked triumphantly up the steps into the Abzu Complex. Waving to Vorin and Phosop, Arden stayed below with his mom, watching the Blood Amaryllis.

"So, what happened?" she asked him.

"We found Eresh. Or a version of her. Then we rescued Vorin and Astarte from the Black Hand, and I passed out. It's a long story," he answered briefly, not wanting to explain. "She wanted me to come to a secret location she gave me coordinates to. Me and Rynn—no one else."

His mom breathed deeply and exhaled. "Passed out? Never mind. I don't want to know." Pacing in a circle, she continued, "I don't like it. Neither of you is experienced enough for this. Stay close to Rynn though. She's very good for being so young." *I would be too, if you taught me more. But whatever.*

"That might be a problem," he said. "We had an argument. Daryala tried to squeeze me for info. She said we could be thrown in jail. And a bunch of other things I don't know what to think about. I blamed Rynn for it. Said some things."

His mom shook her head and gritted her teeth. "That woman... Daryala... has gone through a lot. She's ruthless and tenacious. Put nothing past her. Be extremely careful." She patted him on the shoulder. "I'm sure Rynn will be okay if you talk it out. Just don't be an idiot. Every possible meaning."

Arden felt his ears redden. He wanted desperately to change the subject. "Any news on Nora, Aella, and Connie?"

She shook her head. "We have Vidaya looking. She thinks she might be getting close, but no luck so far. Our Lightborne friends have also been quiet."

"I meet with Vidaya for my practical soon. I'll ask," he told her. "And if I learn anything later today, I'll let you know when I get back."

"Okay, Arden Arinza. Stay safe."

"You too, Reina d'Martest. After I get some practice in, I want a rematch."

"You're on."

Together, the two walked up to the Irkalla Tower lift and into a new day.

29

IRMINA FAUST

T HE MAIN ROOM IN Irkalla Tower stood nearly empty. Arden guessed that the voting day revelers were at home sleeping off the prior night's festivities and preparing for their resumption today. Banners hung from four locations displaying voting results, but he shrugged in disinterest. Instead, he sauntered in front of the world clock where Noire had given him a high-level explanation of how time worked in the Abzu and Infra. His thoughts were held captive for a moment by the idea that so many places all over the world could be connected to this smidgeon of space called the Abzu Complex. While the clock marched forward to time's beat, he mindlessly watched the seconds slip past.

The timepiece read eight-thirty in the morning, which meant he had thirty minutes before his orientation session with Vidaya was set to begin. At first he considered contacting Rynn and trying to set things right, but he wasn't ready. Not owing to anger or resentment, but entirely because he didn't know what to say to her. Instead, he pulled Noire into a direct call using the KALM-ER phone.

"Hey, Noire. Can you and Tuck meet me in a private place for a quick talk? I'm in the tower and I only have... twenty-nine minutes," he said.

Her voice sounded worried. "We went back to Medical Services this morning, but you were already gone. Meet us at our spot in the Ledge."

"Be down in five," he said, striding toward the elevator.

When Arden exited the lift, it took him a moment to get his bearings. After taking the wrong turn twice, he remembered the way, and a few minutes later knocked on the door and entered the room where his two friends sat waiting. They greeted him with smiles. Somehow, yesterday's events with Reshenu seemed to have happened weeks prior.

He exhaled, puffing out his cheeks, then told them in a hushed voice, "Daryala wants me... or us... to give her info about anything we find in the Infra. She threatened to throw everyone involved in prison, and even brought up execution. I wanted to warn you—see if it might not be a good idea to be somewhere else for a while."

Tuck's smile had faded from his face as Arden talked. "Damn. Not sure what to think about that."

Noire grinned sarcastically. "At least you won't have to worry about being poor anymore, Tuck."

"Not quite what I imagined," he replied, stretching his hands above his head. "But thanks for the tip. I think it might be time to go on a long Delve, Noire. They'll be watchin' us, but they can't follow everywhere. Branthumville? See if Beyd can hook us up with one of those fancy portable Fabricators."

She bobbed her head in agreement, fully serious now, "Right. We need Deveras to deactivate these Edict implants. We'll have to be discreet. Can you call him while I show Arden what we found?" Tuck sidled over to a corner of the room to contact the Seeker mission leader.

Arden's ears perked up. "You found something? About the Ten or the Linzers?"

Noire shrugged. "The second one. Maybe. When you mentioned seeing Nora Linzer in the Compendium, I had an idea. Based on your story that got us into this Edict mess"—she cleared her throat to drive her point home, then went on—"we looked at CADS records. There was information on N. Everton from California, an Aboveworlder who had given birth to a Darktouched child. The record is very redacted, but we were able to dig up the daughter's Darkname. Irmina Faust. She Disavowed."

Running a hand through his sandy brown hair, Arden spoke deliberately. "The Linzers had a daughter. Her name was... bah!" *But if I can't say her Abovename, does that mean she's still alive?* "Anytime they spoke of her, they seemed sad. It fits too well not to be part of our puzzle." *The Linzers had a Darktouched child. No wonder they were protective of me.*

Noire was peering up at him questioningly when Tuck stole her attention. Scratching his head, he stated, "Deveras said he'd have Beyd remove the implants. We should go while the gettin' is good."

Noire jumped up from her seat. To his surprise, she gave Arden a quick hug. "I'm sorry we couldn't help you more. Be safe, idiot."

Tuck giggled. "Take care, kid. We'll be fine. Thanks—and no thanks—to you. We'll see you soon."

"Thanks for everything. Hopefully this Daryala thing blows over," said Arden. They left the room, Arden heading back to the elevator and his friends slipping off to the spiral staircase.

When Arden returned to the tower's main level, still ten minutes early, Vidaya was already waiting. Her back was turned to the elevator. Sensing an opportunity, he snuck forward to stand next to her. He saw her eyes shift left, watched as startled realization hit her, and laughed when she gave a tiny squeak.

"Good morning, Arden Arinza," she said snippily. "First the wings and now this. Children nowadays have no respect. Stop giggling like a schoolboy," she went on chastising him. "On the elevator. Floor 12 for the Child Assignment & Disavowed Support main offices. I hate the acronym *CADS*."

Even though he was facing away, Arden felt her eagle-like gaze fixated on him. During the ride up, he shuffled awkwardly until saying guiltily, "Sorry, Vidaya.

I shouldn't have snuck up on you." *I need to remember to ask her about Irmina Faust.*

"It's fine. Come now, I have much to show you this morning," she told him, stepping out of the compartment. "My office is just over here." They walked across the footbridge to the outside ring of the tower and into a cozy, warm office. A round, brightly colored mandala rug occupied the center of the room, and the spicy aroma of masala chai permeated the small space.

Vidaya motioned for him to sit and called a black display panel down from the ceiling. Without bringing anything up on the screen, she began to talk. "We of the... *CADS* discipline administrate Darktouched child placement and Disavowed services. This includes not only placing liberated children, but supporting mixed families as well as those Darktouched who opt to give up their offspring."

Arden shifted uneasily in his chair, unable to resist the urge to ask questions. "After being here a bit, I understand liberating Darktouched children. I don't really agree with it, but I get it." He tapped a finger on the wooden chair arm. "Darktouched giving up their kids seems almost worse. How is that okay?"

Vidaya sighed. "That is difficult. The chances of a child who does not possess the Right inheriting it are infinitesimal. Those parents are forever bound to a world that their children cannot inhabit. It's a cruel twist of fate, and one might argue our response to it is equally cruel. I have nothing more to say. It is what it is. I would like to discuss Disavowed Services, which is my primary focus."

Arden rocked back in his seat and nodded. "Everything concerning CADS is the hardest thing for me to accept about this place."

Vidaya shrugged and looked at the floor. "Sometimes, it is for me also. Before we go further, let me explain some things that you probably missed because of how you reached the Abzu Complex. The Darktouched missions operate nearly everywhere in the Aboveworld. Our maximum population limit is unknown, but we average perhaps nine thousand, plus or minus. Thus, each mission has to be efficient to function." As she tipped a cup to her lips, her eyes went wide. "I must apologize, Arden. How rude of me. I did not offer you any refreshments.

Please." She slid a tin across the desk and rose from her seat to pour him a cup of tea.

Arden opened the container and removed a thin, parallelogram-shaped white pastry. Taking a bite, he found it just the right amount of sweet. As it melted in his mouth and the milky, nutty flavor ignited his taste buds, he immediately popped the rest in his mouth and grabbed another. "What are these? They're delicious." Taking the cup Vidaya offered, he took a sip of chai.

"Kaju katli. They're made of cashew flour mostly. I'm glad you enjoy them." The smile that had briefly lit up her face disappeared as she returned to business. "Mission efficiency is possible because of how our world works. There are Abzu Hubs dotting the entire globe. Compendium records suggest you met Charon in the outer ring of the Flagstaff Hub, so you've seen a smaller one. Each of the Hubs has an outer ring that connects to the main station. All of these stations route to the same arrival terminal just above the top barrier. This would be impossible if the Abzu Complex were only a geographical location."

Arden reasoned, "So, somewhere between each station and the Complex, everyone enters a kind of shared space."

Vidaya nodded. "Something like a server instance for a website. But that's very technical," she said. "You can also think of it this way. We Darktouched inhabit the inner fabric of the world. Its soul, if you want to be spiritual."

Arden recalled Ninazu's words and spoke them out loud. "Not only beneath the world but also within it."

"Precisely. I could not have said it better myself," she proclaimed. "I say this because the Darktouched Right has both corporeal and spiritual components. When a person Disavows, for example, we can cover up the physical and mental entanglements. Abilities sealed. Memories forgotten. However, an extreme longing for this place remains. We do not have a way to solve that problem. The unfulfilled Right is beyond unbearable for most Disavowed." Arden began to ask another question, but Vidaya stopped him. "Before you say anything, I want to share something highly confidential with you. As you know, Deveras and Reina asked me to find Nora Linzer and two young people I understand to be your friends."

"Right," confirmed Arden. "We grew up together."

Vidaya rubbed her right forearm across her eyes. "No one else knows this, but Nora came to me days ago. Your friends are safe in hiding."

"What? How? The banished Lightborne sent us a note saying the Linzers betrayed us," he said dubiously.

Her eyes became puffy, eroding her eagle-woman persona. "I concealed them because I do not agree with Malank's plan. Not to excuse their actions, but I believe Alan and Nora had similar reasons. Please, let me explain." Arden saw the image of a young woman appear on the display panel. "I believe you saw this woman in the Compendium yesterday. It is not, as you believed, Nora Linzer."

Suddenly comprehending, Arden blurted out, "Irmina Faust. It's her daughter. I think she's still alive."

Vidaya gulped and then uttered, "You and your friends have been diligent indeed. Yes, Irmina. Hers is a tragic tale. Like you, Malank believed her an ideal candidate." *Ideal candidate for what?* "A Darktouched girl with a Lightborne father. You can imagine how his penchant for luck made that appetizing."

Arden interjected, "I'm sorry, Vidaya. No one has ever told me what their plan is. I have no idea what you're talking about."

She leaned back in her chair, tears welling in her eyes. "It is hardly my place to tell you this, but they believe *you* are the key to unlocking the Source. True Darkness, where, according to our myths, the deepest wisdom of the world resides. You and Irmina are highly attuned to Nabucite. They want to grant you Light's Gift... to make you both Darktouched and Lightborne at once."

"If it's that easy, why hasn't it been done before?"

"It *has* been done before. Many times over the centuries, if I had to guess. I have never seen what happens with my own eyes, but I know the result is always death, without fail." Tears were streaming down her cheeks now. "For this reason, over their protests and claims she would be safe, Irmina ran from her destiny with Nora's help. I have hidden her ever since. When Deveras came to me, after the death of the last boy, I couldn't say no lest they suspect my earlier... indiscretion."

Arden stood, his legs and voice shaky. "Why me? Other than an attunement to Nabucite, there's nothing special about me. Is there?"

Vidaya wiped her face and eyes. "Malank thinks you are extraordinary. For you see, the Darktouched Right came to you on the very day that boy died."

"You're telling me *this* is why the Reclaimers came to my home?" Arden spoke quietly, processing more than asking. "My entire life is a mess because one crazy banished Lightborne thinks I'm his good luck charm?"

"In a word, yes," answered Vidaya. "For these reasons, I hid Irmina. But I was unable to do the same for you. They watched you more closely. Treated you with greater kindness. Kept your parents uninformed, I believe. Reina, at least, seems to know nothing." Reaching for a tissue, she blew her nose. "Why the Linzers decided to betray the plan, I cannot say with absolute certainty. Nora asked me to hide your friends and then left. I do not know where she went."

Arden paced the room, unsure what to ask. *At least my friends are safe. That's one less worry.* Distracted, he banged his shin against a squat end table and swore. *Mom said that Deveras believed in the plan and that it was risky for me. But this sounds like walking in front of a firing squad and hoping they miss.* He sat down again, grabbed another pastry, and swallowed the entire cup of chai. *Maybe I am special though, somehow. There must be more than luck behind what Malank and Fiala believe.* As the thought entered his mind, he wondered silently whether it developed out of ego or logic.

Vidaya's eagle visage had returned now, although pity still tinged her eyes and brow. "Arden, please listen. I realize this is a heavy burden, but I wanted you to know the truth to the extent I know it. There may be things beyond my understanding at work. You need to talk with the Lightborne. Do not worry—they cannot give you the Gift without your acceptance." She blew her nose again and then added, "And do not forget who the real enemy is. The Lightwatch is the cause of all of this. They hunt us, steal what they can, and kill or sell our people for ransom once they've used us up. The banished Lightborne are also subjected to terrible, unspeakable atrocities if caught. That is everything I know."

Arden finally found his words. "Thank you for being honest with me. It means more than anything. It's difficult for me to ignore that they're all using me. Sending me to my death probably. I mean, they say that I have a choice, but do I? As for the Lightwatch, what are they really after? We fear them, hide from them, some are even preparing to go to war with them. What's their goal?"

Vidaya slumped in her chair, looking like she might cry again. "I'm sorry, Arden. I don't know. I'm not sure who would except for the banished Lightborne." For a moment she stopped, seeming to wonder whether her next words were worth speaking. "When I asked Beyd for permission to run this orientation, it was so I could see you, meet you, and try to help you. I've done what I can. I'm not even sure it was the right thing to do. Please, tread cautiously and be safe." Holding up the index finger on her left hand, which remained resting on the desk, she said, "By the way, the practical sessions are not required to pass orientation. I made that up so you would talk to me today. I am sorry for that also."

Arden forced a smile onto his face, put his hand over hers across the desk, looked her firmly in the eyes, and walked out of the room.

30

WISDOM'S BOND

CRIMSON POOLS FORMED IN fields of white. Beginning as mere dots, then expanding, converging, and spreading to the edges, puddling lifeblood on the cavern's surface. For an hour, Arden sat alone on a bench overlooking the faraway blossoms. Occasionally, the tapping of footsteps would ring through the nearly empty chamber and a person would pass by, briefly obstructing his view.

The events with Reshenu now seemed a lifetime away. *What am I doing here? Will Eresh have answers? Or do I have to choose between death versus a life in hiding, like Irmina?* Knowing that answers would elude him forever if he remained idle, he fought the salty, nauseating feeling rising from his salivary glands and called Rynn. When she answered right away, he was plagued by anxiety.

Quietly, he said, "Can you meet me at the benches underneath the tower? I'll explain what's going on."

"I'll be there in ten minutes," she replied, and dropped off the line.

Mindlessly, Arden ambled through the revolving doors and stepped onto the lift. Just to feel something other than dread, he leapt off the platform and let himself fall, not opening his wings until he was two-thirds of the way down. Reminded of his dream the night prior, but also fearing the utter finality of playing the game too long, he relented, gliding to an easy landing not far from the benches where he planned to meet Rynn.

She arrived minutes later and sat down on the same bench, leaving a space between them. "Where are we going and why?" she asked brusquely.

Swallowing to suppress the cocktail of vitriol and gloom rising in his throat like bile, Arden looked at her and spoke quietly. "I was wrong this morning, and I apologize for the ugly things I said. When Daryala threatened me and my family, I lost my head and took it out on you." He paused to let the words hang in the air, but Rynn made no sign she heard him. Eyes now turned toward the ground but seeing nothing, he continued, "The bracelet was given to me by Eresh. She asked that we seek her out together, you and I. I'm sending you the coordinates now."

Rynn scoffed. "Eresh. Really? You're out of your mind."

"Yeah," he said. *Let it go. It won't matter soon anyway.* "It's fine if you don't believe me. She told me to bring you. Said the bracelet was how I'd convince you."

She faced him now, brow furrowed in doubt. When their eyes met, her expression changed to one of inquisitiveness. "What happened to you? Something's off."

He began to speak, but hesitated. *You can trust her more than anyone. So said the owl! ... I really am insane.* Mind made up, he answered, "I'll tell you on the way. Do you know where those coordinates are?"

"Zone Ganzir. It's at least a four-hour trip. We should go," she told him.

They traveled separately while talking over the comm, shadesurfing further than Arden ever had before. Eventually, they passed through a portal. He told Rynn the entirety of his tale so far. However, not fully trusting her or his owl visions, he withheld Vidaya's admission that she had secreted away Irmina and now Aella and Connie. Once he had finished, they carried on in silence for another hour. When a second portal crept into sight, he followed her lead and shadesurfed in.

On the other side, Rynn spoke in an even tone. "It's still another hour, but that was the last portal. Your story is a lot to take in. I need more time." They fell into a companionable silence for the remainder of the way, advancing through broad swaths of Infra where only an occasional tiny floating island interrupted the nothingness.

Arden swiveled his head, listening for the sound of beating wings and scanning for anything unusual. Once, far in the distance to their left, he thought he saw a faint light glide past. But because the KALM-ER suit's advanced HUD wasn't displaying anything, he ignored it.

They had been traveling for three and a half hours when a structure materialized on the horizon. At first, he thought it was a large hourglass hovering in the darkness. But as they drew nearer, he realized it was actually two pyramid-shaped buildings joined at their pointed tops, mirroring each other.

In his HUD, Arden opened the instructions given to him by Reshenu. Ending the hush, he said to Rynn, "Eresh says we enter via the orb where the two pyramids come together. The words are cryptic after that. They read, 'Together and alone, extinguish the light. Then the way will open.'"

"That makes as much sense as anything else you've told me," she replied. "At least there's something out here. For a long time, I thought we'd only find empty space."

Arden stared up and down the object, alternating his focus more rapidly the closer he and Rynn came to the enormous hourglass. Visions of the buildings collapsing into each other, killing him and Rynn, played out in his mind. Reaching the center did nothing to ease his apprehension. The mirrored structures were built from a white metallic substance and connected by just a few square feet at the tip of each. A Nabucite sphere encased the coupling and was bordered by a hovering catwalk.

They touched down on the walkway, and Arden heard an unfamiliar voice in his head. "When you are both ready to proceed with the test, touch the orb at the same time. Do not forget that failure is death."

Rynn turned toward him, tapping her right index finger against her ear. "You heard that?" Arden confirmed that he had. "Are you ready for whatever this is?"

He shrugged. *It's not like I have a real choice anyway.* When he put his hand on the Nabucite, she did the same.

Suddenly, Arden was separated from his body. The conscious part of him soared high into the upper pyramid, pulled into its center. Surrounding him was penetrating, scraping darkness, like that of the Deep Infra. Here he was blind. Upon his body, he wore heavy equipment wholly unlike his KALM suit. Power coursed through him, but his movements felt slow. A shield like a scutum, nearly as tall as he was and glowing around the edges with a soft red light, grew out of his left arm.

From behind, he heard a soft noise and spun to face it. Before he could remember to raise the shield, a force impacted his legs, sweeping him off his feet. Pain coursed through his ribs as he landed awkwardly on the ground. While climbing to an upright position, he heard another sound and twirled around, looking for danger without knowing what it was.

Rynn's voice touched his brain. "Arden, can you hear me? I can't see anything. Whatever is in here is kicking my ass."

"Do you only have a shield too?" he asked, raising the defensive implement against unseen threats.

It was then that he understood. A small section at the top of the shield offered him a limited view into the darkness. Spinning around, he saw that he was trapped on a round, floating platform perhaps fifteen feet in diameter. Something flitted across his narrow field of vision and streaked to his right.

Rynn answered. "No, I have a spear. And I can kind of see now. There's a small window floating around in front of me."

Arden felt a blunt force impact him from behind, nearly knocking him to the ground again. Regaining his balance, he spoke urgently. "I think we're connected somehow. Wherever I point this shield, I can see. Keep your eyes on the window. Stay centered. Kill anything that moves."

Straining his senses, he waited for another stirring in the darkness. "Three o'clock," he shouted, whirling to his right and keeping the shield lifted. A human figure in Reclaimer garb bore down upon him, swinging a cudgel made of light at his head. Bracing for impact, he ducked under the blow. From nowhere, the glowing shape of a halberd shot toward the attacker, impacting it squarely in the chest. With a burst of light visible only through the shield, it was gone.

"Is it over?" Rynn's voice asked.

Arden felt a vibration in the air behind him and swiftly faced it. Just in time, he saw red needles flying toward him and positioned the shield to intercept them. "Are you okay?" he called out to Rynn.

"Yeah, barely. Don't forget to call out directions. I can't see without you, remember?" she said back to him.

He heard footsteps to his left. "Ten o'clock!" Two strikes crashed against the shield at the same time, causing his teeth to rattle and his arm to ache. Driven to one knee by the brutal force, he pushed back with both arms. The halberd swung in front of him and removed the head of one enemy. While it exploded in a burst of light, the weapon flashed in and out of sight as Rynn brought it slicing down into the shoulder of the other. It collapsed to the floor, dead, and then dematerialized as its companion had.

Seconds passed, and Arden neither heard nor saw anything. But he sensed danger regardless. The hair on his arms and the back of his neck stood on end. An audible emptiness emanated from directly above. Raising the shield overhead, he saw a man with glowing white skin and unnaturally blue eyes clothed in radiant white. "Straight up, Rynn. Watch out!"

The man approached like death—slowly, deliberately, and relentlessly. Without a sound, he surged toward Arden with unexpected speed, causing his legs to buckle. As Arden crumpled to the ground, he saw the halberd leap into the air, but the robed man effortlessly evaded Rynn's strike and vanished beneath the platform. No more than a second later, Arden signaled to her and crouched low as the monster attacked again. This time, he tried to dodge, but the enemy anticipated his movements and struck his right leg, toppling him over.

Sharing the blow, Rynn screamed in pain and called out, "It's a Severed! I've never seen one in person, but they're very deadly. When it comes again, you're going to have to man up. I'll take care of the rest, but you need to give me an opening."

Wincing and favouring his left limb, Arden stood, the dull ache in his right fibula almost unbearable. "Got it," he said. "I don't think I can take more than a couple more hits." Overwhelming terror gripped him again. "Five o'clock!" Pivoting rapidly, he stiffened his body with his full might. The Severed grew blindingly bright as it battered the shield—swiping, punching, and clawing—trying to rend the darkness and the Darktouched cloaked in it. Exhausted, arms numb, Arden felt his legs buckle. Then, in his peripheral vision, he watched as the halberd slashed through the midsection of the robed figure, rending it in two.

The instant it died, Arden was pulled back into his body. No pain remained from the battle. Rynn returned also, and they removed their hands from the Nabucite orb at the same time. The voice from before once again sounded in Arden's head. "Congratulations. You have exemplified Wisdom's Bond and proven yourselves worthy to train as Sentinels. Please proceed to the Cradle."

Within the Nabucite, a shimmering blue portal emerged. Neither of them said anything as they strode through together.

31

THE CRADLE

ARDEN AND RYNN WALKED into a wide cavern mouth. Straight ahead stood an enormous sealed gateway constructed of the same greenish-blue stones as the buildings in old Y'Sham. Familiar with the ancient doorway markings, Arden moved toward the righthand side of the main gate. The stones moved aside and allowed them passage through a long corridor that sloped upward. *I wonder if they reacted to my suit or me.*

At the end of the hall, there was a familiar blue barrier. Arden crossed the threshold, and Rynn followed a few steps behind. The walls opened around them in the shape of a circle as wide as the Abzu Complex's cavern. Looking up, Arden began to comprehend the scale of the place. The stonework towered so high that it seemed to have no end. From his vantage point, no elevator or stairway was available to assist in the ascent. On the floor in the center of the structure, markings signified what he imagined to be massive gateways leading into the Infra.

They did not have to imagine for very long. Within a minute of their arrival, a lone woman descended on a platform of pure darkness tethered to two serpentine dragons. Garbed in a deathly black gambeson that was cinched at the waist, abyssal plate armor, and a horned helmet with a face mask, she struck a menacing figure. The dark halberd slung across her back, outlined in glowing red like the one Rynn had wielded during the earlier battle, made clear how lethal she was.

Gliding to a halt ten feet in front of them, she smoothly leapt from the platform and strode over. Her helmet dissolved in accord with some unseen command, and the face of a lithe, pretty woman with long hair tied into a single braid greeted them. She appeared to be in her forties, but Arden knew she was many times that age. Even though she maintained a neutral countenance, her eyes were sad and marked by crow's feet. Arden found her voice soothing.

"Welcome to the Cradle, Arden Arinza and Corynna Darkspear. I am known to you as Eresh. We meet at last. Come." Turning her body, she motioned with an arm for them to join her on the carriage platform. Without hesitating, they stepped onto the chariot of darkness. Issuing another silent command, Eresh bade the dragons to rise, and they slowly ascended the mammoth chamber. Each floor of the towering building measured thirty feet high, and Arden noticed ovular indentations in the floor as well as massive tubes running outward from them.

Perceiving his curiosity, Eresh told him, "Before the Reshaping, we bred dragons and other creatures of the depths here, both for defense and exploration. After I forged the Second Covenant with Tiamat, everything stopped. It had to. Although, as you can see, some of the creatures remained our friends." She looked at Arden and Rynn for a moment, and then added, "You can remove your suits. This is a sanctuary for all creatures and people. Even Lightborne."

Rynn withdrew her gear first, a look of consternation on her face. "Aren't you supposed to be the founder of the Darktouched? You really consort with *them*?" By now, Arden had removed his suit as well.

Eresh's mouth turned up into a thin smile. "For one who knows so little, you seem to know much. Don't worry, Rynn. You'll understand soon." Rynn folded her arms across her chest, obviously seething.

"Where is this place?" asked Arden, thinking back to his conversation with Vidaya. "We can't be in the Infra anymore. Is it below the Abzu?"

Eresh shook her head. "An extension of it. In the Aboveworld, there is something called the Milwaukee Depth. It is the deepest point in the Atlantic Ocean. Far under the water, there lies an ancient remnant of Y'Sham. For invited guests that know the way, those ruins offer a way into the Cradle."

After ascending for five minutes, living stones in the ceiling opened up. The group dismounted in an area with many small rectangular buildings spread out in every direction. At one end, a staircase rose toward a palatial structure.

"These were once the homes and facilities of our soldiers, support staff, and their families. For centuries, we maintained a strong alliance with the people of Y'Sham. And yes, even the Lightborne for a time."

Rynn and Arden both stared in surprise when they saw people milling about in the distance. Eresh smiled again and told them, "As I said, this remains a sanctuary for *all* people. Of course, now most are Darktouched. In the past, we sat together in the roost below and watched races between our fastest riders. It was a better time, in some ways."

Following Eresh, they ascended the palace staircase and entered a room with a long table placed in its center that was encircled by many ornate chairs. Her armor dissolved as the helmet had earlier, revealing tight-fitting black clothing that covered her entire body except her hands and head. Bypassing the main hall, she brought them into a side room with a smaller table and six chairs. A cabinet-sized Fabricator rested in one corner.

"Please, make yourselves at home," she said, kneeling down next to the machine. "Would either of you like anything to eat or drink?"

Rynn shook her head, but Arden lit up at the chance. "Both, please. I haven't eaten anything in hours. I don't mind surprises." *Although that might have to change, all things considered.* Eresh smiled and input an order into the Fabricator.

Once they were settled, Rynn and Arden waited for their host to speak. When she did, her only words were, "Let's begin with questions *you* must have."

Rynn spoke up immediately, a fierceness in her eyes. "If you really are Eresh, why aren't you helping your people? The Lightborne have been hunting us for centuries. My adopted family... How did you get the bracelet?"

Eresh smiled, a touch of pity in her eyes. "Since the Reshaping, which is now more than fourteen thousand, two hundred and three years ago, I have kept a constant watch over the Darktouched. My goal has been preserving my Second Covenant with Tiamat, ensuring the Abzu Complex and Irkalla Tower remain at peace and unscathed." Pausing to take a sip of water, she let her smile drop. "As for your adopted family, an effort *was* made. When our people from the Cradle arrived, they were already dead. Strange behavior for Lightwatch Reclaimers to kill without first taking their due, wouldn't you say?"

Rynn frowned, answering coldly. "What are you not saying?"

Eresh shook her head. "For now, I will tell you nothing more. But I promise you, before you leave this place, you will know."

Her focus shifted to Arden. Taking the cue, he asked, "Why did you invite us here? Speaking for myself, I'm nothing special."

Her knowing smile had returned, and Arden felt uneasy. *Kilk was right. It's maddening.* She looked him in the eyes and answered, "A plan was concocted long ago by a great man with a noble vision."

Arden interjected indignantly, "If you mean Malank, I know about his great plan for me. He's a gambling lunatic and I'm a sacrifice."

Eresh glared at him, and the room grew cold. Like a scolded child, Arden shrunk in his chair and became utterly silent as she said, "Please, do not interrupt. It is in poor taste." Her smile returned and the chill abated as she spoke again. "A plan that has since been taken up by fools, as you so eloquently point out. But, flawed though he may be, Malank Linwell has a good heart and is more right than wrong. Fiala Vihur also." She stopped talking to cough a few times, then continued, "That said, they are not the only ones who have... appropriated said plan. The one calling herself Daryala Gindir is playing a dangerous game— Please do not interrupt me again." Eresh glowered at them and then sipped her water.

Arden glanced at Rynn and smirked. He was surprised when she smiled back. Seeing them, Eresh said, "You two *are* special. It has rarely happened that two individuals with such strong Nabucite affinity also have the potential to invoke Wisdom's Bond. Your performance in the trial earlier is testament to your innate abilities."

Rynn raised her hand smugly. Unamused, Eresh waved a finger, signaling her to speak. "What does that mean? Wisdom's Bond? And what's a Sentinel?" asked Rynn.

"It means that in tandem you are far more powerful than you can ever be apart. In a sense, you are fated to be together. Before either of you asks, Wisdom's Bond cannot be mistaken for romantic feelings. But one thing can reinforce the other, in theory." Eresh smiled again, seeming to take pleasure in the embarrassed silence she had created. "It means that as one of you learns new abilities and grows in strength and knowledge, so does the other in equal proportion. While you don't share a consciousness, you are two-as-one, and one-as-two. There has not been a Wisdom Sentinel pairing since before the Reshaping. My sons, in fact, were the last."

Arden, unable to resist, pressed further. "How would we become Wisdom Sentinels?"

Eresh shook her head again. "Before either of you leaves this place, I will show you. But you must decide individually and together. I cannot force you." Abruptly, she got up from her chair and walked out of the room, calling around the corner, "I apologize, but it seems we have unexpected guests. Please wait."

When Eresh was out of earshot, Rynn whispered to Arden, "I'm sorry too. For this morning, I mean. This is crazy, right?"

He grinned for a moment and replied, "Just a bit. Being a Sentinel sounds kind of awesome though, doesn't it?"

"I'm not gonna lie. It really does."

When Eresh returned, she had two strangers in tow that wore long, dark hooded cloaks and face coverings. The taller of the two reached a hand up to expose their face, and Arden's mouth gaped. The guests were Malank and Fiala.

He felt a lump forming in his throat and rage welling up from within. "You! Why are you here?"

The smile that had begun to form behind Malank's thick, red beard vanished instantly. "Oh, no. Wait... kid. What's your Darkname?"

"Arden," he replied curtly. "Have you two been hiding down here the entire time? I thought you were looking for my dad and Alan."

Fiala answered him. "Hello, Arden. And no. We've been searching up top this whole time. *Someone*," she looked askance at Malank, "insisted we come down here. Going on about destiny's winds, as usual."

Holding a hand to the charm around his neck, Malank said defensively, "Well, look! They're both here. A fated meeting." *Both? They know Rynn too?*

"Are you for real?" Arden shot back. "I found out about Irmina Faust. Was what you did to her *fate*?"

Malank scratched behind his right ear nervously. "We've made mistakes over the years, Fi and I, but this time is different. Please, look at Alazar's charm. The only other time this happened was the day the Darktouched Right passed to you, Arden." Grabbing the oblong teal pendant hung around his neck, he displayed it to everyone in the room. The light within was dazzling.

With a murderous look on his face, Arden flew from his chair and punched the much larger man squarely in the face. Malank made no effort to stop him, taking blow after blow seemingly unphased. When Arden had worn himself out and retreated to his chair, Malank smiled down at him, saying, "I'm sorry, Arden. But please listen to what we have to say. All of us." Reaching up, he lifted the leather strap over his head and set the pendant on the table.

From the jewel materialized the image of a man. He looked much like Arden, but with darker hair and eyes. The voice that left his lips was soft but forceful.

"So the secret's finally out, eh, Malank?" Eying Arden, the illusion said, "He's not just some fate-obsessed fool, Arden. Well... he is, but it's warranted. I'm Alazar Almaz. Or I was before I died. Let's catch you up, shall we?"

32

THE SEVEN THAT WERE TEN

T WO SMALL PITCHERS OF ancient brew, drinking cups, and three plates of flatbread and cheese rested on the small table. Alazar's image floated above the porcelain dinnerware that subtly reflected the fate charm's soothing teal light.

Arden sat quietly between Eresh and Rynn, his anger having subsided, munching and taking an occasional swig of beer. Between bites, he would sometimes stop to examine his bruised knuckles and then scowl at Malank, who looked totally unscathed. Mostly though, he stared at the intricate silver patterns inlaid in the pitchers. Flowing lines depicted the Hulpa spirit when it yet lived, surrounded by humans and creatures of the dark.

The Lightborne had removed their cloaks and now lounged casually in their chairs. Both looked drained, and Arden wondered whether it was because of the past nine days or being below ground, out of their element.

Alazar's projection was tall enough that he looked down on those seated around the table. When everyone was settled, he began speaking. "The easiest place to begin is the beginning. The Ten's beginning, to be precise. Do you have a question, Arden?"

Arden, his interest piqued, leaned forward in his chair. "Eresh, Ninazu, and her two sons were four of the Ten, right?" He looked at Eresh, who remained expressionless. Malank and Fiala glanced at each other briefly but said nothing.

"Not quite right. Eresh's sons were not of the Ten. Let me explain," said Alazar. "In a time before Y'Sham existed, a coalition of many nations was formed. Not entirely dissimilar to today, wars raged and disaster loomed. Desperate, this league assembled several handpicked units. These groups were to seek out and retrieve lost technology from sites already considered mythical. It was sanctioned looting. One squad, blessed or cursed by fate, found something." He paused to glance at Eresh, who maintained her unreadable expression. "In that place, the raiders met fierce resistance from nature and beast alike. But they persevered, cutting their way deeper until they arrived on the edge of a lake filled with liquid light. A voice called to them from a place unseeable, telling them not to fear, to step forward onto the lake's surface. One of the Ten, named Bau, bravely did so, amazed that she remained upright. Afterward, the Ten walked together to the lake's very center, anticipating treasure, plunder."

Eresh raised her eyes to Arden and Rynn, then continued the story in Alazar's place. "There, they found a soft, pulsing light. The voice offered them a choice. They could accept Light's Gift and use it for the betterment of mankind, or walk away forever. All agreed to take the Gift." A sad sigh escaped her as she breathed her next words. "Tragically, they were attacked while leaving the sacred place, and Bau gave her life to save the others. Before the Ten ever exercised their newfound power, they were cut to Nine."

Seven, Eight, Nine, Ten. The thought reminded Arden of Tuck and Noire. He visualized them arguing over something trivial while Delving inside of a Branthumville ruin.

Alazar sat cross-legged now, facing Arden and Rynn. "With the Gift, they were remade by the Light and gained access to the Lightwatch. In that place, where they possessed immense power, they learned to harness the Light to predict future events. For the power of Light is knowledge." With a forlorn, faraway gaze, he went on, "At first, they were reckless, giving their Gift freely and commanding their followers to do the same. The more people who possessed the Gift, the Nine reasoned, the greater their knowledge pool. Eventually though, they came to understand that data is not meaning."

Arden remembered Alan Linzer's words. *The Lightwatch leaders live in an echo chamber. Every single one is greedy for data that will fix the future before it's broken.*

Eresh once again spoke, her tone somber. "Yes, young Darktouched, the Nine were the original Lightborne. As the centuries wore on, they limited their council to mighty lords, intervening to prevent many wars and disasters. Still, no matter how many tragedies they averted, more loomed. Vexed, two of us turned to the Darkness in search of wisdom, hopeful to complement what the Light lacked." She paused to take a breath, then told them, "Through a pact with the Darkmother, a being named Tiamat, Ninazu and I subverted our Gift. Yet True Darkness and wisdom remained out of reach, for we had merely created Light's shadow. A paltry imitation. Now, only seven remained in the Light."

She turned to Alazar to continue the tale. He spoke quietly, and Arden thought he seemed ashamed. "After the Reshaping, I was elected to lead the Seven. Eresh and I remained friends, but at her request I withheld this from the other six. With her family gone, she sought solace in solitude. Not knowing what else to do, I led the work of gathering knowledge and preventing catastrophe for millennia. We became excellent, I think, at identifying key individuals—Lightborne candidates—who could help us make a greater impact. But I had begun to think it was all for naught when a notion struck me. In the centuries that followed, I analyzed data, grew my lineage carefully, and at last came upon an answer. In order for it to work though, a series of events, including my death, had to occur." Alazar now rotated to face Malank and Fiala. "I think the rest of the tale is yours."

Malank drained his glass and began to speak in his deep, rumbling voice. "After Al passed away, we six did the best we could to stay the course." He glanced up at Arden and nodded. "Yes, Fi and I are of the Ten. Anyway, we elected Chen Huang to succeed in leadership. He did admirably at first. But as his frustration with our limitations grew, his methods turned severe. He became obsessed with the Darktouched, viewing them as thieves. Rats, he called them. The Reclaimers were established to take back what belonged to the Lightwatch, in his view. For the Dim, as we call those who lack the Gift, he was a worse kind of

monster. To stop bad things, he did terrible things. Millions died. In the year…"
He glanced at Fiala.

Tapping her foot, Fiala offered up, "Around AD 1645."

"Right," said Malank. "Three of us broke away, giving up our right to enter the Lightwatch. Banished. A Lightborne with no access to the Lightwatch is a miserable creature, but Senna found ways to tide us over. Through her inventions, we've been able to survive and even grow small lineages. The Linzers are of my Gift's family tree, so to speak. And there are others. But you must understand, for the lesser Lightborne, being unable to enter the Lightwatch is a source of punishing unfulfillment. It's similar to being Disavowed, but worse."

Arden interjected, "Hold on. Why does Chen think the Darktouched stole from him? And are Connie and Aella suffering? Alan said they were Lightborne."

Malank rocked his chair onto its back legs, and it creaked so loudly that Arden thought it would break. "Eresh, can you explain?"

"The Lightborne cannot enter the Infra safely, nor can they acquire its knowledge passively," Eresh said. "Without Light, they see nothing, know nothing. During the Reshaping, many technologies, information stores, and other things that Chen Huang covets were pulled into the Infra. To the Lightwatch, this is an unforgivable theft."

"Thank you, Eresh," said Malank. "As for your friends, Arden, they aren't Lightborne. But we expected them to be at some point. Aella's father is of my lineage. Conleth's uncle is of Fiala's." Complex emotions stirred within Arden as he considered how much of a sacrifice Nora Linzer had made to hide his friends. *She tried to spare them a terrible future. The Linzers both did. Just to shield me.*

Fiala tapped her foot again, more impatiently this time. "We finally got our feet under us, and then Malank told us what he knew of Alazar's plan."

Malank bobbed his head and muttered, "We were always close, Al and I. Like brothers. He gave me the fate charm and just a bit to go on before he died. I wanted to do right by him, because I believed in him. What was it you said, Al?"

Alazar responded, "That the key to my plan is a person who will inherit both True Light and True Darkness. I saw it in the Lightwatch predictive models, and thankfully everything has played out just so. More or less."

Seriously? What about the people who died because of your plan?

"We searched for inroads to the Darktouched, considering them friends with a common enemy," Malank said, continuing the story. "After years, we made contact and, with their help, began looking for the right person. We've found six over the centuries. But each time Light's Gift passed to one of them, they went mad and died." He was about to slam his huge fist on the table but thought better of it. "There was a time that I did doubt fate was on our side. When Irmina Faust, the Linzers' daughter, disappeared, I almost gave up. I began to think we were no better than Chen. Senna *had* given up. But Fi convinced us to try one more time." Arden felt a lump in his throat, because both Malank and Fiala looked ready to weep. "Another death! That poor child. And that was it. Senna walked away, and we haven't spoken since."

Fiala ran an index finger under her left eye and wiped it on her pants. "But then the pendant came alive, and Alazar spoke to us. He said it was time—the moment we had been working toward, hoping for, believing in. With his help, we found Eresh. Then the Darktouched Right passed to you, Arden. And you were born, Corynna."

Eresh stood, holding her gaze directly on Rynn. "I think now is a good time to answer your question from earlier. Lightborne, especially under Chen Huang, do not kill without first extracting information. Not ever. But someone trying to run their own version of Alazar's plan might, if their goal was to draw you closer. To control and use you. Beydin and I believe that Daryala Gindir is somehow connected to Senna."

Malank and Fiala stared at Eresh, shocked looks on their faces. Even Alazar appeared concerned, and his normally calm voice was shaken when he uttered, "Hidden in the shadows. Lightwatch predictive analytics couldn't have seen this coming. What is this Daryala doing? And why didn't you tell Malank and Fiala?"

"It's a Darktouched problem," Eresh replied curtly. "According to Beydin, she's trying to find a way to steal Lightborne power and weaponize it. There's a new KALM suit prototype. What she plans to do with it is unclear to me."

The spears and armor from the R&D lab!

Rynn leaned forward in her chair, the fierceness from earlier shining in her eyes. "If that's true, I'll kill her myself. And if Sabrath was part of this..."

Eresh shook her head, growling, "Don't throw away everything for a moment of revenge. Existence itself hangs in the balance." Returning to her chair, she spoke decisively, "If you become Sentinels, you must seek out Tiamat. Learn the truth. Become stronger. Only True Darkness can complete Light's Gift."

"And what if she succeeds?" asked Rynn. "She might be able to kill us with those weapons. I can stop her."

The room was becoming colder, and Eresh clamped her jaw shut in frustration. Closing her eyes, she spoke again. "That is extremely unwise. Beydin, at my direction, has been stalling the equipment's development. We've also been feeding bad information to the Compendium through Kilk Branthum. The old fool, obsessed with his legacy, cannot tell the difference anymore."

A silence fell over the room and Arden felt a question rising. He knew it was an inappropriate time but asked anyway. "Is Beydin a Lightborne too? One of the Ten?"

Alazar answered when Eresh remained quiet. "No, Arden. Beydin is a friend, but certainly not a Lightborne or one of the Ten."

Eresh waved a hand in exasperation. "That's not important right now. I need a break from this talking. And you two"—she pointed to Arden and Rynn—"have a very important decision to make. You must choose soon." Without another word, she walked out of the room.

"I have more questions," said Arden. "Two things have been bothering me. First, what's your plan's goal, Alazar? Second, what is Chen doing with this data?"

Alazar stood and replied, "Revealing the details now could undo the entire scheme. Please trust that my secrecy hasn't been without cause. As for Chen, your question is valid. We don't know yet, but the Lightwatch has to be stopped.

Even if their intentions are good, their methods are evil." With a bow, he concluded by adding, "I also need rest. This form is very limited." His image faded away, and the gem's light returned to a faint pulse.

Malank tapped the table with this finger. "Before we end, Arden, I have something to tell you. We found where your dad is being held. Deveras and Reina are working on meeting their demands. Do you want to be there for the exchange?"

Arden locked eyes with him. "Yes. When do we leave?"

"Tomorrow," Malank answered solemnly. "Whatever needs doing, do it before then."

"What about Alan?" Arden asked.

Malank shook his head. "We don't know for sure. None of our contacts know anything. He may be working with the Lightwatch now. That, or he ran." Arden leaned back in his chair looking dazed, and Malank patted him on the shoulder. "I'm sorry. We'll leave the two of you alone to make your big decision. Fi, I think it's time you and I had our own little chat. If the Darktouched upper ranks are compromised, that complicates things. Also! No funny business, Arden and Rynn. There's no time—well, not unless you hurry."

Arden's skin grew hot, and he fought his natural instinct to glance at Rynn. When he finally took a peek, he saw that she was also staring a hole in the floor. Laughing boisterously, Malank grabbed the jewel from the table, excused himself, and was gone. Fiala followed close behind.

When they were alone, Rynn said to Arden, without looking at him, "I want to become a Sentinel. You decide for yourself. If this is true, whatever it takes, I will kill Daryala Gindir." Then she too marched away, leaving him alone in his thoughts.

33

WISDOM SENTINELS

T HE CRADLE'S RESIDENTIAL AREA was laid out on a square plot measuring roughly half of a square mile. The houses were small, with no yards and constructed on a well-planned grid that maximized space utilization and efficiency. Services were located in the precise center, forming a tiny town square.

Arden wandered aimlessly, paying little mind to his surroundings. From the palace, he descended the steps and then walked clockwise around the perimeter. He saw very few people, and those he did seemed to shy away from strangers. Twice, when he passed houses with people out front, they quickly skittered inside and let the living rock doors seal shut behind them without a word.

In his mind's eye, he envisioned the Cradle in ancient times. Soldiers rushing about dressed in dark gambesons, plate armor, and cloaks, wearing horned helmets and wielding fearsome halberds. Fabricators churning out food and drink, providing succor to troops arriving from the battlefield. Meanwhile, well-rested men and women descended on black wings to the dragon roost below, gliding to mount dark chariots readied by expertly trained and experienced support teams. The well-oiled war machine hummed.

The Cradle had bustled with ceaseless activity as, whether above into light or below into darkness, soldiers soared to battle. They would strike at the heart of whatever nation or alliance had cropped up as the most recent threat to sustained peace and prosperity. Combined with the might of Y'Sham and the immeasurable body of knowledge held in the Lightwatch, the Darktouched of that era—allied with those creatures of the deep able to reach the surface—would have been a terrifying enemy for any opposing force.

Still, their power had not been enough to win the war. In spite of their ferocity, prowess, and dedication, they had fallen short. And their failure had left the world in such a dire state that Eresh and Ninazu had called upon Tiamat and her children to wipe the slate clean. The entire ancient world had vanished in an upwelling of darkness, leaving behind scattered fragments and lingering memories. An event so horrible that, even in modern times, myths and legends both in the Aboveworld and the depths somberly articulated the lessons to be learned from unwise decision making and recklessness.

Yet the opposite was also true. The ferocity of the conflict, the hopes and desires of those who participated, the strength and valor of survivors, heroes, and the dead—in an unending chorus blending the voices of future warriors, soldiers, civilians, historians, and so many others—echoed through the millennia to the present day.

From the bottom of his heart, thinking of his own experiences and yearning for free will, Arden wondered whether enforcing the designs of the Lightwatch by using the power of Y'Sham and the Darktouched had indeed been the right course of action. Had he been an inhabitant of that ancient past, would their forceful and controlling methods have worked on him? *Who decides what the ideal future is? Why does one small group, even if they know so much and can see so far into the future, get to tell millions of others what to believe in, what to strive for, and which endeavors and struggles are worthwhile?*

Even though Arden had traveled little, other than his adventures in the Abzu and Infra, he had seen throughout his life that peace could be weaponized to maintain a status quo advantageous to a small few. As he roamed, he pondered which side of the war he would have ended up on. *If those same events happened again tomorrow, what would I be fighting for? Freedom?*

Absorbed in his reverie, he at first failed to see the white owl perched on a house nearby. Not until it swooped down directly in front of him did he heed its presence. Its haunting voice spoke to him, "Arden Arinza, Lucas Devlin. What is freedom?"

He continued walking, letting the creature glide along behind. Rather than speaking, he reached out with his thoughts. *The ability to choose my own path without someone standing in my way. The opportunity to play my role well and experience the results of my efforts.*

The wingbeats made no sound above him, but Arden knew the bird was there. "What if your choice, your role, your efforts... are counter to those of another? What if, without malice, judgement, hatred... you stand in the way of another's freedom? Are others less worthy than you?"

He was now halfway around the perimeter of the residential area. *In that case, I suppose we're both free to choose our own path, to strive for our goals and beliefs—and to succeed or fail.*

"And if you succeed at another's expense, detriment, defeat... would that bring you peace? Does being strong, intelligent, cunning... mean that you are better? Are people truly born as equals?"

Human nature is competition. One has to win, and another has to lose. Everyone is good at something though, and they can excel at that thing. Also, being strong is no excuse for trampling over others or bullying. That should be stopped. It's not right.

"But if you stop, curtail, slow the aggressor... are you not stealing their freedom? If you aid, support, enable another... are you not choosing who is free? Are you not controlling events, picking sides, determining right and wrong?"

Should I do nothing then? Is my only real freedom to sit and watch? To go about my business and ignore everything else?

"No, negative, not. You must accept, tolerate, own. In choosing your path, you pick a side. What do you believe in? What is worth fighting for? What is worth the risk of failure?"

Then the owl flew away, and Arden continued his walk. By the time he reached the palace steps once more, he had his answer.

When Arden entered the main hall, Rynn and Eresh were sitting together at the long table, conversing. They both looked up at him expectantly.

He spoke unfalteringly. "I've made my decision. I want to find the truth, wherever it is. I want to protect my family and friends in the Abzu, Infra, and everywhere else. And I want to stop the Lightwatch from deciding how everyone else should live. I'm willing to fight for and, worst case, fail trying to accomplish those things. Not for my own freedom or survival, not for world peace, and not for revenge. That's the side I choose. If you agree, Rynn, then I want to become a Sentinel with you."

Eresh looked at him approvingly, and Rynn rose to her feet, pacing for a moment before answering. Her voice was calm and resolute. "I have to confront Daryala Gindir. It's not about revenge. I just need to know the truth. Otherwise, I agree with everything you said. Is that okay?"

Arden nodded, saying, "I get it. I have to help rescue my dad."

Eresh stood now, a smile on her face. "Follow me then. There's no time to waste."

Gracefully, she led them directly toward the back of the room and through a tall set of ornate double doors. They hugged the lefthand wall of an audience chamber with four thrones placed against the far wall. When they reached the corner, living rock shifted to the side, revealing a steep, narrow staircase. For several minutes, they descended into the structure. Finally, they turned a corner, and a few more steps brought them through another passageway. The small space they entered into reminded Arden of the dark room in his backyard, except that it had a strangely high ceiling.

The only thing in the tiny area was a stone archway, barely taller than he was. Standing next to it, Eresh motioned with her hand for them to enter. "You must both pass through. The rest will be made clear once you're inside."

Arden and Rynn glanced at each other skeptically, because they could clearly see through the archway to the wall behind it. Shrugging, Rynn went first, with Arden following immediately after.

When he crossed the threshold, a comforting feeling of warmth surrounded him. The entire space was dark, and he couldn't see anything in any direction.

Then, on the floor, a series of red circles appeared. Following them, he walked alone in the blackness until he saw a raised staircase made of the same white metal as the pyramidal structures from the Infra. The steps led to a raised platform perhaps three feet in diameter. Ascending carefully, he came to a rest at the top. In front of him was a shadowy veil hung like a curtain.

A voice reached out to him: "Arden Arinza, if you wish to share Wisdom's Bond with Corynna Darkspear, tear the veil."

Heeding the command, Arden stretched out both arms and grabbed hold of the gossamer material. With controlled force, he ripped the abyssal fabric and saw Rynn do the same across a wide chasm. The instant their eyes met, a red thread extended from the center of his chest to Rynn's. The warm feeling grew intense, and he could feel something tearing loose at the core of his being. A formless, shadowy haze left his body, traveling along the thin line.

Over the center of the divide, his phantom joined with Rynn's. Pulsing with energy and writhing like the darkness of the Deep Infra, the mass tore into two equal portions. One piece floated toward each person, and when their bodies absorbed the energy, everything vanished, and they once again stood in front of the stone arch.

Arden felt the difference immediately. Rynn's many years of weapons training, experience with KALM tech, and her refined battle sense made him more lethal. He knew it was true—there was no need to scrutinize or test. Her knowledge of the Abzu, Infra, and even things about the Aboveworld and Lightwatch augmented his own understanding. By looking at her, he could tell she was having the same experience. His many years competing in swimming and other sports, studying textbooks at his mom's insistence, and everything he had learned in the past days transferred to her.

But there was more. His control of darkness felt robust. Summoning his KALM gear was like raising his right arm. Unfurling his wings was like walking. With a thought, dark armor like they had seen Eresh wearing materialized to protect his body, and he gripped a dark halberd in his right hand. Stepping a safe distance away from Eresh and Rynn, he twirled it around his body and high overhead, tossing it in the air and catching it effortlessly as it spun back to him.

Without navigating a HUD, he sensed the presence of other Darktouched and was able to reach out to them with his mind.

Now, after becoming a Sentinel, Arden felt confident he and Rynn could make the journey into the deepest abyss where Tiamat awaited them.

He heard Rynn speaking in his head. "I feel like something's been missing until now. This is unreal."

With feelings not words, he told her that he agreed. Although his thoughts were his own, the barrier separating his being from hers was no longer extant. The tearing of the veil had caused them to be, in so many ways, one person.

One-as-two, and two-as-one.

Back in the smaller room where they had met the Lightborne, Eresh instructed them, "Your potential is great, but it is unrefined. Do not think that you are invincible. Remain cautious and vigilant. This is perhaps the most vulnerable time for you. Although you will leave and go your separate ways for a while, you must promise me to come here before traveling below. I will do what I can to augment your strength, and I will accompany you part of the way." Arden and Rynn quietly swore to return, and then Eresh excused herself, leaving them alone.

"When will you head back?" Arden asked her. "I guess I'll be here until tomorrow, if you wanted to maybe have that second date."

Rynn scoffed. "Now? Here? Isn't that a little weird? Besides, who says I forgive you for being an ass?"

Laughing softly, he said, "We may not have another chance for a while. But fair points otherwise."

She reached into her pants pocket, retrieving the cedar bracelet. "Tomorrow, I'll confront Daryala Gindir. Even as a Sentinel, that'll be dangerous. Who knows how Sabrath will react. And you could find trouble too." With the index finger of each hand, she rotated the bracelet like a wheel. "Fine, walk with me."

Together, they ambled down the palace steps and toward the town square. They entered an old mess hall, and Rynn issued commands to a Fabricator while Arden sat on the counter, watching her. "Today was quite an adventure," he finally said. "I'm glad you came along. Sorry again for all of that this morning."

Rynn looked up at him from the machine, shaking her head. "You don't have to keep apologizing. All's forgiven." The Fabricator began to whir, and she let out a cheer. "It still works. Amazing! What would you like to eat, sir? We don't quite have the selection of the Yum, but we can offer a fine dusty gruel." Her laughter echoed through the empty space.

"How about pizza?" he asked. "I haven't had any in ages. Almost a whole two weeks." *Not since the day this started.*

"Hm," she answered, "no pizza. It looks like the options are more Y'Sham-y. Here's a soup. Let's try that."

A moment later, she carried a tray with two bowls and a small loaf of leavened bread resembling rye. Moving carefully, she set it down on a table close to the counter. "Dinner is served," she said, straddling the bench.

Arden slid off of the counter and sat down facing her. "Thank you very much. Itadakimasu." He ate a spoonful of soup. "Wow, this is really good even though it's not hot. It's like a better minestrone. I wonder what the meat is."

Rynn smirked. "Giant rodent jerky. Why did you speak in Japanese before eating?"

Arden shrugged and shook his head. "A friend of mine growing up would always say that. It became a thing."

"Ah," Rynn said, looking sad. "I hardly remember anyone from before the attack. There was this one girl I was friends with. She would always have a chocolate bar with her lunch. And she'd fold the paper in this very specific way." Sighing, she forced a smile onto her face. "After that, my life was discipline, training, and Black Hand this, Lightwatch that." She broke the bread in half and handed him a portion, dipping hers into her soup.

"I'm sorry," Arden said, empathizing with her. "That sounds hard. I guess, compared to you, I've been really lucky."

Rynn shrugged. "It wasn't so bad. Like I told you before, Sabrath is harsh, but also fair and honorable. If Daryala really did what Eresh thinks, I have a hard time believing he knew. I hope not. I don't think I can raise a hand against him."

Looking into her eyes, Arden said, "I understand. Alan and Nora Linzer helped raise me. There's no way I can imagine them betraying my family, but if they did..." He rubbed his hands on his knees and sat that way for a time.

Reaching out, Rynn placed a hand on his, leaving it there. "We're in this together now. We'll make it through."

After they finished eating, they walked around the square, between houses, wherever their feet took them. As they had that first night in the Jumble, they told each other imagined histories. Musing about past inhabitants of the Cradle and Y'Sham, and dreaming of days so long gone they seemed to have taken place in a different universe. As the hours passed, they gradually grew tired and sought out a place to sleep.

Arden pointed to a small house with a crumbled door. "This looks good enough to me. I'm worn out."

Rynn agreed and passed over the verge. "I'm taking the master bedroom. The bigger one, whatever that is."

Arden followed her inside and chuckled. "However many thousands of years later, a home is a home." He peered into the kitchen area and again saw Rynn inputting something into a Fabricator. "Still hungry?"

The machine whirred and she approached him, something clasped in each of her hands. "Yes, but this isn't food." She opened her right palm and extended it to him. In her hand was a pendant in the shape of a white raven that looked to be carved from bone. A simple leather strap was threaded through a hole in the bird's wing. "This is Yéil, a trickster raven that many First Nations people in the Pacific Northwest tell stories about."

"Tell me," Arden said with genuine interest.

"There are probably hundreds of versions, but in the one I know, Yéil hatches a plot to shine light from the sun, stars, and moon down on the earth." She motioned with her hands as though light was sprinkling down from above. "One day, he flies into a rich man's house, and sees the sun, moon, and stars in cages. One cage is hung high in the rafters, another is on the floor, and the third is outside near the river. The next day, Yéil transforms into a beautiful eagle, and parades in front of the rich man. Seeing him, the man puts him in one of the cages, releasing the moon. That night, Yéil transforms into a fly and flees the cage, leaving behind a single white feather. The second day, Yéil transforms into an albino wolf and approaches the man as though hungry. Seeing the wolf's beautiful pelt, the man tosses him in a cage, releasing the stars. That night, Yéil transforms into a mouse and sneaks away. The third day, Yéil transforms into an enormous beaver. The man's daughter sees Yéil and wants to make him a pet, so the man opens the cage near the river, releasing the sun."

"Nice," said Arden. "Clever bird."

Rynn put a finger to her lips. "Shush, there's more. When Yéil saw the light shining on the earth, he turned into a fish and tried to swim away, but the man caught him in a net. Realizing he had been tricked, the man tried to cook Yéil alive in his hearth. Coughing and spluttering from the smoke and soot, Yéil transformed one more time. This time, he became a particle of ash and floated away on the wind. However, the fire had turned him black. And that's why the raven is black to this day. Still, Yéil succeeded in freeing the light. Just like you and I will someday."

Arden applauded in a lighthearted way and grinned at her tale. "That's great. Nicely told."

Rynn reached up to show him a black raven pendant hung around her neck. "I made a copy of mine. Promise me you'll wear it. Yours is white, mine is black. Two ravens, the same but different. Doing whatever it takes."

"I promise," Arden told her, putting on the necklace. "Until the end."

"Until the end," she repeated. "It's time for bed. Thanks for today." With a quick step, she closed the distance between them, gave him a peck on the lips, and wished him goodnight as she walked into one of the bedrooms.

"Goodnight, Rynn," Arden said. Then, he went into the other bedroom, plopped on the plant-like bedding material Kilk had spoken of, and immediately fell asleep.

34

BEWARE THE GREEDY ONE

THE WHITE OWL FLEW ahead of him between the treetops, threading a path through the pine forest. Lucas raced along, urgently trying to catch his winged omen but always falling further behind. With a flash, the creature disappeared, and his heart sunk. Now he was truly lost in the wilderness. Shaking off despondent feelings, he surged forward and broke into a clearing.

Abruptly, the scenery changed, and he was hovering over a scrub desert. Straight ahead, an enormous raven glided down from above and to his left. He followed it instinctively and they landed close to each other near a crossroads. It had perched on a saguaro arm, pecking at insects crawling over budding flowers.

Beneath the cactus, Mai ran circles and barked at the black bird. In this low desert habitat, her half coyote genes sprung fully to life. She sat back on her haunches, panting and staring up at the raven.

"Why, why, why are you running around down there making such a racket?" the raven called down to Mai in Rynn's voice.

Mai replied, sounding like Noire. "The cactus is a friend of mine. Tuck, are you okay?"

Lucas laughed, but no sound came out.

Tuck's muffled voice said, "Yeah, yeah. I've had worse days. As long as the bird doesn't crap on me."

Projecting down from high overhead, the white owl's shadow flitted past, and it dove at the smaller bird. Settling on the bough of a mesquite tree, the owl stared at the scavenger with wide eyes.

"Hey, hey, hey, why are you attacking me, oh Wise One?" squawked the raven, who had hopped to a different arm of the saguaro. "We deserve to eat too! You just want this for yourself!"

The owl's haunting voice made the air heavy, like breathing mist. "Foolish crow. I don't eat insects or cactus flowers."

The raven tilted its head back and looked at the owl with one eye. "Not a crow, Wrong One. I am Marasa, the raven, and so is my twin."

"I'll bet you are," said the owl, eying him hungrily. "Be careful, Marasa. Words have many meanings. It must be fate to find two meals that share one delicious name."

Marasa ignored them all, returning its focus to gorging on insects. Mai barked at the raven, "Glutton. Why don't you share with us?"

"Why, why, why would I share with any of you?" Marasa replied. "The owl wants to eat me, you don't eat insects, and the gangly two-legs is merely a wanderer here."

Lucas answered, but again no sound left his lips.

"Fine," said Mai, slinking away. "I'll go find my own food. I don't need you." Lucas followed his coydog friend for some time until she finally acknowledged his presence. "Oh, it's you. The one who abandoned me."

Lucas motioned with his hands that he couldn't speak.

"Don't be silly. Your voice sounds like garbled nonsense on the best of days. Use your brain."

Oh! I didn't abandon you, Mai. The Lightborne attacked us. We had to run.

"Excuses. I fought them. The least you could have done is help me," she sniffed. "Oh, look there. Another glutton."

A few feet away, a white raven was nibbling on a ripe prickly pear. It peered up at them. "I'm Marasa. You've met my twin. There's plenty to eat. Join me." This bird had Malank's voice.

Mai walked over and picked a cactus fruit, and Lucas did the same. The barbed hairs on its skin pricked his fingers and he let it drop to the ground. The coydog also dropped the fruit, licking her fur. "The spines are murder. I guess being half coyote isn't enough," she lamented.

The white Marasa screeched with laughter. "Weaklings. I knew you couldn't tolerate the devil's-tongue. How unlucky. Go find some carrion to chew on."

From a patch of brush further in the distance, they heard rustling and branches snapping. Something was approaching. They smelled the source before they saw it. With a snort, acting as though they were invisible, a javelina sauntered into view and began munching on the fruit. The white Marasa cried out, "Hey, mister. I was here first. Find your own meal."

The javelina spoke in Kilk's voice around a mouthful of food, having moved on from the cactus's fruit to its pads. "It seems I have found it. In fact, I believe every prickly pear in this desert belongs to me." Flashing razor-sharp tusks at them warningly, the peccary returned to its feast.

From behind them, the black raven and the owl both hollered, "Run! Run, all of you!" In the distance, an impossibly large golden eagle pursued them. Even the javelina looked up in fright and scurried away. Soon, they were sprinting as fast as their legs could carry them. Lucas, in defiance, turned to face the colossal bird of prey.

The owl yelled back at him, "No, Arden Arinza. You are not ready for this battle yet!" With a long, terrifying shriek, Lucas's omen doubled back and threw itself at the eagle's face, clawing at its eyes. "Run, Child of Shadow, or you will die here!" The eagle screeched in pain, grabbing at the owl with its tremendous talons. Flinging the smaller animal away in a bloodied heap, the colossal predator returned to the chase. Lucas ran swiftly, somehow able to keep pace with Mai.

He saw a figure burst from the underbrush toward him and dodged too late to avoid it. The javelina tore at his legs, and he crumpled to the ground, unable to go on. It snorted, then said, "Better you than me. I'm not meant to die today. A few more meals, and I'll be remembered as the most voracious eater ever!" Scurrying away, it left him for dead.

As the eagle neared, talons open and plummeting at blinding speed, Mai leapt in front of him with her hackles up and fangs bared. "Live on, Lucas. It's all up to you now." Lunging forward, she snapped her jaws at the eagle's legs, rending the killer's flesh. Not wanting to forsake her twice, Lucas also attacked the monstrosity. A black halberd materialized in his hand, and he stabbed at the eagle. To his dismay, he quickly realized there was no use in the attempt. As if immune, the monster paid him no mind, displaying not even a scratch from the attack. Within moments, Mai also lay spent, her lifeblood seeping into the earth. The javelina cackled at him from its hiding place under a creosote bush, watching the slaughter.

Methodically, the eagle strode over to him, a slight limp hampering its gait. Deadly talons clacked with each step, and Lucas knew the end had come. The winged hunter's voice was that of Eresh. She declared, "Death awaits everyone who stands against the Ten, little boy. You should have escaped when you had the chance. Such a waste of life." Flaunting bloodied claws in front of its next kill, the eagle readied a deathblow. Then, at the moment its final strike was imminent, the bird erupted in a horrific scream.

From above, the Marasa twins plummeted like missiles and gashed the creature's eyes, blinding it with a single coordinated strike. The white twin croaked at him, "You cannot kill this beast yet, only starve it. Leave now." As quickly as they had arrived, they were gone.

Eresh's voice roared, and the desert turned to ice. "Ingrates! I gave you everything, and you repay me with betrayal?"

Lucas was now fleeing across an icy lake. Cracks began to form in the surface but didn't slow his steps. Although blinded, the ferocious giant followed him via sound, his every footfall a beacon. As it plunged toward him, he crouched down and rolled to the side just before it impacted him. The bird crashed through the ice, taking him with it.

Falling ever deeper into the water's embrace, Lucas watched the light fade above him. Blue turned to black turned to the scraping darkness of the Deep Infra. A petrifying roar vibrated through his entire body and a voice touched his mind: "Wisdom Sentinels. I am the Darkmother, Tiamat. Find me before it is too late. Be wary of the Ten. Without my power to aid you, their machinations will unravel everything that you know. The threads of fate can yet be wrenched from your grasp. Do not squander this chance, for there will never be another. And trust not the Greedy One! That one's schemes will be the undoing of us all."

Tiamat, I swear we will find you and set things right. But please tell me, who is the Greedy One? It seems nearly every Lightborne and Darktouched could be the one you speak of. The growling, groaning of the unending abyss stole Lucas's ability to think, and he felt his vision dimming.

"Those borne up by the Light are a scourge upon the land, but that one hides in the darkness. Find me. Do not tarry."

Wait! Is it Daryala Gindir? Another Darktouched leader? Is it Eresh or Ninazu? It could be anyone!

But Tiamat was gone, and there was no one left to answer. With a feeling of hopeless frustration, as the earth moaned and shadewinds buffeted him, Lucas closed his eyes and let the abrading blackness take him.

Awakening in a cold sweat, Arden slid out of bed and rushed to find Rynn. The KALM-ER watch showed it was four in the morning. Stumbling through the ancient house, he yelled into the room where she had gone to sleep, but no one answered. Peering inside, he found it empty. She was already gone, off on her lone mission to confront Daryala. Part of him was dejected she hadn't woken him to say goodbye, but he also understood. *Sometimes talking can kill motivation.* He reached out to her with his mind, not expecting it to work, but was still disappointed when the attempt failed. A brief look outside offered nothing unforeseen. The residential area looked exactly as it had the night before.

Deeply concerned about the dream—and especially unnerved by Tiamat's warning—Arden returned to his room and lay back down. Toying with the white raven pendant around his neck, he pulled the phone from his pocket and tried to call Rynn, but the device showed she was out of reach. *I guess I'll have to trust her judgment and believe she'll be okay.* With his mind still full of troubled thoughts, he searched once again for sleep.

Just as he was finally dozing off, Arden was overcome by the strange sensation that someone was watching him. He sat up in bed. Scanning his surroundings, he was startled fully awake to find himself surrounded by darkness. Unsure if he was dreaming again, he eased out of bed and gingerly let his feet touch the blackness. It was solid. Not far from him stood a white platform similar to the one inside the stone arch. When he stepped onto it, Rynn was already waiting for him a few feet away.

"Arden, I'm sorry I didn't say goodbye," she said. "Eresh taught me a few things before I left. We can enter this place and communicate over any distance. I'm already back in the Abzu Complex."

Arden shook his head. "No problem. I had the wildest dream just now. Tiamat spoke to me. She told me not to trust the Greedy One and said that person is hiding in the darkness. I don't know if it means anything, but be careful."

Rynn nodded somberly. "I will. That doesn't sound like just a dream to me. I have a really bad feeling. You be careful too."

"Always," he said with a laugh. "By the way, how did you get back so fast? It took us forever to get here. Relative to the Infra, we don't even really know where *here* is."

Rynn shrugged. "I don't know how it works exactly, but Eresh showed me a secret pathway between the Cradle and home. The doorway back is always the same, she said, but the ones leading into the Cradle are constantly changing. Only those she trusts can find and use them." With a warm smile, she waved. "I have to go now. The pendant looks good on you. I'll talk with you again as soon as I can. Be safe. If you kick the bucket, I won't be powerful anymore. That'd be a shame." With a wink, she was gone, and Arden was back in the Cradle.

35

THE COUNCIL ROOM

THE LIFT FROM THE cavern floor of the Abzu Complex glided noiselessly, and Rynn momentarily let her guard down. Subconsciously, her hand sought the cedar bracelet in her pocket. Time was marching forward, and she needed to speak with Sabrath Nulne, her adopted father and the Black Hand's second-in-command, before the day began in earnest. In a few minutes, it would be half past four. Her conversation with Arden had done nothing to lessen her worries. *The Greedy One hidden in darkness. Could it be Daryala?* The elevator stopped and she stepped off, ignoring the familiar scenery.

While snaking through the narrow cobblestone streets on the south end of the Jumble, Rynn plotted contingencies if the conversation with the Black Hand commander went poorly. *The elevator is a trap, so I'd have to take the stairs. The barracks and armory are directly below headquarters. That leaves up. But I'd never make it past the security checkpoint on B1. Beyd helped Arden. Maybe he'd help me too.*

As Rynn climbed a flight of stairs, reached a landing, and then climbed another, she frustratedly pounded on her wobbly legs to wake them up. *Now's not the time to be weak.* For a moment, she gazed to her left over the verdant wall that separated the Jumble from the Greensward. False morning light painted the sky a dull blue, and the lush, diverse greenery stirred awake. Fabricated plant life filled the entire area, making it a tribute to rare, precious, and extinct life forms. More than that, it was a place for Darktouched to enjoy a small bit of nature in the Abzu Complex, far from the surface and natural sunlight. Rynn often lingered at the entryway to her home, like now, breathing in the sweet aroma of freshly watered greenery. Peace would have to wait, though—she had things to do.

The front door opened, and she crossed the threshold. A blended aroma of coffee and leatherworking materials tickled her nostrils and brought her a smidge of comfort. As long as she had known him, one of Sabrath's hobbies had been crafting pouches, satchels, and other small items from Fabricated supplies. "It clears the mind," he would tell her, a focused scowl warning away anyone who might think to disturb him.

His other passion was coffee. She scanned the kitchen and found two French presses on the counter. Only one of them was steeping. A water kettle remained on the stove. She sloshed it around to check how full it was and then, satisfied it held sufficient volume, turned on the burner beneath it.

Sabrath strode down the hall and greeted her. "Morning," he said quietly. "Just getting in at a quarter to five?"

Rynn leaned back and tapped her fingers on the granite countertop. "Yeah," she answered, then walked over to stand next to him near the French presses, scooping some coffee grounds into hers.

"Nulne o'clock. Coffee hour has arrived." Sabrath sighed contentedly. He depressed the plunger and poured java into a gray mug, taking a small sip. "Give me one last cup, and I could die a happy man." Squinting slightly, he examined Rynn's face. "What happened? You've been a little off since yesterday morning." On padded feet, he moved around to the other side of the tall counter and sat on a barstool chair facing her.

Rynn turned off the burner, carried the kettle across the kitchen, and slowly let water fall over the coarse grounds. "Council Room?" Sabrath nodded and picked up his mug, proceeding down the hall. Rynn grabbed her French press and a red cup, then followed him.

Eight paces and a left. Since her first day in Sabrath's home, she had counted the number of steps and floorboard slats between the kitchen entryway and the room they mutually called the Council Room. At ten years old, it had taken her as many strides to cross the distance. The unexpected memory made Rynn smile. In reality, the Council Room was a small library and office with two beanbag chairs in the center, one red and one gray. Whenever the two had serious matters to discuss, no matter what they were, this was where it happened.

Sabrath had already landed in the gray chair, the gray mug secured firmly in his right hand. Without setting down what she was carrying, Rynn smoothly lowered herself, coming to rest cross-legged on the red seat. Facing him, she placed the press and cup on the floor and puffed out her cheeks.

"I met Eresh. *The* Eresh," Rynn began quietly. "And learned a lot." Sabrath sat up straight and took a large gulp of coffee. Through silence, he willed her to continue her story.

Avoiding specifics about Alazar's plan, she recounted her journey into Zone Ganzir with Arden. Although she felt some guilt as a result, she altered key details in the retelling. *Sabrath might be working with Daryala. I have to protect Arden and everyone else.* In her revised version of events, she had faced the trial alone, carried Arden on her back to the Cradle, and become a Sentinel after impressing Eresh. As proof, she summoned her black armor and halberd.

"Oh, my." Sabrath hungrily eyed the weapon. "I need one of those. Anyway, you were saying."

Rynn continued her story. "At one point, Eresh mentioned a plan that involves me." She analyzed Sabrath's face but saw only surprised interest. "With this," she said, raising the halberd as a symbol of her Sentinel powers, "they think I can find the Source and then receive Light's Gift. I'd become both a Darktouched and Lightborne. We could defeat the Lightwatch!" Withdrawing her Sentinel gear, she added pointedly, "Eresh thinks Daryala knew about this."

Sabrath's visage wrinkled in skepticism. "Knew? How?"

I can't tell him about the Ten. "She's not sure," Rynn lied. "But she believes Daryala orchestrated the murder of my adopted family. With the goal of controlling me."

Glugging down the remainder of his drink, Sabrath scowled. "The Daryala I know would never do anything like this. I can't believe you'd even suggest it." Rising to his feet, he ambled across the room and lifted a framed picture from a bookshelf. "When she first suggested that I take care of you, I was... opposed. Remember when we took this?"

Rynn looked at the photo. Sabrath, still with a hint of hair, and her ten-year-old self sat smiling together against the backdrop of cerulean ocean waters. "I do. Saint Thomas. I was so depressed at first, and this trip really pulled me out of it."

Sabrath smiled warmly at her. But then it faded, and he massaged his brow. "Rynn, I've known Daryala most of my adult life. She's definitely changed since the attack, but this is hard to fathom."

Rynn pressed the plunger on the French press and then filled her cup. The soothing scent filled her sinuses, and the bitter taste stirred her senses, emboldening her. "You never knew anything about any of this, *right*?"

Sabrath hung his head. "No. This hasn't come up." His large, gray eyes stared directly into Rynn's, searching. For an unnervingly long time, he gazed at her, trying to make up his mind. With a wag of his head, he uttered, "Still, whether you think of me as a father or not, you're my daughter. And I trust you." Rynn began to speak, and Sabrath stopped her with an upraised hand. "We're going to follow the chain of command. I'll talk to her myself."

"I want to be there," she said. "I *need* to be there."

"That's a bad idea, Rynn," he cautioned. "What if she reacts badly? You know she's not entirely..."

"Stable?" suggested Rynn. Sabrath opened his mouth to protest, but then closed it and nodded in agreement.

Should I tell him everything? No. If my feelings about him are wrong, then it's over. Pushing away her misgivings, she partially hid behind the steaming cup.

"I plan to head to the tower at six. Do you want to go together?" he asked.

Rynn shook her head. *I need to talk to Beyd.* "I'll meet you there. Thank you, Sabrath. You're like a father to me."

Why can't you just say it, Rynn? He's your dad in every way but blood.

Sabrath's shoulders slightly slumped, but the corners of his mouth turned up anyway. As he headed for the door, he chuckled. "I always said you'd be the death of me. I'm going to hit the head and get dressed."

36

THE DEVIL'S TRIANGLE

ARDEN TRIED FOR ANOTHER hour to find sleep and ultimately accepted failure. Instead he walked to the palace, looking for Eresh, and found her sitting at the long table in the main hall. "Good morning, Arden," she greeted him. "I'm sure by now you know that Rynn has already left." With a discerning look, she added, "You seem to have a question."

Arden nodded. *I can't tell her about the dream.* "Morning, Eresh. I do. How does Wisdom's Bond work? Rynn said you taught her how to talk to me over long distances. Wouldn't that mean I know too?"

Eresh stood with her arms folded. "Consider what it's like to learn a new skill. Your body may not remember how to do it consistently without several repetitions, right? Wisdom's Bond can be fickle at times. But, simply, until you and Rynn entered that place together, neither of you really knew how." She sighed, rubbing her hands together. "Try to look at it this way. The greater *your* proficiency in something, the more Rynn can tap into that skill. She may need a little practice to also master it, but learning would be like shaking off the rust of disuse. As if she knew and forgot, rather than learning something entirely new. Does that make sense?"

"Yeah, I think so," he said. "And knowledge that we gain... That's shared immediately?"

She tilted her head back and forth with a slight shrug. "Yes and no. You know what Rynn knows and vice versa. That does *not* mean the instant you learn new information she's alerted to it. That would be a nuisance. With the Bond, the knowledge is there when you need it. At times, you may be pleasantly surprised to discover that you know something you never learned."

"I wish I had that skill," said Malank's voice from behind them. Arden was surprised at how quietly he moved, given his size. "Then Fi wouldn't always have to keep me in line." His boisterous laugh filled the room. "Hello, Arden. I hope we're good now, you and I. Today, we rescue your dad."

Arden shrugged, speaking candidly. "We're okay. I've made peace with how I got here, and I've decided what my own goals are." His hazel eyes glinted as he frowned at Malank and added, "But you did lie to all of us. Who actually knew your plan? Did the Linzers even know?"

Fiala walked into the room as Malank answered, "No, no one else knows all of the details. To be honest, after Irmina, our relationship with the Linzers was... strained, to say the least."

"Why not just take back the Gift, then?" Arden asked, glancing at Eresh as he did. She closed her eyes and slightly shook her head, sitting down next to him.

"They were friends. And they truly love you," said Malank. "Besides, that's not how it works. Death is the only way to give up the Gift once it is bestowed." Using the toe of his right boot to hook a chair, Malank pulled it toward himself and straddled it. "Here's an example. I'm the First in my Gift's lineage. Alan is my Second, and because Irmina vanished, I chose Nora as my Third instead of her. If Alan dies, I can choose a new Second. If Nora also dies, she can't be replaced until I give my Gift to someone. One chooses two. Two chooses three. And so on. Each time the Gift is passed forward, the power received is diminished. Significantly."

How can he be so matter-of-fact about it? I don't even want to think about Alan and Nora dying.

Fiala tutted. "Which is a lesson *someone* needs to learn. That is, be very careful who you give the Gift to. Or be prepared to take it back."

Malank turned to face her, exclaiming indignantly, "If we did that, we'd be no different than Chen and his parrot crew!"

"I know," said Fiala calmly. "It was a figure of speech. Relax."

Arden pulled up a chair and sat down, facing them all. Until now, the fact that he was speaking casually with three of the Ten had not fully sunk in. "I still can't believe the Linzers really betrayed us. Isn't there any chance we get them both back and sort this out?"

"Maybe," said Malank. "The person we'll be making the exchange with is Chen's Third, a man named Mammon Ryker. His interests are more... material than most high ranking Lightborne. For him, nothing is without a price."

Fiala tapped her foot. "We searched for days, Malank. Alan either doesn't want to come back or the Lightwatch has him."

"Right," said Malank, eyes far away. "There are no good scenarios."

Eresh cleared her throat, inserting herself into the conversation. "Afterward, your plan is to bring them to the Cradle, no? I fear that Daryala Gindir may already be hunting Arden and his family. After today, Rynn as well."

"We can't possibly *carry* all four back down," Fiala said, caution in her voice. "Only Firsts are able to transport people. You know that, Eresh."

Clearly frustrated, Eresh retorted curtly, "You have no plan at all then."

Malank held up his hands, palms facing outward, motioning for them to slow down. "We're paying Mammon for safe passage. Deveras and Reina have a plan for where to go and how to get back underground."

"Fine," said Eresh grimly. "Just know that if Arden is captured by either side, it's the end of everything. He should just stay belowground."

"About that," Malank admitted sheepishly, "Mammon won't make the deal unless he meets our young friend. I agreed. The charm spoke to me. Destiny's tailwinds are pushing us forward."

Eresh spoke gently but skeptically. "Malank, I think the charm is just our dead friend's way of guiding us to follow his plan. It's not, as you like to say, a weathervane for the winds of destiny." Sensing she had crossed a line, she continued, "Alazar was just trying to push us onto the right path. We've found it now, so why risk losing our way again?"

Malank stood from his chair, scolding her, "How can you say that? Al saw more, I'm sure of it. We need to have faith."

"It doesn't matter anyway," said Fiala. "Arden won't get his father back if he doesn't play along. Let's just get it over with." She sighed. "I can't believe I'm saying this, but right now I wish Senna was still with us."

Arden also got up, agreeing with Fiala. "I'm tired of talking. I'll be fine, Eresh."

"We'll protect him with our lives, Eresh. You have my word," said Malank. He frowned at Fiala. "Wherever she is now, Senna chose her own path. I just hope that we're still on the same side."

Eresh threw up her hands and shrugged, defeated. "You and the girl are as stubborn and reckless as my sons. Do what you wish." Arden could see her willing herself to say more. "And be safe. I will see you soon."

Light like fire, white at the center gradating into yellows and reds as it undulated outward from the eagle's heart, encased Arden. The enormous, winged familiar clutched a blazing capsule in its talons, and he rode inside. From within, he was reminded of the bubble shield Alan had summoned during the Reclaimer attack on the Devlins' home.

They passed through the dragon roost at immense speed. In a blink, the bottom of the tall structure came into view. They flew through the floor, which opened below them, and then raced down a corridor similar to a subway tunnel. In seconds, the passageway ended at a junction with another vertical shaft. Their momentum was so great that, on the upward turn, Arden didn't feel like he was traveling higher but was instead still moving along the ground. The dull roar of air rushing past exhilarated him. As they accelerated further, he called his KALM gear just to see the HUD reading. *Six hundred miles per hour and rising. I hope he's not a clumsy flier.* By the time they reached the next bend, the air had begun to ripple around them, creating pressure waves in their wake.

The tunnel widened but maintained its tube-like shape. They progressed first through a series of defensive barricades with gates placed at different heights and locations. Turrets mounted at strategic positions held ancient armaments, and Arden imagined their function while passing by and around them. When the tunnel ended, they passed through a flat area constructed entirely of the greenish-blue stones of Y'Sham. A wide staging area quickly opened up, and a blue barrier rippled in front of them.

Malank called down from above, "I think you're going to like this, kid. We're coming out onto the ocean floor in the Milwaukee Depth."

Surging through the writhing blue wall, they entered deep, dark water. A maelstrom raged around them, forming impassable walls. Arden knew that—whether in a KALM suit or encapsulated in the light of the Ten—any attempt to break through would be fatal. Lightning crackled along the edges of the storm, and he was reminded of his mother's story of Nuzum.

The eagle familiars maintained their rapid ascent for perhaps a minute, then steadily slowed until they barely moved at all. Eerily, the maelstrom quieted around them, and debris began to sink back to the ocean floor. The lull in the murderous, surging energy released ship hulls and masts, airplane fuselages and engines, unrecognizable bits of wreckage, plastics, metals, stone, dirt, and a multitude of dead sea creatures. Electricity still leapt across the dark, murky depths.

A soft blue glow appeared in the distance. Below, two more lights blinked on, then three more to the right, then more and more until they were surrounded. Creatures with humanoid features and glowing, translucent skin emerged from the darkness, lighting up the seawater. Their wild hair, like the stinging tentacles of a lion's mane jellyfish, floated in every direction and was wrapped around their bodies. Their torsos and arms, covered in scales and jagged spikes, appeared to be coursing with electricity. From the waist down, they were a wriggling mass of tentacles, reminding Arden of a squid.

One creature advanced until it was only a few feet away, and a voice touched his mind. "You three have been granted safe passage by Eresh. Please, follow me. You will not be harmed." They followed behind the creature, progressing rapidly toward the surface, until light began to stretch down from above. "Farewell. Until we meet again," their guide said as it broke off and gradually disappeared.

Below them, the tempest swirled once more. From above, Arden saw that their movements distorted light, creating an effect similar to graphical glitches in a three-dimensional rendering.

When they broke through the water's surface, Lucas looked around and realized he could no longer see Fiala. *And we're officially back in the Aboveworld.* Flipping through his HUD settings, he found her floating a few feet away. Relieved, he said to Malank, "Okay, you were right. That was amazing."

Malank laughed from deep in his chest. "I never get tired of it. You know we're flying over the Devil's Triangle, right? Sometimes those sirens get a little carried away with their... exercising."

"Nice." Lucas laughed along with him. "Where do we go from here?"

"San Francisco," he answered. "Mammon Ryker is quietly a very successful businessman, if you want to call it that. He'll do anything to turn a profit. We're just lucky Darren wasn't handed over to Hiram Lud or Almon Cain." The eagle turned towards the west and screamed up and forward. Below them, the world was a blur. "Chen probably would have replaced Mammon long ago, but he funds most of the surface operations for the Lightwatch."

Seconds later, Lucas's HUD alerted him that they were passing over Florida and nearing the Gulf of Mexico. "I've been meaning to ask you something. How are Severed created?"

Malank was quiet for a moment before answering. "Without understanding how the Lightwatch works, that's difficult to answer. Let me try." He sighed. "Our entire lives are happening at once, reflected in light. Conception, birth, life, death. In sequence and an instant. Even the Ten... Nine, as long as we've hung on. Our lives are nothing more than a flash of light." They were halfway over the United States now, according to the HUD. "At the same time, for

Lightborne, there's a related, second life happening in the Lightwatch. Now, imagine a thread between your beginning and end self. Severing is like cutting that thread. The two selves never meet, endlessly longing for each other, endlessly persisting. Driven mad but unable to expire, the Lightwatch self breaks free, becoming like a raging spirit."

Like a beautiful, angelic figure robed in white with glowing skin and blue eyes. Lucas said solemnly, "A soul with no self. It sounds incredibly cruel."

"It is hell epitomized, not just cruel," Malank said, his voice breaking. "Chen and his cronies didn't invent the practice, but they... After Alazar died, so many good people were Severed. Their screams never leave you. The haunting stare of empty eyes. People that were your friends. People you loved."

"Can they be killed?" asked Lucas. "To end their misery."

The Golden Gate bridge appeared far below them, and Malank directed the bird toward the ground. "Of course," he replied. "With great difficulty, unless you're very powerful. As a Sentinel, you're well equipped for that battle, but hope you never cross paths with one. You will never be the same. There's a price to killing that is far greater and lasts far longer than the act itself." They touched down in a quiet side street, and Lucas withdrew his KALM gear. Malank, a shadow over his face, said, "Union Square is just over there. Tara and Asante should be waiting for us." Then, he walked ahead of Lucas on his own.

Fiala landed next to them, glanced at Malank, then said quietly to Lucas, "Did something happen? I haven't seen him look like this for a long time."

"I asked about the Severed. Was that wrong?" he asked.

Fiala took a deep breath and shook her head. "No. Someone he cared about a lot was Severed."

"By Chen, right?" Lucas pressed. They stopped at a crosswalk, still standing out of earshot from Malank.

Fiala shook her head again. "By him, at Chen's orders. I don't think he'll ever get over it." A walking-man icon appeared across the street from them. "We should move. Come on."

They crossed Stockton Street and climbed the stairway to Union Square. Standing there waiting for them were Asante and his mom. Like the first time he had seen them in the Abzu Complex, their appearance was off-putting to him at first. He tried to remember what they looked like in the Darktouched world, but he was frustratingly unable.

Asante reached out and grasped his shoulder. "Are you ready for this?"

Lucas replied with a confident smile. "I think we're going to find out soon, one way or another."

They strode together into the square, the Aboveworlders around them oblivious to their identities and shared purpose.

37

THE TRUE NATURE OF NABUCITE

RYNN BOUNCED TOWARD THE gondola station, newfound vigor in her legs. Caffeine and a small breakfast fueled her body, and Sabrath's willingness to help bolstered her spirits. When Beyd answered her call immediately, she began to think that fate was on her side.

It was five-thirty in the morning, and she made the short journey in solitude. *I wonder if Arden's left the Cradle already. I hope our talk with Daryala doesn't make things impossible for him.* The gondola held only one other passenger, but neither of them acknowledged the other.

On the tower's main floor, she stepped briskly to the elevator and entered the carriage. The information-desk attendants weren't due until seven a.m., so Rynn was able to pass through unseen. Apprehensively, she told the elevator to take her to B10. Seconds later, she breathed a small sigh of relief at arriving without issue in restricted R&D. Beyd sat on a desk in his tweed suit and fedora, waiting for her.

"Good morning, Rynn," he said cheerfully. Reaching behind him, he tinkered with a machine and then waved her along. "Follow me. I just disabled the security checkpoint."

They bypassed a series of workstations and walked down a hallway that led them to a plain wall with a door centered in it. Although Rynn had never been in this place before, she recognized it from memories shared via Wisdom's Bond.

Peering to her left, she saw another doorway and knew with certainty what was behind it.

Beyd stopped and turned around to face her. "Since you're a Sentinel now, I guess you know what's in there, eh?" he said, pointing over his shoulder at the Everdark room. Rynn confirmed that she did, and Beyd walked them toward the area housing Black Hand prototypes. "If things go wrong, wait for me in front of Branthum's legacy," he said derisively. "I have an escape plan that I'm ninety-nine percent sure will work."

He's almost totally sure it might work. Good luck on your own, Arden.

Beyd unlocked the door and ushered Rynn inside. "Now, two more things. First, take the wristwatch and phone on that table. The KALM-ER Sentinel combination is choice."

Rynn swapped out her bands for the new gadgets and summoned the suit. "I love this upgrade, Beyd," she gushed.

"I made some adjustments to yours that I wasn't able to make to Arden's. Summon your Sentinel equipment, please," Beyd directed her.

When the black armor and halberd materialized, Rynn was awed. "The armor feels lighter and stronger at the same time. And the halberd is even more like an extension of my body."

Beyd grinned. "You can concentrate energy into it now too. Give it a go."

Rynn focused her mind and channeled power into the halberd. It began to hum with a swirling, menacing darkness. When she struck the air, a shockwave rippled along the ground, cracking the floor and wall in front of her. "That is sweet!"

"Right?" said Beyd, eyeing the damage. "Now, the second thing. The prototypes in this room are half rubbish, but their design intent might be revealing."

"You mean that Daryala's trying to steal Lightborne power?"

Beyd shook his head. "No. Many of the designs are suited to Infra warfare. I don't know why, but it can't be good."

Rynn frowned. "Eresh didn't mention this. Does she know?"

"Not every detail," Beyd replied. "I wanted to understand more first. That said, if things go wrong with Daryala, use this." In his outstretched hand was a partially translucent sphere the size of a table tennis ball. One half was black, with a yellow sun formed within it, and the other milky white with a purple moon. "It's a type of stun grenade that should work on Darktouched and Lightborne. Don't use it now," he warned her. "But if the time comes, throw it at the floor and run. Look away or you'll be stumbling around like you're pissed."

"Thanks, Beyd. I think I have a chance now," Rynn said.

"No worries. Oh!" he said abruptly. "Your modified suit lets you bypass Abzu Complex security stations. But people can still see you, so don't be daft. Kia ora, Rynn."

Rynn entered Black Hand headquarters via the stairs at exactly six o'clock, and laughed to herself when Sabrath exited the elevator at the same time. They saluted each other and walked purposefully around the circular walnut table, both gazing at the red hand emblazoned on the floor as they did. When they reached the entrance to Daryala's office, no guards were stationed outside.

Sabrath leaned toward Rynn and whispered into her ear, "Are you ready for the guillotine?"

She smirked, replying mischievously, "Are you?"

With a shrug, Sabrath climbed the steps and she followed on his heels. Daryala glanced up at them, and Rynn's skin crawled at the sight of her Nabucite eye. Every meeting with Daryala had been the same. No matter how hard she tried, Rynn never became accustomed to the woman's appearance. *Something feels more wrong this time, but I can't place it.*

Flanking the Black Hand commander were two men who shared an uncannily similar appearance. *Castor and Pollux—the fake twins. They look blank as ever.* They were exactly the same height and moved in the same stiff manner. Both wore their black hair trimmed high and tight, and both had round, dark brown eyes. The only striking differences between them were that Castor had a dimpled chin and Pollux a crooked nose. *We could really confuse people and break Castor's nose a few times.*

Both Sabrath and Rynn saluted. Daryala made no attempt to return the formality, but Castor and Pollux were outranked and did, begrudgingly.

Thirty seconds of silence later, Daryala spoke. "Do you have something to report, Corporal Darkspear?" *Corporal? But I'm...*

Sabrath's normally quiet voice boomed. "Commander Gindir, do you not mean Lieutenant Darkspear?"

Daryala scoffed. "Actually, *Private* is more appropriate, given her failure to perform her duty."

"What duty do you mean, Commander?" Sabrath asked.

"To report any and all activity of the traitor, Arden Arinza, and his allies." Daryala's Nabucite eyeball stared directly at Rynn, but her good eye seemed unfocused. "Perhaps she is one also."

Sabrath began to turn red. *This is bad.* "My daughter is no traitor. We came here in good faith to ask you something. May we?"

Daryala waved a hand lazily at them. "Please do. Humor me."

"Did you... Were you involved in what happened to her Darktouched adopted family?" he boldly questioned.

Daryala shrugged. "What if I was? Sometimes sacrifices are needed to ensure the greater good."

Rynn, unable to choke back her venom, said rancorously, "According to Malank, that's exactly how Chen Huang thinks. If that's the side you're on, then I'll kill you here and now!"

Swept up by her emotions, Rynn called her Sentinel gear, pointing the abyssal halberd at Daryala. Focusing her power, she attempted to sense Darktouched in the vicinity, already plotting her escape. The skill was new to her, and her mind was strained by the effort. Yet, like a battering shadewind gust, comprehension slammed into her, robbing her of breath. Although the HUD identified the one-eyed woman and her guards as Darktouched, she realized that there were only three other Darktouched in the room.

Sabrath, Castor, and Pollux. That's what's wrong! She's not different, but I am. She's not one of us!

Daryala winced almost imperceptibly. "Chen Huang? You'd compare me to *that* butcher?" Light began to radiate from her body, filling the room. Her good eye was no longer wandering, no longer unfocused. It gleamed deadly in the soft glow. "I'm *far* more precise."

"I'm sorry, Dad. I didn't tell you everything," Rynn said, channeling dark energy into her weapon. Sabrath looked at her incredulously and then shook his head and smiled, drawing a black cudgel.

"So, who are you?" Rynn demanded. "One of the Ten? My guess is Senna. Actually, maybe you're just a lackey."

From behind the desk, applause rang out and Daryala stood. "Senna, of course. *Lackey?*" She feigned being emotionally hurt. "Since it seems we aren't friends anymore, I'll *show* you what the Ten can do." Daggers of light appeared in both of her hands. She blinked her good eye and focused it on Rynn. "I should thank you before I kill you. I've grown tired of pretending. Tired of only being able to see through this ridiculous Nabucite eye. Tired of everything. Malank is a fool and Eresh a relic." She shook her head, as if in despair. "Before I watch it slowly fail one more time, I'll abort their plan with my own two hands. I'm doing this *my way* now, girl." Her face remained cold and expressionless. "Just so you know, I killed your family myself." She brought one of the daggers level with her own throat and winked. "Both of them." With a commanding voice, she said to her guards, "Execute these traitors."

Rynn focused power into her halberd and swung toward Senna, but she easily deflected the shockwave. The powerful force, however, surged toward Castor. Caught flat-footed, he dodged too late and was killed instantly by the impact. In the same moment, Sabrath hopped backward and raised his guard as Pollux edged forward, black sword threatening. He charged Sabrath, who slipped around the attack and began bludgeoning him.

Seeing this, Senna grinned wickedly and stepped from behind her desk. Rynn heard her taunts clearly. "Is that really all you can do? Not even Light's Gift can make up for how utterly *deficient* you are. Malank's plan is even more inane and hopeless than I thought."

It's time to run. This had better work, Beyd! As Senna charged at Sabrath, Rynn threw the stun grenade and shielded her eyes. The room exploded in light and shadow, sound and silence, energy and abyss. Blinded and stunned, Senna backpedaled to the far wall.

"Run, Rynn!" Sabrath bellowed at the top of his lungs. "I'll slow her down if it kills me. Just get out of here!"

Tearing her soul to pieces, Rynn sprinted away from them, desperate to reach the stairwell. Panting, crying, and seething at once, she dashed toward the floor above. Through metal door after metal door, past a security checkpoint, and down a corridor, Rynn ran until she was looking at a plain wall.

Beyd bounded down the hallway behind her, yelling, "That was quick!" He flung open the door and pushed Rynn inside, then returned moments later. Liquid Nabucite began to fill the chamber. "Theoretically, a Sentinel should be able to travel through Nabucite. The blue portals use a similar principle. We need to watch out for Zezaht though. I created her to purge bad data from the Compendium. She'll think you're a corrupted record and try to eliminate you."

The darkness was now so thick that Rynn could barely see, even with her upgraded armor on. Beyd's voice entered her mind. "Follow me. Ignore everything else." A pulsing shadow crossed her vision and moved rapidly away. *He should have run into a wall.* "Hurry. And don't watch the lights!"

Rynn struggled to keep her eyes trained on the dark, formless guide. The further they progressed, the brighter and noisier the Nabucite became. Like will-o'-the-wisps, lights of many dazzling colors streamed around her. They took the shape of strangers, friends, animals, plants, buildings, tablets, books, food items, and sundry others. *I'm seeing everything ever logged in the Compendium.* Voices thundered and reverberated. Above her, Eldras Shurali delivered a bombastic speech about the importance of preserving knowledge for future generations. To her left, a chorus of nearly mythological Dark-touched leaders opined on the issues of their day.

Overwhelmed by sound, light, and her own emotions, Rynn collapsed to the ground and covered her ears, shutting her eyes. A shadowy force plucked her up and set her on her feet, and Beyd's voice again touched her thoughts. "Follow me, Sentinel. Or you'll die." Together, they picked their way through the madness for ages.

A frightful bellow ripped through Rynn's consciousness, scattering the lights and silencing the clamor. Beyd yelled, "Bugger! Zezaht. Run!"

Although they galloped ever onward, Rynn never grew weary. Not physically. But her mind began to fragment. Dreams and visions clouded her eyes, and several times she startled as though awakened. Zezaht drew nearer, threatening to end her story. To erase her. To remove that which did not belong.

In the distance, a blue glow welcomed them, but it was too far. Rynn crumpled once more, succumbing to the mental burden of being inundated by millennia of compiled information. Its caretaker, loathing her presence, desired only to expunge her. Her dark guide lifted her up once more, bore her to the portal, and threw her in.

When Rynn woke, she was alone in an unknown, cold, dark place. In the distance, buildings made of greenish-blue living stone seemed to float in the abyss. Willing herself to her feet, she plodded toward them through the scraping, groaning darkness.

38

RYKER'S REQUIREMENTS

T HE FIVE LINGERED AROUND the Dewey Monument in the heart of Union Square, the Greek goddess Nike towering over them on her columnar perch. Malank remained aloof while they solidified the details of their plan.

Asante informed Fiala, "Toyo agreed to the Fabricated items our friends requested. They'll be delivered when we're sure Darren is alive. I'm carrying samples." He twisted slightly to point out the backpack slung over his right shoulder.

Fiala, stone-faced, said, "Good. You'll need these." From her pants pocket, she retrieved three pairs of discs made of a clear, scaly material. Each one was about the size of a contact lens. Handing one set to each Darktouched, she instructed them, "Put them in both eyes. They'll fall off after a day."

When Lucas held one of the scales over his right eye, it leapt toward his eyeball, grabbing and adhering to it. For a moment, his vision exploded into thousands of colors. He blinked several times, and when the world had returned to normal, he put the other in his left eye.

His mom quickly did the same while coaching him, "Inside, don't use your Abovename. Darknames are fine, and aliases are probably even safer." Asante gave a thumbs up to signal his agreement.

Fiala spoke again, "Without the scales, you'll be blind where we're going. Lightborne don't need them, obviously."

Lucas stared at Asante, who had just put on his own pair, trying to glimpse a visible difference in the other man's eyes. There was none. Swiveling his head, he searched the sky and buildings for something new and previously unseen, but remained disappointed.

Tara questioned the Lightborne with impatience in her voice. "My husband is waiting. Can we lock in our plan for egress?"

"A Returner can send you anywhere you've been on the surface. I assume you have a destination in mind?" Fiala inquired.

"Yes," nodded Tara. "Do you want to know where?"

Fiala turned to face Malank, who said only a single word, "No." When she crossed her arms and tapped her foot, even though it was only once, he grimaced and added, "Alazar told me that if we know, it could alter key details of his plan."

Rolling her eyes, Fiala asked him, "*Alazar* told you?"

Malank shrugged. "The fate charm did, then. Also, it's time." He took off the pendant and handed it to Lucas. "This belongs to you now. Whether you believe in it or not, I only ask that you keep it."

Lucas reached out his hand slowly while the other three watched wide-eyed. "Are you sure?" he asked the red-maned Lightborne.

Malank grunted a response. "No. But Alazar— *The charm* said you needed it more than me. Promise me, and it's yours."

"I promise, Malank," Lucas said sincerely. "You can have it back when this is over." He dipped his head to put on the necklace and pulled the oblong jewel along the leather cord so that it rested next to the white raven pendant Rynn had given him.

Shaking his head, Malank said quietly, "I don't think that's how this goes. But thanks. We should go get your dad." He began to walk away from them but stopped and turned back. "One last thing. Mammon has no interest in Chen's war, but that doesn't mean he's not vindictive. We don't know how much Alan told them or how much they forced out of Darren. Assume the worst." Then he once again bounded away, the others following behind.

Once across the square, they descended a stairway. As they walked along, Lucas noticed the signpost overhead read Geary Street. At the corner, a blinking hand icon warned them they only had ten seconds remaining to cross. Casually, they sauntered in the direction of a building that to Lucas resembled a giant layer cake from which someone had cut two thin, vertical slices. He imagined the twin rectangular prisms on the left side of the building staring resentfully at their plump, cube-shaped sibling on the right. Behind them, a much taller building loomed over the siblings. Asante, who was last in the group, jumped onto the curb just as the timer reached its end.

Proceeding along Geary Street, they stopped in front of an open section of wall between two sets of double doors that may have been delivery entrances. Fiala reached out with her right hand, grabbed onto something invisible, and pulled. A door appeared before them, swinging open on unseen hinges. With a wave of her hand, she motioned them inside. A narrow hallway wide enough for two people to stand abreast beckoned them forward. At the end of it, a lone guard wearing full Reclaimer gear stood beside an elevator door. When the group approached, the guard pressed a button and the elevator opened. Without speaking, they entered the compartment and the doors closed behind them.

Lucas never felt a lurch or the movement of the lift ascending, but within two seconds of the doors closing, they opened again. This time, guards stood on both sides facing them, and the lefthand one waved them inside. Immediately, Lucas felt warmth around him. While less intense than during the Reclaimer attack on his home, the light still felt like the hot summer sun on his skin. They were passing through an enclosed walkway, the floors, walls, and ceiling of which were transparent.

Ahead of Lucas, Malank seemed to be floating in open air over the cityscape below. While this was startling to him, he reasoned it was no more exciting than his first steps onto Irkalla Tower's pure Nabucite main floor. Instead, what truly captivated him was the appearance of the scenery itself. The world beyond the footbridge looked like the color negatives of old photographs his parents kept in their garage. Everything took on a reddish-brown tint. Above, the sky was distinctly red, the clouds black. Below, the asphalt appeared white and plant leaves almost blue. Unable to help himself, Lucas reached out a hand to touch the wall and was surprised by how cool it felt.

From behind, he heard Asante say, "I haven't been this weirded out since I was eight. It's like the world's turned inside out."

Fiala whispered, "What the Dim and Darktouched see is only a mirage. This is closer to the true nature of light."

"Ironic, though, isn't it?" asked Tara.

Fiala half-turned to face her and shrugged. "I don't get it. What is?"

"That from up here, the Darktouched are white and you all the opposite," Tara mused.

Malank laughed from down the hall in front of them, remarking, "In my many years, I never thought of that. Maybe we were the bad guys the whole time."

Fiala snapped at them, her tone stirring in Lucas the same feeling as her foot tapping, "We're almost across. Pay attention."

They progressed the remainder of the way in silence, entering into a circular chamber with yet two more guards stationed on either side of the doorway. A few steps further into the room, they were greeted by an athletically built man with wavy, shoulder length blond hair and a tanned complexion. Remarkably symmetrical facial features and large, alluring blue eyes reminded Lucas of the movie and boy-band stars Aella had gushed over when they were growing up.

Wearing a toothy smile while casting an openly contemptuous look at them, the man said, "Welcome, traitors and rats. I am Adonis Mallory, Fourth in the lineage of our Pathkeeper, Chen Huang." Shedding any false pretenses, he continued in a condescending tenor, "Also, attendant to *His Greatness*, he of many forms, Mammon Ryker, Third in Chen Huang's lineage. Please, follow me."

Lucas saw Asante and his mom look at Fiala with concern. She gave them an almost imperceptible shake of her head, demanding silence, and signaled for them to follow Adonis.

Near the middle of the room, they formed a curved line in front of an enormously obese, patchily balding man seated on a padded golden throne. Lucas instinctively knew he was Mammon Ryker. Perhaps because of the Lightborne scales on his eyes, he saw a wide bubble surrounding the self-styled sovereign. Guessing it to be some kind of protective ward, he dismissed his initial read that the glutton was an easy mark. A cunning, deadly glint in Mammon's deep-set brown eyes belied his amusingly repulsive presence.

Adonis strode gracefully to stand beside his master, whose sticky voice reached out and slathered over everyone directly in front of him. Food particles clung to his chin and the collar of his white suit jacket and tie. "To business, then. You, boy." He pointed at Lucas. "Come closer." Lucas glanced furtively at his mom and suppressed a smirk before taking two long steps forward to stand just beyond the shield's edge. With the finger of his right hand, Mammon summoned him closer. "Come, little Darktouched. Adorable, isn't he, Adonis?"

Adonis sneered as Lucas stepped inside the bubble. "Yes, Master Mammon. But try to remember why they're here. Almon will be upset if—"

"Almon has no authority here!" said Mammon, spitting. "The only person I bow to is Chen, and even then only when necessary."

As they argued, Lucas realized the bubble was more than a defensive mechanism, if it was one at all. Instead, it was a trick of the light—an illusory mirror. From within, the hideous Lightborne rivaled Adonis in his handsomeness. Well-muscled, with a strong jaw and full head of black hair parted perfectly on the left, he struck an imposing figure. Rather than slopping over the arms of the golden chair, Mammon's body reclined mightily upon it, one elbow bent and his head lazily resting upon a closed fist.

He stroked his chin and smiled warmly at Lucas. "Were I interested in such pleasures, you might be my Ganymede. The beautiful boy who, although mortal, became the cup-bearer and lover of Zeus. Alas, such things no longer entice me. For you, I have a different game in mind."

Malank raised his voice warningly. "There were no games in our arrangement, Mammon. We agreed to terms. My friend here has your samples."

Asante paced forward, the backpack held in front of him. "In this bag is a perfectly re-created section of Picasso's *Women of Algiers*. And, as requested, a sprig of Roman silphium. The dodo clone is in holding. Your full demand will be met when we see that our friend is alive."

Mammon waved a hand and Adonis took the bag, looked inside, and nodded. "It appears to be as he says." Upon receiving another signal from his master, Adonis disappeared through a doorway directly behind the throne. Moments later, he returned, roughly pushing an exhausted-looking Darren forward until he crumpled next to the throne.

When their eyes met, Lucas had to fiercely resist the urge call out to his father, to run over and help him to his feet. *Don't give the bastards the satisfaction.* He gritted his teeth and stared daggers at his father's captors.

Adonis declared, "Everything is in order, Lord Mammon. Shall we formalize the exchange?"

"No," said Mammon. "There will be no deal until my requirements are satisfied. That means blood sport. Show me what you're capable of, eh, boy?"

Malank growled, saying, "If it's conflict you want, let *me* oblige you."

Mammon waved a hand dismissively. "I know what the Ten can do, fool. Besides, you haven't set foot in the Lightwatch for centuries. I doubt you could even kill Adonis." The blond man scoffed from his place beside the throne, and Mammon returned his gaze to Lucas. "If you want to save your pathetic excuse of a father, you'll step through the door." As he dramatically pounded his left fist on the throne three times, a Reclaimer appeared from the right side of the room, revealing a previously hidden pathway.

Lucas's mom shook her head at him, eyes full of fear, but Asante moved close to him and whispered in his ear. "Be careful, kid. We have no idea what this is all about. This Ichabod is up to something." *Ichabod? Does he mean Mammon? But in "The Legend of Sleepy Hollow," Ichabod Crane was tall and gangly. If that's how Asante sees Mammon, then he must look different to everyone. I wonder which Mammon is the real one.*

Telling himself that it didn't matter, Lucas dipped his head and shrugged. "Like always, what choice do I have?" *At least I'm a Sentinel now. I might not die.*

One shaky step in front of another, Lucas walked to the door and onto a transparent footbridge like the one they had just passed through. This time, though, a staircase led up through the color negative scenery, and he glowered at the red sky above, irritated at his fate. Without truly realizing it, he passed through an inky barrier and continued his climb. *How many times will this amazing plan leave me stuck holding the bag for everyone else's mistakes?*

His thoughts stopped cold, just as his feet did, when he reached the top of the stairs and found himself staring across the room at a Severed. The creature charged Lucas instantly, its empty blue eyes and ear-destroying scream paralyzing him. He barely had enough time to summon his armor and halberd before the first blow struck and he was thrown backward, high against the wall. Falling hard to the floor below, the breath knocked from his lungs, he struggled to regain his composure. The creature was upon him again, tearing and flailing at his throat and heart, trying to end his life swiftly. Lucas frantically attempted to draw out some unknown ability, but nothing happened.

The Severed abruptly broke off its frontal assault and flew high into the air. It plunged toward him, giving him a small window to dodge. Spinning to his left at the moment it struck, Lucas avoided major damage but suffered a graze to his right forearm that slowed and weakened his counterstrike. Even so, the robed spirit stumbled backward with a shriek and quickly retreated across the room. Using the moment to recover, Lucas breathed deeply, quickly formulating a plan. *How can I turn its speed and aggression against it?*

Remembering the Wisdom's Bond test, he sidled around the perimeter of the room toward the Severed. *Defense and quick counters. Even when they dodge to the side, they're trying to attack.* When he was within twenty feet, the monster again surged toward him. Jabbing quickly with his halberd, he grazed its torso, then prepared for the next attack. Anticipating a shift to his left and another flurry of blows, he slashed fiercely in an arc, this time gashing the monstrosity's thighs.

Now furious, the beast leapt into the air and again plummeted. Instead of trying to dodge, Lucas carved the air with an upward stroke, forcing the creature to abandon its assault and evade to the side. Remembering Rynn's semi-circular cut, he spun rapidly with all the strength left in him. A wail filled the room as the abomination's legs were both badly cut. Barely able to move, it desperately pressed the attack. With a ferocity that shocked Lucas, it surged forward and latched onto his arm. In a second, it was scrambling onto his back, threatening to choke the life from him.

Lucas knew he had the advantage, so he didn't give in to panic. With both legs, using the power of a swimmer's wall kick, he vaulted rearward. The adversaries slammed against the wall viciously and the creature fell, briefly stunned. With a sharp twist and blind thrust, Lucas pierced the abomination through its liver and pinned it to the wall. But as he watched it die, utter horror overcame him, and he sank to his knees. In death, the spirit's rage quelled, it remembered who it was.

Lucas was staring into the bloodied, broken face of Alan Linzer.

The last shred of the man who had been a grandfather to him weakly lifted a hand, pleading for him to hold it. When their fingers touched, they were suddenly sitting on the Linzers' front porch. Alan stood next to Lucas looking as he remembered him, wearing a baseball cap, Hawaiian shirt, and cargo shorts. The only difference was his eyes. They remained the deep, hollow blue of a Severed.

Alan spoke softly, as though from far away. "I'm sorry for everything, Luc. Nora and I wanted to protect you, but we made a mess of it." Lucas shook his head, and a sickening upwelling of despair choked his throat. Words failed him, and Alan kept speaking. "We wanted to spare you kids. To help you in a way we failed to help our Jamie. We lost her, and we weren't going to lose you too. Those people who used you from the time you were born needed to be stopped."

Lucas continued shaking his head, managing to choke out the words, "Jamie's alive, Alan. Vidaya Murtabak hid her. She thought it was the only way to keep her safe."

Alan looked up at him in bewilderment and elation. "What? Our Jamie is alive? Vidaya saved our Jamie? Does Nora know?" His voice broke and he collapsed to the deck boards, the edges of which were slowly dissolving into particles of white light.

"Vidaya said it was Nora who helped Irmina escape her destiny. I assumed you both knew," Lucas said. The dream world was eroding around them, counting down the seconds to its end.

"No," Alan gasped. "She never told me, but I accepted my fate long ago. I deserve this end for what I did to Nora and Jamie. And the poor boy who replaced her. And to you. My death was acceptable—I just wanted them all to suffer. Even the ones who called themselves your parents. *Especially* them. That's why I sought out the Lightwatch. Nora told me not to. She told me they'd betray us, but I wouldn't listen. I'm so sorry, Luc."

Lucas stooped down, grabbed Alan's hand and lifted him to his feet. Their time was almost up. "You can rest easy, Grandpa Alan. The plan is different now, and I have someone I can trust. Thank you for everything."

Alan smiled. "I love you, Luc. You be strong. I wish this old man could've done more to help you. Goodbye."

"I love you. Goodbye," said Lucas numbly.

As the last bit of Alan left the world, Lucas opened his eyes and realized he was back in the room where he had battled the Severed. Tears were streaming down his face as he descended the staircase, passed the Reclaimer guard, and returned to face the ones who had murdered his grandfather. The monsters who had used him to deliver the killing blow. Through a haze, he saw the stunned faces of Malank and Fiala, and the vengeful rage in Asante's eyes. His mom was sitting on the floor supporting his dad in her lap, eyes red and mouth trembling.

Mammon Ryker now appeared to Lucas as a gloating, jeering sports fan dressed in a basketball jersey and baggy athletic shorts. He was flashing dollar bills in his right hand—each finger was adorned with a gaudy ring. Bouncing animatedly on his golden throne, he was clapping and cheering at a holographic display of the makeshift arena where Lucas had killed Alan Linzer. Adonis backed away with a smile on his face, willing Lucas to end his lord's life.

Lucas pointed his halberd at Mammon. "How dare you. How dare you end that man's life in that way. You have no right to play games with our lives, you faceless coward. I should kill you right now."

Mammon grew quiet, and his voice when he spoke was deadly serious. "I did you a favor, rat. That traitor became a Severed before Chen Huang and his lapdog, Almon Cain, found out about your plan. If they knew, we'd all be one step closer to non-existence."

Malank and Fiala stepped between Lucas and Mammon, shielding him from the Sentinel's retribution. "What are you talking about, Mammon?" Fiala asked him. "What is Chen's goal now?" Asante moved forward to stand with Lucas, placing a hand on his shoulder.

With a gluey cackle, Mammon told them, "He's given up on saving the world from itself. Now, he wants to pull off the Lightborne equivalent of a Reshaping."

Malank stepped forward, and his body shimmered against a faded background as he summoned a battle-axe made of white, dazzling light. "What does that mean?"

Mammon shook his head disdainfully. "Chen's trying to find the land where the Ten first received the Gift. He believes that it's deep in the Infra, and he's been frantically snatching up Darktouched trying to find a way down." He leaned back, grabbing a straight-brimmed ball cap from the arm of his throne and placing it at a strange angle on his head. "After stealing the power he thinks is there, he intends to burn the world's tapestry and weave a new one. All that the light has ever touched—the story of this world—wiped away in a flash. Poof! In that scenario, you'd better hope Chen writes you back into the story. You might not be *you*, though."

Shucking off anguish, Lucas snarled at him, "Then why play games with us? Why not just help us or fight alongside us?"

Mammon shrugged. "The Lightwatch can't be beaten. And I'm too old and tired to fight a war, boy. I thought it would be fun to stick it to them before they find me out. They will. From the snake behind me, most likely." Adonis flinched at the indirect mention of his person and slinked off down the hall behind the throne. "I wanted to see for myself how capable you were. You're not bad, but not good enough to win against *them*."

Fiala interjected, "Where is your pet snake going? We still need to use the Returner."

"Ah, yes," Mammon laughed, his bejeweled right hand now holding a gold vape pen. He took a deep draw from the device and slowly blew nicotine vapor into the air. "The Returner is down that hallway. I suggest you hurry and catch him. The Reclaimers follow my orders. They won't hinder or help you. Good luck."

39

RETURN TO THE START

T HE WORLD CRUMBLED INWARD from its edges as Lucas witnessed events unfold around him. Like a heartbeat, necessary and relentless, time's pulse moved his companions forward while he reeled from Alan's death. In the pit of his soul, he yearned for a moment where everything stopped, where he could sit, think, and mourn. Yet, in a blur, Malank and Fiala vanished in pursuit of Adonis. Asante raced to Tara's side, crouching on one knee to help Darren to his feet.

In the rush, Mammon called out to Lucas, beckoning him nearer. Not thinking, he shifted closer to the hideous Lightborne and entered his deceptive bubble. When he did, his dark Sentinel armor and halberd dissipated, leaving him with little defense and no means of attack. Still dazed, he hardly noticed his extreme vulnerability. When Mammon's left arm stretched toward him, he recoiled reflexively.

"I mean you no harm, boy," Mammon cooed, then puffed on the vape pen. "Consider this my last will and testament. I offer you a glimmer of hope. Seek out this place when, if ever, you and your friends are ready to challenge the Lightwatch."

Lucas forced himself to remain motionless as Mammon's body briefly glimmered and the world turned dull behind him. Light pooled into a seed-shaped conjuration held between the Lightborne's index finger and thumb. After depositing the bead of light into Lucas's palm, Mammon forced him to shut his fingers around it.

A warm light shone briefly from inside of Lucas's closed fist, and his mind's eye traveled to a small complex of domed buildings huddled together deep underwater. In the same instant, he became aware of their precise location.

Mammon seized his arm and gripped it tightly, saying, "Do not take *too* long, boy. Save our memory—all who have wandered in this rotten world. Even those of us who deserve it least." Then he released his grip and through some unseen force pushed Lucas backward, darkening the ward around his throne so that only his silhouette was visible. "Now go. Let me enjoy the little time I have left."

From somewhere far away, he heard Tara and Asante calling out to him, but his mind failed to process their words. The jewel around his neck pulsed brightly and he heard Alazar's voice. "Lucas, you need to move. There will be time for thinking later."

Jarred awake, he willed his feet to life and caught up to his parents and Asante just as they reached the doorway leading to the Returner. "Will Dad be okay?" he asked, stepping around them and into the color-negative corridor.

As Lucas summoned his armor and halberd, his dad croaked an answer, "I'll be fine. Just need a beer."

Lucas surprised himself by giggling. "Good," he said. "Then let's get out of here and find some."

Progressing rapidly down the pathway, Lucas scanned for threats. He still saw no sign of Malank and Fiala, but a section of floor lit up with a fiery glow, drawing his attention. Not wanting to get too far ahead of the other three, he waited in silence. Moments that felt eternal crawled by, but soon they were standing together inside of the flowing red light. Then they were hurtling up and forward on a direct line toward a tall, pyramidal structure towering over the cityscape.

When the platform stopped, the four Darktouched stood together within a spherical chamber situated high above the monolithic building. Malank and Fiala awaited them near a pedestal in the center of the room, holding Adonis Mallory captive on the ground between them. The blond man tilted his bruised face up at them—his mouth twitching into a bloody grin that lingered—but said nothing. Rope made of green light held his hands together behind his back, and a less-noticeable green patch covered his voice box. Lucas hoped the restraints numbed and stung like the green needles he had been shot with days earlier.

Fiala addressed the Darktouched as they approached, "This will be adieu for a while. After we go, one of you needs to touch the pedestal and think of a destination. The Returner will light up. As long as each of you has been to the chosen place, you'll be sent there instantly."

Malank circled around Fiala and wrapped his right arm around Lucas. "I'm very sorry about Alan. Fi and I never expected this." He backed away and bowed his head. "Be safe, young man."

Fiala's hand made contact with the pedestal. It shimmered against a faded background, then disappeared behind undulating light. Asante hurriedly asked the Lightborne, "Where will you go? How can we contact you?"

"Somewhere safe, until the dust settles," Malank said. *The Cradle? No, it must be somewhere else.* "Take care." Picking up Adonis with one hand, he dragged the man into the blinding glare, both of their bodies cloaked in radiant light. With a twinkle, they were gone.

"Be careful in the dark. Our other Sentinel may have kicked the hornet's nest already," Fiala said. In a blink, she also disappeared, and the room darkened.

Tara stepped forward to tell the Returner their intended destination, and the light blazed again. Asante, still propping up Darren, turned to Lucas and asked, "What did she mean?"

"Rynn planned to confront Daryala Gindir," he responded. "It's too much to tell right now. We need to move quickly. I know the way." *Or I hope so, anyway.*

Treading forward, he felt himself being disassembled into molecules and shot high above the earth. Briefly, he saw a concave reflection of the world below. In color-negative hues, a second San Francisco reflected the one beneath, and then vanished into a distorted swirl. A tingling sensation enveloped him, and his feet touched the ground. Overhead, the morning sun broke through the clouds, pricking at his skin. He was standing in his own backyard.

Not waiting for the others, Lucas marched to the toolshed and threw open the door. Before entering, he vainly searched for Mai but saw no trace of her. *Be safe, girl. We'll meet again someday.* Battling his desire to call out to the coydog, he pushed inside. Footsteps followed behind him as he flung open the hatch and dropped to the floor below. Asante's voice touched his mind: "Scout the passageway to the outer ring. I brought your dad's KALM bands, but we still can't fight or move quickly."

Lucas responded over the comm, "Already on it!" Striding briskly, he was in the simulator room within seconds. As he neared the opposite side, the hatch swung open, and he slipped through. Head swiveling and weapon ready, he advanced down the cement path soundlessly. When he reached the wide divide, he easily hopped across. The shuffling of feet echoed down the path from behind him—Asante and his parents had reached the entrance.

Moving cautiously but swiftly, Lucas progressed to the next doorway and paused at the fork in the path. Curious and with a moment to spare, he turned left and scouted ahead. A few steps down the hall, another metal door awaited. Ignoring his inhibitions, he hurriedly ran to it and was shocked when it swung open. Inside, he glimpsed piles of books and shelves filled with cuneiform tablets and Uldu scriptstones. Against the wall to his left sat a desk. Bewildered, he peered down at it for a few seconds. *What is going on here?* Lying in plain view was a semi-translucent gem very similar to those he had spied in the R&D lab. Those that had been attached to Black Hand prototype weaponry.

Sensing a presence behind him, he whirled and raised his halberd. Rather than an enemy, he faced his mom. On a private channel, she said to him, "Kilk has been paranoid for months. Thinks he's being played for a fool because no progress has been made on Everdark. I think he's right."

Lucas nodded. "Eresh has been feeding him false information. Daryala believes she's using his Delve finds to develop those gems," he said, motioning toward the one on the desk. "Beyd thinks she's trying to steal Lightborne power and use it against them."

His mom shook her head. "I don't think that's right, Lucas. Based on my analysis, they're only able to store a limited amount of light energy."

"I don't understand."

"I'm not sure either," she said. "I have theories, but now's not the time. We have to go."

Grabbing his arm, she pulled him out of the room and back down the path. They took the right fork and met Asante and Darren as the cement floor turned to gravel and the cavern widened. No Lightborne pursued them this time, but even in the dark stillness they remained quiet and alert. Not waiting for the lift, Lucas leapt from the ledge and summoned his wings. Below him, the platform ascended to meet his three companions. Swooping down, he landed effortlessly on the ground below and quickly made his way to the writhing blue barricade.

"All clear to the end," Lucas informed them. "I'll check on Charon."

On the other side of the barrier, Charon's purple-and-pink luminescence greeted him. When he reached out with his mind, the ferrybot spoke to him in unnecessarily hushed tones. "Ah, you have a Darkname and Abzupass this time. Good for you, lad! All for naught, though. They've closed the gates at the Complex terminal. The entire city is locked down."

"Do you know why?" asked Arden. *Because I'm pretty sure I do.*

"No," said Charon. "Early reports are vague, but supposedly there's one dead Black Hand and another clinging to life in Medical Services. A perpetrator has been detained." *Oh, no. Rynn actually did it. And she got caught besides.*

Arden questioned him urgently, "Are you able to drop us off between the Abzu Hub and the Complex terminal?"

"Headed for the Cradle are we, young Sentinel?" the ferrybot asked shrewdly. "Don't look so surprised, Arden Arinza. Beydin Krenneth *is* my creator, after all. I am quite splendiferous, am I not?"

Grinning behind his suit, Arden declared flatteringly, "You're amazing, Charon!" Pointing at his parents and Asante, who had just passed through the barrier, he said, "Can you take us all at once?"

Charon cleared his nonexistent throat, and glowing nanobots swirled to envelop them. "I can indeed transport you! Although, I should warn you that there are guards at each main station. We may be in for a bumpy ride."

As they whooshed through the water, Reina asked Arden, "Where are we going?"

Arden shrugged. "Not totally sure, but I'll know it when I see it." When she huffed disapprovingly, his anger stirred. "There are secret doors to a sanctuary called the Cradle, and only people close to Eresh can find them. Since the Abzu Complex is locked down, we have to go there instead."

"What? Why?" Her voice held great concern.

"I think Rynn might have attacked Daryala Gindir. There's no time to explain. You have to trust me," he said firmly.

Charon's voice boomed around them. "We're almost to the station entrance. Brace yourselves." Accelerating rapidly, the luminescent cloud turned a threatening crimson color. It carried them through a security checkpoint, knocking down two guards dressed in Black Hand uniforms and forcing a third to dodge out of the way. Rounding a curve, they began to descend with stomach-wrenching velocity. When the water turned to a cascade of droplets all around them, Charon slowed and spoke again. "We are almost there, young Sentinel. Fear not. You will know how to find the door." The ferrybot released them and surged back toward the Black Hand guards, still far in the distance. One tossed a dark object at the nanobots and they began to spasm and flicker, then turned black.

"Charon got us this far," Arden shouted. "Let's move!" They swam and floated through the remnant mist of the Abzu, which fell simultaneously downward and upward around them. Swirling dark water mixed with abyssal shadow embraced them. In the distance, Arden sensed the doorway summoning him. With no assurance he was right, he led them further on. They followed unquestioningly. Sentinel powers alerted him to the guards closing in behind them, and he raced ahead. But the portal—their only chance at escape—remained invisible.

He began to despair. *I can't find it! We're going to be caught. If Rynn's already captured, this is the end.* But just when he had almost given up, a faint blue glow in the distance held his breath captive. Using his HUD, he made sure the sighting was real before allowing air into his lungs. Turning around, he dashed back to his parents and Deveras, directing them over the comm, "It's not much further. Hurry!" The guards were quickly drawing near. With his dad hampered, Arden would need to buy time.

Flying past his mom, he drew his halberd and steeled himself for battle. With a strike readied, he tucked his legs into his chest and kicked, propelled forward by his Sentinel armor at frightening speed. Unexpectedly, a sparkling light emanated from the fate charm, glittering on the mist. A life-sized version of Alazar materialized, and his voice rang out, "Run, you fool pup! I'll slow them."

Summoning twin swords of light, Alazar charged two Black Hands, incapacitating one with an unavoidable blast of heat, light, and sound. Arden slashed at another, who scurried backward to safety. Spinning around, he dashed toward salvation.

Propelled again by his black armor, he arrived at the door and pulled it open. A familiar blue portal appeared some feet inside the doorway. While Alazar's projection harried their enemies, Deveras flung Arden's dad through the gateway and then leapt in after him. Arden saw a flicker of white beneath him. As Reina approached, his eyes latched on to the snowy white owl. *Not now, you damned bird!*

His mother yelled, "Arden, we have to go!"

"It's the owl again. I'm going after it," he said calmly. "I love you, Mom." Abandoning everything else, he dove in pursuit of the winged messenger.

Her reply reached his mind. "I love you, too, Arden. Be strong." Somehow, he was aware the very moment that the blue portal dissipated. *At least they're safe now.*

Behind him, the guards continued their chase. A faint light returned to the fate charm, and Alazar's voice spoke to him. "This was not in *any* predictive model. Are you sure you know what you're doing?"

"No. Now shut up and let me do this!" Arden said.

The owl floated on fully spread wings and he mimicked it. For a time, they danced together on the edge of Abzu and Infra. And then it took a nosedive without any warning. Panicked, Arden boosted himself, rushing after his omen, willing himself to fly faster. He felt the Black Hands breaking off their pursuit. *Maybe they're afraid. Maybe I should be too.*

Ahead of the owl, a blazing white image appeared. Arden recognized it instantly. It was a four-pointed star with three wavy lines extending from between each point, enclosed in a circle. *Just like the stone dais. It looks like the sun.* The bird flew unswervingly into it, and then exploded into thousands of glowing feathers.

Logic told Arden to slow down, but an inscrutable feeling rising within him disagreed. *You only die once.* Recklessly, he accelerated. Where the owl had impacted, a distortion like cracked leather appeared. Plunging into it, he heard a deafening crack and felt intense pressure around his body. On the other side, the clawing gloom of the Deep Infra scraped against him and shadewinds battered him from all directions. Then, as though satisfied with the toll they had extracted, they ceased, and absolute nothingness enfolded him.

40

CHILD OF SHADOW, BRINGER OF LIGHT

ARDEN'S FEET TOUCHED DOWN on the stone dais. He gazed up at colossal pillars from the sun symbol's heart. The gem hung around his neck shimmered silently, casting its light upon the white raven pendant. Vainly, he tried to contact Rynn, knowing that he was cut off from the world, alone in this place. The memory of Alan's death tore into his conscious mind, and despair again clutched at his throat. Sinking to his knees, he let the tears slip down his cheeks and onto the cold surface of the dais.

Gliding down on open wings, the white owl landed in front of him. Its melancholy voice freed him from misery's embrace. "Child of Shadow, Bringer of Light. You have arrived, journeyed, returned. Now you are ready to uncover the Ten's truth. Piece by piece, bit by bit, little by little."

Arden looked forlornly into the raptor's eyes. "And then what? How will any of this help me find Tiamat or stop the Lightwatch?"

The bird flapped its wings. "Knowledge, wisdom, truth. These are the keys to your fate. And to the plan, scheme, plot of the man whose remnant hangs around your neck. You have found, carried, brought his light. Together, we three will open the path. Awaken, Alazar."

Heeding the owl's call, the fate charm dazzled, lighting up the ten towers surrounding the circular platform. Arden believed now more than before that the enormous columns were holding up the entire world, eternally supporting the Infra, Abzu, and Aboveworld. A life-sized Alazar again materialized from the gem, and its light gradually ebbed. He spoke to the owl. "I see now. This place embodies *our* story. That would make you one of us then, no?"

The owl flew high up into the air. "Perhaps, possibly, maybe. Before that, Alazar, the boy must hear *your* tale. Arden Arinza, Lucas Devlin, now you will begin to see, understand, grasp how the threads of fate came to be placed in your hands. Then the next path will open before you."

With a scream, the winged creature flew into one of the titanic supports, causing it to blaze in the darkness. Arden and Alazar strode toward it together. When they reached the edge of the stone dais, the pillar seemed to shift away from them. After a few seconds, Arden realized that it was falling. Air pushed out around it as it tumbled faster and faster into the black. With a booming crash, it impacted the abyssal sea and settled. A bridge of light extended before them, and they crossed over. They walked in silence, the white owl flying in circles overhead, watching over them from above.

Glossary of Terms

Darktouched Terminology

- ABOVEWORLD: Term used by the Darktouched to describe everything above the Abzu. In effect, this is the earth's surface and all civilizations built upon it.

- ABZU: Dark water beneath the earth that is typically only navigable by the Darktouched. Serves as the main entry point into the Darktouched world, including the Abzu Complex and Infra.

- ABZU COMPLEX: The Darktouched city that lies between the Abzu and Infra. Consists of Irkalla Tower and the residential ring surrounding it.

- ABZU HUB: A series of entryways and connected underwater pathways (also called the "outer ring") where some Light can still reach. Abzu Hubs center around a main station, which is the primary entry point into the Abzu and Abzu Complex. The Darktouched consider Abzu Hubs the aboveworld's bottommost layer.

- ABZUBALL: The primary sport of the Darktouched. Played inside of a spherical playing field composed entirely of water.

- COMPENDIUM: A Nabucite construct that stores all information collected by the Darktouched in the aboveworld, Abzu, and Infra.

- DARKTOUCHED: Those who have inherited the Darktouched Right and gained the ability to navigate and thrive within the Abzu and Infra.

- DARKTOUCHED PLEDGE: For those who have received the Darktouched Right. The oath taken against a subset of laws critical to the preservation of Darktouched society and life in the Abzu Complex and Infra.

- DARKTOUCHED RIGHT: The passing of Darktouched power to a new host when the previous owner dies.

- DISAVOWED: The collective group of individuals who have been banished from Darktouched society. Their Darktouched abilities, as well as all memories of anything related to the Darktouched, are sealed via Edict. They are permanently banned from entering the Abzu Hubs, Abzu Complex, or the Infra.

- DISCIPLINE: A profession recognized by one of the missions. Only sanctioned disciplines are eligible for monetary compensation and professional rating.

- EDICT: A set of terms established by one or more of the mission leaders that is enforced via insertion of an implant. If the person receiving the Edict does not follow it, the implant will cause them to enter a coma and/or die.

- FABRICATOR: A machine that uses Nabucite to create items. In Darktouched society, Fabricators are the primary source of daily-use goods and foodstuffs.

- FUNNEL, the: The gateway into the Infra located at the bottom of the Abzu Complex.

- HEADS-UP DISPLAY (HUD): A series of visual overlays served up by KALM technology to help Darktouched navigate and perform disciplines within the Abzu and Infra.

- INFRA: A place beneath and within the earth where Light does not reach. Only a Darktouched in full KALM gear can survive and thrive in the Infra, and it is the primary location where they perform the daily tasks of their chosen discipline.

- IRKALLA TOWER: The heart of the Abzu Complex and command center for mission leaders and other high-ranking officials. Irkalla Tower also houses critical facilities, services, and restricted-access information.

- KNOWLEDGE ACQUISITION AND LIFECYCLE MANAGEMENT (KALM) TECHNOLOGY: The gear used by Darktouched within the Abzu and Infra. Primarily consists of a full-body suit and HUD. The label is also applied to Darktouched machinery.

- LEDGE, the: The nickname that Delvers have given the records access floor inside of Irkalla Tower. The Ledge serves as a starting or jumping off point for most Delver jobs, as well as those of other missions and disciplines.

- MISSION: For the Darktouched, one of five functional groups. Each mission has a leader and its own strategy, goals, and objectives. There are five missions, each with a clear role in society and a set of responsibilities it must uphold: Delvers, Seekers, Black Hand, Surface Affairs, and Support.

- NABUCITE: A mineral of pure darkness that is essential to Darktouched power and society.

- REDUCER: A machine that decomposes matter to a molecular level, thereby allowing for its reuse in a Fabricator.

- RESHAPING: An event occurring many thousands of years in the past that most Darktouched believe to be mythological.

- SHADESCREEN: A disorienting defensive capability of the KALM gear.

- SHADESURFING: A transportation capability of the KALM gear. Shadesurfing is the primary means of travel in the Infra.

- SHADEWIND: A surge of energy occurring in the Infra due to strong gravitational—and other—forces.

- WISDOM'S BOND: A connection between two Darktouched that draws them to one another and, if strong enough, allows them to become Wisdom Sentinels.

- WISDOM SENTINELS: A rare coupling of Darktouched wherein the barrier between their individual existences has been removed. Wisdom Sentinels share strength, abilities, and knowledge.

LIGHTBORNE TERMINOLOGY

- DIM, the: The Lightborne label for individuals who have not inherited Light's Gift.

- LIGHT'S GIFT: The means by which Lightborne pass their power to new individuals.

- LIGHTBORNE: Those who have inherited Light's Gift. The Lightborne loyal to the Lightwatch have been, for centuries, the enemies of all Darktouched.

- LIGHTBORNE CANDIDATES: Individuals that have been identified by Lightwatch analytics as ideal inheritors of Light's Gift.

- LIGHTWATCH: The seat of power for the Pathkeeper and the Lightborne loyal to him.

- PATHKEEPER: The elected ruler of the Lightwatch.

- RECLAIMERS: A military organization commanded by the Pathkeeper. The Reclaimers are responsible for hunting both Darktouched and banished Lightborne, in order to retrieve information for the Lightwatch. Derisively called Shepherds by the Darktouched.

- RETURNER: A Lightborne transportation device.

- SEVERED: A rageful, dangerous spirit created by the Lightwatch.

General Terminology

- SCRIPTSTONE: An ancient device of the Uldu used to store and access information.

- ULDU: A term coined by Beydin Krenneth for the ancients who inhabited the world prior to the Reshaping.

- Y'SHAM: An ancient civilization and former ally of the Darktouched.

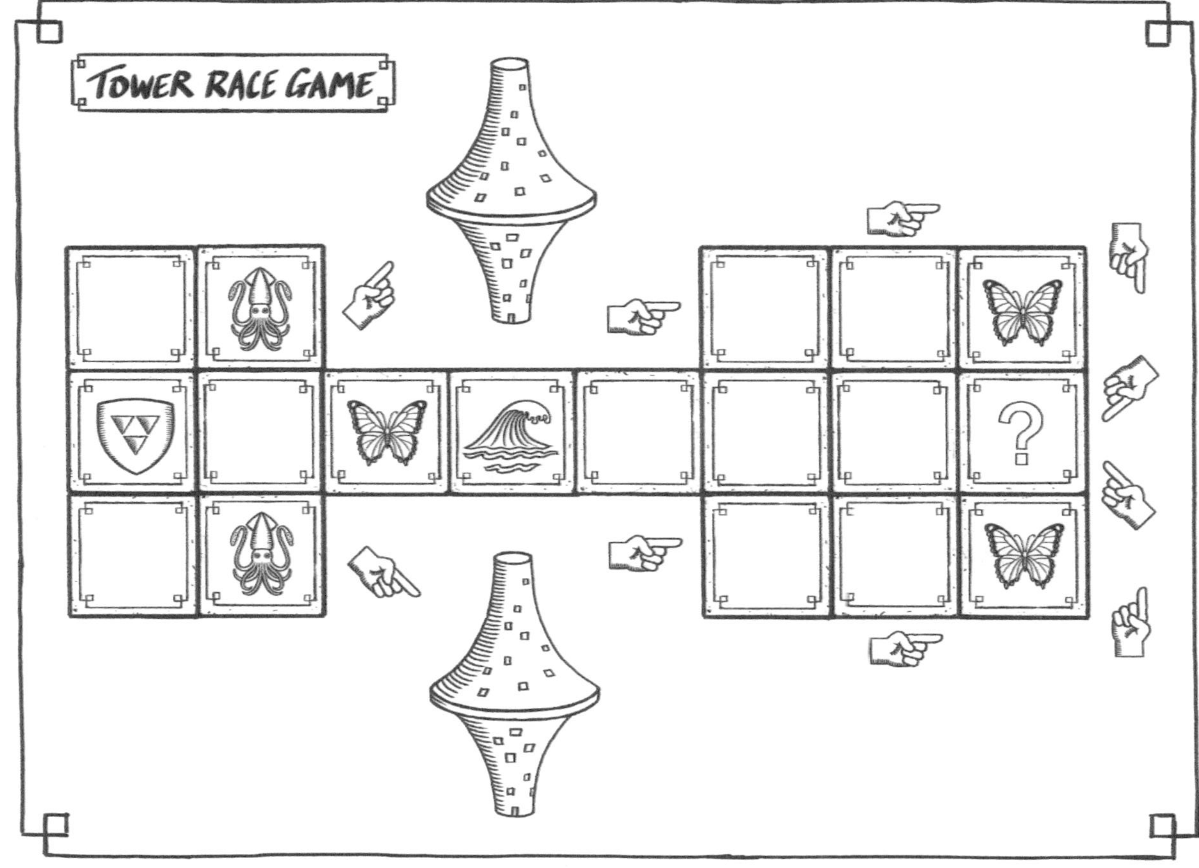
TOWER RACE GAME

TOWER RACE RULES

GENERAL RULES

Objective: Players attempt to move all seven (7) of their game pieces onto the board and save them by reaching the Irkalla Tower on their side. The first player to save all seven pieces wins.

- Pieces move based on the roll of a six-sided die.

- Both players roll to determine who begins the game. Highest roll wins, and players repeat the process until there is a winner.

- Players receive one roll per turn; a roll cannot be split among pieces.

- Players cannot position two of their pieces on the same square.

- Players must roll the exact number needed to leave the board.

- If, based on their die roll, a player is unable to move a piece that is already on the board or bring a new piece onto the board, their turn is lost.

- If a player lands their piece on top of an opponent's piece, this engages a **pounce**.

  - A pounce is resolved by each player rolling their die until one player wins by rolling a higher number. The loser's piece is cleared from the board and returned to start.

- If a pounce occurs on an effect square and the current occupant is defeated, the new occupant engages the effect. If the current occupant wins, no effect is engaged.

SPECIAL EFFECTS & ICONS

- The game board has a total of five (5) special effects—each of these is represented by a specific icon. **Float, shield, and ink** remain in effect until the end of the player's next turn.

- **Pointing hand icon.** Signifies the direction game pieces move on the game board.

- **Butterfly icon.** Engage **float** and receive an extra die roll.

  - Extra die roll must apply to the game piece that engaged the float effect.

  - The float effect grants a game piece <u>immunity to **dash, tsunami, and pounce, but not to ink**</u>. When the float effect ends, the game piece no longer benefits from immunities.

  - **Float pounce.** If a floating game piece lands on an opponent's game piece when the float effect ends, a pounce is engaged even if the opponent's piece is shielded. Following the resolution of a float pounce, the player's turn ends.

  - Float can stack if two effects are engaged on a single turn.

- **Question mark icon.** Engage a **random effect** based on a die roll (see explanation below):

  - **1, 2, or 3:** Piece cleared from board and returned to start.

- **4 or 5:** Move ahead three (3) spaces, unless the space is occupied by one of the player's own game pieces.

- **6: Dash** to shield icon and clear all opponent game pieces touched, returning them to start, even if shielded. If the space with the shield icon is occupied by one of the player's own game pieces, they must stay on the random effect square [**Note:** In this scenario, opponent pieces are still cleared.]

- **Wave icon.** Engage **tsunami**. Push all pieces on center line away two (2) spaces, except those who are floating or shielded. If any piece falls off of the edge, it is cleared from the board and returned to start. Game pieces pushed onto a special effect space by **tsunami** do not engage the special effect.

- **Shield icon.** Engage **shield**. Safe from all effects for one (1) turn. Cannot be pounced while shielded unless a float pounce occurs.

- **Squid icon.** Engage **ink**. All opponent pieces currently on the board are blinded for one (1) turn and unable to move.

ABZUBALL

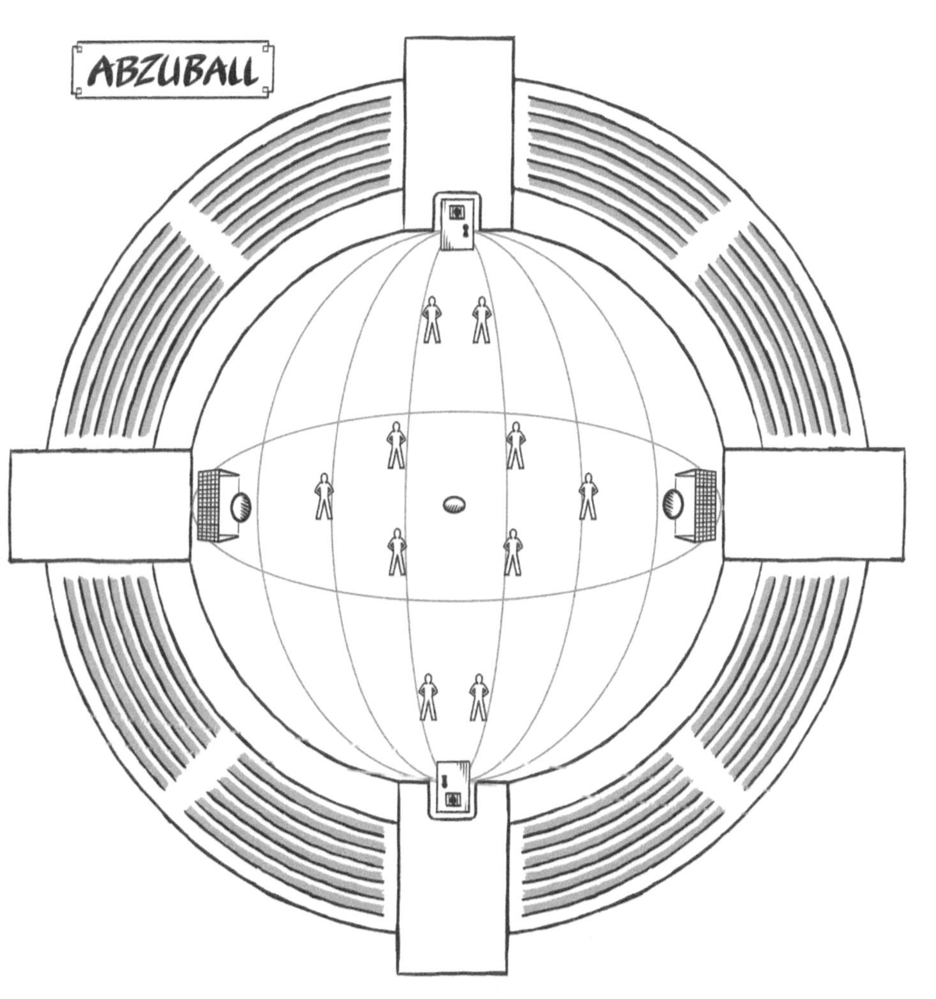

Abzuball Rules

Objective: One team must win two out of three (2 of 3) periods to win the game.

- Each game period is ten (10) minutes long.

- Teams consist of five (5) players.

- Period wins are awarded to the team that scores the most points within the allotted time.

- Points are scored when a team retrieves a ball from its starting location and returns it to their **goal zone** while maintaining physical contact with the ball.

- There are two (2) types of game balls, each worth a different point value:

  - **Midball**—placed at a starting location in the center of the arena—is worth one (1) point per score

  - **Farball**—placed at a starting location inside of each team's goal zone—is worth five (5) points per score

- Scored balls return to their starting location and become playable after a ten (10) second delay.

- Any ball left untouched for five (5) seconds or that goes out of bounds is returned to its starting location.

- There are two (2) **jails** situated within the arena, one for each team.

- Players will be sent to jail for thirty (30) seconds for all of the following reasons:

  - Leaving the field of play, whether forced or of their own volition;

  - Standing in a goal zone for more than ten (10) seconds; and

  - Being the fifth player to cross the vertical midline on either side (i.e., causing a full overload into either the offensive or defensive zone).

- Kicking is not allowed (neither the ball nor other players). Offenses result in a one-minute penalty.

- Each team has two (2) one-minute timeouts available per period.

- Each player receives two (2) **shadescreens** (*see Glossary for definition*) per period.

Acknowledgements

The adventure of writing this first novel has been a dream since I was a young boy. In all of the time between then and now, I knew with absolute certainty that I would struggle to pen these few words. But, Alazar has advised me to start at the beginning—and so I shall.

Without Jane and Caleb, I could never have begun nor completed this project. In so many ways that go beyond the sum total of words on a page, they are what brings this tale to life. Telling the story of Darktouched and Lightborne, of Lucas and Rynn, is as much for them as for the pursuit of my own dreams.

For equipping me to navigate life's journey, I want to thank my parents, relatives, friends, and everyone else who contributed to my upbringing, growth, and maturation as a human being. Of course, my personal experiences give texture and meaning to what I create, and my life has been rich in experiences and learnings thanks in large part to you all.

Before I run out of words, a few shout outs are in order. Ron: Early on when my own insecurities were gnawing on my ego, your feedback gave me enough validation to keep moving forward. Greg: Without really knowing me, you offered a hand up. Your willingness to offer sage advice lit the path for this "green-to-the-publishing-industry" writer. And, to all of my beta readers, especially Dan and Sarah: Thank you all so much!

I am uplifted and excited at the prospect of continuing this adventure with you all. Cheers!

ABOUT THE AUTHOR

R. Roland Finch is a speculative fiction author from Flagstaff, Arizona. *Light's Shadow* is his debut novel and the first book in the Raiders of Light Series. Although he has dreamed of writing professionally since he was a grade schooler, his path to publishing his debut novel took a circuitous route over the course of many years as a project/program/portfolio manager and, currently, business architect. Synthesizing many disparate elements into a large, working system is something he enjoys very much. He draws inspiration from his various travels and adventures, his upbringing, and his family. You can find him online on Facebook or on Twitter and Instagram at @RRolandFinch.

www.ingramcontent.com/pod-product-compliance
Lightning Source LLC
Chambersburg PA
CBHW020246010826

48973CB00006B/1674